Praise for
Donald E. McQuinn's
previous novels

With Full Honors

"*With Full Honors* is military SF written by a man who's been there and done that, and it shows. It's also *space opera* in the best sense of the term. The society in which the action takes place is carefully detailed, and the intricate blend of action, politics, and religion is full of surprising twists that will keep you guessing throughout. This is one to look for."
—HARRY TURTLEDOVE

"A rousing, slam-bang science fantasy, full of combat and political intrigue."
—JULIAN MAY
Author of *The Galactic Milieu* trilogy

"*With Full Honors* is a superb book—McQuinn's combat is brutally realistic; his characters and the problems they encounter are original and completely true to life; his descriptions are sensually vivid, and the cultures he skillfully moves us through are as masterfully developed as anything in current speculative fiction."
—CHRIS BUNCH
Author of the *Shadow Warrior* series

*Please turn the page
for more rave reviews . . .*

Warrior

"An impressive debut ... McQuinn builds a convincing world and fills it with believable characters [and] superior action scenes."
—*Chicago Sun-Times*

"*Warrior* weaves a fascinating tale of post-nuclear culture made chillingly real by its rich detailing of an emerging situation."
—JOHN SAUL

"Terrific, the kind of exciting, involving tale that keeps you up nights ... *Warrior* is a book that deserves to be read."
—TERRY BROOKS

Witch

By Donald E. McQuinn:

TARGETS
WAKE IN DARKNESS
SHADOW OF LIES
WARRIOR*
WANDERER*
WITCH*
WITH FULL HONORS*
THE PRISONER WITHIN*

*Published by Ballantine Books

THE PRISONER WITHIN

Donald E. McQuinn

A Del Rey® Book
THE BALLANTINE PUBLISHING GROUP • NEW YORK

A Del Rey® Book
Published by The Ballantine Publishing Group
Copyright © 1998 by Donald E. McQuinn

http://www. randomhouse.com

Library of Congress Catalog Card Number: 97-94496

ISBN 0-345-40044-5

Manufactured in the United States of America

First Edition: February 1998

10   9   8   7   6   5   4   3   2   1

For Noreen, and our shared memories of Helen

CHAPTER 1

Immaculate in dress greens, Captain Lannat of Rifles halted at rigid attention with a crack of heels and reported to the major in charge of the escort: "Prisoner at the line, sir."

The major executed a smart about-face. "Prisoner detail: Ready *arms*." At the word "arms," the twenty-four Rifles in formation each drew a heavy broadsword from a belt-hung scabbard. The metallic hiss of metal against metal whispered across the sunlit parade deck in front of the stark white barracks. The brilliant day was suddenly rotten with threat.

The major went on. "Detail, *posts*." On the double, the Rifles moved forward, forming two columns. They flanked the two officers, ten troopers to a side. At proper march interval, two troopers ahead and two behind closed off the ends of what had become a rectangular enclosure. The major moved to the head of the new formation.

Captain Lannat of Rifles was alone, enclosed behind walls of guards. Brothers-in-arms. Troopers who had admired and respected him once. Men who heard his name mingled with the word "treason." Now they rejected his gaze. Good men; they would kill a traitor with the fearsome, detached vigor that distinguishes those trained to violence.

At the major's "Forward, *march*," the sonorous thunder of katun drums provided the formation its slow, studied cadence.

It was the hypocrisy of the accusations that seared Lannat's spirit. His every action had been planned and executed to further the emperor's rule. It was Mandro Ta, the Tyrant of Donia, who had collaborated with Commander Etasalou of the Elemental Guard to attack the planet Paro. It had cost almost every man of Lannat's command on Paro to frustrate their invasion. So who became the scapegoat? The junior officer involved.

The prisoner formation marched through the arched gateway in the wall surrounding the barracks grounds, executing a precise right turn. The move sent them down the deserted boulevard leading to the Parneon, the administrative hub for the entire Homeric galaxy. Blinding white under Collegium's tropical sun, as were most of the city's buildings, it rose in the distance like a mountain. Or, Lannat thought, as a mountain would look if the gods were architects. More specifically, architects from Home, that myth-shrouded origin of humans, lost to this galaxy for dozens of generations.

Passing between two buildings that made the katun drumbeat reverberate, Lannat almost lost the cadence. He resisted the urge to look back, where the drums followed. Even they were part of the deception swallowing him, he thought. He remembered the times he had followed his father's parades, when the katuns were truly drums. Huge things, tall as a man, they rode on carts, with drummers mounted alongside to wale away with clubs like bats. It took a man to play a real katun. Now they were electronic toys, hung around the neck like huckster's trays. The so-called drummer tapped his fingers on the black, featureless surface. Speakers did the rest. Electronic cheats, no bigger than a hat.

For a moment, the falsified drums symbolized everything that had happened, and Lannat felt the control that sustained him so well to this point crack and tremble. He wanted nothing in the world more than to dash through the end of the formation and break those lying, artificial drums.

He didn't because the men escorting him would cut him to pieces if he ran. He, Captain Lannat, brought shame down on them. All the published testimony defined him as a traitor. An officer. One of theirs. They would be terminally intolerant of suspicious moves.

Lannat willed his mind to near blankness. He concentrated on the heat reflecting from the buildings. He took it in, let it melt wire-taut muscles, soothe raw nerves. By the time he reached the top of the one hundred stairs leading from street level to the thirty-foot-high entrance of the Parncon, he was almost relaxed.

Silently, yet so swiftly that they generated small tornadoes of dust across the marble walkway, the doors opened at the formation's approach. Beyond them stretched the central hall. Normally Lannat liked to linger in the huge, cool space to admire the intricate inlays of walls and floor, the carved pillars and magnificent stained glass ceiling, its heroic-scale illustrations dedicated to details of the galaxy's colonization.

This wasn't a normal occasion; he almost grinned at the understatement.

Then he heard the drums again, and amusement withered. The drummers reduced the volume to a galling unmilitary pittypat and quickened the pace. The synchronized footsteps of military cadence echoed strangely. There was no Elemental Guard to keep away gawkers inside the building, as there had been for the length of the boulevard. A sparse crowd watched the unit and its enclosed prisoner pass.

The sibilant chatter of the spectators made Lannat think of nervous birds hiding in the bushes as a team of killhawks swept overhead. It was to be expected; for weeks all of Collegium jangled with tension. Rumors that renegade Rifle units would attempt to free their popular captain flashed through the city. No one wanted to be too close, just in case.

Of all men, Lannat knew the idiocy of such tales. Yes, he was a popular officer. Past tense. Operative word: *was*.

Since being arrested on his return to Atic from Paro, Lannat had had plenty of time to think about his situation. Angry and rebellious at first, he soon settled into the dogged, steady work of clearing his name. He schooled himself to think of the situation as combat—which indeed it was—where emotion was controlled, lest it forget to be a friend and turn into a deadly enemy. A foot soldier learns quickly that dash and posture gets the applause, but it's muscle and blood that does the job. Lannat settled in for a tough fight. By the end of his second week of confinement to quarters in the central barracks of the Rifles, he finally admitted to himself how desperate his situation was.

His only friends were the surviving men and women who had seen what he saw on Paro. All, including Nan Bahalt, the woman he loved, were made to understand that they were within an inch of joining their precious Captain Lannat in a charge of treason. Not one of them flinched; they all defended Lannat. To no purpose: The powerful figures who accused him cared nothing for ordinary people. Or ordinary truth. What did enlisted personnel know of galactic policy? As for the Bahalt woman—well, she *was* a doctor, one of Lumin's priestesses, but she was a "liner," and a black one, into the bargain.

No one criticized families that worked toward a semblance of ethnic continuity—not openly. Nevertheless, it was fair and proper to point out that she was a beautiful woman, and everyone saw how she looked at Captain Lannat. Did anyone really expect the truth there? Especially from a liner—*Let's be reasonable about this, shall we?*—one already stepping outside the family tendency?

His future would be settled with words. Lannat understood that the end, if he lost, was the same as if it were a matter of knives.

Lannat thought of himself as born to soldiering. Life was always one of the counters on the board, along with honor and pride and all the unspoken, treasured things that make a man and his unit one. His deepest pain came from the awareness that he could fail this test. He was innocent. That fact was drowning in lies. Only in this extremity, facing the name of traitor, had he truly come to understand how complicated, how fragile, was the construction called "life." It genuinely surprised him to discover how cheaply he held the actual living, if they took away what he stood for. Then there were the other times, the awful, dark moments, when he wondered exactly what he did stand for, if anything was worth dying for.

It never occurred to him to wonder how he saw himself, though. If the tribunal called him guilty, the world would officially call him traitor. Those who had fought the battles with him knew otherwise. Dead and living, all were witness to the truth. That could not be changed.

Outwardly stoic as he marched along the Parneon's great hall, Lannat managed to cut glances at the spectators. A few Elemental Guards, gloating, not entirely successfully hiding their edginess. Civilians: some titillated by the sight of pride brought down, others sympathetic, understanding his hurt on more human terms.

At the door leading off into the tribunal room, the major bellowed a command to halt. Boots crashed on the Parneon's polished marble. Hard echoes battered back from walls of art and culture. The troopers closing the forward end of the rectangle moved aside to the right. The major took post to the left and ordered, "Prisoner. Forward, *march*."

Lannat obeyed, halting at the doorway. "Prisoner at the line, sir."

"Proceed to the defendant's bench, Captain Lannat." As Lannat passed him, the major muttered something that nearly caused Lannat to stumble. Lips barely moving, features frozen, he said, "Good luck."

Still uncertain he had actually heard the words, Lannat moved past courtroom benches to his seat at the defendant's table. He exchanged greetings with his counsel, a lieutenant colonel of Rifles named Eylah. The colonel was a swarthy, taciturn man from the planet Syrac who had told Lannat where he stood at their first meeting. "I've interviewed everyone I could about the battle of Whyee Valley, Captain. Well fought, even if it did degrade to the use of plasguns. I've always held to the Blood Father's proscription against missiles. The closest any Rifle should get to that sort of thing is the crossed rifles that make up our insignia. That goes for hair-splitters who approve of railguns because they're crew-served weapons, too. When you allowed the use of missiles—even plasma missiles—in Whyee, you cheapened us all."

Having said all that, Colonel Eylah settled into his assignment as defense counsel. He wasted little effort hiding the fact that he believed with all his heart that Lannat was guilty.

Indeed, all the pretrial testimony left little room for question. The official Parovian deposition stated, quite honestly, that Lannat's Rifles had effectively destroyed Paro's armed forces, leaving the way open for the rebels who raised Prince Casey to take over as ruler. King Casey could only acquiesce to their wishes, since Lannat had also crushed the expeditionary force of imperial forces sent to quell that rebellion. Even Lumin, the state religion, got in a few good strokes. Sungiver, the Lumin High Priestess, blamed Lannat for the new popularity of the cult of the Seeker on Paro.

When Lannat asked Colonel Eylah what he thought the present day's session might bring, the older man leaned closer. "I've thought this all through, Captain, and I've made up my mind. There's no more testimony or depositions to be heard. The tribunal may come in with a verdict today, they may ask for more testimony, they may simply recess for more deliberation. Here's my plan. Everyone knows you're a favorite of the emperor's because you saved his nephew's life on Delphi." He paused and couldn't resist adding "That's where you got mixed up with that Seeker cult, isn't it? That could hurt us, you working against Lumin. After all, that's the only real religion; Lumin brought us to the light, and ever will. But never mind; it's not like we had much choice."

Lannat interrupted. "We've had this conversation before, Colonel. I didn't betray the emperor. We were attacked on Paro, and we defended ourselves. I won't plead guilty to something I didn't do."

Colonel Eylah made a face and waved both hands as if dispelling a bothersome smell. "Of course, Captain." The colonel was cursed with an inability to meet the gaze of another when lying. Right now he studied the *Courts and Boards* manual on the table in front of him, the ceiling, the tribunal desk, his fingernails—anything but Lannat. He went on, "We've no proof of your story. Of course, the Rifles with you confirm your version of what happened, as does Doctor Bahalt. None of that proves your innocence."

"I've told you a thousand times; it's not 'my version' and it's not a 'story.' It's the truth, by all the light I ever hope to see. All the prosecution has done is parade people through here to lie about me. It's the prosecution's job to prove me guilty." As Lannat finished, he realized he was massaging the scar that cut a thin stripe from high above his left eye down and across the right one, where it turned vertical, falling to just below the heavy cheekbone. It was a nervous habit, touched off by anger or irritation, so he knew it was also glowing red. He pulled his hand away abruptly.

The colonel had the grace to wince at Lannat's description of the trial. "Innocent until proven guilty is the theory. Unfortunately, we're confronting very powerful forces, and their version contradicts yours in every point. Bluntly, their case is stronger than ours."

"Because they're high-ranking people repeating the same damned lies. Everyone who testified against me has a position to protect or hopes to earn favors. I protected the emperor's interests. They're trying to destroy me because I ruined their plans."

Colonel Eylah put on his official expression. It was essentially indistinguishable from his ordinary look, but it required that he sit up straighter. "You fought and destroyed imperial forces. Your version of the intent of those forces contradicts the word of those who committed the forces to Paro. Trust me: Capitalize on your position with the emperor. Plead guilty. Ask for direct intervention by the Exalted. If he—"

The order to stand to attention broke off the argument. Lannat and Colonel Eylah rose. The tribunal entered from behind the official desk on its dais. There were seven people, as required by capital offense trials. They wore shapeless black robes that reached from shoulder to floor and hoods like pillowcases. Further anonymity was assured by throat microphones that altered voices to hollow, metallic tones.

Lannat disliked looking at black, faceless things that held his life in balance. He particularly hated listening to those droning simulations of human speech. The fact that he knew the tradition behind it all didn't help.

During the early days of colonization of the galaxy, vendettas and feuds had been commonplace. The Blood Father decreed that all personnel judging capital offenses be unidentifiable. Over hundreds of years the practice of feud disappeared, but the uniform and secrecy dictated by the Blood Father remained. Sitting members of a capital case, such as the present tribunal, were drawn from a pool of twenty-one officers. There were always eleven Rifles and ten Elemental Guards. Each was an officer chosen by lot from his or her parent unit. Each was sequestered in solitary confinement during the tribunal, assuring that no one knew which seven were selected actually to conduct the trial. Absolute anonymity was the goal, and it had not been compromised since its inception.

It was not a popular assignment.

A voice, electronically distorted until it sounded like muted, chilled brass, rang down from the dais, filling the room. "The imperial tribunal of Emperor Halib is in session. Its word is the emperor's word, and the Homeric galaxy will hear and conform. To all who hear these judgments, this tribunal is beyond appeal. Decisions are final."

The seven officers sat down. When the spectators on the benches and trial participants did the same, the sound of their combined action made a noise like wind-worried leaves. Lannat, his gaze locked on the black figures, repressed a shiver.

The central figure at the tribunal table said, "The prisoner will rise."

Pushing on the tabletop with the knuckles of clenched fists, Lannat stood. This was the way every day started in the tribunal. He was surprised at his inner relief; there was no hint of a decision. Until then he had been genuinely unaware of how much he dreaded the final moment, the announcement of finding. At attention, he fixed his gaze on the wall directly over the left shoulder of the central figure. Now was when the president of the tribunal got things under way by asking if each counsel was ready to proceed.

Again, the words without a voice. "The tribunal finds the accusation is proven. The prisoner will be escorted to Imperial Prison Seven-J, where he will be executed by beheading in the ancient manner prescribed by the holy dictates of the Blood Father. The date and time of execution are set for exactly one week from now. Imperial Counsel, mark the time."

Hearing his life terminated—defined to the minute—was unlike anything Lannat ever imagined. It was as if his body turned to ice, while his mind, blazing like plasma, screamed for relief, for correction, for help. Sheer shock, reaction far beyond anything his will might have accomplished, held him at rigid attention.

He was innocent. He had fought for the emperor. They were going to kill him.

He was *innocent*.

Knees wobbled. Breath caught in his throat. His heart was storm-surf, crashing through his chest. The churning, disbelieving mass that was his brain seemed to be losing all contact with reality. He slumped, shamed by his shocking weakness. Barely catching himself, he braced against the heavy table. A shove from behind nearly dropped him. The effort to turn and discover who pushed him took incredible energy. Colonel Eylah lay on the floor. A long slick of drool drained from his open mouth. He snored.

Madness. Lannat continued to turn, spun to a supine fall on

top of the table. An outstretched arm merely slowed his decline, made his collapse slow-motion comedy.

The room whirled. Everywhere, spectators dropped. No one cried out. The falling bodies raised soft, dusty sounds.

Straining mightily, Lannat rolled over toward the tribunal dais. Five of the hooded heads reposed on the official, almighty tribune table.

Lannat blinked and beat back an insane giggle. He tried to focus, tried to speak. Someone grabbed him under the arms. Other hands hoisted his ankles. Then everything was a dull blur and a blackness that pressured his skull until his brain exploded in a bright red flash.

CHAPTER 2

Emperor Halib shook with rage. Unable to speak, he raised a hand, the fingers splayed wide. Slowly the fingers curved inward, clawlike. When the whole was a white-skinned fist, he drove it down onto his desk with a blow so hard it jarred the delicate porcelain teacup in its saucer. The purity of that chime made telling contrast to the imperial primal scream that overwhelmed its silvery note.

Distorted features emphasized the fact that Emperor Halib was not a handsome man. As echoes of his fury died and his face returned to a semblance of normal, it became clear that he tended to jowls and the bright, demanding eyes had bags. For a man in his mid-forties, he appeared more fleshy than fat, however, and the blow to the desktop testified to considerable strength hidden under the ornate clothes of imperial office. When he pivoted purposefully, directing a searing glare at each member of his audience in turn, he did it with the instinctive authority of fourteen generations of supreme authority. He commanded.

The four men and one woman standing in attendance quailed, save for the man farthest to the emperor's left, a silver-haired, jut-jawed figure at professional attention in the dress greens of the Rifles. He wore the star within a circle of a general on his collar. It was to that man the emperor addressed his first hoarse words. "Rifles. Mutiny."

General Jerlow, Commandant of Rifles, colored as he spoke. "Not Rifles, Exalted. I stake my integrity on it."

The emperor was at last coherent. "Curse your integrity. Your life is at stake. When my investigators prove Captain Lannat was spirited away by other Rifles, you'll kneel beside him on the executioner's stage."

Jerlow spoke with ill-concealed offense. "Two innocent men will die."

The emperor jerked as if electrified. The rest of the audience gasped. The lone woman, dressed in multilayered flowing robes of orange and yellow, actually leaned slightly away. Something like distaste touched her features, a reaction that seemed strangely suited to her. Her beauty was that of a fully mature woman, secure in her position, but it suffered a chill austerity. Her place at the far end of the line of five made her movement particularly obvious, but the emperor was unaware. He had eyes for Jerlow alone. He ground out words. "You admit it, then; you believe Lannat innocent. You support the traitor."

"I believe Captain Lannat's version of what happened on Paro. I did not arrange his escape from imperial custody, nor do I condone that escape. The honor of the entire Corps requires that he clear his name in a fair trial."

There was enough accent on the word "fair" to energize the

middle figure in the group facing the emperor. In the same colors as the woman in the line, he wore an orange long-sleeved blouse with an open vest of yellow. His trousers, bloused into polished black boots, matched the vest. He said, "Exalted, he insults you to your face. He as much as said the trial was unfair. That's why he engineered—"

An imperial hiss cut off the speech. The emperor, dressed all in black, wore a robe with a high collar that extended above his head, curving to partially enclose it on the sides. Notwithstanding the glittering diamonds studding the edges, he stared out of that enclosure as if peering through the embrasure of a bunker. Worse, he was solemn now, speaking with quiet venom. "Commander Hano, I have ears. Your perceptive interpretations are unneeded, unwelcome, and extraordinarily unwise. I need not point out that the only indication of the truth of Captain Lannat's version of events on Paro is the unfortunate disappearance of Lumin's own Commander Etasalou, your immediate predecessor. How mysterious that no trace of him was found in the ashes after the fire and explosions that destroyed Lumin's secret Elemental Guard training facility. I should like very much to see him interrogated. With requisite rigor."

The woman spoke up. "Lumin is blameless, Exalted. We have held to our heritage as the bringers of light, the caretakers and dispensers of all knowledge. The Blood Father's word made it so for all eternity. Whatever others have done, Lumin—"

"I wondered when you'd start to chirp." Halib swiveled to face her. "We'll have our own private conversation in a few minutes, Sungiver. I am offended by these fools. You are a different story altogether."

Fear touched Sungiver's eyes. She recovered her glacial haughtiness quickly. Nervous twitching at the corners of her mouth betrayed fraying nerves.

Emperor Halib was already addressing another man, this one in a close-fitting tunic and trousers of dark blue with black trim of the Elemental Guard. "Administrator Ved. As second-in-command of the Elemental Guard and assistant to our newly promoted Commander Hano, you are personally responsible for determining how this disgrace occurred. You will also find Captain Lannat."

Administrator Ved coughed, stuttered. "It will take time, Exalted. The Guard is understrength . . ."

"I don't care if it takes lives, Administrator. Including yours. Your Guard is understrength because it is fragmented, combatting open dissension on five of the remaining eleven—did you idiots all take note of the word 'remaining'?—planets under direct imperial command. Lumin is our state religion, our receptacle of all knowledge. You are losing the faith of the people and you know *nothing*!" Emperor Halib was on his feet, gesticulating, spraying saliva in glittering mist. "All of you. Get out. Not you, Sungiver. I have words for you. For the rest, I have contempt. Disgust. Get *out*. Find me Lannat. Find my betrayers. Get out."

The men left. All but the Rifles commandant strained for a quick glance at Sungiver.

Emperor Halib suppressed a smile. Even in their present extremity, the bootlickers assayed the prospects of one of their number. He could practically hear their thinking: If Sungiver was to have a private audience with the emperor, who would benefit? Or suffer? How? Would an enemy be advanced? Impeded? There would be no concern for friends. At the level of power held by the departing quartet, the word "friend" was bait.

The emperor shifted his attention to Sungiver. He smiled and took an extra moment to enjoy how the malice of it frightened her. "Alone at last, eh? A couple of certifiable survivors. You on one side, me on the other. Do you think we simply wear well, Sungiver, or are we so much more clever than those around us?"

Sungiver's responding smile was tentative. "I was never on a 'side,' Exalted, unless it was yours. I'm not sure I understand what you mean about surviving. My connection with the expeditionary force to Paro was minimal, at best. I cared only about the success of Lumin's—and the imperial—ministry there. I warned Commander Etasalou and Mandro Ta that they were exceeding their authority."

Halib continued to smile. "Is that what you told them? Exceeding their authority; nicely put. My understanding of the situation was that you were part of a trio, that your goal was to yank me off the throne. But I see now I was mistaken. You simply got confused, took a few insignificant liberties. Does that sum up your plan? I have to ask, because I don't really understand 'exceeding authority,' since mine is limitless. Life and death—that sort of thing. But we're talking about you, aren't we? You and the plan to depose me."

"I knew nothing of any such plan. I tried to stop them, Exalted; to contain them, if you will. I argued and reasoned until I was exhausted. As Lumin's female leader, one of my primary roles is to maintain peace. I never forget that. I kept reminding both of them that our purpose in life is to promote the good of the empire, and that the good of the emperor is key to that obligation. They told me nothing of their plans, or I would have told you, Exalted."

Halib sat down and slumped, chin on his chest. The posture distorted his words, but he was understandable. "I'm not going to have you killed because you will serve me better knowing that I need only the flimsiest excuse to make me change my mind. You are a bore, Sungiver. Too cowardly to strike your own blow, too stupid to find a competent ally. You are no danger to me. I, however, am a constant danger to you. Remember that, and preserve your pointless life by assuring that Lumin serves me constantly. Now leave." He maintained his position, not bothering to look up. Sungiver had no way of knowing that he squinted at her through slitted eyes past lowered brows. Always watching. Always evaluating.

For some time after the door closed behind Sungiver, Halib didn't move. He willed relaxation, filling his lungs with deep, deliberate breathing, feeling muscles go slack. Little by little he descended from the emotional peak of rage. Only when he was completely calm did he abandon himself to savor. He reveled in the new, burgeoning conspiracy growing around him. Plotting. Scheming. That was life. He tingled with a sensual, stimulating awareness of danger.

The new game was under way. Life was rich.

A tiny sound, a squeak that would have gone unheard only a few feet away, broke his train of thought. The noise was an alarm, set in the back of his chair, initiated by an ultrasonic signal.

Reluctantly Halib opened his eyes and sat up. Composing a properly statesmanlike manner, he called out, "Come in."

A section of the bookshelved wall swung open like a door. Administrator Ved stepped out of the hidden passage. His hand was on the hilt of his sword, and he scanned the room with the quick, insistent eyes of a predator.

Halib laughed at him. "Would I call you in here if there were anyone else to see?"

Ved stepped clear of the secret door as it closed. He said, "Safety is assured by precautions, Exalted, not assumptions. There are voice duplicators."

Sobering quickly, Halib nodded. "There are many things, old friend. Does it ever bother you that we, too, are deceivers of the worst order?"

"In my weaker moments." Ved shrugged, and light played off polished leather cross-belts. "We were born to what we do, you to rule, me to act in your behalf. For us, there are no rules. There is only winning."

"Or losing. But you never consider that, do you?"

"No, Exalted."

Halib shook his head. "Perhaps that's why I trust you. You're the only man I can say that about."

Ved grinned. On anyone else, the expression would be terrible, wolfish. Between Ved and the emperor, it was understood to be confiding. Ved said, "Likewise, Exalted," and both men laughed wholeheartedly at the cruel truth.

When they quieted, Halib asked, "What news, Ved? Is it Hire? Ilion? Perhaps Agamem? Do we know where he's bound?"

"Hire, Exalted. As you suspected."

"It seemed the most likely. No planet has a more repressive regime than Hire. Counsellor Ullas is most scrupulous in observing the rituals of obedience and loyalty to the throne. Have you ever met Ullas?"

"When he came to Remembrance, several years ago."

"His son was a warfighter. I remember his last match. Very brave, very good. I thought the referees stepped in a bit early."

"One does not let the son, even the younger son, of a planetary ruler die without good cause, Exalted. He was badly wounded. You did know he's on Atic again? Senior member of the Hiran Cultural Sibling Group."

Halib brightened. "I'd forgotten. The Hiran CSG? We have a hostage of more than ordinary importance then." A glance at Ved told Halib his idea was ill-received.

"It's been at least two centuries since an emperor used that gambit, Exalted. Anyhow, Ullas always struck me as a man who'd welcome martyrdom. For someone else."

"As you say. However—to the main point: Exactly how will Counsellor Ullas support our traitor? How long before we feel Etasalou's influence in the empire once again?"

"Hire is a very fertile field for a man of his skills, Exalted. Despite Counsellor Ullas's repressions, resistance exists. It lacks organization. Knowing our man's skills, it won't take him long to insinuate himself into the counsellor's administration. Etasalou would be a rebel's worst nightmare. And Ullas's nemesis."

"You think Etasalou would actually seek to rule?"

"He came close to ruling the empire." It was a cold message, intended to shock. It succeeded.

Halib protested, "Paro is a backwater, nothing. There was no danger of immediate revolution. We would have gathered our loyal forces . . ." Uncharacteristically, he let the sentence slide away. His gaze turned vacant, contemplative. He reached to pinch pursed lips between thumb and knuckle.

Ved resumed. "It's not enough that we capture Etasalou, Exalted. He must be eliminated."

Halib stopped massaging his lips. "Eliminated? Not made an example of?"

"We need no martyrs. We need dead villains. We should send a man to kill him."

Skeptical, Halib shook his head. Before the emperor could speak, however, Ved's intensity overruled his protocol. "Exalted, I can't prove a word of what I'm about to say, but I can't keep silent, either. I think Commander Etasalou salvaged most of the data, equipment, and personnel on Hector and smuggled everything off. I think it's on its way to Hire, closely followed by the commander himself."

"The mind-control work? You yourself reported it destroyed. You told me how distraught Etasalou was. You said it was a major factor in his decision to flee rather than fight to maintain his status here at the heart of the empire. Now you tell me this? Explain yourself, Ved. This is unprofessional. And disturbing."

The lean, hardened features weakened. "I feel it, Exalted. I have no information. I know him, though. All these years, I stood beside him, ate with him, drank with him. Yet I never knew him. Nor he me. He didn't want to know anyone outside his family. His life is compartmented beyond belief. I think the training facility on Hector was one such compartment. I can't believe it was destroyed. My bones tell me I've been lied to."

"How do I know your bones aren't simply crumbling from old age? An assassin eliminates only the personality. The laboratory lives on. All the more reason to send a force after him."

Grinning ruefully, Ved said, "You may be right about the age of the bones, Exalted, but not about the message. But if I may make a suggestion: If we send a force after Etasalou, he and

Counsellor Ullas will hide everything. We'll find nothing. We need Etasalou dead in any case. Send a man after him. The man will have to learn where Etasalou lives, where he works, whom he deals with. Once Etasalou is dead, seize the laboratory and everything connected with it."

"What if there is no laboratory, no scientists?"

Once again Ved's wolflike grin bared his teeth. "Etasalou's death will satisfy me."

"I'm sure he'd be proud to hear it. Let me think about this. You know I have little confidence in assassination. It always sounds so pristine, but it's the very mother of unforeseen consequences. I'd have to be very secure in my mind about the man you sent; that's paramount."

"Once the Exalted has had the opportunity to consider all the possible ramifications of this new concept, I can assure him he'll have no doubts concerning the man I propose to send."

Eyebrows rising in surprise, Halib said, "You know the man already? He must be very good, indeed. Have I met him?"

"The Exalted has dined with him, here in the palace." Ved hesitated, extending Halib's suspense that extra, most delicious moment. "The man who will kill Commander Etasalou for you is Captain Lannat."

CHAPTER 3

Lannat knew about oneway cells, of course. Everyone knew. The people who experienced them were a much smaller minority. Lannat hated being among their number.

He wondered how long he'd been in the black, featureless box. The optical properties of the glass walls permitted passage of light and vision from the outside. To the eye of the prisoner inside, the shining surface was like the surface of a lake, receding to dark murk.

Four sleeps on the blanketless shelf that jutted from one wall. What did that mean? There was no way to know how many hours he was awake or slept. Nor any way to know if the food that appeared on a tray through the slit in the door came on any schedule. Or if it was drugged in order to further disrupt his circadian rhythm. From his first minute in the cell, he tried to keep organized; escape could hinge on knowing if it was day or night. He carefully noted when he felt most alert. The problem was, he knew there were two maximum-wakefulness periods, one from nine to eleven in the morning and a second between seven and nine in the evening. At first he thought he could space the two apart by noting the lowest energy period, soon after lunch. The sheer boredom of the place undermined his plans. He simply fell asleep or woke and prowled. He quickly had no idea of hours or days.

Beard growth by this time suggested he was into his fourth day. Or maybe the fifth.

Dressed in drab gray knee-length shorts, sandals, and baggy shirt, he sat in the surprisingly comfortable chair of plastic tubing and connecting straps. The crashing headache was finally gone. Vision was steady again, so nausea didn't trouble him anymore, either.

He'd been there long enough to grow tired of washing with tepid water at the sink bulging from the wall next to the automatic toilet. He almost wished the latter stank in the familiar way toilets were supposed to stink. Sanitary to a fault, this one flushed with a chemical mess that utterly sterilized the bowl and gave off fumes that burned the eyes and breathing passages, as if getting even with the prisoner.

Even more than all that, Lannat despised the reason one-ways were so named. Although he looked at a glass-smooth, practically indestructible surface and saw nothing but a dim reflection of himself, the ceramet walls were transparent to the patrolling guards outside.

Lannat was reasonably certain there was a strong ceiling light outside his cell, just above one corner. Sometimes he could swear he saw a shadow when a booted guard paced by. Aside from the unannounced appearance of food and drink, the passage of the guards was his sole contact with an outside world. Spaces between the oneways assured prisoners couldn't even discover each other by tapping code messages. It surprised Lannat to realize how quickly those cadenced boots and that shadow, real or imagined, dominated his time. He was already to the point that the steps woke him from sound sleep. Longingly he followed them, left to right, right to left, imagining faces, body shapes, destinations, points of origin. Anything.

The rhythm was always the same. One person. How did other prisoners come and go?

The question preyed on him. Were there other prisoners? He never heard one.

How long could they keep a man like this?
What would prevent them from doing anything they wanted?
They. Them. Who?

Four days. Five? He wanted to howl, batter the lying walls that denied his humanity. Submerged in silence, his thoughts curdled. Minutes and hours ceased to be measurements; time was interminable not-knowing.

Pride held him together. And stubbornness. So far.

The inner desperation grew stronger every time he closed his eyes and opened them to find nothing changed. Madness touched him, the scratchy patter of invisible insects across his skin. The first time it happened, he looked. Now he simply brushed at it, knowing there was nothing there, afraid his mind would invent something.

Was the prison winning?

What prison? Where was he?

Tears actually burned behind his eyes. Humiliation. Rage.

Other men had called him brave once. Now this. Four days? Five, at least. Surely five.

Shadow. At the corner. No boot noises. Lannat bent forward in a crouch, barely touching the chair, taut muscles vibrating under strain. His mouth was suddenly dry.

The leading edge of the food tray appeared in the slot. Then, as the rest came through, Lannat was surprised to see a piece of cloth. A voice said, "Put on the hood. Draw the string tight," and even as his need for human contact seized on the sound, part of his mind dictated great caution. For one thing, the amplified voice came from hidden speakers; it was everywhere, overlapping, disorienting. More than that bit of psychological destabilization, there was the overriding question: Why was this happening?

Picking up the hood, Lannat pulled it on, blindfolding himself. His hands wanted to shake. He wouldn't let them. When he finished, he said, "Now what?" and was proud there was no quaver.

"Don't move. You will be escorted. Do not move until told to do so; punishment will be inflicted. Make no sound."

Noises. Door opening? Scuffling of feet? Strong hands gripped his wrists and shoulders; two men, one on each side. "Straight ahead." As before, the hidden speakers. Carefully Lannat stepped off and was guided through the door. The air outside had no chemical stench. Institutional smells: cleanser, wax. The men holding him: soap, clothes, sweat. It was an indescribable relief, almost as wonderful as seeing something different. The hands turned him to the right. The amount of light filtering through the hood suddenly increased. He decided that had to be the light outside his cell; he had been right about it all along. He congratulated himself, counted his discovery a victory. His captors weren't infallible.

He beat them once. He'd do it again. *Beat them.*

His sandals slapped on a hard, smooth surface. The escorts continued to shuffle, almost completely silent. Padded slippers, then. To keep other prisoners unaware, isolated. Lannat wondered what would happen if he yelled.

He was turned right again. This time they walked much farther. Yet another right turn, and he thought he felt the guiding hands tighten. He tensed to resist. There was a popping report, and in the instant it took him to recognize it as an injector, a pinpoint on his thigh burned. Bellowing, flinging his right arm like a flail, he reached for the drawstring of the hood with his left.

He was unconscious before he touched the knot.

Awareness returned with a slow, eerie sense of time lost and a flood of disconnected realizations. He was in a chair. It was dim, almost dark. He blinked several times, assuring himself it was the illumination, not his eyes. There was an awful taste in his mouth, bitter and dusty. Suddenly he was fading away, and he made an embarrassing sound in his throat, afraid of falling back into unconsciousness. He wondered if he was dreaming.

After that small backward step toward sleep, he recovered very quickly. He noted that the dimness was intentional; it assured he couldn't recognize anything about the figures opposite him. Then, when he tried to adjust his position, he discovered he was bound to a chair, a strap across his chest, more straps at ankles, wrists, and biceps. Covertly, with gradually increased effort, he tested the one at his right wrist. It had no more give than steel.

One of the figures spoke. The voice was almost normal, but there were telltale hitches and unnatural glottal stops that told Lannat it was mechanically altered. It was a man's voice, loftily superior, and it said, "The fibermet bands incorporate an array of sensors, Captain. We have a complete medical Patient Individual Systems Recorder mounted on the wall behind you. We are reading your physiology at all times. You'll be pleased to know the effects of the injected narcotic are completely gone. Your pulse rate, blood pressure, and breathing are admirable, considering your circumstances. Your blood chemistry, on the other hand, is a pharmacopeia of anger and fear-related natural emissions, and your brain wave indications read like a hurristorm warning. Frankly, I'm rather glad you're tied down."

For the first time, the tiny peeps and dings of the PISR penetrated Lannat's consciousness. The knowledge that he was displayed as a series of colored lights and fluctuating gauges filled him with a strange, raging embarrassment. It was worse than being bound and helpless, it was being exposed. He heaved against the restraints. "If I could just get my hands on you. Who are—"

"Quiet." Amplification turned the second voice into thunder. Lannat reeled. Ears ringing, he concentrated to understand what followed. "What would you give to clear your name?"

"What kind of question is that? You scum invented the lies that put me here. Why pull me out of a courtroom where I was already convicted?"

"Answer me."

Lannat said, "I assume the sensors include a stress analysis. Watch it, and know I'm telling the truth. All I ever had or wanted was honor. You took that from me. I can't buy it back with greater dishonor. I won't be a tool. I'm resigned to dying. You don't frighten me."

One of the figures moved as if suddenly uncomfortable. The one asking the questions said, "What if you could prove everything you claimed in court? What if you could avenge yourself on the man who destroyed you, who was responsible for the deaths of so many young Rifles?"

Lannat laughed. "Etasalou? He's dead." Another idea struck him, and he changed from scornful to icily enraged. Muscles bulging, he strained at the strapping, and his eyes glared hatred. "The emperor. I'm unjustly convicted, so you think you can use me to attack him. I should have known. Only the highest-level nobles could pull off the operation that brought me here. You rotten bastards. For the last time, listen to me: I never betrayed my oath to Emperor Halib."

"Very pretty." The first speaker regained his voice and his

condescending attitude simultaneously. "What if I told you Commander Etasalou lives?"

"What if I told you you're a liar, and not a very good one?"

The offended silence thickened the air of the small room. Lannat was reminded of his toilet, and almost laughed. He was wondering if that meant he was close to hysteria when the first speaker resumed. "Etasalou lives. So long as he does, the emperor is in personal danger, his rule threatened."

Despite the arrogant superiority of the speaker and the additional burden of electronic voice alteration, Lannat caught a sense of something beyond the words. For the first time, he felt truthfulness. And more than that: concern. A faint breath of hope skimmed across his thinking. He dared to wonder if this patronizing dolt might actually be interested in the emperor's well-being.

Lannat responded carefully. "If you saved me from that courtroom in order to send me after Etasalou, you don't understand me at all. I'm a Rifle. I fight for the emperor. Killing is part of that. Murder isn't. The distinction may escape you."

"Refuse this task, and you'll be found dead in an alley, dressed in the uniform we took off you when we brought you here. You'll think of that as murder. I'll think of it as your execution, carried out in an unorthodox manner."

Before Lannat could answer, the second man spoke. Having shouted once, he seemed assured that his authority now controlled the situation. Such a quick assumption made Lannat think; only a man accustomed to taking command easily would react that way. Strange, impossible theories whispered through Lannat's brain. He forced them aside to listen. The speaker said, "Think back to the last celebration of Remembrance. Were we in a state of war, Captain?"

"No, sir, but—"

"I'm not finished. Just answer. You killed a man. Since it wasn't war, could we call it murder?"

"No, sir."

"Commander Etasalou is dedicated to the emperor's destruction. He has, in effect, declared war. He is in hiding, in sanctuary provided by a hypocrite, where he plots and builds his strength. Would you, as a Rifle, execute a combat order to engage the emperor's enemy in whatever guise the battle required?"

Lannat struggled for an answer. Finally, gaze fixed on his sandals, he nodded. His answer started as a mumble, gained strength as he went. His head rose slowly. "I know Etasalou for what he is. You're right about my dead Rifles; he's responsible. I would kill him here, now, for simple revenge. For my Rifles. For my life. I make no apology for that. But what you ask— pardon me, what you suggest—is assassination. I'm a plain soldier. Don't ask me to explain my acceptance of one and my repugnance for the other. I cannot."

The first speaker exhaled. Lannat thought it might be a sigh. Then the man said, "You refuse? Knowing what will happen to you?"

Smiling, Lannat wondered if they understood the pain behind his expression. He said, "I'll do it. I don't believe for one minute that, if I succeed, you'll clear my name; whoever you are, you don't have either the legal or the moral authority for that. Neither do I accept your rationale that assassination is merely one more killing in a war. I will hunt down Etasalou because I am the emperor's man. I swore the oath. I will hunt down Etasalou because my dead troopers require it. And when I am done, when you are wondering how to rid yourselves of me, think on this: Remember what Captain Lannat of Rifles was once. Ask yourselves if you would ever have the heart to do what I will do. Ask yourselves if you were right to ask me to do it."

Cloth rustled. The men stood. A dazzling beam of light shot from between them, blinding Lannat. When the light went off, he could barely make out the advancing guards. He snarled impotent fury at them but offered no resistance when the shiny injector touched his leg.

CHAPTER 4

Emperor Halib followed the oblong of light along the fitted stone floor of the passageway. Movement ahead of the flashlight's beam startled him. He made a sound in his chest and stopped so suddenly that Administrator Ved bumped into him.

Twin orbs, like glowing drops of blood, suddenly leaped into view. An animal—a pale, lank thing—rose on its hind legs with startling swiftness, forepaws extended. Bared fangs gleamed. It squealed threat, the arrogant ruler of its dank kingdom.

Halib disabused it. He threw the flashlight. The black passageway exploded with crazily dancing light, the beam spinning this way and that, too fast to track. Sound erupted, as well, enraged and frightened shrieks that gave the beast its common name. "A kreech," the emperor said, the word a loathing. "I never saw one . . ." He caught himself; there were things about the palace's secret ways that even Ved could not know. He made a fake coughing sound and went on. ". . . so bold." He hurried forward, retrieved his flashlight.

Following, Ved chuckled. "Good stuff, rulite; a plastic or glass lens couldn't have handled that toss. I'm glad you missed the thing."

Over his shoulder, Halib asked, "Are you that fond of kreeches?"

Ved made a rude noise. "Had you hit him, there would have been a mess. I know who would've had to carry the flashlight then."

Halib sniffed imperial disdain.

It took awhile to reach the video monitor bolted to the stone wall. A small control box hung next to it. There were three glowing buttons and two slightly larger spoked wheels. Halib pressed his right index finger to the second button. The screen leaped to life with a picture of his library. In the upper right corner of the image, a small green light informed him that heat and motion sensors had detected no unauthorized presence during his absence. That facet of the security system energized only when Halib slipped out through the secret door. Turning the two wheels, he changed the direction of the camera lens, scanning the room and the balcony outside. The lens was hidden in the eye of one of the many characters painted on the room's ceiling. Satisfied there was no one present, he touched the bottom button with his left index finger. The bookshelf/door swung open.

Stepping into the room, Ved said, "Someday you'll have to tell me what happens if you use the wrong finger on those print-readers."

Smiling, Halib didn't answer.

Going directly to his desk, he touched yet another control. A decorative wall panel next to him opened down its center, swung apart as doors. A bar silently slid forward. Halib poured two large portions of whiskey into magnificent crystal tumblers. He handed one to Administrator Ved and saluted him with his own. Formalities observed, Halib put down a hearty swallow. "What a thoroughly unpleasant experience. I don't think anyone has ever so completely exposed my impoverished ethics as Captain Lannat just did. I can't thank you enough."

The jesting sarcasm didn't affect Ved's concerned frown. "He's useless. He'll never last on Hire. And if he did, he'd never eliminate Etasalou. Somehow he'd think of a way to give that kreech a fighting chance."

"Let's not mention kreeches." Halib had a bit more whiskey. He held the tumbler to the light, admired the luminous amber fluid. "Straight from the keg, this one. Twelve-year-old, from New Bourbon's north corner. Significant restorative powers. Which I sorely need." He sipped, turned to Ved. "Exactly what are you saying?"

"I don't want to use Lannat, Exalted. I misjudged him. He reeks of too much concern about right and wrong. Eliminating Etasalou is no job for a man who intellectualizes the matter. I've just made things worse."

"I disagree." Halib settled into his desk chair, waving at Ved to pull up a seat for himself. "You and I would do what needs to be done almost instinctively. Men like Lannat do what they do in order to assure that we continue to rule. I understand him. As I understand you, old friend." He broke off suddenly. Busily, hands as imprecise as moths, he pushed papers and paraphernalia about on his desk. He looked deep into Ved's eyes before speaking again. "Do you realize I can call no one else 'old friend'?"

Nodding slowly, Ved said, "And anyone else who says it of me is misled. We're a matched set, Exalted. The art of rulership exemplified. Rulership: Is that a proper word?"

"If it's not, it should be. Don't distract me." Halib was brisk. "What you failed to see in Lannat is that close combat is a test of more than mere physical courage. For the person with any human qualities whatever, there is another requirement, perhaps a harsher one: to retain one's self under the psychological impact of the carnage and loss. There must be a transcendent *need* that justifies the slaughter: the cause. Lannat needs a cause. We supplied him with part of one this morning. We must assure he has more than Etasalou to keep him focused."

Ved simply frowned his confusion, waited.

"Name the person most helpful to Lannat in the matter of the Parovian debacle," Halib said. "Name the person Etasalou has reason to hate more than Lannat, more than me."

"The woman, the Lumin priestess. Doctor Bahalt. Doctor Nan Bahalt. Etasalou's niece. That imbecile colonel defending

Lannat made her look like a lovesick girl, wasted her testimony entirely. How is she supposed to help us?"

"You, with utmost secrecy, will have Bahalt admitted to see Lannat. Arrange for a guard to solicit a bribe from Lannat or some such—I don't know—make up a scenario. Lannat doesn't know he's going to Hire; theoretically, we have no idea where Etasalou's gone. There's no reason, therefore, for not sending Bahalt to Hire. Arrange it."

Ved almost choked on his whiskey. "Bahalt? To Hire? Why?"

"Lannat must go on his quest convinced that the danger to my person is overwhelming. Neither of them has any idea Etasalou's on Hire. Lannat must not know that fact until he's finished training and physical alteration for the mission. Then he must discover that Bahalt is on Hire, within Etasalou's grasp. Given both factors, he'll have his cause, cast in concrete."

"But if I arrange a meeting in the oneway, and he tells her he's being sent to . . ." Ved stopped, thoughtful.

Halib grinned. "Exactly. Lannat and Bahalt are exploring a budding romance. Is it likely he'd tell he's agreed to murder her uncle? Not while there's light in this world."

Undaunted, Ved argued on. "Etasalou puts family kinship before everything. What if he forgives this niece? She may betray Lannat. Or what if he kills her to avenge what he considers his family honor before Lannat can save her?"

"She won't betray Lannat. If she were going to do that, she'd have done it already. And if Etasalou kills her, Lannat will be all the more motivated to do what we want."

Shrugging resignedly, Ved turned his attention to implementing the plan. "It'll take some time to find a plausible excuse for Bahalt's transfer. She's under Sungiver's command. While it's being worked out, I'll have Lannat moved to another cell. Oneways are unpleasant."

Halib shook his head, stood up. He asked, as he moved to the book-lined walls, "How's he handling the situation?"

"Not well. Solitary confinement is contradictory to everything in his psychological construction. I don't think there's any danger, exactly."

Running a finger across the spines of the volumes, Halib considered Ved's response for a while before deciding. "Let him ripen."

"He's going to be very angry, Exalted. Oneways do things to people's minds."

"I would certainly hope so." Halib wondered if he should try to explain to Ved. While thinking it over, he tilted his head back to scan the ceiling, with its paintings of the original colonizers of the galaxy. Central to the huge, arching picture was the original starship that brought the Blood Father to Atic. Hovering in the distant sky—a totally fabricated artist's conceit—were the ships that went on to the other inhabitable planets of the galaxy. The Blood Father stood in the center of an admiring, smiling throng.

Halib's attention was drawn again to the false image of the loitering starships. He wondered what else in the painting was untrue, and how many—if any—of his ancestors had known. And what they had done to disguise it. In the end that was always the way of things, he told himself. The Lannats of the world fought and died seeking tangible truth. The Halibs ruled, wresting power from the sacrifice of others with filmy lies. So be it.

"If Lannat's gibbering with rage, so much the better," he told Ved. "As much as I admire the man, he must serve the destiny of empire, or he has no use. You understand. I cannot afford ordinary concepts. The fate of a dozen planets and their cultures rests on me. That is what I am. That is what Lannat is for."

Ved raised his tumbler in silent acknowledgment. Sunlight fractured on the edges of the cut design, launching multicolored darts in random fantasy as he drained the whiskey. Rising, he bowed low, then made his way to the secret panel. A moment later Halib was alone.

He pushed the button to retract the bar. Dark polished wood and metal, crystal decanters and beveled mirror, multicolored liquids glittered good night as the door panels closed. He stared at the spot for a while before finishing his whiskey. Then he pushed the button and raised his tumbler in silent greeting when the bar obediently reappeared.

The door to Lannat's oneway flew open. Startled, he leaped from his chair and turned to stare in stupefied wonder at Nan Bahalt, framed in the opening. His thought processes were little more than crackling explosions; he lifted a hand, unable to move further, or to speak.

He'd given a guard his buy card number for the promise of this moment. Now that it was here, he was afraid to believe. Vision mocked him. No skin had that luscious brown richness. No eyes gleamed so, none were so wondrously deep and alive. No figure was so full, so ripe with promise.

No lips ever called his name with such sweet, hesitant hope.

A hard shove sent her stumbling toward him. He leaped to catch her. Holding her with one hand, he raged, strained for the door with the other. It slammed shut, almost catching his fingers.

Nan pulled him back. For an instant they looked into each other's eyes, then embraced in a kiss that was reunion, passion, and despair. It was Lannat who finally pulled away. Again, his gaze devoured her for the briefest of moments before searching the gleaming walls beyond her with hatred.

"We only have an hour," she said. "Don't waste any of it on them. Are you all right?"

A smile broke through the anger. It suffered for the experience. Still, it was a smile. "I never missed anyone before. Not like this."

She kissed him lightly, then put her head against his chest. "Your note said they were going to free you. It didn't say who they are. Everyone's looking for you." She stepped back suddenly, eyes wide in fear. "The Peace/Order surveillance cameras. I was so excited I never even thought . . . Did I lead someone to you?"

"If you were under any sort of surveillance, the bloodbeetle I bribed wouldn't get within a mile of you." He forced a laugh that came out too sardonic. "I'm already a prisoner. Anyone who wants me has to free me first, right? Don't worry; I'm all right."

She giggled nervously, then reached to touch his face. "I never thought of you with a beard. You look different."

He bent to kiss her, long and hard. When they parted, she laughed some more, heartily. Looking deeply into his eyes, her own sparkling with mischief, she said, "Oooh, variety. I like that in a man," and he kissed her again. They held that embrace a bit longer than before, and this time when they separated Lannat's eyes remained hard closed. He shivered like a man freezing. He collected himself with effort. Rasping, grudging, his tone acknowledged their present reality. "Has anyone given you any trouble?"

"No, it's been fine."

The lie offended him. "Don't do that. I have to know, Nan."

Stepping close again, holding to him to hide her face, she said, "They took me from my old medical service, the one that used to be under my uncle's command. I'm part of Sungiver's medical staff now. They haven't been especially friendly." She looked up, attempting to blunt the truth. "You can't blame them, Lan. My uncle disgraced Lumin. No religion can tolerate an apostate. He betrayed everyone, everything. Anyhow, rumor says I'm being transferred to Hire."

Lannat accepted that with a mix of dismay and relief. The thought of her so far away was poisonous; at the same time, anything that distanced her from Sungiver was good. Anyhow, he thought grimly, when this was all over, he'd go to her wherever she was. He let his feelings about Sungiver break through. "Sungiver has to have been in on the whole Paro thing. She knew exactly what everyone was doing, all the time. Hypocritical old witch. As soon as I'm cleared . . ." He stopped, then said lamely, "I told you in the note. They're giving me a chance to prove I'm innocent."

"Who?" She moved away to the shelf-bed, perched on the edge. "I'm afraid. You trusted them all before—the emperor, the Rifles, Casey. Look what it got you. Now it's 'they.' I know it's dangerous, or you'd have already said what it is. 'They' don't care if you clear your name. You know I'm right."

Lannat laughed, breaking off as soon as he saw how it affected her. It shocked him to realize how harsh, how brittle he sounded—and that he couldn't remember the last time he had laughed aloud. Softly, his tone making the apology he would never find in words, he said, "It's the only chance I'll ever get. I have to take it." He shifted awkwardly, looked around as if seeking escape. Sullen, dark anger melted. When he met her gaze at last, it was pained, pleading. "They robbed me, Nan. Everything I knew or wanted is gone. But I spend most of my time remembering us, on Paro. I still have to clear my name. I couldn't live with myself, much less live with you, with those lies hanging over my head. You probably don't understand that. All I can do is ask you to bear with me."

He stopped there, looking off at the door to the oneway, and there was a ferocity in the expression that made Nan straighten involuntarily. Her hands, on her knees, gripped tightly. Still, she waited silently until he continued. "I wanted the first time I told you I love you to be a special moment. It was going to be romantic and wonderful, a thing we could look back on and treasure for the rest of our lives. They stole that opportunity, too; I waited too long. Now I have to tell you here. I hope I can tell you again, somewhere better, in a place that's just for us. I love you."

Nan was crying. And smiling. "Nothing else matters. I love you." She came to his waiting embrace. This kiss was lingering, confiding. Committing. When they stopped, they walked to the shelf, holding hands, where they sat beside each other, her head on his shoulder, his arm around her. She said, "I keep thinking about Delight, the little girl Sungiver thought was a telepath. Did you know the emperor reunited her with her parents? He's a good man, Lan; I can see why you admire him." She paused, shifted her position, hesitant. When she resumed, there was a wistfulness in her tone that nearly broke Lannat. She said, "I want us to have a girl. Like Delight. I want to watch you spoil her. All my life, I want that."

He said nothing.

For a long while, they shared the silence. Finally, they talked some more. They spoke of a future as if it actually existed. They tried to forget they were providing entertainment for those outside.

Unable to sleep, Lannat pretended. It was a game. The guards weren't aware of it, but that was immaterial. The important thing was to win. Any way he could hide the truth from their prying eyes, the unceasing monitoring of their listening devices and cameras—that was winning. It was the only way he could contend.

He rolled over on his side, admitting that it didn't matter at all if they believed he was asleep, awake, or pupating. It was his one mode of resistance, but it wasn't really important. Importance was physical. If he could just get his hands on one of them. Just once.

How many sleeps since Nan's visit?

Sometimes it seemed he had dreamed that whole hour.

Ten sleeps? Twelve? For a while he tried to keep count by making small tears in the hem of his shirt. Soon after he woke with a thudding headache that made him think of drugs and discovered he was wearing a new shirt. He was pretty sure there had been six rips in the old one. But it could have been five. Or eight. By the time the headache went away he decided not to bother anymore.

He thought about time less each day. Whatever a day was. Mostly he wondered if the promise to free him and send him after Etasalou still held. When he wasn't thinking of Nan. There were other thoughts, of course. Of finding the oneway

door unlocked and stealing through the p
the first guard he came to, take his weapo

Sitting up, he flung himself off the she
sink. The bearded, haggard stranger in t
him. He washed up, slicking back his hair
only unkempt, he felt foul; he was allowe
often as he wished, and clean clothes were ncoming without delay when requested. Nevertheless, no bath, no shower, no shave, and no haircut was disgusting. Even in combat, even during the long, arduous campaign on Delphi, he had managed to stay shorn and shaved. He'd never seen himself like this.

He was seated in his chair, daydreaming about hot tubs and massages, when the speakers startled him. "Stand in the center of the cell, back to the door."

Because this was such a unique event, Lannat hesitated. The voice was annoyed. "Move."

By angling to one side, Lannat was able to watch the door in the mirror inset above the sink. Another victory—perhaps a very important one. He spread his feet for better leverage.

The speakers said, "You are dismissed. Turn slowly, take the hood from the guard. Put it on. Obey, or your dismissal is revoked. Punishment will be inflicted."

An electric current of excited, tangled emotions nearly staggered Lannat. Cursing his gratitude, straining to hold back any visible semblance of relief, he did as told. The door moved, so slowly, tantalizing. When it was fully open, a guard in a tight, hooded uniform stepped into view. Lannat noted the material; nypro was reasonable proof against edged weapons, and it was slick, hard to grasp. Silently the guard extended the familiar black hood. Lannat donned it. He took the opportunity to check the man's footwear: cloth slippers.

Lannat didn't smile at the confirmation. It was an act of massive will.

The walk seemed interminable this time. There were different turns, more of them. And then fresh air. Clean, rich with

ts—mown grass, earth, water. He heard the rhyth-
atter of a sprinkler. He was surprised by all of it. He'd
med he was in the city. An engine roared to life, making
him jump. The whine of the antigrav followed. So he was going somewhere in an elcar or eltruck.

It was night. No hint of light penetrated the cloth or leaked
through the puckers where the hood gathered at his throat. The
certainty of knowing the time of day was intoxicating. For the
first time in—how long?—he knew it was dark. He wanted to
reach out, seize the aromatic blackness in his hands, and
squeeze.

Hands guided him to steps, up into a truck bed. He heard
men settle on the fore-and-aft benches of what he was sure was
a standard military troop carrier. No one touched him or spoke.
The truck howled aloft. Inertia told him when they started forward. Wherever forward led.

He estimated they were under way for thirty minutes, con-
ceding that his sense of time was grossly questionable. When
the machine descended, echoes told him they were between
solid obstacles. The city, then; tall buildings. The eltruck
bumped to a stop. The engine continued to run. Lannat was
helped to negotiate the eighteen inches of hover maintained by
the vehicle, then marched a few paces away. Someone pushed
him face forward against a wall. A voice said, "Don't move
when you hear the eltruck leave. You're being handed over to
others. If you move or speak, we'll come back to return you to
the oneway. Understood?"

"Yes."

Moments later, the vehicle lifted off and sped away. Alone,
Lannat listened to distant city noises. Surface speeders roared,
squealed around corners. Elcars and eltrucks filled his ears
with wildly shifting doppler effects. Somewhere a heavy engine chugged and thumped.

Nevertheless, he heard the stealthy footsteps approaching.
No slippers on these feet. Boots. At least two pair, probably
four. The advance stopped. A hoarse whisper commanded,

"Stand fast. We're boxing you, taking you with us. Don't try anything."

"I won't."

With two men ahead and two holding his biceps and wrists, Lannat was hustled along on a street-smooth surface. There were no curbs, many twists and turns.

Lannat was completely disoriented when the attack came. There was barely time for one of his escort to shout a curse, and everything was chaos. Lannat was tumbled. He struggled with the hood as he was knocked around helter-skelter, unable to avoid anything. Just as he tore it off, a man screamed, the gurgling terror of a cut throat. A heavy impact drove Lannat flat on his face. His hand struck something metallic, wet. A sword blade. He found the handle and rose to a squatting position, backed against a wall, weapon extended in defense.

The struggle continued in a bizarre near silence. Men grunted, groaned. Fell. Lannat watched two kick their lives out in the alley that stretched away in both directions. The only illumination was diffused backscatter. Two men, back to back, wore the light-colored garb he'd seen in the oneway. Four darker-clad figures hacked at them.

Someone shouted, "Yerot, finish Lannat. We'll handle these."

One of the four darted to the fallen and bent over them. A pencil-thin beam of light played on the wide-eyed face of a dead man. Lannat half rose and cocked his sword arm. The face above the flashlight pushed forward, twisted up toward Lannat.

Lannat lunged at the line where dark shirt ended on the neck. His victim made a surprised sound. The flashlight dropped, rolled against a body. Lannat was already stepping across the man, who was trying to hold his throat together with both hands. The three figures engaging his former escorts had no idea what was happening behind them. The attacker closest to Lannat would never find out. An overhand slash split his skull. Freed of his foe, the man in the nypro whirled to help his companion.

He and Lannat were a moment too late.

Nypro resisted slashes quite well. Unfortunately, a hard, direct thrust usually wedged its way through the overlaid fibers. That was why one of Lannat's escort died when one of the attackers threw his entire weight behind a thrust into his stomach. Nevertheless, the material seized the blade. The killer, reluctant to release his weapon, went ahead with it as the dying man fell away. He had no chance to protect himself as the last survivor of Lannat's original guards chopped into his torso with a sideways slash.

The only attacker left turned to run. Catlike, Lannat leaped, slashed. Right arm almost severed, the escaper went sideways into a building, his sword clattering on the cement. He bounced, twisting to face Lannat. In the dark, his mouth was a shrieking blackness against pallid flesh. Lannat stabbed him just below the sternum. The mouth closed, the sound ended in the instant, fluid slump of the body. Lannat had to put a foot to the man's chest to yank his sword free.

Behind Lannat, in the cul-de-sac of a freight-loading dock, an antigrav engine howled to life. Startled, he spun around, recognizing the sound as an elcar, expecting it to attack. The vehicle was hidden from his view; the soft light created by its luminous navigation screen overflowed into the alley. The surreal, electric blue glow touched on two sprawled bodies. Beyond them, propped against the wall opposite the cul-de-sac, the surviving nypro-clad guard glared helplessly at the escaping vehicle. He managed a weak swipe at it, the sword flying from his hand when it clanged off the roof. The darkened elcar lifted off. In the enclosed alley, the reverberating roar of the engine screaming to achieve vertical liftoff was deafening. As soon as it rose above the adjacent rooftops, it spun wildly and sped off.

Breath wheezing raggedly, the surviving guard waited for

Lannat. His voice was harsh. "I thought you'd help them. You're a prisoner."

"Was a prisoner. They meant to kill me. At least you people are keeping me alive. Where were you taking me?"

"You're still my prisoner."

"I can hear your chest sucking wind, trooper. If I leave you, you die here."

The man fell silent. Lannat was about to speak when the man said, "You try to run, I'll bet a month's pay I outlive you. Give it up. Strapped to my belt, in the back. Radio. Turn it on, say, 'Bustout grab.' Turn it off. They'll already have a fix, come for us. Be quick. The Peace/Order cameras won't stay knocked out much longer. And you have to put the hood back on. And give me the sword. Prisoners don't carry weapons."

Lannat exploded, but he bit back the words, allowing no more than an exasperated grunt. Gathering himself, he dropped the sword to the ground and made the necessary call. The guard said, "The hood. You have to."

Mumbling, Lannat found the thing. He put it on like a hat, waiting. As the eltruck settled toward them, he got an arm around the fading guard, held him up. The hands that helped him into the vehicle were much more considerate than before. Still, they avoided speech or contact. And they pulled the hood down securely over his face.

The second ride was very short, and when the vehicle stopped, he was instructed to keep the hood on. He was certain he was alone after that, a suspicion reinforced by a long wait before a single pair of hands led him off. They walked a long time, and then he was stumbling awkwardly down stairs, a long flight. When he complained, his escort said nothing. Then there was a long, horizontal walk in a place that smelled of cold, dead stone and moisture. More stairs, leading up. Narrow, twisting passages. Lannat was certain he was in tunnels, secret ways.

Through the hood, intense light was a palpable shock. Lannat's hands came up involuntarily. The person guiding him shoved him from behind. He staggered forward. Another pair of hands steadied him, fumbled at the hood drawstring. Lannat reached to help. The other hands fell away, and Lannat heard someone retreat. It took a moment for his eyes to adjust to the light, and when they did, he couldn't believe them. He stammered, found the right word. "Exalted."

Standing in front of his library desk, Emperor Halib held up wadded, protesting fists. Features twisted with shock and rage, he rasped words. "What have they done to you? By the light, Captain, they'll pay."

CHAPTER 5

Lannat accepted the proffered pinfruit brandy in its handcut Syrac crystal goblet with a grimace. Words tumbled out, just short of babbling. "I'm filthy, Exalted. I'm embarrassed to touch anything so handsome. I'm embarrassed to be seen like this."

A distraught emperor waved dismissal. "I don't even know who was holding you—some fringe group of imperial extremists, I'm told. More dangerous than helpful, as a rule, but they have their uses. It was they who discovered Commander Etasalou's escape. They convinced me of your innocence in the Parovian business. Then, when they sent word to me that you, of all the empire, were willing to serve me once more, I was overwhelmed. But they abused you. How could they? I'll hear no more of your embarrassment, Captain. The empire is embarrassed, and I am ashamed of it. How could this happen?"

Lannat took refuge in his drink. When the huge brandy balloon touched his lips, his nose was literally inside it. He inhaled carefully. After the bland deprivations of the oneway, the exotic mixed scents were an assault. Vanilla and strawberry; and under them, something floral, and the sharp tang of alcohol. The smell alone dizzied him. Not that he cared. Not just now. He cut a glance at his surroundings.

Books. A huge room, the arched ceiling resting on walls at least twenty feet high. Walls of books.

The oneway. Nothing to read. What was one book worth then?

Behind a large, wonderfully proportioned desk of the finest dark pollumwood, the emperor waited patiently. Lannat savored the faint muskiness that gave pollumwood its fame. For a moment that lulling aroma combined with the undercurrent of alcohol in the brandy to twist his thoughts. In an instant, he was on another planet: Delphi. The mysterious temple of the Seeker. He had been wounded then. Alcohol lingered on the flesh around his bandaged chest, and the acid tinge of newskin. His plain chair was pollumwood, and a silver-haired woman of ancient beauty spoke to him of valor beyond cut and thrust. She was dressed entirely in black, and blind. Beside her, a chorus of similarly dressed priestesses sang beautifully intricate hymns.

Astara. Of the Seeker.

Her name rang in his mind, a clarion of yearning.

Warning.

Lannat swallowed hugely, abusing the quality of superb brandy. It was medicine at that point, needed to clear his head.

To his right was a wide opening onto a balcony. From where he sat, Lannat saw only stars and silhouetted mountains in the distance. Glow-light told him he was looking across the city from a great height. From up here, it was all serene. He turned his attention back to Emperor Halib.

Why would he think of Astara now? Why did the thought come wrapped in the dead-cold grip of fear?

Awkwardly, leaning forward onto his desk in his intensity, the emperor attempted to explain without apologizing. "For the first few days of your disappearance, I confess I thought your Rifles were behind all this. The people who held you—they did tell you Etasalou plots against the throne?" He cocked his head to the side. Lannat thought it a birdlike move, but predatory. An eagle, focusing imperial eyes on something small, distant.

"Yes, sir. I was told that. I was asked to . . . track him down."

Gusting an almost explosive sigh, Halib leaned back in his chair. He looked up, past Lannat. At last, he asked softly, "And you agreed? After all the empire has done to you."

"Not entirely out of altruism, Exalted. I want to prove I did nothing contradictory to preserving the emperor's authority. Etasalou is as important to me as to the emperor."

Muttering, Halib said, "Exactly so. And perhaps for better reason."

"Sir?" Lannat bent forward, unable to hear clearly.

Halib cleared his throat. He turned those hard, penetrating eyes back on Lannat. "Let me make sure you understand your task. You find Etasalou and you kill him. There will be no reputation-saving trial, where the evil traitor confesses all and reestablishes your honor. Eliminate him, and I'll see you exonerated. Fail, and you die as a renegade and traitor. All of that, and yet there will never be any connection between the throne and you. You were never here. I never spoke to you. That is the way of power. I cannot fail, cannot even appear to fail, because I must retain my power. I must not die, or then my power flows to others, so I cannot permit one who would kill me to live. I will sacrifice you to bring him down. I will send you out to sacrifice yourself. We both do what we do for the empire, for duty. Do you see how callously I make use of you?"

Draining the brandy, Lannat said, "I understand completely. I have the emperor's personal promise, a thing I would never have hoped for. Where do I find Etasalou?"

"And there it is." Halib studied his splayed hands on the polished wood desk. "Commander Etasalou and a number of his staff from the Lumin training facility on Hector fled. We're following several leads. He'll be found soon. You'll receive the best the empire can provide to assist you in your task." Halib stopped, looked away, and sighed heavily. "You leave here with my eternal gratitude and admiration. Still, you must replace the hood, much as it distresses me. You cannot know how you came and left; in Etasalou's hands, you would eventually answer any question. Again, my world cannot acknowledge men such as you, no matter that I trust you."

Lannat put the mask on. The emperor waited while Administrator Ved reentered and helped Lannat through the secret door and into the passage behind it. When they were gone, Halib sat in his chair, staring at the meticulous rows of books across the room. Long minutes dragged by, became more than half an hour. When the signal sounded in his ear, he jumped, despite anticipating that very signal. He greeted Ved with a questioning "So?" and indicated the chair where Lannat had been.

Ved sat. "He's on his way to a safe house."

"Don't be obtuse. Explain the ambush."

White lines appeared beside Ved's nose, accentuating the sudden and uncustomary glow in his cheeks. "We're getting identifications on the bodies now, Exalted. One's a habitual criminal. Convictions for assault, armed robbery, drug peddling—no political crimes, though."

"Are you saying this was a simple robbery? An accident?"

"No, sir. I know coincidences happen, but I never believe it."

"Then your organization is infiltrated. How else would anyone know you were moving Lannat tonight? More important, is there any danger of your personal exposure?"

"There are far too many levels of security protecting me to ever be breached, Exalted. You know full well my family has served the dynasty in my capacity for generations. We are not discovered. As for someone discovering Lannat, I have only five oneway locations. It would take effort, but one or more may be compromised. If so, anyone suspecting I held him could watch us easily."

Halib rose, walked to the door leading outside, stalked back, flung himself back in the chair. "A spy, no matter how you cut it." He made it accusation. "This is very dangerous."

Coloration more pronounced than before, Ved said, "Every person connected with this entire operation is locked down, Exalted. Interrogations are already under way."

"Good." Halib nodded brusquely. "What are your plans for Lannat?"

"We'll redesign his fingerprints—there's a photoetching technique that lasts almost two years—and clear away that facial scar."

Halib interrupted. "Give him a different one."

"I don't understand."

There was no reasonable explanation. Nevertheless, Halib felt in his guts that Lannat should bear visible proof of combat. There was something in the younger man that spoke to other men of battle, of ultimate risk. Halib knew it, knew he would never experience it within the constraining requirements of his own life, and couldn't bear to cheat Lannat out of it. How could he explain to Ved? Ved would understand that difference, but he must never suspect that the emperor he served so faithfully did. Emperors weren't allowed envy. Halib said, "He must be unique, as the present mark makes him unique. Anyone who looks at the new man must believe completely he sees that man only, to the exclusion of all others. In fact, when this is over, I want the old scar replaced. Captain Lannat will be exactly as he was."

Accustomed to imperial weirdness, Ved merely said, "It shall be." He sat silently for several long breaths, waiting for Halib to stop staring into space and say something. Then he gave up, breaking the silence with a rather hollow chuckle. "I can't believe he's going to do it. There's almost no chance at all he'll get anything from Etasalou to clear himself. I admire his determination, but he's a fool."

"Yes." The emperor was contemplative, almost distracted. He continued in a musing voice, aimed more at empty air than Ved. "When's the last time we talked about my sons? Do you remember?"

"The last time? It's been years. Why do you ask, Exalted? There's not another problem, is there?"

Halib waved airily, still looking deep into the gloss on the fine wood surface. Then he raised his gaze with stiff-necked deliberation, waiting until it was full on Ved before answering. "You might want to think about my sons and think on how infrequently I mention them, before you let me hear you ever again call Lannat a fool. Give the matter your strongest consideration, Ved. But I'm holding you from too many things— an investigation and the preparation of our captain for his mission. Forgive my rambling."

The discomfited red glow was long since drained from Ved's cheeks by the time Halib finished. The pallor that replaced it was enough to absorb the previous lines by his nose; his whole face was pasty. He rose jerkily, a chastened man in the presence of a ruler with the power of life and death. "We'll get to the bottom of the ambush, Exalted. And I promise that, when we're done with Lannat's disguise, his mother wouldn't be able to pick him out or trip him up on his cover story."

Halib smiled. "Take care of it, Ved. I trust you."

Ved left much more quickly than usual. Halib barely had time to reflect that he'd told two men he trusted them that night. A record. Not the saying of it, of course; the fact that he meant it.

After waiting a few minutes, Halib pressed a button to summon a servant. The man arrived quickly and Halib ordered a light snack sent to his bedroom. They left together, taking different directions at the hall.

While Halib was automatically returning the salute of the two guards posted outside his bedroom, a man named Mard huddled behind a tree in an unlit park in a remote part of Collegium. Mard focused intently on a distant, brightly illuminated gate that pierced a high wall.

In the light, the wall was ice-white. A full hundred yards long and ten high, the ends abutted more darkened park grounds. A considerable distance behind the wall was a building, all but its upper stories obscured. Softened by the night, the severity of its architecture was nevertheless apparent. Smears of light poured from draped windows.

Mard shifted but was careful to remain within the shadows. He knew he was safe in the park; the thermal imaging detectors mounted on the gate's wall were aimed at the street. Similarly, light amplification devices at the corners of the walls were aimed parallel to the sheer surface. He also knew that the warning equipment was hooked to a defense system. Most homes had alarm mechanisms. Official buildings were allowed defenses, and no building was more official than this one. Trigger any of its detection devices and high-voltage wires atop the walls were activated. Electronically controlled land mines on the grounds were armed. There were other nasty surprises, including trained slinkats from Atic's own mountains. Low-slung, stub-tailed, heads too large for their bodies, eyes too large for their heads, they made people who saw them for the first time laugh at their comical ugliness. When they discovered the razor-sharp spurs on their muscular hind legs, the laughter faded. If they saw the scissorlike fit of the slinkat's four-inch-long teeth, the same people frowned. No one who saw a slinkat's lightning-quick rush and kill ever considered laughing at one again.

Mard had no intention of risking any of those deterrents. He wanted—needed—escorted admission. His future rested inside that building. Lumin maintained two separate but equal headquarters. This one was the official domicile of Sungiver.

Changing of the guard was an informal event. An elcar delivered a new guard, picked up the old one, and that was that. The new guard strolled about, loosening up. Mard waited until she settled down. Then, as if strolling a boulevard, he headed directly for her.

The young woman yelled at him that he was approaching a forbidden area. Mard raised his hands high, continued forward. The guard reached for a communicator and called for support, simultaneously drawing her sword and extending it. Stopping, Mard said, "I have vital information for Sungiver. Her only."

By then elcars were roaring over the wall, four of them. They dropped to a routine hover, eighteen inches off the ground. Twelve armed guards enclosed Mard in a semicircle. A burly man put the tip of his sword to the intruder's throat. "Drunk or sober, don't move. You're on holy ground."

"I have to speak to Sungiver. I have information—" Mard yelped, stepped back, only to find another sword jabbing him in the back. The hand he raised to his throat came away bloody. "I mean it. I'm Elemental Guard, the same as you. She needs my information."

"She needs?" The burly guard laughed. Others joined in.

The woman on post said, "Where's your uniform?"

Mard glanced around nervously. "You must have a scanner on post; check my identification wire." Trying to watch everyone at once, he held out his left hand. The woman retrieved a device from the sentry booth just inside the gate. Dull black, it was about the size of a deck of playing cards. She touched the small end to Mard's ring finger. The top of the scanner lit up, revealed itself as a small vidscreen. The large guard loomed over her shoulder, read the tiny print on it. "Sergeant, are you?" he said. "Well, Sergeant Mard, you're in it up to your eyes. This says your i-wy's been in the bone for six years. Security requires rewiring every five."

Confidence strengthened Mard's voice. "Keep reading. I was on Hector the whole time. Perfect security. No need for replacement."

The burly guard's expression went from suspicion to concern as it dawned on him that there was potential for personal disaster in this situation. Gruffness acquired a peculiarly plaintive undercurrent. "You were hand-picked by Commander Etasalou?"

Mard said, "It's on the i-wy. I'm not saying any more until I see Sungiver. Tell her I have a message from the commander himself."

The woman said, "Let's get inside, out of all this light. This stuff's not covered by the general orders. I'm calling the guard commander. It'll do the bastard good to get waked up."

Within the hour, Mard was linked to two Elemental Guards by long chains leading from his wrists to theirs. The guards each kept one hand on his sword handle and one on the chain, as if Mard were a captured animal. Before they started their journey, Mard had been stripped of his own clothing, examined by ultrasound and magnetic resonance machines, bathed in a shower that sprayed him with sterilizing compounds as well as antibiotics, then redressed in the present loose, floor-length robe. Now they stopped at a polished bronze door. A golden sunburst gleamed from its surface.

His skin still tingled from antiseptics when he was ushered into a circular room at least fifty feet in diameter. The predominant color was a hot orange. There were no windows. The guards told him to move ahead of them and stand in front of the red, yellow, and orange upholstered chair that was the room's sole furnishing. The chains checked him five feet short of it.

The chemically impregnated upholstery material was sensitive to minute changes in illumination and pressure. Recessed in the domed ceiling, small bulbs beamed subtle, ever-changing light levels at the chair while fans assured constant air movement. The degree of change in both stimuli was undetectable by human senses. The sensitized cloth responded continuously, however, giving the chair a disturbing appearance of living flame.

Sungiver entered unannounced. Regal, forbidding, she swept to the chair. The material of her outer robe was sensitized in the same manner as the upholstery. As she moved, it swirled constant color change, and when she settled onto the chair, she became one with the flame tableau. She gave him a few seconds to appreciate the splendor of her presence before speaking. "You told my security people you have a message from Commander Etasalou. You speak for the dead?"

Mard stared at her like a chastened puppy. "Don't you remember me?"

"Why would I do that? You presume to know me?"

"When I was a Lumin acolyte I was recruited to work for your division and instructed to penetrate as deeply into Etasalou's division as possible. You touched me. With your hand. Here." Mard raised his hand to his forehead. Links of chain tinkled derision.

Sungiver had the grace to try to disguise her ignorance. "Now I remember. You've changed, matured. That was . . . a long time ago. As I recall."

"Six years. All of it on Hector."

Surprise wiped away Sungiver's facade. "You were on Hector? And you say Etasalou lives?"

"He does. And he has many of Hector's scientists with him. He means you harm. You, the emperor, and the Rifles captain named Lannat."

Sungiver sniffed. "Lannat's come up in the world. What does Etasalou propose to do about him, especially since Lannat's disappeared?"

"Commander Etasalou ordered us to kill him. We failed."

Sungiver told the guards, "Fix his chains to the retainer rings and leave us alone." That done, she studied Mard with a probing interest that made him feel as if his flesh were flaking off like paint.

When the guards were gone she spoke again. "Can you prove Etasalou lives?"

Mard shook his head. "Sungiver, I beg forgiveness. I have no message from Commander Etasalou. I know the name and location of the man who sent us to kill Lannat. I can give you the names of the other men I was with, the names of many of the scientists and doctors who fled Hector when—"

Sungiver's raised hand and sudden smile stopped him. She said, "I never believed you had a message. Of course I forgive you. And I'll protect you. You're here because the attack on Lannat failed."

Stammering, gesturing so wildly his chains clanked and clattered, Mard answered in a rush. "I was doing what I promised to do. I abandoned my true mission—spying for you—because I couldn't be effective any longer. And, yes, I ran here because I'm in danger. Commander Etasalou—I mean, his people—never intended to take us off Atic. Even if we succeeded, there was no one at the extraction site when I got back. Etasalou left us here with no protection at all."

Sungiver leaned back, almost lounging, in the heavy chair. Her languor made the play of flame-color vividly incongruous. "You did right, coming to me. You've served me well. The lie was necessary. Lumin understands, because it is Lumin that brings light to each of us, each of us to light." She fumbled at the collar of her robe, pulled an amulet into view. Speaking into it, she said, "I want Sergeant Mard taken from my interview room, unchained, and then escorted to Doctor Otab's offices where he will record all he knows of Commander Etasalou's work on Hector and the commander's further adventures since the battle on Paro. Also, everything Sergeant Mard knows of Commander Etasalou's supporters on Atic and the other planets will be recorded. Doctor Otab will arrange quarters; Sergeant Mard is immediately promoted to captain in my personal security force with all appropriate pay and privileges." She lowered the amulet, smiled at Mard. "Does that reassure you?"

Forgetting his restraints, Mard tried to move forward. Held in place, he fell to his knees, arms wide in supplication. He was still babbling thanks when the guards led him out.

Sungiver waved cheerfully as the door closed. When it thumped shut, she addressed the amulet once more. "Further instructions for Doctor Otab: Mard may have some use beyond what he knows of Hector. I shall think on it. Once I'm sure he has no more to offer us, use him to exercise the slinkats. And this time be sure he's naked. Remember the last clothed man. I will not have another valuable animal choke to death."

CHAPTER 6

The doctor said, "Nothing to it, Captain. Just put your hand through that slot. We'll be done in a few minutes."

Light and heat leaked around the edges of the material covering the opening. The shiny metal box smelled like an overworked toaster. Lannat turned from it to look up at the doctor. " 'We,' Doctor? You're putting your hand in there, too?"

"You'll hardly notice it."

"I thought so. 'We're' going to fry 'our' hands, but I'm the one who'll 'hardly notice' it. Let me get this straight: This thing flash-burns off skin, then laser-etches new prints. Right?"

"Crudely, yes. You see—"

"Crude's good enough for me. How long do I broil in this thing? How long do the fake prints last?"

The doctor's strained patience frayed even more obviously. "The prints are replacements, not fakes. They can last a full two years. Longer, with minimal friction."

"Shorter, with intense use, I'm told. And they burn off very easily."

The doctor threw up his hands. "What do you want, perfection? We're doing all we can."

Lannat rolled up his sleeves. "Damned right I want perfection. These prints fail and I'll be getting my dental record rewritten by mouth-breathers who drag their knuckles when they walk." He jammed his hand through the slot, fingers spread, as previously instructed. The light flared brighter.

He jerked and silently cursed the reaction. The pain was rough, but no more than he expected. Acceptable.

The optically guided and computer-controlled laser took off a single layer of cells. After each pass, a spritz of anesthetic partially numbed the hand before another layer was pared off. Once the existing prints were gone, the hand was ready for the next step. A colloidal suspension of his own cells was applied and, while it was still in a gellike state, new whorls and ridges were burned in.

They would identify him until his true prints reasserted themselves. Then he could be himself again.

Whether he wanted to or not.

Everyone had warned Lannat about the stench. His stomach churned at the smell of his own hide searing. No one had ever mentioned the noise. The meshing gearworks controlling the laser's movement whirred and purred with a hateful sound of self-satisfied amusement.

By the time the second hand was done, Lannat was a bit unsteady.

The doctor wasn't entirely without feelings. He hoisted Lannat upright with a hand on his elbow and led him to the door of an adjacent operating room. Inside, Lannat stretched out on the table. An anesthesiologist clapped something smelly— Did everything in this building stink?—over his mouth and nose. A voice said, "Count backward for me, Captain. Start with seventy-three."

At seventy, Lannat decided this was simply boring, and they'd have to find something stronger to knock him out. At sixty-eight, he changed his mind; it was funny, actually. Really comical. At sixty-five he made up his mind to tell them to give it up. Then he opened his eyes and wondered how he'd gotten into a different room with a window looking out at a rainy day. And his face hurt.

He reached to touch it. Bandaged fingertips contacted bandaged features. The sensation brought him to complete awareness. He sat up, forging through nausea and pain, and spotted the mirror over the sink in his room. Lurching to it, he examined himself.

Hairline pushed back. Hair darkened a bit. Eyebrows to match. Gingerly, wrapped hands all too clumsy and all too sensitive, he eased off the bandage covering the old zigzag scar that ran from just below his forehead down to his jawbone. Gone. The skin where it had been was blush pink.

It took a few moments before he found the courage to look under the bandage on his right jaw. That was where the new scar was carved. He winced when he saw their work. No favors there. Much shorter than the old scar on the left side, the new one was wider and welted. A stabbing blow with a heavy sword, Lannat thought.

He didn't consider himself especially vain or vainglorious, either, but he mourned the old mark. It was familiar. He was used to it. This new thing was cheap. Fake. Aloud, he said, "Ugly, too, damn it."

"Are you talking about the new scar or the whole view?"

Lannat whirled to face his doctor. The quick movement sent an entire storm of pain and dizziness pounding through his head. It did nothing to sweeten his mood. "I want my gear. I've got work to do."

"Healing comes first. Take care of the hands, in particular. Damaged prints won't match the ones in the data bank. However, we can start drilling you on your new identity and cover story."

Lannat brightened. Pain and dizziness were forgotten. He was startled and somewhat concerned to realize his first thought was of reunion with Nan. That was self-indulgence, and this mission offered no room for such weakness.

The second thing to come to Lannat was concern over the

mental manipulation involved. One of the secrets of Hector was Commander Etasalou's research into the brain. Lannat shuddered, remembering the Elemental Guard troopers who fought for Etasalou. Troopers without fear, without concern. Human beings who barely acknowledged pain and fought as viciously while dying as they did when there was hope for life. The qualities of humankind married to the unswerving goals of robots.

Briefings and instruction began that afternoon. They continued for six grueling weeks. Despite his intense application to the job, Lannat badgered everyone for a specific release date. No one bothered to hint when it might come. Then one night he was wakened by a blinding light aimed directly at his face. He vaulted out of bed to confront the intrusion. Several men appeared from behind the wall of light while he was still gaining his feet. They seized him. Sheer numbers flattened him, ignoring his struggles while roughly binding him with thin cords he instantly recognized as metlin. Lannat knew better than to struggle against that. Thin as wire and unbelievably tough, it cut like a knife. He allowed himself to be thrown back on the bed. The men disappeared back into the light.

Shouts and other noise told Lannat the raid extended to the rest of the facility. Squinting in order to avoid the full dazzle of the light, he wondered how long before imperial rescue forces arrived.

A sneering voice said, "You've discovered the metlin restraints; you show good sense not struggling. Tell us what identity you were assigned and your mission. All we want is to abort this stupid game and send you back to face your legitimate sentence."

Lannat shook his head. "My name's Val Bordi. I'm being trained to infiltrate the underground on Geron."

"Don't waste my time." Something popped behind the light, a crackling noise. Lannat registered it as a zapper at the same time the dart pierced his skin an inch or so from his belly button. The electric shock battered him flat, stiffened his muscles like wood, then, just as quickly, left him bonelessly limp. Fighting for consciousness, he howled. The dart continued to send hard, sharp jolts of reduced-level voltage through him.

Salt-copper blood taste filled his mouth. A low moan trickled over a torn lower lip. Clearing his head, fighting to ignore the dart, he repeated his name. The syllables hiccuped, jarred out of him by the painful shocks.

This time he yelled at the sound of the zapper, the sound going shrill when the second dart impacted his left shoulder and delivered its full charge. When he collapsed his heels dug into the sweat-soaked sheet. Scuffling backward, he wadded the material in a heap, grunting with effort and the ongoing punishment from both darts. Eyes closed, he continued to heave back against the wall. When the electricity stopped flowing through the darts he slumped, panting like a dog. Sweat coursed down his face and neck, created growing stains on his pajamas. Frothy saliva and blood flecked his lips.

The interrogator's voice remained calm. "We already know you're supposed to assassinate Commander Etasalou. I told you we didn't want to hurt you. This is all because of your stupidity and stubbornness. We're here to expose that pig Halib's incompetence. Our master knows you're just a tool. Tell us how you've been trained to perform, and we'll leave. All we need is the information. Once we have it, you're useless to us and to the emperor. That's our only objective. And this is just the beginning."

Lannat shook his head. When he spoke, the pitiable weakness of his own voice shamed him. "I don't know anything about a commander. Don't hurt me anymore. Please. I'll tell you anything. No more. Please."

Once Lannat admitted the pain to them, spoke aloud of it, it was almost impossible to stop speaking of it. He turned his head away, pushed the lower part of his face hard against his shoulder.

The interrogator said, "You don't understand. We have all night. There won't be any rescue, Captain. I have to break you.

I will. I promise you, when I leave, I'll have what I want. And you'll be a wreck that cowers at every unexpected sound or movement. Save yourself useless torture. Your mission is already compromised. It doesn't exist. Will you make me destroy you simply to spare that fool Halib a moment of disappointment? I assure you, he'd put up with no inconvenience to help you. Just tell me where he was sending you."

"Geron." Lannat barely understood the word himself. "I go Geron. Inf 'trate. Unnergroun'. Swear's true."

"You swear it? How sad. They've already capitalized on your loss of honor, haven't they? Your word comes cheaply now, doesn't it?"

Without warning, both darts delivered full charges, the second one cutting in a few seconds after Lannat fell limp from the impact of the first.

He screamed. Cried for help. Bellowing, his voice was molded into drumbeats by the rhythmic hammering of the little darts, he insisted he was Val Bordi, destined for Geron, the emperor's spy. He named his contact, described his bona fides.

Begged them to stop hurting him.

Different noises, far away, broke past his preoccupation with pain. He wanted to believe the sounds were important.

A cooling draft swept over him, made his wet pajamas clammy. He thought he heard a door close. Agitated mumbling reached through the blinding light, confused him. He tried to shut it all out, rolled over on his side.

The light went out. For a moment he thought the darkness was blessed unconsciousness. The returning pulsing of the zapper darts said that was not to be, and he almost wept his disappointment. Clashing metal against metal stirred him. The sounds of fighting were like a memory. Shouting came closer, and the pounding of running feet. He looked up, his eyes unable to focus well. There was new light, the rectangle of an open door. Figures poured into the room.

Someone cursed. The darts were pulled out of his flesh, the

last small pain welcome. Still unable to see well, Lannat registered being helped to a sitting position, felt the metlin bonds slashed free. Rough, considerate strength bundled him to a chair. The normal lights came on in the room. Lannat squinted up at someone in the red and yellow of Lumin. His doctor, disheveled, said, "Who were they? What did they want?" As he asked, he was opening a small bag, hauling out a diagnometer.

Lannat sagged, closed his eyes. "They wanted to know my name."

Emperor Halib rose from his magnificent bed with the stealth of a practiced burglar. It offended him deeply, but his own security system required it. The megarmor door with its fingerprint-activated lock was proof against interference from outside. Inside was the problem. Although it would take at least an hour for anyone to break into the room, everyone insisted his breathing and temperature be monitored. His saving grace was the concession that nothing be attached to him. Accordingly, bending close to a panel in a closet, he whispered a code word. The machine behind the panel recognized voice and command; it switched on devices to provide recorded data of a sleeping Halib. That done, he crossed the room and whispered another message to yet another hidden machine, this one behind a decorative panel. It responded by opening a secret door, revealing an ominously black passageway.

The door snicked shut behind Halib. Inhaling deeply, he closed his eyes. The warren of clandestine ways throughout the palace delighted him. The rough walls, the aroma of their stone, the very act of being there, a presence outside the knowledge of humankind—it reached to the deeper roots of his soul, nourished his obsession with all things covert.

Opening his eyes, reaching with total familiarity for the flashlight in its receptacle next to him, he reconsidered the notion of being outside the knowledge of all others. It wasn't precisely true. Administrator Ved knew perhaps half of the tunnel network. Still, he couldn't tell when or where his emperor might be within that maze.

There was another who knew. She knew where he was at all times. More than that, she called to him, mind to mind, in a voice he could neither escape nor deny.

An emperor should not be at anyone's beck and call.

Certainly not that of a blind hag.

Halib repented of the unworthy thought instantly. Simple-minded pride, he scolded himself, and switched on the light. She was very possibly the key to everything he hoped to accomplish. The thought gave impetus to his pace. Despite the steep pitch and meager handholds of the descending stairs, he hurried along. Descent brought cold, a penetrating dankness that contrasted wildly with the splendor of the surrounding palace. He was tempted to stop at one of the many spyholes, simply to enjoy the thrill of seeing without being seen; he confessed the character flaw with no qualm whatever.

Fourteen generations of absolute dominion taught that although emperors were remembered for their character, they survived through timely intelligence.

An image of Captain Lannat plucked at his mind. Halib scowled, dismissed the unwelcome intrusion.

At the lowest level of the stairs, Halib braced against the unvarying sensation of other presences, other times. Previous reigns had created dungeons this far under the palace. Halib often wondered at the mentality of men who wanted their victims so close yet went to great lengths to hide them and assure their agonies went unheard. He wondered what his ancestors would say to him, knowing that he couldn't come here without hearing those cries and moans, the grate and rattle of infernal devices. Ancestral voices never came. Only those of their victims. He refused to consider any implications in that.

Pressing ahead, Halib came to a small wall-mounted box. He spoke into it. A bit beyond, two massive stones, laser-welded together, slid back to reveal an exit. Rollers sighed softly under the weight. The only other sound was Halib's rushed breathing. When he switched off his flashlight, a soft glow marked the doorway. He bent low, stepped through it.

Straightening, he looked past the seven candles burning on the floor of the small cave and into the blind-white eyes of the woman who called him here. He said, "I come, Astara. You called."

The woman was elegant. Clothed entirely in black, she stood as straight as the head-high walking stick in her right hand. The pitch of her body betrayed a secret; she had need of the prop in order to remain so erect. Still, her beautiful features carried haunting serenity. When she bowed acknowledgment of Halib's greeting, the silver hair cascading down to her back and shoulders shifted and shimmered like molten metal in candleglow. Her voice was low, melodious. "I request, Exalted. You honor me by extending that privilege. I would never 'call.' My respect is too great. Yet to be true to myself, I must tell you I am gravely concerned. It must be said, Exalted: Ends do not always justify means."

Halib flushed. "Pretty compliments. Rude criticism. Which one did you think I wouldn't notice?"

Sadness glossed her answering smile. "Both are heartfelt. Only one is important. Those who care for each other exchange compliments because it gives them pleasure. Only those who care can exchange honest criticism. What you have done to Captain Lannat is very hurtful. Do you feel it necessary?"

"He cannot be recognized; you grant that? The operation, the altered fingerprints—I know it's painful, but necessary for his safety. The indoctrination to acquire a new name, a different history, is difficult—"

Astara interrupted. "In my blindness, I know you blush. I know you speak around me, not to me. I know why. The Seeker has too many friends, too many eyes for this sort of subterfuge. I speak of this last shamefulness, the interrogation in the middle of the night."

"He was magnificent." Halib blustered. Simultaneously, he was surprised by his own pride in the statement. He hurried on.

"He had no idea it was a test, yet he never wavered. I concede the harshness of my methods. You must concede their effectiveness. The end did indeed justify the means."

"One day he will ask himself what you would endure on his behalf. You send him to commit murder. You torture him to discover if he can withstand it. You risk the woman he loves."

Sharp pains touched Halib, two of them. One at his left shoulder, the other in his midriff, just above his belt. The urge to touch them was maddening, but he had a terrible suspicion that Astara had something to do with them. He gritted his teeth and forced himself to address her remarks while ignoring the other matter. "You enjoy a very convenient set of standards. You find it appropriate to condemn what I do, yet you and your cult are quick enough to enjoy the fruits of my efforts. Etasalou is no less the Seeker's enemy than mine. Tell me you'll mourn him."

"Tell me Etasalou's death is your only goal in this matter."

The twin hurts flared, then disappeared. Flinching, Halib took a step back. Hoarsely he said, "You can't know my mind. You mustn't. Our pact forbids. Here, in this cave, you promised me as you promised my father."

"My word is good." Asperity sparkled in the words, as did censure. Astara paused long enough for Halib to absorb both before continuing. Her tone softened. "I infer your plans because I understand your intentions as well as your temptations. Your goals are the highest, the most noble of any dynasty. They make me proud to know you. I would have you use proud methods. When I see things that remind me of the Blood Father's cruelties, I fear for you."

Hands raised as if warding off danger, Halib glanced around. "You mustn't, Astara. Not even here. He is holy, he is—"

"Dead these hundreds of years," she finished for him, the words harsh. "A heartless man alive, a bitter legacy dead. Your mythic Blood Father fomented a mutiny that conquered a fleet of convict hulks. That was his accomplishment. His ways are the dark part of all humans. It is the rule of the beast. You, and your father before you, have set yourself against it. This empire would have collapsed generations ago but for the effectiveness of Lumin in its discriminatory education policies. That, and direct imperial control of all starships. Now you face a rogue technician, one who has the power to reinvent everything you call empire, even that which you call humankind."

Halib wiped his brow, watching Astara with a caution that bordered on suspicion. "You know I agree with you about the empire. It must change. People should not live or die at the whim of any one man or under laws not of their own making. We are one in that. Nevertheless, your chosen quest is the heart and mind; you struggle to make each person rise to their potential for goodness. I live on a battlefield, where the sword is never grounded, never sheathed, and the prime factor is that very evil you admit dwells in all of us. I plead for the help of the Seeker, but I will fight my way. Help me. Or stand back."

Chuckling, Astara took the three steps necessary to bring her to him. Again her unsteadiness made the necessity for the tall staff brutally apparent. She reached to touch him, the hand going unerringly to his cheek. She said, "I have loved you since you were born, my devious, deceptive friend. I cannot always approve of you. Sometimes I admire you, sometimes I deplore you. But I love you. Whatever plans you have for Captain Lannat—especially whatever you haven't told him you expect him to do—I ask you to think through. He is mine, too, you understand. Oh, he resists me and the Seeker. But he is mine, and therefore, Exalted, he is yours. Be careful, please. For both of us."

"I shall. But now I must go. His testing is over. He leaves tomorrow. If it's in your power, watch over him."

"For his sake? Or for your goals?" She laughed, brushed at the lines of his frown with fingertips that had the delicacy of a breeze, then said, "I will do all I can."

Halib stepped away from her caress with embarrassed quickness. Inside the passageway, he watched the dual blocks of stone, each a full cubic yard, whisper back into place. Utter

blackness swarmed over him, set off a touch of vertigo. It
passed quickly. He stood for a moment, unmoving, wracked by
doubt and surprise. Aloud, he murmured, "I believe her; she
would never reach into my thoughts. Then how did she know I
want—*need*—him to strike at the other, as well? She wasn't
guessing. She *knows*. Am I so transparent? Does anyone else
suspect?"

He shrugged massively, decisively, flicked on the flashlight,
strode down the tunnel. Then, almost imperceptibly, he
slowed. Soon he was shambling. He stopped. "Damn you," he
said, and again, "damn you." He slapped the wall, the report
echoing frustration ahead and behind, lost in darkness. " 'Be
careful,' she said. 'For both of us.' Which 'both,' damn it? You
and him? Or you and me? Diabolical old hag. And you call *me*
cruel."

The rest of the journey to his bedroom was escape.

CHAPTER 7

The first warning klaxon alerting all hands aboard Starship *Socrates* blared through her cargo bays. Lannat looked up
from his cleaning rag to watch the other cargo snuffs begin
checking tie-downs and scaffold rigs. He picked up his own
cleaning materials—a bucket of soapy water, a brush, and the
wiping rag—and turned them into the gear locker. A fat snuff
took it with a look of frozen boredom. Lannat was glad to see
the stuff go, even if it meant they were headed into passage.

This was the last one.

An image of Nan, a fantasy, crowded out everything else, and he felt his entire body grow warm. In the next instant, harsh reality broke the daydream.

A year gone. A year with her on Hire, where the man who hated her had fled. Ever since learning that, Lannat's every thought of her brought its bitter aftertaste of fear, of despair.

If she was safe, did she still think of him? Care at all? A year. A little more than a year. People changed. Had she met someone?

Lannat stretched, listening to joints crack, feeling muscles strain. Physical stress cleared his mind.

Could the mission be so close? First there had been the two months of training. Then the five-month trip to Hire. They said he couldn't disembark then, however. Etasalou and Counsellor Ullas paid particular attention to anything coming from Atic. So Lannat, working under the name of Galvos, watched the blue-green of Hire heave into view, then disappear, knowing Nan Bahalt was down there. Vulnerable.

Then, after the pain of watching Hire recede into the void, three months to Geren. Finally—*now*—back to Hire. Eleven months on the starship, his stomach knotting at every thought of her.

In a few hours it would be over. No, not over. But he'd be involved. He could *do* something.

The klaxon sounded again, a double blast; thirty minutes until the ship entered grip, the first stages of passage, that near-mystic journey through the space-time anomaly that permitted intragalactic travel. Without such rents in the fabric of space, humans would still be restricted to Home. Even radio waves depended on commbuoys positioned on either side of an anomaly to transmit from planet to planet in months rather than years.

Passage was the door to space exploration.

Under the best of circumstances, it tested machine and mankind to the ultimate limit. Lannat had never heard of anyone who survived if he wasn't strapped in when the maniacal forces of the anomaly seized the ship.

He moved a bit more quickly to his cargo section. The entire hull of *Socrates*, as a cargo vessel, was packed with stacks of metal cargo containers; the cargo snuffs called them bright cans. Each standardized rectangular box measured ten feet by twelve feet by thirty feet. *Socrates* carried hundreds of them, racked on top of each other, separated fore and aft by lanes wide enough to provide access to cargo lifters. Cross-ship alleys were just wide enough for a man to walk through. The effect was of a city as precise as crystallography.

Lannat hated the sight.

He quickly examined the fibermet bands holding everything in his section in place. There were sensors that measured the tension of every strap, but safety demanded human checks. The same held true for the scaffolding surrounding the cargo containers. Lannat scampered up and down and across his assigned areas. He was fast, but he was careful. No one wanted to think about a stack of cargo containers shaking free when *Socrates* writhed and yawed through passage. If the ship lost her precise center, where all those forces impacted each other to create a tenuous balance, she ceased to be. When a ship failed, there was never any way to know what happened. But if she was a cargo ship, cargo snuffs all over the galaxy wagged heads and muttered something like "Loose goods probably started it. One of them bright cans comes loose, and she'll rip through your hull like it was made out of fog."

Snuffs were very careful about secure cargo. Ship's officers double-checked the snuffs constantly.

As Lannat trotted to his bunk, the last of the cargo officers finished inspecting.

Strapped down, Lannat closed his eyes. The final klaxon blasted. He jumped. Cold sweat tickled at his temples, and his throat was as dry as a jet exhaust.

He was sure he felt the tug of grip. The point of no return. The ship was committed to her plunge into the anomaly. It would, it was hoped, fling her out light-years closer to Hire. He knew that the bridge crew fed data to the ship's computers and reported her course, speed, and attitude in growing tension. Once in grip, they simply aimed her. And prayed.

Twisting his arm against his straps, Lannat reached to touch the hull. He felt her first groans as the maelstrom laid hold of her. She bucked, settled for a while, then rolled sickeningly. Tortured moans and squeals raced through her skin, her ribs, the struts and frames that were her bones. Cables and piping slammed and chattered.

The forces tearing at the ship reached inside her, as well. Bombarded by immeasurable energies, the human mind shut down. Isolated in private thoughts and terrors, Starship *Socrates*'s human companions fell unconscious.

Lannat woke instantly, jerking around to assure himself *Socrates* still existed before intellect reminded him that, if *Socrates* didn't exist, neither did he. She was there, so he was there.

Good.

He threw off the straps and practically leaped to his feet. Only hours, then orbit over Hire. Nan.

He hurried toward the cargo bay. The forthcoming mission was so close now. In his speed, he reached for it. In his need to survive, he feared it. Yet, beyond all that, he wanted to shout for joy that his eleven months of waiting was coming to an end.

When his duties were done, he settled in the nearest cross-ship alleyway. Cautiously, keeping his back to any watchers, he drew the ceryag knife from the scabbard under his left arm. The blade, a meld of synthetic ruby and ceramics, had an oval cross-section and lengthwise ribs for strength. The material still snapped too easily. On the plus side, ceryag didn't set off metal detectors, and the edge was awesome. For a few moments, eyes slitted, he stared at the scintillating sharpness as if expecting wisdom to drift upward from the material like smoke from fire.

He put the knife away, frowning darkly. There was arguably something wrong with a man who could lose himself in admiring a killing piece. Unconsciously he raised a hand to touch his scar, then caught himself. He smiled. Fingers with false whorls rising to a false wound.

His fingertips felt wrong. No one ever told him how his sense of touch would be different. When he complained, the spymasters ran test after test, "proving" he was perfectly normal. He knew better. The fingertips felt different, whether their fool machines detected change or not. He couldn't get used to them, and it wasn't because he was neurotic, no matter what they whispered when they were sure he couldn't hear. He simply didn't want to be someone else.

With preparation for off-loading done, the lucky snuffs scheduled for landfall were getting ready. They polished shoes, adjusted the hang of cloaks, perfected the tuck of a shirt here, the drape of trousers there. Once more Lannat wondered why the cargo workers were all male. The spymasters assured him it was some sort of guild rule, and a good thing for him. They said it made it easier for him to hide in the crowd. Lannat didn't question any of the crew about it; as with everything else, he kept to himself.

As a man staying aboard, Lannat dressed much more casually. His trousers were of plain, coarse material. His lar-flannel shirt was equally rough, a product of the planet Geren. Lar stalks, properly treated, produced a fiber with such a high silicon content it actually offered some protection against edged weapons. Also, Lannat wore a jacket of thick, incredibly tough leather. He had to protect it from theft at all times; Donian-worked zard skin was expensive, and cargo snuffs were less circumspect about stealing from a new guy than an old hand. Despite his eleven months among them, he was still called a fing. The origin of the term was lost in antiquity; it served the snuffs as an all-occasion insult.

That reminded him—and bothered him—how much he disliked his fellow cargo snuffs. It made him wonder if he was

some sort of snob. His only impression of them was of ignorant, venal men who took pride in their vices. He was quite
aware that none of his own Rifles spent their free time singing
in choirs, but most of them knew the difference between cruelty and hardness. Still, there was advantage to the vague an-
tipathy he shared with the crew. He wouldn't be missed until
Starship *Socrates* was long gone from Hire. There was a reasonable chance he wouldn't be reported absent for a full day.

Lannat strolled to a viewport. The cargo lighter was already
in view, coasting toward them. Beyond it, gloriously bright and
beautiful, the planet Hire.

Nan.

He couldn't let himself dwell on her. On Hire he must be yet
another man. There was a mass of new data to remember. Parents, schools, relatives, addresses. ID numbers, comm numbers, buy card numbers. Security people, asking, asking. Hire
allowed no mistakes.

Suddenly he was shaking.

Control. The spymaster said survival under cover was 80
percent a matter of control.

Misdirection. That was another 10 percent, they said. It was
why they insisted he land on Hire on *Socrates*'s return trip from
Geren rather than on the way there.

Then they laughed and said the final 10 percent was
dumb luck.

Cold-blooded bastards.

Lannat grinned wryly. Just like Rifles, he thought, and
cursed them some more, as a matter of form.

With the lighter flashing visuals to indicate ready for link-
up, Lannat edged into an alley between stacked cargo containers. Out of sight of the rest of the crew, he raced to a particular
tower. Scrambling up the webbing and scaffolding, he made
his way to the top. There was barely room between the ceiling
and the crown of the container for him to squeeze between.
Wriggling, he made his way to a small loading hatch. Ignoring
the handle and its telltale electronic monitor, he maneuvered

alongside the entry. From inside his jacket he drew an object that appeared to be a flashlight. When he turned it on, however, it made a high, buzzing noise. Lannat touched one end of the device to the thin gap between the door and the rest of the container. The buzz turned to a throaty growl.

Vibration soon nudged the hinge pins free. The hatch sagged open. Lannat lowered himself inside, careful to protect the integrity of the monitor. Producing a pencil-light, he replaced the pins. A quick search of the crowded interior brought him to his goal, a large tube standing on end. Lannat grabbed the two protruding hand grips that were there for the obvious purpose of opening the thing. A few sharp spins had the top screwed off. Feet first, he lowered himself into the padded interior. Once inside, he could barely move. Reaching up to secure the cover was hard work. Getting his arms back down to his sides to activate the controls at waist level brought sweat.

Tiny lights, called blip lights, directly in front of him signaled that the temperature monitor, the heater, the gas chemistry balance equipment and its attendant oxygen recirculator were operational. That done, he fumbled with the cross-chest harness until he was firmly strapped in place. The back side of the buckle centered above his diaphragm. It held sensors to monitor breathing, body temperature, and perspiration chemistry. Should he exceed specific parameters, the sensors triggered other blip lights. Lannat seriously questioned the practical value of a light that flashed on to tell him "Neener, neener, neener; you're scared spitless."

He told himself to settle back and enjoy the ride. Excellent minds went into the preparation of the escape transporter. It wasn't all that uncomfortable, actually. All a person had to do was close his eyes and stop thinking about being utterly helpless in total darkness. Not exactly helpless; just unable to move. Inside a can. Completely dependent on a battery half the size of a fist. With one's nose almost in contact with the insulation. Untested insulation. Well researched, however; everyone said so.

Who could worry?

The blip lights flickered.

The impact of a robot cargo lifter ramming its forked nose under his set of stacked containers set off a tremble of eagerness through Lannat as well as the bright can's metal walls. He inhaled deeply, quickly. He fought against images of a toppled load, a crack in his escape transporter. Then he was moving.

The transfer went smoothly, with a minimum of thumps and rumbles. Still, when he heard the cargo lifter growl away, he discovered his hands were so tightly clenched it hurt to splay the fingers. For one horrible moment a calf muscle tried to cramp. Sweat seemed to boil out of him.

The blip lights blazed. The faintest touch of hysteria touched his mind, insisted that the tiny lights were scolding him. He told himself that was idiotic and cursed back with equal fervor.

Secretly, underneath all that, he was grateful for the faint illumination they provided.

Next came the unmistakable siren warning that the starship outloading hatch was about to close. Cargo snuffs in the tunnellike lock connecting starship and lighter had thirty seconds to get inside. The siren was largely superfluous; people rarely stepped past the outloading hatch.

Too soon—how could thirty seconds go by so quickly?— Lannat heard the lighter's corresponding hatch unlocking.

Unable to resist, he sucked in air greedily, held it. All around him there was an almost explosive sigh. The air within the tunnel and all the containers on the conveyor belt was simultaneously gusting out through drain vents into space.

Lannat was in a vacuum.

Silence. The terrifying, airless silence of space. Of eternity.

Steady vibration told him the conveyor belt was moving containers into position to be picked up by one of the lighter's robot cargo lifters. Some more jounces and some stomach-roiling rocking back and forth passed before everything stopped with a final jar. Lannat was aboard the lighter.

The Hire-bound durable goods moved in what the transport

people called a free bay. The lighter crew controlled its doors and other machinery from a tractor rig. The detachable free bay had enough structural strength to handle cargo and enough hull to provide aerodynamic quality. It was entirely no-frills, certain death for anything alive. Such as stowaways.

The lighter's engines kicked in. Lannat clenched his teeth against the vibrations. His thoughts went to the katun drums. He specifically remembered burial processions. When the drums passed close by, one felt—rather than heard—deep throbbings that tore at the very fastenings of the guts.

The reaction was true of all katun drum occasions, not just funerals. But that was what he remembered. He couldn't get the image out of his mind.

He forced himself to review his instructions. Remain in the container until signaled clear to exit. Three sharp raps. Pause. Two more raps. Get out fast. Dispose of all ID used aboard *Socrates*. Get new papers now from pocket in container's insulation.

On Hire, he would be Val Bordi. Starship *Socrates* would report a man named Galvos missing, presumed to have jumped ship. She would continue on to Atic. Investigation would show that Galvos never existed, but it would take awhile. By the time that word reached the authorities on Hire, Lannat hoped that Val Bordi would also have disappeared, replaced by a redeemed Captain of Rifles.

The lighter buffeted viciously on reentry into Hire's atmosphere. Once more the ardent little blip lights jittered to life, telling him he was overexcited. He shouted at them pointlessly, then stopped. Staring straight ahead, looking far beyond the critical bulbs, he endured.

Antigrav engines howled the lighter to a soft landing. Lannat recognized the sound of a crane and the shouts of landing pad workers. Chain rattled and cable dragged across metal with its own peculiar buzz. Lannat's container was lifted, transported. He didn't like the swaying motion. There were some slams and shakes when the massive box was lowered again, then forklifted into place.

Grunting and yanking, Lannat twisted open the tube lid. He crawled out silently, listening for the signal that would free him to leave the bright can. Hours passed. Visions of betrayal plagued him. Eventually he quit checking his watch.

When the rapping finally came, it startled him. No approaching footsteps, no questions. Just tap-tap-tap. Pause. Tap-tap. Much softer than he expected, much closer together. In his mind he saw a furtive, timid figure doing what he must, then sprinting for safety.

Lannat sympathized.

His exit was as cautious as his entrance. Poking his head out of the hatch, he examined his surroundings. A cavernous warehouse surrounded him, filled with hundreds of containers identical to his own. Because of the windowless gloom, broken by a few dim lights, the place was worse than the hold of *Socrates*. The containers formed a surreal landscape of geometrically sheer cliffs and mysterious crisscrossing canyons leading to darkness.

Lannat's container stood apart from the others on the concrete floor. Looking up at the number of containers stacked on top of each other, he breathed silent thanks. There was no webbing here; even if he had been on top, able to open his hatch, the climb down would have been nearly impossible. The efficiency of the emperor's undercover operatives impressed Lannat more than ever. A surge of optimism sent him scurrying through the dusky alleys between stacks, looking for a door.

He found one quickly. Before he used it, however, he removed everything identifying him as Galvos from his wallet. Each item was individually plastisealed; not a universal practice, but common enough to warrant no particular attention. Using the ceryag blade, Lannat carefully split each article free of its wrap, piling the collection of photos, buy cards, and identification on the concrete floor together with the plastic. That done, he searched for a water faucet of some sort. He had little

time for that task and abandoned it quickly. The spymasters
had already provided another answer to his problem, empha-
sizing that all this action must take place in an absolutely secure locale; there must be no possibility of observation. Lannat
was confident the warehouse was perfect. Taking a step back,
he urinated on the collection.

The result exceeded his imaginings. The spymasters said all
the material would rapidly and totally decompose once exposed to any liquid with a high oxygen content. The insistence
on utter secrecy apparently had something to do with the immediate appearance of wild, multicolored flames a foot high.
Lannat tiptoed backward with as much speed, style, and grace
as his circumstances permitted. Unfortunately, that was very
little. He slammed into a container.

Sheer good luck prevented him from soiling himself or his
clothes. Watching the fire sputter out, he thought longingly of
the spymasters and fond reunion.

As for his identification material, the chemically treated articles were fine gray ash. Even magnetic strips and the micro-
chips encased in the buy cards were essentially vaporized. He
gave the mess on the floor a wide berth as he left, wrinkling his
nose at the stench. Before he stepped outdoors, he transferred
Val Bordi's papers from his pocket to his wallet.

He inspected each document with meticulous care. The
identification booklet carried by everyone on Hire carried a
coded optical strip, updated annually. When inspected, it revealed that person's history and present. Failure to carry it or
tampering with it in any way seriously imperiled that person's
future. The official term for the document was "lifeline." It was
small exaggeration.

The spaceport's landing pad lights on their high towers created a dazzling island in a black sea of night. It took Lannat a
moment to recall that Hire had no moon. Some small asteroids
trapped in its gravitational field whizzed past, gleaming coldly,
but no one counted them as real moons. In fact, no one counted
Hire itself as very much. Lannat met a few Hirans on Atic. He

found them all to be withdrawn, uninterested in any world other than their own. They had a reasonable argument for their insularity: Hire was scenically grand. Two of the three primary landmasses featured several mountain chains separated by immense, wide valleys rich with forests and nourishing rivers. The third landmass, the smaller, presented a more docile landscape. Marked by rolling hills, lakes, and spring-fed streams, it was named Kull, and was literally Hire's food basket. The bulk of the population lived there.

Exercising the social reticence—some called it plain good sense—that marked their native character, the Hirans sited both of their spaceports and the planet's administrative headquarters on the wilder shores. That way fewer acres of arable land were paved over to provide office space for bureaucrats. Better yet, more people were distanced from the trappings of government. In light of the repression by the present dynasty, the separation was more benevolent than anyone originally planned. The briefers on Atic said Etasalou could be expected to hide on the largest continent, called Goliphar. It was the most rugged of the three and home to the capital, Liskerta. Presently that metropolis was a faint glow to the southwest.

Starlight was enough to give some indication of reaching mountains to the east and north, once Lannat had the spaceport's lights behind him.

No one paid any attention to another rider when he joined those catching an elbus for town. By the time the racket from the bus's antigrav engines leveled off, Lannat already noticed that his fellow passengers were more than reserved. The psychological distance they maintained was the equivalent of isolation. They read. They dozed. They stared out the window. When the elbus stopped to pick up new fares or let out old ones, most of the window gazers turned their attention to fingernails or clothes or something else. If they did continue to look outside, their disinterest in other humans was ostentatious. Similarly, they appeared unaware of the frequent Peace/Order cameras flashing past on posts and rooftops, nor did they seem bothered by the constant, low-level mumble of the propaganda broadcast coming over the elbus's speakers. It was Lannat's understanding that the very quietness of the continual indoctrination made the subconscious more receptive. He listened for a few minutes and decided it was such inane twaddle it was harmless.

Nevertheless, the behavior of his fellow riders strongly suggested they believed the admonition that "There is no law higher than social harmony; all crime grows out of nonconformism." They certainly heard it enough on the elbus.

At the small mall that was his stop, Lannat fell in with the handful of debarking passengers. He strolled toward a restaurant called Mikey's, which advertised its presence with a rotating neon sign atop a pole in front of the building.

No one would have noticed Lannat's quick, sidelong glance at the pole. If they had, they still would have attached no significance to the innocent graffito—"JJ + GK" enclosed in a lopsided heart. To Lannat, however, the message signaled that it was safe for him to enter the restaurant, sit in a booth, and order dinner.

The customers were exactly like the elbus passengers. People conversed with companions, very quietly. Those who were alone avoided eye contact as if they feared damage. The waitress was as cordial as anyone could be who refused to look directly at a patron. Lannat decided it was all for the best; if the locals chose not to see him, so much the better. "Inconspicuous" was the magic word that might save his life.

Halfway through his meal, Lannat saw a man enter and was sure he must be his contact. Slightly more than average height and weight, dressed much like Lannat himself, he came through the door quickly, darting a glance at his watch with obvious irritation. He was the very picture of a man late for an appointment. His blond hair was cropped close; heavy cheekbones, full lips. A gold disk with an off-center blue stone dangled from a short chain attached to an ear stud. The decoration was common on Hire.

Lannat sensed much more behind the ordinary exterior, as one predator senses the reality of another. When the man scanned the room, settled his gaze on Lannat and smiled, it was more than proof of Lannat's theory. The gaze was also a measuring, a speculation.

He slipped into the booth across from Lannat. Smiling broadly, he said, "I missed the early elbus. Couldn't find my house key. It was under today's mail."

The identifying phrase was in order. Lannat responded as instructed. "I've had the same thing happen to me. The last time I found it in my pocket."

The other man continued to smile, but as soon as he heard Lannat's correct response, something changed in his expression. There was relief and satisfaction. Lannat saw more. It took a moment to identify. Eagerness. The man burned with anticipation, as if this meeting was a promised beginning. He said, "Glad you made it. Took a lot of guts. My name's Jarka."

Nodding, Lannat bent forward a shade, lowered his voice. "Glad to be here. You're taking me to the apartment?"

Once more Jarka worked some subtle adjustment within his steady smile. The back of Lannat's neck tingled. Even so, he was unprepared for the enormity of Jarka's next words. "You've been lied to. Everyone who set you up for this mission was lied to, and they passed it on to you. Now that we've got our hands on you, *we* make the rules. Cooperate, and you'll be taken care of. Give us trouble, and . . ." He shrugged. The smile disappeared, leaving only steel-gray eyes that stared full into Lannat's. "Give us trouble, and we'll give you to Etasalou."

[faint text from previous page showing through]

CHAPTER 8

The chaotic jumble in Lannat's mind finally focused on one thing: Nan Bahalt.

Her dependence on him kept him from reaching for the throat below the infuriating smirk across the table.

Control. The people who planned all this said the key was control.

They were also the ones who bought everything this liar told them.

Mentally shouldering aside growing rage and apprehension, Lannat realized that Jarka's threat revealed more than it should have: Jarka and his friends had to know that Etasalou was the target, but they obviously understood that Etasalou was more than that. They, too, knew he represented evil. And the idea of Etasalou as threat probably meant the original mission was still in place.

Jarka's menace, then, was mostly bluff.

Lannat needed only a moment to wishfully convince himself of that notion. It calmed him, reestablished his resolve. Control, he suddenly realized, meant more than managing his own behavior. It also meant directing the behavior of others.

Nan Bahalt. Whatever happened, she had to be gotten clear of her uncle's reach.

Lannat asked Jarka, "What do you know about me?"

A faint wisp of surprise touched Jarka's superiority. "You're a member of the Elemental Guard, recruited by the emperor's intelligence personnel to come here and eliminate Commander Etasalou. You're doing it so the Guard can regain the emperor's favor."

At least the spymasters hadn't compromised the cover story. "My mission has the personal wishes of the emperor stamped all over it, and I am the emperor's man. Can you understand that?"

"You're a long way from the emperor. Naked without a friend. One word from us—"

"No more threats," Lannat interrupted. "If you didn't need me, your counsellor's police would have me inside already." A sudden, unexpected image darted across his mind; he recalled the all-clear signal tapped out on the side of his bright can, how the sound made him think of someone terribly afraid tapping. The memory was so strong he decided to take a chance with it. "You're afraid, and you think I have to be just as afraid, or I won't work with you." He paused again, just long enough to wave away Jarka's red-faced burgeoning protest. "I've been afraid since I agreed to come here. Meeting you and listening to you dump ballast isn't even a twitch on the scared meter, so don't waste your air. Tell me your terms. But remember, I already know you for a lying cheat. Whatever comes up, you'll understand why I'll never let you get behind me."

Jarka's high color turned to cold pallor. "We'll see how brave you are."

Half rising to leave, Jarka checked at the sight of an unmoving Lannat. He frowned and sat back down quickly, glancing about to see if he was noticed.

Lannat wondered about the same thing, but kept his gaze locked on Jarka, asking him "You going somewhere?"

"Where you're wanted. Come on."

There was no choice. Lannat smothered a grimace. Still, he couldn't resist one last remark as he rose. "It'll be worth the trip just to find out what sort of people you work with." He gestured the fuming Jarka ahead of him. At the cashier's post he experienced a sharp jolt of panic when he couldn't recognize the bank logo on any of his buy cards. Once he thought, however, he remembered being briefed that all three were universally accepted on Hire. It was another hard reminder about control.

The transaction between himself and the cashier was another reminder, this one about life on Hire. Lannat extended the buy card. The woman placed it on the photo-register. This was an acid test, a moment Lannat steeled himself to get past. The false thumbprint, false signature, and false identity number went to a central registry as well as to the proper bank. Not only was he paying for his dinner, he was verifying to the law enforcement authorities of Hire that he was exactly who he claimed to be. And where he was. And what time he was there.

No one over the age of twelve was allowed to use cash on Hire. From thirteen on, anyone without a buy card had no official existence.

The soft ticking of the photo-register sent a shiver up Lannat's back. It wasn't so distracting that he missed seeing the holovid camera hanging from the ceiling behind the cashier. That was another record of his presence and appearance. He avoided looking directly into the lens, feeling more like a native Hiran already.

The spymasters spoke of repression, walked him through similar situations time after time. The actuality of the experience crushed their best efforts to condition him.

It took two seconds for the electronics to accept the false identity. Two seconds. A lifetime.

Lannat was sweat-damp leaving the building.

Jarka's elcar was in the mall parking lot. Lannat moved as nonchalantly as possible while surreptitiously searching for surveillance cameras. Muttering, Jarka told him, "You pretend they're not there. The concept is, if you're looking for the cameras it's for a reason. The Advisors will want to know what that reason is."

"I'll tell them I was just curious."

Sneering, Jarka steered him in a different direction. "Boy,

that's clever. The Advisors never heard that one, I'll bet. Look, it doesn't make any difference what you tell them. Try to get that through your head. If they dock you for any reason at all, they run a whole background check. So do what you're told."

Lannat couldn't decide which he despised the most: this place or this man. He thought about it, getting into the elcar, watching Jarka draw a course and altitude on his planner screen. The Hiran punched the button to send it to the central radar control and switched on the anticollision equipment. The screen flashed approval before Jarka had the engines running. Once they were under way, Lannat resigned himself to his situation. Shoving aside his irritation, he said, "Just so I know where I stand, how long have you known Etasalou was on Hire?"

"We knew he was coming before he got here—a year, a little more. When his scientists and doctors landed from Hector, the counsellor put them in an old elcar factory. The Hiran resistance—we call ourselves the Free—placed people on the workforce that rebuilt it to the scientists' specifications. Etasalou's people were anxious to see their commander had proper quarters. They threw his name around to get what they wanted. Pretty stupid, considering how bad the emperor wants his blood. Typical Elemental Guard approach."

The attempt at insult was doubly painful. Lannat's pride in his Rifles' background almost erupted and he bit back the urge to correct Jarka. Mildly he asked, "Do you still have people working there?"

"No hope." Jarka banked in a sharp turn, avoiding Liskerta itself, headed for a heretofore unobserved range of mountains, far to the southwest. Lannat remembered them from his training: the Marnoffar range. The vehicle leveled, slowed. On Jarka's side, the city flowed past, a concentrated dazzle of lights that dwindled into outlying suburbs and randomly spaced brighter nodes that defined smaller business enclaves. The whole was tied together by bands of traffic at different altitudes; altitude alteration sites, like small whirlpools, permitted direction changes. Jarka turned off all the interior lights. The control screen dimmed. Still clear, however, was its pulsing red line that indicated the vehicle's permitted course and a blue dot showing its exact position. Dual blue numbers flashed at the upper left corner, giving the proper as well as the true altitude.

When Jarka spoke again, his tone startled Lannat. Harsh disapproval was replaced by surprisingly quiet reflection. "I turned off the equipment so you could see better. This is my home. We've always been a peaceful people, not especially interested in what goes on in the rest of the empire. If the counsellor would just understand that's the way we want to live, we wouldn't have a problem."

Jarka paused. Lannat knew better then to press; he waited. Skimming along in an elcar with its night-navigation aids darkened was serious encouragement for shouted instructions to forget musings and pay attention to driving, but Lannat needed information. He hung on and hoped his driver knew what he was doing.

Suddenly multicolored beams of light split the darkness off to their left. Jarka explained, "That's coming from the counsellor's compound. It's both his home and administrative headquarters, called Court. Some ancient conceit or something." He gestured, the movement a symbol of disgust.

The pillars of light coalesced, changed colors, eventually forming a pattern. The show was pure propaganda. A golden armored figure such as Lannat had seen only in encyclopedias rode a horse across the sky. That winked off to be followed by a green and gold banner—the official colors of Hire—with an open book in its center. The pages fanned open. That became a face, limned in the same colors. Jarka said only, "That's him." Then, the words appearing one at a time in searing scarlet, the counsellor exhorted all who watched: LIGHT IS LIFE! KNOWLEDGE IS LIGHT! LUMIN!

As quickly as it appeared, the display was gone. Jarka went on, dripping contempt. "Counsellor Ullas is very devout."

He flipped on the night-navigation equipment. The enhanced vision screen lit up, startlingly bright. The jagged peaks, heretofore almost totally invisible in Hire's deep darkness, were presented by the computerized color compensation electronics as if caught in full daylight. Lannat relaxed his nervous grip on the armrest as Jarka resumed his earlier discussion. "The starship that brought Etasalou carried a little over two hundred Elemental Guards. They take care of all maintenance and security. The counsellor's the only nonprisoner Hiran to set step on Lumin's new grounds since Etasalou arrived, and that was before the screens went up over everything."

"What screens?"

"Antivision screens. They ran heat-conducting wires from the fence to a spine mounted above the factory building. At night they run electricity through the wires; their closeness to each other messes up image enhancers pretty well, and the heat completely screws up thermal detectors. Then there are highspys hovering all around the place. Between them and the foot patrols, no one can look down from the surrounding hills and see what they're doing in there. Your former boss is very big on security. Should make your job interesting."

The last phrase proved Jarka's organization didn't intend to prevent his original mission so much as they expected something additional of him. Lannat tucked the information away and moved quickly to the next reasonable question. "Etasalou never comes out?"

"Rarely. Officially, he's not here, of course, but it's pretty hard for him to disguise himself. We only have a few 'liner' families on Hire, and any family that marries along physical distinction lines is well known. Just the fact that Etasalou's so dark-skinned makes him stand out. When he does leave the laboratory, it's unannounced, always to Court. Each time he's taken a different route. There are at least six elcars, all alike; one carries Etasalou, the rest carry Guards. I'll give them this—they're disciplined. They won't talk. Scary is what they are."

If you only knew, Lannat thought, but kept that to himself. It was unlikely that even Jarka's friends had penetrated the depths of Etasalou's work. Lannat repressed a shudder at the memory of his own contact with victims of the commander's mind-control experiments; no one should die as those people did. Again, treacherous mental process diverted his thoughts to Nan Bahalt. He practically blurted, "Has Etasalou contacted any other Lumin representatives on Hire?"

"That's one of the things we're confused about. There's been no observed contact between Etasalou or his people and Lumin. In fact, they avoid anything Lumin."

"Does anyone have any idea what the counsellor and Etasalou are planning?"

"Rumors say they want to create an independent planetary home for Etasalou's version of Lumin. Some say they mean to capture a starship and stage a coup on Atic." For the first time, Jarka looked at Lannat as if speaking to someone worth talking to. "They say a small, disciplined force, smuggled onto Atic and attacking with surprise, could take the palace and the emperor before anyone knew what was happening. What do you think?"

"It could succeed. The attackers would have a life expectancy of about fifteen minutes once the alarms went off, and they'd accomplish nothing. The emperor has three sons."

"One of them is here."

Lannat croaked. "Here?"

"Big secret." Jarka flashed a lopsided grin. "Came in on a starship from Agamem almost a year ago. Supposed to be one of their nobles, visiting Hire. We spotted him as soon as he landed."

Lannat couldn't restrain himself. "What the hell is wrong with you people? You knew Etasalou was coming here, but you didn't want to tell the emperor. You know the emperor's own son is here, and you haven't told him. Whose side are you on, anyhow?"

"Our own." Jarka almost shouted the words, but as forcefully as he spoke, the way he bit down to stop whatever was to follow was equally impressive. Narrowed gaze fastened on the elcar's instrumentation, he boosted forward speed until the combination of engine noise and roar of air across the hull precluded more conversation.

Lannat resisted the temptation to speculate on what any of the evening's events portended. If there was a bright spot, it was Jarka's news that Etasalou was avoiding Lumin. It suggested the commander didn't know his niece was on the planet.

He slumped in his seat. There had been a gritty, dark feel to this mission from its conception. All war was killing, no matter what the politicians or scholars said. Taking out an Etasalou was less of a moral challenge than engaging some other frightened fool to decide whose leader was "right." That was why the men and women who had died in the Whyee Valley deserved to lie easy in their graves, no less than their leader needed to clear his name. The stench of murder and the sense of being unclean wouldn't quite go away, though.

The necessity to protect Nan was the only thing that gave the mission what little luster it had. If that was jeopardized . . .

Control is 80 percent, the spymasters had said.

Lannat told himself he could maintain control. He could be patient. He must.

But there was the matter of the 10 percent they had mentioned last: luck. He had the sickening sensation that, no matter what he did, he was going to need a full 100 percent of that last 10 percent.

CHAPTER 9

The elcar swept up and over a sawtoothed line of foothills to descend in a belly-wrenching slide toward a pair of strobe-lights. Lannat was certain Jarka deliberately yanked the nose up in order to add some dash to the final approach. As it was, they flashed over the first light and bore down on the more distant one like a killhawk after prey. Visible on the elcar's navigation screen, although not to the naked eye, a large building loomed just beyond the second light; Lannat had no inclination to study it just then. Since the elcar lacked any sort of friction for braking, it was obvious Jarka needed some intense maneuvering, or their entrance into the building would be the stuff of high drama. Whipping the vehicle in a sickening turn, Jarka swapped end for end, so the thrust engines now tried to drive them away from the impending crash. Slammed into his seat restraints, Lannat determined to die in silent dignity. The elcar bucked, twisted, shuddered. Finally, with Jarka's hands and feet dancing feather-light across the controls, it hovered. To add to Lannat's irritation, Jarka spun the machine on its center point to face the building once again, cut the antigrav, and brought them to touchdown with the airy gentleness of settling treecotton.

Switching off the engine, Jarka plunged them into momentary darkness. The strobe light, some distance behind them, continued to flash, but at a reduced rate of one burst every five seconds or so. Jarka leaned back, hands still on the wheel, and sighed. "I'll probably drill this howler into the dirt someday. Until I do, I just can't land it on auto. That's too much fun." Belatedly he turned official. "We're here. You can get out."

"Here where?" Lannat opened his hatch, swinging his legs free, stepping onto earth, not concrete. The two-story building, perhaps thirty feet away, was dark. Blasts of light from the strobe behind the two men gave it a weird mobility, brought it threateningly close with illumination, only to thrust it back into darkness. Beyond it was a star-blazed sky and dim, silhouetted peaks. A forest ranged the clearing that enclosed the building and landing strip.

A rumbling basso roar sent Lannat backward, feeling for the elcar hatch. "What's that?" The question squawked.

"That's a lyso. We'd best get inside." Continuing to speak over his shoulder—with Lannat stepping out smartly to keep up—Jarka explained, "Vegetarians. Dangerous if they're disturbed. He sounds far away."

For Lannat, it was the building that was far away. He was pleased when Jarka didn't knock and wait for an answer.

Once inside, he wasn't that sure of his choice. Lights came on far overhead, multibulb chandeliers barely bright enough to reveal a large, ornate lobby. Gold leaf glowed warmly from picture frames, statues, deeply carved pillars. The duller gleam of silver added depth to the works, and infrequent jewels sparkled. Straight ahead were more doors, closed. Jarka led the way through them.

Again, high, faint lights came on, revealing a large, empty auditorium sloping down past terraces of seats to a stage. A man walked out onto it. Stopping, facing the pair at the entrance, he spoke in a deep, resounding voice. "Welcome to Hire, Val Bordi. Welcome to the headquarters of the Free Hire Army."

Lannat said, "The emperor was assured of your support. Now I'm told I'll be delivered to the emperor's enemy if I refuse your orders. Your welcome is as invisible as your army."

The man answered easily. "The army exists. The welcome

is up to you." He gestured, walking off the stage. Jarka touched Lannat's arm, saying "This way." He led the length of the auditorium. At the end, they went through an exit into a hall even darker than the room. Lannat pressed his arm against the reassuring bulk of the ceryag blade. Reason told him it would be suicidal to fight in such a situation. Nevertheless, he was decided. He remembered the oneway. More clearly—and far more frighteningly—he remembered the men who'd been mentally restructured by Etasalou and the way they died. If it came to that, being torn apart was the cleaner alternative.

The hall led to a small room. The man waiting was the one from the stage. He was taller than Lannat by a full head. Dressed in shirt and slightly tapered trousers, he was broad-shouldered, narrow-waisted. He moved with athletic grace, lighting a candle on a small table. Pale hair, not so blond as Jarka's, caught the light. Putting on a perfunctory smile, he gestured the pair to seats. The chairs were large, leather-upholstered, luxurious. Lannat noted the table was the same pollumwood as the emperor's desk back on Atic. The paneled walls were congrain, a dramatically striped lumber. Candlelight played off fittings and fixtures—brass lamps, framed prints, yards of bookshelves. A den or individualized office. Lannat felt himself relaxing, relieved to be free of the echoing space of the auditorium and the confining hallway.

The man across the small table bowed his head. "We serve the Seeker." The voice, at least an octave deeper than before, drummed around the room. "We seek truth, knowledge, and faith. From darkness we must escape. Our destiny is light."

Lannat responded. "Light is life to all things, and the way of the Seeker."

Jarka's stunned look was an instant of wry amusement for Lannat. Actually, he was as surprised as anyone by his involuntary recitation of Seeker liturgy. He'd rarely done that even when he was on Delphi, surrounded by the Seeker priestesses. He put the whole thing down to stress and warned himself to get a better grip on things.

Smile a bit warmer now, the tall man reached past the candle and extended a hand to Lannat, who shook it with basic civility. If the man was offended, he gave no sign. He said, "My name is Betak. I need your help. To get you here, I have broken my word. A man such as you understands the pain that brings."

"You lied to people who trusted you, people I trusted. Do you imagine I care if that causes you pain?"

Betak jerked as if struck. Jaw jutting, he continued. "I've been Emperor Halib's intelligence chief on Hire for years. For the last decade, I've tried to make the home government understand that the people here can no longer accept the repressions of Counsellor Ullas. Even in an environment such as this, desperate people will find a way to hide, to organize, to strike back. To us, Commander Etasalou is a minor irritant. His elimination solves nothing."

Lannat leaned forward in his chair. "Wonderful. Your personal problems make you uncomfortable, so the galaxy must wait its turn. If you want to learn what true horror is, let Etasalou live on as Ullas's ally. Soon your living will envy your dead and curse your name with every breath." He looked to Jarka. "You're crazy, but you could still learn a lot from this man." Then, again to Betak: "You don't have any idea what harm you've done me. Or yourself."

Rising, Betak studied the floor as he paced, refusing to look at Lannat. "Our goals extend beyond Etasalou's death. We need more from you than an assassin's stroke. My profession, like yours, frequently demands sacrifice. Hate me if you choose, but do not test me. You will accomplish nothing by it, save your own destruction. Work with me for our mutual benefit. What we ask is simple: Use your experience to train our warriors."

Wearily Lannat threw out objections. He found little strength for it, convinced now that his course was decided and there was nothing he could do about it. "Under the surveillance I hear about? Everyone I've seen on this planet is too afraid to make eye contact."

Betak rose. "Our people," he shouted, "are going into Etasa-lou's laboratories. No word of their experience comes out." Advancing with the stiffness of someone injured, Betak stopped in front of Lannat and bent to put his face within inches of the other man's. "Some of our number have brothers, fathers, sisters in those laboratories. Have no fears for our dedication. Should we weaken, our strength is restored by our faith in the Seeker. The emperor called your mission a blow at evil. All we ask of you is that you help us do as much. In exchange, we shall support you completely."

"But your needs come first. Right?"

A shadow that could have been guilt flicked across Betak's features. He straightened, stepped back. "It must be that way. After all, you didn't expect to creep inside the lab and poison the commander's breakfast, did you? There must be an attack, a diversion, an escape route—a plan. That requires trained personnel, and we have none."

"Why me? There are plenty of retired Guardsmen. Rifles. Even more troopers who served a hitch, got out, and came home."

"Hire is unlike anywhere else, as you may have noticed. For example, you must understand that this dynasty has always scrupulously observed the Blood Father's edict against missile weapons. There are exactly five railguns on all of Hire. No plasguns, no slug guns. Five years ago, the Advisors collected all weapons. Swords, ancient spears, battle maces—anything. Nobles and Advisors may own swords. All are registered and equipped with transponders. Advisor Central can locate any approved sword on the planet at any time. No commoner family may own an edged tool larger than a butcher knife, and only one of those. Axes are registered; so are hatchets, pruning hooks, shovels, pitchforks, and 'any tool, hand or power, deemed a potential weapon.' Discussing any martial art is a misdemeanor crime against civil tranquillity. Teaching or studying them is a felony. A fistfight in a bar is worth two years in an Advisor work camp; only one year if you can prove you were struck without any prior involvement whatever. As for your returned Rifles and Guards, they are very carefully monitored."

"Petition the emperor. He's a humane man."

"The emperor thinks that, since Hire isn't in open rebellion, as half his empire is, then it's obvious we're docile because we're happy." There was passion in Betak now, not anger. Stiff, formal demeanor melted away. "I'm telling you, if I can establish that the emperor covertly helped end this regime, I have a chance of keeping Hire loyal to him. You remarked on the timidity and isolation of the people you saw tonight. Can you envision their ferocity when they learn they can fight their way free of Counsellor Ullas? I hope to control that repressed explosion. But it's coming, controlled or not."

Withdrawn until that moment, Jarka broke in. He addressed Lannat. "Look, I'm not feeling very proud of myself right now. All I thought about when Betak said we were going to use you to create our own resistance fighters was that your Elemental Guards trained the Advisors to be what they are. All I saw was using the emperor's own against him. What you thought didn't matter, you know? I still think we're doing the right thing, getting you to help us, but maybe we didn't go about it the right way. You two are arguing about the empire—I don't give a damn about it, one way or another. All I know is, this place is rotten. What's happened between you and me is done; why look back? We're all in it now. You can't do your job or get off the planet unless you do what we want. We can't get rid of the counsellor without your help. It looks to me like none of us has any choice."

The logic was irrefutable. Lannat continued to curse Betak's calculated underhandedness, even so. What he couldn't decide was how to confront the matter of Nan. He'd envisioned himself working with a small, trustworthy team of people who knew Hire well enough to help him spirit her to some safe place. That dream was finished. A person didn't go into combat and hope to live unless there was complete faith in one's comrades. Trust and confidence meant more than blood and bone. He found himself remembering things about the Seeker cult. The spymasters used them as prime examples of their craft. Spreading across the galaxy, the priestesses avoided apprehension as effectively as smoke. And the resistance on Hire apparently were devout cultists.

Control. He couldn't control a thing outside his reach. Betak's resistance organization offered the rich possibility of controlling the personnel, perhaps Betak himself. Levers and fulcrums, Lannat thought. From the corner of his eye, he saw Jarka shifting uncomfortably, and for a moment, he felt a sudden, inexplicable sympathy. The blond man's features were tight, determined. Despite his dislike for Jarka, Lannat saw the man's soul riding lightly on his face. It shone with the insufferable arrogance of the pure-hearted believer, the achingly vulnerable courage of the faithful. Lannat wanted to tell him to get away, that the whole game was false and nothing like what he believed it to be. He wondered if Jarka had ever seen another man die.

Rising, using movement to break that morbid train of thought, Lannat told Betak, "Jarka's right. Our responsibilities outweigh our differences."

Unsmiling, Betak nodded. He made no offer to shake hands. "An inauspicious start to a campaign designed to rid us of two completely evil men. We can—we will—rise above our problems, now and in future. Hundreds of thousands of lives depend on it."

Following Jarka out of the room, Lannat thought, We already have our first major disagreement, Betak, my new very best friend. I'm finding it very hard to concern myself with any lives beyond two. All I want is Nan and me out of here. You and Halib and Etasalou and this counsellor—all of you: I wish you darkness eternal.

CHAPTER 10

Watching Counsellor Ullas eat, Commander Etasalou amused himself by imagining how his host should die.

There were many reasons for disliking the counsellor. Etasalou confessed to himself he had myriad reasons to be genuinely grateful for haven and support. And, for all the counsellor's minor quirks and foibles that made him unpleasant company, there was really no particular reason to hate him. Nevertheless, he did, with a fervor that was nearly sexual in its urgency.

That was absurd on the face of it. Etasalou asked himself what rational man would fantasize rising from his chair, smiling pleasantly, and sinking a table knife in that wobbling, bouncing, disgusting Adam's apple so temptingly in reach?

It wasn't the sober mastication, with its machinelike jaws grinding their way through one blue-green nasul after another that was especially irritating. Actually, the metronomic dip of the bony fingers into the jeweled bowl—and the insectile scratch of fingernails on the metal—was more disturbing. No, the infuriating aspect of Counsellor Ullas at table was his ardent devotion to the task at hand. He did not speak. He did not change expression. He kept his gaze locked on his food as if its destruction were his holy mission.

Finished with the bowl of nasuls, he pushed it away with a forefinger. A trembling servant leaped to snatch the rejected dish.

Ordinarily, Etasalou coveted nasuls. Their spicy-sweet flavor defied imitation, and the small globular fruit wouldn't keep for the voyage from Hire to Atic. No preservation technique captured the intense savor.

Watching Ullas eat eliminated appetite. Even for nasuls.

Etasalou sighed. Ullas was a burden to be borne. In the meantime, personal elegance must always be pursued. Etasalou leaned back gracefully in his chair, the better to compare his own lithe leanness with Ullas's thin angularity. Lanky, Etasalou decided. But deceptive. There were many stories of Ullas's surprising physical strength. Graceless, however. Etasalou thought of Ullas's walk, the high knees, the clunk of large feet and heavy heels, the pale head perched forward on the end of the gawky neck.

Not a pretty sight.

Impressive, in a brute-force sort of way, but then, so was a well-thrown rock. Yes. Counsellor Ullas, the galaxy's only primitive weapon with the power of speech.

Feeling better, Etasalou dropped his gaze to survey himself. In deference to the counsellor's devotion to Lumin, he continued to wear the flame hues of the state religion. He indulged his own sense of style, however. The short-sleeved red tunic buttoned tightly over a long-sleeved blouse of yellow. Full trousers of a lighter yellow, nipped tight at the ankles, featured a sword belt of red, studded with golden disks. The sword scabbard was enameled, a dazzling glitter of vines and roses, the holy flower of legend and Home. Etasalou admitted the vanity that delighted in hot colors. They played wonderfully well off his burnished dark-brown complexion. That thought reminded him of another point against Ullas. White, almost transparent skin, with raised blue snakelike veins everywhere. Sometimes Etasalou thought he could feel the heat from those ropy blood vessels as they went about their work.

He stole a glance at Ullas. If the color tan in all its varieties ceased to exist, Ullas might very well be forced to go naked. Didn't anyone ever tell him his dead white hide wrapped in blandness gave him the look of trampled weeds? Assuredly not. No one intentionally irritated the counsellor. Ullas looked dull. Behind those inexpressive features was a mind as cruel as one could imagine.

A tiny frown squirmed across Etasalou's brow. His thoughts linked Ullas's cruelty with the treacherous transponder hidden in the knurled silver handle of the sword at his hip. It galled to know that the weapon informed Ullas's snooping Advisors of his every move any time he strapped it on. He banished the frown, treated himself to a tight-lipped smile; when the time came to use the sword, Counsellor Ullas would be beyond caring.

A large splash of red would liven up those boring clothes.

Etasalou turned his attention to the room. It seemed grossly unfair that a dynasty reigning for eight full generations never produced an heir with good taste in decor. Perhaps someone else admired the ostentatious swoops and curves, the juxtaposition of geometrically precise lines and sweeping arcs. But was it absolutely necessary that everything shine so? Admittedly, it was a carefully orchestrated glow. Simply too simple; the style called attention to itself. Etasalou wondered if it reminded him more of an operating room or a laboratory.

"What progress on the experiments?"

The counsellor's brisk, penetrating voice jarred Etasalou out of proportion. He started, knocked a fork to the floor. He failed to hide his ire. "Obviously, if I haven't mentioned my work, there's been no progress to report."

Ullas's look revealed nothing, nor did his characteristically quick response. "I am interested in hearing what progress you make. I am equally interested in knowing when you make no progress. In fact, 'no progress' intrigues me greatly. At the risk of sounding crass, Commander, you are an open wound in the body of my finances. It bleeds more treasure—my treasure—daily. Progress, and quickly, is in order."

"This is science, Counsellor. I understand your concern as

much as I appreciate your support, but every step must be measured carefully."

"I wish you'd measure your expenditures of my funds with equal care. You promised more than reports. You said the prisoners I've supplied you would spearhead the destruction of the rebels."

Pretending to sip his wine—local swill, past its prime—Etasalou cursed Ullas under his breath while he prepared an answer. Lowering the goblet with exactly the right combination of flourish and unconcern, he was careful to smile. "We're close to providing you the people you need. Would you honor us by coming to my laboratories, that I may demonstrate our work?"

Ullas was genuinely caught by surprise. "When did you have in mind?"

"At your convenience, of course, Counsellor. Would tomorrow afternoon be suitable?"

Another solid blow. Etasalou gloated. Ullas considered long and hard before answering. "I'll cancel my appointments. Perhaps I'll have something interesting for you by that time, a sort of expression of union. For the present, I have other things to discuss. You knew, of course, your presence on Hire has been reported to Emperor Halib?"

"He gets constant word that I'm on every planet in the empire. He's no danger."

"I am less confident than you. I have more to lose."

Etasalou nodded. It was a fair statement, from Ullas's perspective. "I know how the emperor thinks. More than that, I know how weak he is. I have said it before, Counsellor—the throne is there for the taking."

"And I told you before, I want only dominion over Hire, Geron, and Pylos and a starship to keep them under control. Halib—or anyone else—can have the rest."

Such generosity, Etasalou thought. He said, "Unless we kill Halib, you cannot rule, except on Hire, and then at his pleasure. Believe me . . ."

Waving a hand, Ullas interrupted. "I believe what I see. Show me how you mean to revenge yourself on Halib and open the way for my dream."

"Tomorrow, then, Counsellor. I am not satisfied with our progress, but I can show you where we're going. A little more time. That's all we need."

"Time works for the rebels. I hear disquieting rumors."

Etasalou couldn't resist. "It's too bad we have no reliable informants among them."

Ullas didn't bother to look up from his contemplation of a fleck of nasul skin lodged under a fingernail. " 'We,' Commander? There is no 'we.' My informants are my concern. As are my rebels. That is why I have you. Providing you asylum assures me the power to crush the resistance. Unless you accomplish that, your stay on Hire must become insupportable."

A full squadron of eleven Advisor elcars rose from the landing field adjacent to the Court in inverted arrowhead formation and howled off toward Etasalou's laboratories.

Etasalou and Ullas rode in the third from the front elcar of the right wing. Ullas remarked on Etasalou's insistence on such security measures. Etasalou responded, "I have no faith in luck. Good planning, good luck. Bad luck, bad planning."

"Not a deeply religious statement for someone who was the senior male figure in Lumin," Ullas said.

" 'Was,' Counsellor. What I have seen convinced me that man is all the god there is. Or needs to be. No more mystic dithering for me. I control. You shall see."

There was little room for Ullas to back away; what there was, he used. He avoided looking directly at Etasalou after that.

The trip north to the Fols Hills took only minutes. Etasalou hopped out nimbly, eagerly. He rubbed his hands together. Guards stood at attention at the polished brass gates. The gleaming bars swung open in welcome, giving an uninterrupted view of more guards lined along the walk to the former factory's front entrance. Etasalou beamed. "Never looked like this in the old working days, did it? It does you honor, Counsellor. My laboratory, but your glory. You'll see."

He stopped talking. The disapproving set of his companion's jaw was a minimal clue to Ullas's feelings, but Etasalou was sure it meant he was calculating the cost of the cleaning, the painting, the new fittings. A bizarre image of the counsellor hunched over a dimly lit ledger popped up in Etasalou's mind and refused to go away. He pretended a coughing problem so he could dislodge it.

Guards, positioned ten feet apart, snapped hands to heart as the pair passed. Progress was routine until the two men were halfway to the door. From the corner of his eye, Etasalou watched Ullas glance at a man and hesitate. When Ullas turned, walking back to stare disbelief at one statuelike guard, then another, it was too much for Etasalou to bear in silence. He laughed aloud.

Ullas faced him, spare features pale. Half drawing his sword, he spoke to the c-button on his lapel. "Code A. Code A."

Elcars howled wildly, stormed aloft on the other side of the gated fence. The fine wire screen over the compound shimmered in the sudden shift of wind currents.

It was Etasalou's turn to pale. "No, Counsellor—no! There's no danger. This arrangement is for your entertainment, not to threaten. Believe me, there's no danger to you here."

Frightened sincerity rang in the words, and Ullas relaxed slightly. Not entirely reassured, he spoke to the c-button again. "Hold position. Keep me in view. Attack at your discretion." Then, to Etasalou: "These men are Hirans. Did you think I wouldn't recognize them? Explain, and quickly." His hand remained on his sword hilt.

No guard moved. Still at attention, completely ignoring the byplay, they stared straight ahead.

"I wanted to wait until we had many more such examples to show you, Counsellor, but my impatience has overruled me," Etasalou said. "I couldn't wait to show you what we've accomplished and how we do it."

"It's true, then? You really alter men's minds?"

"Restructure, Counsellor. Restructure. These men still think their own thoughts. The difference is, now their every act is filtered through a new set of standards. Whatever they do, they consider beforehand if it will benefit Counsellor Ullas. You want soldiers? These men live to conquer in your name, to defend your holdings. They fear death, or they would be valueless, but they love you more. There is no sacrifice they will not embrace unhesitatingly."

"These men hate me. Their fathers hated me. I cannot believe they aren't merely waiting for an opportunity to strike."

"Test them. Order it, and they will fight to the death. It will be a terrible waste of my efforts, but if that is what it takes to convince you, I insist."

Ullas took his hand from his sword, raised it to fondle one of the gold buttons on his loose jacket. "They'll attack one another? To kill?"

"I guarantee it."

Something like a smile moved across Ullas's lips. Etasalou looked away from that, and his attention caught on the change in Ullas's eyes. Where Ullas's weird smile chilled the heart, his eyes made it race. They widened, glistening. They darted, feverishly unstable, fixing on everything, on nothing, flickering so quickly Etasalou wondered that the man saw anything clearly. Ullas pointed, wet tongue working back and forth across that smile. "That one. He cursed my dynasty in open court. Cursed me, my family. And him, over there. He killed an Advisor. Tell them to fight. Make them kill each other."

Etasalou marveled. The man spewed venom like a Syrac grass-snake. Never raised his voice, never changed expression. Etasalou lamented that the instruments in his laboratory would never inspect Counsellor Ullas's brain. He told Ullas, "They are my creation, Counsellor, but yours to command."

Ullas said, "You four," selecting from those standing a bit farther away, "stand here, between me and those two." Once he had a protective wall in position, he ordered the other two to perform. "You two: Draw your swords and fight. No quarter."

The pair raised hand to heart in salute, then drew weapons.

Etasalou was disgusted. There were easier, better ways to demonstrate the mental reconstruction of the men. To set them at each other was shallow and wasteful. A leader understood that dead enemies were lost slaves. Ullas would never grasp even so fundamental a concept.

Months of work had gone into each of the two men circling each other, looking for an opening. It would take more months to repair their injuries, assuming they survived. At least the event would provide the proof Ullas needed to convince himself that the laboratory—and his boon friend, Commander Etasalou—were indispensable. Two lives was a small price, seen in that light.

CHAPTER 11

Etasalou was pleasantly surprised by the quality of the duel. He resolved to compliment the Elemental Guard major responsible for training.

Nevertheless, he frowned when one man executed a completely unorthodox parry that turned into a near-killing thrust. His opponent yelled with pain as the sword point lifted a flap of flesh from his neck. Neither the free-lancing maneuver nor the injury caused Etasalou's dissatisfaction. What troubled him was the unpleasant awareness that the two Hirans, unschooled in swordsmanship until recently, were very adept. It made one wonder if the optimistically titled Free Hire Army might not have more skill than suspected.

Another clever move demanded his attention. The shorter of the two men—the one whose neck had just been cut—dropped under a thrust, moving forward in a swift, ungainly scuttle. Inside his opponent's weapon, he drove upward, using his head as a ram. The taller man twisted, bending his arm, so the battering attempt was partially deflected. Still, there was enough energy to knock him off balance; he tried a backhanded slash as he fell away. The short man was forced to parry, but since the blow was a weak one, he was able to continue his offensive move. He whirled his blade, building speed, and hacked at his foe's arm.

The noise of the impact deceived the ear. The crunch of severed bone was subdued, unimpressive. Similarly, the hissing of the honed edge separating muscle fiber as well as uniform material was barely audible. The defeated man's sword arced through the air, glinting and twisting. The hand and forearm that had held it an instant earlier flopped limply to the ground. Already stumbling backward from the previous impact, the wounded man tangled his own feet. He fell backward, sat down hard. Stunned, disbelieving, he grabbed his arm just below the elbow, where it ended. His face contorted as he squeezed to stop the fountaining blood.

The rest of the guards held firm. When Ullas's fascination wavered momentarily, he noted their undisturbed acceptance. A slick of fear whipped across his previous exhilarated enjoyment. It brought yet another realization; the *sound* of the fight was wrong. Except for one pained cry and the infrequent grunts and groans of the combatants, the entire area was cloaked in unnatural silence.

Something stirred deep in Ullas's subconscious, a panic-screeching horror that defied names. He suddenly feared these creatures—human, yet not human—and the mystery that transformed them.

But he wanted the power. *The mind. To control all minds.*

Why, then, did he tremble with dread?

Ullas's disturbed considerations broke on Etasalou's unexpected movement. Completely ignoring Ullas's original intent that one of the men must die, Etasalou shouted at the victor to stand away from the loser. He continued to snap orders, sending for medical technicians, instructing them to bring ice, plastic, and a trauma kit. The designated messenger sprinted off as Etasalou yanked the wounded man's belt from his trousers to make a tourniquet. When that work was started, he gestured to the man who'd done the damage to take over the repairs.

Ullas ignored the instant transition from determined killer to caregiver. With his normal thought patterns firmly reestablished, he railed at Etasalou. "You stopped them. You told me they would fight to the death. Those criminals . . . scum . . ." A cutting gesture finished the brief tirade. His hand went to his c-button.

Etasalou was conciliatory. "Death was assured, Counsellor—a formality. I preserved the man in order to show you how effective our medical personnel have become. You saw that these men are completely prepared to die in your name, literally for your entertainment. Nevertheless, they remain human, and they perform best when their conditioning isn't forced to override their survival instinct. This is a superb opportunity to show you one way we reinforce their will to serve you."

Blinking rapidly, fingers flexing, Ullas considered his words. Gradually his hand slid away from the c-button. He glanced over his shoulder at the poised elcars, then regarded Etasalou with ice-pale eyes. Etasalou told himself there was no expression there to read. Still, he felt Ullas signaled regret that he couldn't unleash his Advisors. Ullas told Etasalou, "We shall see, Commander. I shall not forget this incident. A promise made to me is not an idle thing. Now, show me why you have offended me."

Etasalou led the counsellor directly to the laboratory.

The minute they stepped into that gleaming white world,

Etasalou felt his spirits rise. He basked in the attention of his technicians, in the stark beauty of his empire.

Yes. This was the root of empire. More. It would launch him to godhead.

Muttered impatience from Ullas forced him to confront the present. He took his guest to a black column, a bit over four feet high, two feet square. A flick of a switch illuminated a holovid; inside the column a human brain appeared suspended in midair.

Signaling technicians, Etasalou lectured. "The volume of the human brain is approximately one quart, Counsellor. From that significant little lump has come all we know of beauty, filth, wisdom, folly, and general eruption. Now let me suggest the magnitude of what I bring to our alliance. Under my leadership, these scientists have determined that the brain's one hundred billion neurons interact with each other through one hundred *trillion* synaptic links. Multiply that by the possibility of strong links and weak links as well as differing versions of strong and weak. You see the limitless numbers?"

"You claim you can control the mind," Ullas said impassively. "I'm not interested in arithmetic."

"It helps to appreciate the achievement if . . ." Etasalou let the brittle rejoinder fade away. Ullas, intent on the pulsing brain replicated in the column, appeared distracted. Irritable, Etasalou tried again. "We cannot create thought yet. Not exactly. What we can do, however, is track some—not all—of the synaptic connections." He touched another switch. Dozens of holovid screens on the wall flashed to life, consecutive images of a brain rendered into slices by electronic scanning. "We introduce restructuring candidates to certain stimulating situations. We use drugs, hypnosis, film, and actual events to generate mental responses. The brain can be tricked by induced imagery." Another switch, and the images were suddenly alive with activity. Something like sparks popped and darted across some of them. Others were still. Etasalou went on. "This is a brain being scanned as its hypnotized owner believes he's watching a friend die. Now watch this." Another switch, and the same parts of the brain continued to respond. Quickly Etasalou pointed to other areas. "These reactions are the same man, still hypnotized, watching the same scene. Yet the reactions differ here, here, over here—and we have massive response in this section, and it wasn't involved at all before. The difference is simply that in the second picture, instead of an unadorned death, the subject was told that his friend was dying with honor and glory for a cause he believed in with all his heart."

Pausing, he shot an appraising glance at Ullas, ready to accept expressions of awe and admiration. Instead, Ullas's head was turned away. He was examining the distances of the laboratory with an expression of besieged boredom.

Etasalou launched himself back into his presentation, unwittingly taking on the harried look of a peddler making one last, rending counteroffer. "Here is absolute proof of our command, Counsellor. If you'll look at this holovid for a moment. Please." Slowly, condescendingly, Ullas did so. It was all Etasalou could do to avoid grinding his teeth. He lumbered on. "This is the hippocampus. In this picture, the red area indicates increased blood flow. That tells us the subject is remembering something. In this case, he's recalling an artificially induced event, created by us. Now—this is important—please note that these areas of the temporal lobe are also active. You see? Here? And here? Good." He bent to flick a switch on the holovid deck. What appeared to be the same picture was displayed. "This is the same subject's brain being tested after mere hypnosis. My technicians created the exact same 'memory,' but you see what happened? In this instance, the subject clearly 'remembered' the incident when questioned. But he was lying. Not intentionally, of course. He told us exactly what he was conditioned to 'remember.' His brain knew it was not the truth. See how the hippocampus is as active as before. Then note that the temporal lobe ignores it."

Caught up in the magic of the accomplishment, Etasalou

flung his arms wide, as if to embrace the images on the screen. "We are creating perfect memories. Not even the subject mind knows the difference."

Ullas tugged at an ear. "Interesting. What's the purpose?"

"The purpose, Counsellor, is to feed this data to banks of computers. We map responses. Today we can fairly well duplicate whichever pattern we choose. We condition the human mind to perform as we will it. We create a race of humans that spends its waking moments seeking to live in total harmony with whatever circumstance their leaders decree. The reconstructed men who fought each other at your command have been conditioned to believe their greatest joy is to obey you. We *control*."

Turning his back on the holovid wall, Ullas said, "It is the duty of everyone on Hire to believe their greatest joy is to obey me, Commander. As you describe the end product of all this expense, it is simply an assistance to correct behavior and proper discipline. Those men fought because they knew I would have them killed if they didn't. As much as I admire Lumin and the knowledge our religion provides us, I see this as no more than a scientist's technique for developing a consistent behavior—a faith, one might say."

"My troops will never complain. Or shirk. Or rebel." The last was a step too far, but Etasalou was goaded beyond caring. He saw Ullas's quick blink and readied himself for a potentially ruinous test of wills.

Ullas's contrary mildness surprised Etasalou. "You make a good point. Life would be far simpler if everyone went about their duties without questions." The counsellor half turned, peered back at Etasalou. "You can restructure an entire population?"

"Given time. Two years ago the best we could do was condition a person to respond within fairly tight parameters. Now, as you have seen, we can establish a much wider range." Etasalou stepped closer, lowered his voice. "You will rule over planets where the goal of every man, woman, and child is to satisfy you."

Ullas looked directly into Etasalou's eyes. He, too, spoke softly. More suggestively. "And you, sir; what of you? Your ambitions are like clouds, Commander. They roll and billow over all of us, horizon to horizon, obscuring more than they reveal. What, exactly, is the price of your gift?"

"Nothing more than what we have already discussed. I am obsessed by defining what humankind can be. Should be. A fool can see that some are meant to rule. The rest must do as they are bid. We who are equipped to decide what is best, what is right, must have the opportunity to create. The emperor has no vision, no purpose. His empire is crumbling. His firstborn is weak as water, the other two weaker yet. I want to work with a man who can create a progressive, unified race of humans. I believe you are that man. My price? Help me to help you rule that society."

Ullas nodded. The two men matched stares long enough for the workers to become aware. At the limits of his peripheral vision, Etasalou saw them shifting nervously, sidling closer to each other. Their unintelligible whispered exchanges were like frightened bird twitter. Ullas spoke. "Such power as we discuss here can compromise one."

Etasalou agreed, then moved the conversation to more comfortable ground. "I spoke to you of the morale of our personnel. Come this way, Counsellor, please. Let me show you why your people will fight for you as no others ever have. Or could."

Once again in control, Etasalou moved out of the electronics laboratory and into a hall. Energetic strides carried him up a long flight of stairs in quickstep. He turned at the top and was surprised to see Ullas right with him, showing no sign of exertion.

They entered the medical ward. Etasalou's gesture indicated the twin rows of transparent plastic domes. They looked rather like tubes cut in half and set atop rectangular stainless steel bases perhaps four feet long, two feet wide, and one foot deep. The bases sat on four sturdy legs, with multicolored tubes of different sizes feeding through one of the long sides. The domes rose another two feet above the base.

Ullas squinted against the dazzle of white enamel and polished steel. "What is this? Display cases? Brains? I don't like grisly things, Etasalou. It's not necessary for me to see the messy details of your experiments."

"One doesn't question a miracle's appearance. Come, Counsellor; see. This room is the future."

Reluctantly Ullas followed. When he looked inside the case, he gulped. His words were rough-edged. "It looks like a . . . like one of those medical instruction models. The parts of a leg."

"Exactly." Pride overwhelmed Etasalou's manners. "The primary components of an entire leg, manufactured of plastic. We call it an architecture. Each surface is treated with cells that will re-create nerves, bone, blood vessels—everything. As the cells replicate, the plastic decomposes. By the time the plastic is ineffective, the proper tissue has grown to near completion and the structure can support itself in the nutrient medium. You noted the tubing? That's how we pump in nutrient and extract waste. Look in this tank. An arm. See how it's developing? Look there, the first sign of fingernails. See the way the muscle builds. And bone here, and here."

Ullas stepped back, normal pallor now gleaming like hard wax. Veins worked at his temples and throat. His right eyelid fluttered in minute vibrations. He compressed a question into the single word "Rejection?"

"The cells are from the patient. It is replication. We're on the threshold of rebuilding organs, as well. The prospect of self-genesis beckons."

Features slowly regaining animation, Ullas reached to stroke his chin. "What are you suggesting?"

"Extended life. People—selected people—can have organs regrown. Their own organs, not transplants. For years we've grown newskin on polymer substrates. What is the skin but our largest organ? If we can reproduce new organs on demand, replace worn out and diseased parts of the body . . ." Etasalou let the sentence fade away, made room for Ullas's imagination to seize the concept.

"Constant youth." Ullas was rapt.

Etasalou corrected him sharply. "We cannot reverse aging. I don't believe we ever shall. No, the parts regenerated are the same age as the patient. No older, of course, but unfortunately, no younger. We are mere scientists, not magicians."

The wry humor failed to penetrate Ullas's intensity. "How close are you? Never mind. You must work harder. Faster. Every day lost is irreplaceable." He stopped, leaned into Etasalou, almost touching him. "Who else knows of this? The brain experiments? The life extension work?"

"Emperor Halib knows of my earliest successes with mind restructuring. No one knows of the regeneration project except my people."

"Reduce the number. No, no; ignore that. Do what you think best. Results, Etasalou. We must have results. Quickly."

"As fast as we can, Counsellor." Etasalou bowed, flourishing, the better to hide triumph. When he straightened, Ullas was already turning to leave. Gritting his teeth, Etasalou hurried after, promising himself that he would remind Ullas of his crudity when the time was right. He reflected that patience was reputed to be a virtue. That was debatable. All so-called virtue was. But patience was certainly a necessity.

Cloistered within his own thoughts, Ullas said nothing until they were stepping back outside into a beautiful day. Stopping, he assured himself no one could overhear, then spoke decisively. "Yesterday I alluded to some information that might interest you. Actually, there are two items. The emperor's son is a guest on my planet. He is incognito. I tolerate his arrogant presence because he may prove a handy counterbalance to my own son's assignment to Atic; Prince Dafanil is the senior member of the present Hiran Cultural Sibling Group. Halib is capable of reinstituting the ancient practice of CSGs as hostages. Halib cannot know that my son would die happily, knowing it was for the dynasty. Prince Dafanil would never do such a thing, which makes him a much more effective piece of insurance. He is worthless otherwise. Because I supply him with unlimited entertainment, he considers me his friend. My thought is this: A coup led by the emperor's own son would create far less uproar than one led by a nondynastic outsider. Dafanil, satisfactorily altered by your restructuring technique, will be an extension of my personality. Once you've perfected your self-genesis efforts, I can rule through him as long as he lasts and replace him with another puppet when he's old. I shall have the benefits of imperial ascendancy with none of the responsibilities. I shall make Dafanil available when the time comes. You will see to the arrangements."

Etasalou agreed. "An excellent plan." The news of the emperor's son was helpful. Ullas's notion of using him wasn't without merit. Etasalou pondered that idea and was shocked to realize Ullas was speaking to him again.

". . . knowing how very strongly you feel about family. I only recently learned of her presence myself."

"I'm sorry, Counsellor; who did you say?"

"Your niece. The doctor. Nan Bahalt is her name. She's assigned to Lumin, here on Hire." Ullas paused, cocked his head. "Is something wrong, Commander? The woman is your niece, isn't she? They told me she was."

Roaring in his ears threatened to undo Etasalou. His face and neck burned fiery hot. This was the woman who betrayed her family. Betrayed *him*. And for a nonliner. Worse, a Rifle, a man pivotally responsible for the need to seek refuge on this moonless, misbegotten rock. Rasping, he said, "Give her to me." Instantly he realized his error, amended the demand. "She's more than family. She's a brilliant researcher. I must have her as part of my effort."

Ullas responded with slow deliberation. "That must be

discussed with the proper Lumin officials. Understand: You are apostate. I am not. I cannot—will not—offend the faith."

Etasalou twisted his face into a smile. "You're right, of course. In my eagerness, I overspoke. In fact, it's best if Doctor Bahalt not know I'm aware of her presence. Some discreet inquiries—her situation, her well-being—would be most welcome."

"Consider it done." Ullas smiled. "How soon can you go to work on Halib's brat?"

Etasalou shook his head. "Not for some time." When Ullas's jaw muscles bunched, Etasalou remained firm. "We are only a few scientists, working to our limit."

Lust and dissatisfaction gleamed from Ullas. Then he turned thoughtful. "I can afford some delay. My son returns this year. It would be good if we could preserve his life and not endanger my objectives." He spun and marched away, knees pumping, head poked out ahead of him.

Ramrod straight, alight with chaotic dreams of vengeance, Etasalou reentered his building. Gradually revenge slipped aside, making room for another vision.

Lannat had escaped from his trial. Or had he? The emperor's favorite. Escaped? Or rescued? Nan Bahalt, Lannat's lover, sent to Hire. Coincidence? Etasalou cleared his throat, spat the mess on the floor.

Nan Bahalt's presence meant one thing, and one thing only.

Captain Lannat was coming to Hire—or was already present.

Emperor Halib, the gamemaster. Advanced his queen, set the knight in ambush. Badly played, Emperor. Pitifully misplayed.

Etasalou laughed aloud, drove a fist into the air. He stepped back outside, drew a huge breath, exhaled with sensuous pleasure while scanning the empty road leading away from the building, the blank expanse of the green-shouldered Fols Hills all around. He laughed again. What a bloody future lay ahead for such a dull little gob of a planet.

CHAPTER 12

The morning after his meeting with Betak, Lannat was awakened long before dawn. Following a quick breakfast, he and Jarka stepped outside into a blackness so thick Lannat swore he could feel it. Trailing behind, Lannat at first assured himself that most of his stumbles were really caused by unfamiliarity with the trail and not the result of Jarka's superior night vision. After his second collision with a tree Lannat decided he just wouldn't think about comparisons anymore.

Dawn was gratefully received. Even Jarka was more at ease, lengthening his stride. They covered ground well, forging constantly uphill.

The Marnoffar Mountains of Goliphar's southwest were round-shouldered in their antiquity, shaped by millions of years of exposure. Their temperate forest covering was ancient, luxurious. Moving through such growth, there was no concern for highspys. Taller trees stretched out massive, horizontal branches, absorbing as much nourishing sunlight as possible. Any energy they missed was seized at the next level. The lower plants were spindly, scrubby. They grew far more branches per foot of trunk, and their leaves, alive to the faintest breath of a breeze, scrubbed the air in constant search for life-giving light. Neither infrared detection nor the highest-resolution optics penetrated two such layers of concealment.

When they stopped for their first break, Lannat took a hearty pull on his canteen before remarking on the safety of their trail.

Jarka, wiping his mouth, detached a small plastic box from his belt. He handed it to Lannat. "The newer highspys have a radar that penetrates the canopy, detects movement. When we heard about it, we didn't worry. After all, animals are moving around here all the time. It turns out that nothing moves through the forest like humans. The radar's programmed to seek out steady, directional progress. If something suggests human presence that doesn't belong in a location, it signals the Advisors, and they come looking. That box I gave you is a radar detector. If it buzzes, we stop. When it's not buzzing, we go."

Skeptical, Lannat examined the thing. "Has the radar caught anyone?"

"Why d'you think we carry the detectors? Ten of us the first time, four the second time. Happened a long time ago, when we were just getting started."

Lannat handed the detector back. "Everyone gets one of those?"

"Just when we leave the camp. All you have to remember is, don't move. Standing still you're invisible."

"Don't I wish."

Jarka chuckled, heaving himself to his feet. Lannat followed. It occurred to him that drawing the small laugh was the first time he'd done anything that made Jarka interact with him as if they might get along.

Eight hours after starting, clothes wet with sweat, the pair arrived at the training camp of the Free. A stocky man in loose camouflaged clothes and rough boots watched them climb the last yards. He greeted Jarka warmly. Thrusting a hand at Lannat, he addressed him as Val Bordi, and Lannat almost hesitated, still unable to respond reflexively to the different identity. They shook hands as the man went on, "I'm called Sul. Not my real name, just like Val's not yours, I expect. Never mind. We've got plenty of names. What we need is training. Betak tells me you can help us."

"Maybe." Lannat looked past Sul. "What's the Free's total strength? Weaponry? Experience? How do you get supplies up here? You have medical personnel, equipment?" He fastened his gaze on Sul, made the shorter man match it. "Just exactly what do you expect to accomplish?"

Coloring, Sul lifted his chin. "You don't waste much time, do you? All right. Our total number of supporters is none of your business. All you need to know is that Betak is a very thorough man. He built the resistance over the years, and he fooled both the emperor and Ullas the whole time. We've got hidden fighters in and around Liskerta and other urban centers ready to join us any time we make a raid. Other supporters keep us informed. This camp's the hub of the wheel; there's forty of us, thirty-two men, eight women. We've each got one fighting spear and shield. Everyone carries a sword and a knife. We make more weapons every day and store them. You'll find no coward's missiles among us, either. We have to strike with surprise and deception because we're weak, but we won't break the Blood Father's law."

Lannat listened to the last with more cynicism than he liked. He interrupted Sul. "I hope the Advisors are as scrupulous as you. They have railguns, I understand."

"Five of them, only two on Goliphar. You know better than I, they're not much use against dispersed troops."

Lannat nodded, and Sul continued. "We pack in supplies from four separate collection sites. Our medical people are Lumin converts; they brought what equipment they could get away with. It's not much, but we'll get by. The people are first class." He paused, and the chin jutted again. "We're going to make Hire free. Not tomorrow or the day after, but some day. Our immediate goal is to hit and run. The people have to know Ullas and his damned Advisors aren't invincible, that they can be hurt."

"Do you know what that will cost?"

"You mean the heavier repressions? Certainly. It'll force people to join us."

"And to inform on you. And there's a huge difference between knowing people are going to be hurt and seeing what you're responsible for. I was told things about Ullas. He'll tear your people apart."

Misery and determination swarmed back and forth across Sul's plain features. "We don't have a choice."

"That's right. You don't. Start, and you're in to the finish. Hope everyone in your organization understands that."

"No fear. I can vouch—"

"Like hell you can. You've been hiding out here in the woods while you play soldier, spying on people who don't have any reason to fear you. I'm told your resistance has knocked out a couple of small electrical substations and painted some walls. That's not rebellion, that's pranks. I'll teach you how rebellion works. But Ullas will teach you what war is all about. That's when some of your people will fold. Starting now, you investigate the background of every soul in this camp. A complete check. Then we'll talk about trust. I'm not dying for your cause, and you can take that to the line."

Sul sneered. "Cold, aren't you? Strictly business. Betak sent us a role model."

It was Lannat's turn to color. His neck warmed. Quietly he said, "I think you're a good-hearted man, Sul. I just don't think you really understand what you're in for. Don't judge me quite yet. Now, where do I work?"

Sul led the way. Jarka fell in behind, not before Lannat saw his troubled frown. He wished he could explain to the Hiran why he was being so hard. He thought of his soldier father. He rarely did that, but just then he remembered him saying once "If a leader explains himself after he wins, it's called boasting. If he explains after he loses, it's called making excuses. Don't bother."

Lannat wasn't certain that was always true, but he'd learned long ago that the first thing a good fighting man must learn is to obey, and people don't rush to obey anyone they feel free to argue with. If the Free were to be an effective fighting force, they needed disciplined teamwork. Someone had to be un-questionably in charge.

Lannat spent the remainder of that day and the evening meeting people and learning the camp layout. Sul had posted the satellite schedule, assuring everyone took cover when they passed over. Highspys were another problem. They coursed the mountains in random pattern. Sul had improved on the effect of the two-layer canopy by constructing most of the camp underground. Classrooms, sleeping, eating, hospital facilities, and storage areas were all in bunkers connected by tunnels high enough for the average person to stand. Sul proudly pointed out that all structural logs and timbers were cut far away and stream-floated close enough to be hauled into the camp.

As much as Lannat admired the ingenuity of the place, he ached to get back outdoors. He resolved to never retreat into that complex. He could condition himself to work down there, but he'd never fight there.

The second day in the camp, he went on reconnaissance. Again he mentally applauded Sul's instincts. The camp was on a round peak, only a few yards higher than its nearby companions. Still, it dominated them, allowing excellent concealed observation points; even the least dangerous area, to the south, was well covered by lookout positions. The camp itself faced northeast, toward the capital of Liskerta. The most likely route of approach from that direction was the path Jarka and Lannat traveled to reach the camp. It was under direct observation for miles. Sul pointed out where a pair of convenient forest fires cleared the land. Lannat remembered the location well from his hike into the camp. Sul said, "The blaze made a great choke point in the trail. Steep, treacherous ground on the flanks. Anyone coming that way has to cross in the open or scramble around it. We've got sonic sensors in the trees there, just in case, and more buried in the clearing. If the Advisors ever suspect we're in this area, it'd be just like them to come at us in the night."

"What about patrols?"

Jarka answered first. "They've actually been through the

camp. We knew they were coming and took cover in the shelters. They didn't see a thing."

"Do the patrols ever stay at Betak's building? What's the purpose of the place, anyhow?"

Once more Jarka replied. "Betak is the counsellor's forest manager. The building is sort of a hunting lodge, sort of an ecological instruction center. It's also the headquarters of the Goliphar Hiking Club. For us, it's ideal. We can pass fairly large numbers of people through the building, all with a legitimate excuse—going hiking or camping or hunting—whatever."

"What about actual recreation visitors? What do you tell them?"

"Some days some trails are closed; Betak tells the tourists it's for maintenance. No one asks questions. And anyone using any Planet Wild Reserve has to carry a permanently signaling location designator."

"What about our people when they come up here?"

Sul shrugged hugely, grinned. "We turn them off. Or leave them in one place. Or have one person carry a bunch of them. Ullas's controls are tough, but they're not perfect."

"Remember that. We're going to use the imperfections."

Later, when he was alone, the idea of imperfection came back to Lannat. He recalled the light outside the oneway, a light he wasn't supposed to see. That was an imperfection—a mistake—and it had proved useless to him. After dwelling on that for a bit, he decided there was a lesson there, after all: An obvious error by an opponent wasn't always a golden opportunity. As the spymasters said, control was 80 percent of the game. Always be sure to be in control.

Control. Game.

Spymasters. They had put him here. Bastards.

Lannat called for an outdoor meeting of all nonwatch standers on the morning of the third day. Thirty people were available, laughing and chattering. They looked up expectantly when he approached, flanked by Jarka and Sul. If anyone noticed that the two Hirans wore disturbed frowns, and the way they kept a chill distance from Lannat, they ignored it. Several in the audience did whisper to friends that the newcomer had an almost unfriendly look.

Lannat waited, looking from one to another of the small crowd, until a prickly, nervous silence settled on them. Then he said, "There are three officers in camp: Mr. Sul, Mr. Jarka, and me. Salutes and formal address are not required in the field. Later today Mr. Sul will assign you to squads. Personnel-designated noncommissioned officers will exercise leadership in the training and welfare of their personnel. Failure will result in demotion."

Angry exclamations from various points in the audience melded into one rumble of complaint. A tall, rangy man cranked himself erect. "What the hell's this all about, Sul? We didn't come up here to play soldier with this—"

"Play soldier is all you know." Lannat's expression didn't change, but he projected his voice with the force learned in years of parade deck commands and battlefield orders. The tall man rocked, let his complaint wither. Lannat went on. "We're going after Ullas's Advisors. We're going to irritate them. Confuse them. Hurt them. Kill them. First as isolated victims, one at a time. When we're stronger, we'll kill whole squads. Then platoons. Until they break and surrender. Or join us. We can't do that scrawling slogans on walls or wrecking transformers and forcing a few hundred people to miss their favorite holovid for an hour. Every one of you is hiding out in these mountains because Ullas will throw you into Etasalou's labs if he catches you. Do any of you have any idea what he does to prisoners?"

No one spoke. The sullen expressions defied Lannat. He understood that every one of them stood ready to despise any who cooperated with him. He pointed at a woman. "You. What have you heard?"

She looked left and right for support. One friend refused to meet her gaze. The other shrugged. Nostrils flaring, the woman faced Lannat again. "They're tortured," she said.

"Wrong. Etasalou will torture someone for information. He

uses pain to get what he wants. It's just another technique, and if it maims or blinds you, that's not a consideration. But he has a better use for us. Once his scientists get finished with your brain, you go into combat with no thought but the objective you're assigned. When the battle is over, and if you've survived, you return to the barracks to train and wait for the next battle. You fight because you have no other thoughts: no fear, no feelings, no hope. You cannot surrender, even if wounded. Your own mind will kill you, simply to guarantee you reveal nothing to the enemy."

"What are you telling us?" another man asked. "Who can't surrender?"

"Etasalou's people. They fight to the death. Win or die, literally."

The woman Lannat singled out rose. "You're talking about our relatives. Family. Telling us they're nothing but—but automatons. You're lying. No one can do that to a person." Her eyes pleaded.

"I've seen what he does. Scientists program your mind, exactly as you'd program a computer, so that when a particular situation presents itself, you respond exactly the way you've been conditioned to respond. The restructured ones can't help themselves. And if they fail, they die. They look you in the eye and they scream at the horror of what their mind is doing to them, and they stop functioning."

"That's crazy." It was the tall man, and the fear in his features belied the strength of his denial. "You can't do that to a person. It's impossible."

"It's not necessary for you to believe me. I promise you, when we strike at Etasalou's troops, you'll see for yourself."

"What's all that got to do with officers and squads and stuff?" a man shouted.

"I'm here to teach you how to fight and live. Die if you want, but I won't let you take anyone with you. If you're not a team, you'll hardly annoy a real combat unit. I am not here to teach you how to be a nuisance. When I get done with you, you will be the finest fighters Hire has ever seen, an efficient, self-motivating, unfailing killing machine. Killing is what feeds rebellion. You asked for it, and by light, I'll see you're equipped for it."

Someone else started to speak, and Lannat overrode him. "We're losing training time. From now on, every minute is accounted for. Today we'll start with sword fundamentals. Ten minutes." He turned and left, ignoring the furious growl behind him. It sounded like a beast, goaded to fury.

He smiled to himself. Everything was going fine.

CHAPTER 13

Lannat stood in front of Jarka and Sul, watching the two lines of troops thrust and parry in ritual drill. Actually, he thought with a certain regret, he was only near the other two, not actually with them. He spoke over his shoulder. "You said your medical people are Lumin—you called them converts. Why?"

Sul concentrated on the exercise in progress. "The resistance trusts in the Seeker. Our primary enemy is Counsellor Ullas. Our social enemy, if you will, is a state religion that denies us our faith, dictates our culture, even regulates who does or doesn't get an education."

Lannat ached to ask about Nan. The man called Val Bordi had no reason to know her. The man who was Lannat dared not reveal that he did. "Are you talking about another theocracy to replace the present one? And how long have you known these medical types? How good are they?"

"That woman." Sul nodded. "The one closest to us. She was director of nursing at Liskerta's largest hospital. Our doctor's an older man. He's down in the hospital. And we're not fanatics. Our government will run on merit, not privilege."

"I'll talk to the doctor later. Now I have to go to work." Lannat stepped away from Sul's discomfort with the religious issue. He wondered if the matter of beliefs would turn into an unmanageable issue. There always seemed to be one such in any rebellion. If the history of the Homeric galaxy illustrated one reasonably dependent constant, it was that the children of revolution ended up devouring the parents. If religion was the black hole of choice for the Hirans, it wasn't his concern.

Raising his voice as he advanced, Lannat interrupted the desultory clash and clang of unenthusiastic sword practice. When he had everyone's attention, he said, "You sound like the rhythm band from the Home for the Bewildered. From now on, sword drill is honest work. You pitty-pat each other like sweethearts in the dark. You embarrass me. Until we can outfit you with blunt practice weapons and padded armor, we'll work on unarmed combat. You—you're first." He pointed at a small woman and asked her name.

Wide-eyed, she blurted out an answer. "Trey. I'm a communications tech. I don't know—"

Lannat drowned out her protest. "Lay down your sword and shield. Step out here. The rest of you come close and watch."

Slow, surly, they gathered. Facing Trey, who came to his shoulder, Lannat spoke over her head to the semicircular formation. "Learn this: Thinking wins fights. Strength is secondary." He moved back a yard into a ready stance, telling the woman, "Situation: We've both lost our equipment. We run into each other. I see you're a woman, unarmed, so I hesitate."

A low voice drawled sarcasm. "You? Sure."

When Trey had to look away because she couldn't repress a tight smile, Lannat gritted his teeth. He went on as if unhearing. "You either attack or wait for me. Which will it be?"

Unhesitating, she leaped at him. Lannat ducked a wide-swinging right hand, sidestepped, retreated. Before she regained her balance, he resumed his stance. "Punch," he said. "Drive your fist straight ahead. Get your body into it. Flail your arm out to the side like that, and you're in trouble. Try again. If you're not too tired."

She darted forward again, cocked the right hand. Startlingly quick, she kicked at Lannat's crotch. He retreated, took most of the impact on his defending forearm. A jolt of pain knotted his stomach when her foot made some contact. Lannat hoped he didn't grimace.

The woman was resourceful. Before she had time to fully realize her kick was ineffective, she had already launched another wide-ranging right hand. Off balance, it was a puny effort. Lannat brushed it aside again. Movement accentuated the gripping in his guts but failed to interfere with actions that were conditioned to the point of instinct. By the time he was settled back into stance, the pain was already subsiding. Nevertheless, he decided to slow the action for the moment. He said, "Very good. You made a teaching point. Speed is at least as important as strength. So is unpredictability. Most important, you're thinking about how to win. Want to try again?"

Screaming, arms outstretched, fingers like claws, Trey flew at him. Lannat raised his own hands in front of him, level with his temples, forearms parallel to each other and his torso. He waited until she almost touched him. When he spun to his right, that defense deflected Trey's extended hands and arms without reducing her body's speed. He turned with her passing, making their interaction a swift dance that married grace with ferocity. Before she could check her momentum, Lannat was on her from behind. He looped an arm around her neck. Grabbing that wrist with his free hand, he squeezed.

"Don't struggle," he said. Soft, unruffled, his voice reeked of menace. The small tech's eyes were huge. Fear hid in her expression, not quite ready to break past shock and uncertainty. She held absolutely still.

Several of the watching troops made noises. Lannat moved slowly, bringing Trey with him. When he faced the group, he continued speaking to her. His mouth was only a few inches from her ear; their pose suggested affectionate embrace. His tone shattered that image. "This is a choke hold. If I apply pressure for a few seconds, you lose consciousness. A few more seconds, you die. Struggle, and your neck is broken. And our relative strengths are completely unimportant. You understand?"

"Yes." There was anger and resignation. Lannat was delighted to hear defiance, as well. He released her, quickly stepped around in front. With his back to her, he dropped to his knees. Over his shoulder he told her, "Assume that kick you aimed at me worked. I fell like this. I'm already coming through the pain. As soon as I have a handle on it, I'm going to come at you—and I'm angry. Put your right arm across my throat." When she continued to stare at him, he snapped, "Now. Do you want to be the victim all the time?"

Without answering, furious again, Trey bent and placed her arm as he instructed. He talked her through the choke hold, explaining how the primary purpose was not to cut off wind but to block the flow of blood to the brain. For one troubling moment, he thought she might actually try to knock him out. She didn't, but when she released the hold and stepped back, he was certain there was mischievous speculation in her expression.

Lannat spoke to the group. "What you saw is a metaphor. Small can defeat large, but only if small is thinking—and is skilled. The hold we demonstrated is what we have to do to Counsellor Ullas; we cut the head free of the body. We do it as small defeats large. We do it with agility, mental and physical. When attacked, we avoid or deflect. When we have the correct opening, we attack, always looking to create separation between head and body. Don't be troubled because Trey couldn't do me real harm. Believe me, in a few weeks, she'll be able to beat almost any man she'll meet in combat."

"What about us?" It was the tall, rawboned man who'd complained to Sul in the mess hall.

"I don't know how good you are. I can promise you you'll be better."

"Didn't mean that. We saw you push Trey around. What about someone your own size? You got a trick you'd like to show us?"

Grinning, Lannat raised spread hands. "I wasn't pushing her around. I was just trying to make a point."

The tall, slender man took a few steps forward, separated himself from the others. "What I mean. You ought to make a point for the rest of us." He laced his fingers, cracked his knuckles.

Continuing to smile, Lannat said, "I'm not sure we have time on the schedule. Exactly what d'you want?"

"More tricks. Didn't you hear? I didn't think you were all that slow-minded." The man matched Lannat's grin now. Most of the group smiled as well, enjoying the confrontation, pleased to see Lannat's poorly hidden reluctance. The man said, "If I was to rush you, would you tell us what I did wrong?"

"This really isn't the time or place. I've told you, the training schedule is important."

"Won't take long."

Lannat knew the man was fast, from watching the way he moved. He was long and lean, and everything he did was considered, so he appeared to be awkward and slow. In fact, he was a type Lannat always thought of as heavy machinery, a collection of rocker arms and pistons. Ponderous at first glance, there was controlled power in every function.

More, the man was schooled. Lannat's first response to the attack was to duck under the punch at his head. Practically squatting, pitched forward, he drove forward, intending to bury a shoulder into the oncoming midsection. His opponent anticipated him. He was stopping before Lannat realized it, and the first clue Lannat had that something was amiss was to feel a bone-hard knee rip the flesh of his cheekbone, then slam into his shoulder. The impact spun him wildly. He hit a tree, used it to brace himself.

The tall man was coming on, poised. He launched a whistling roundhouse kick Lannat barely blocked. Undeterred, the man drove a straight punch at Lannat's head. It nicked the bloodied cheek. Already embarrassed, Lannat winced as the new pain sent a blast of angry energy surging through him. That instant seemed to crystallize all his frustrations, and the rawboned man was available.

Stepping inside the edged-hand blow that followed the straight punch, Lannat drove a knee into the man's groin. Grunting, ashen, but with both hands still raised in defense, the man stepped back. Lannat feinted a sweep at his legs, making the man twist. That turned his head, and Lannat drove a fist into the exposed jaw. As his opponent staggered sideways, Lannat followed. While the man tried to steady himself, Lannat said, "You have some moves, but your timing is rotten. After you hit me with that knee, you should have already had a fist coming down on the back of my head." As if demonstrating, Lannat faked an overhand blow with his left hand. When the man lifted his hands to block, Lannat pounded an uppercut to his midriff. Once more the man stumbled away, gasping for air. Lannat went on. "You should have finished me with that kick. You missed because you were too eager. You were acting, not thinking."

Fiery with anger, Lannat leaned all his weight on his left leg, started the sweep that would take the other man's feet out from under him.

Lannat's torn cheek burned. Blood streamed down the side of his face. It made a sticky, unpleasant mess between collar and neck. The pivoting turn pulled on abdominal muscles, escalated the residual pain from the kick Trey had aimed at his groin. Suddenly his anger changed focus yet again. Fragmented thoughts glittered across his mind.

Outsider. False name, false life. Betrayed.

Nan.

These fools. Brainless, untested. Stupid with pride. Laughed at him. Laughed. Pain. Wanted to see him injured. They wanted teaching? They would be taught.

The fight was over. Had been over for a while. Still, fury was fire in his veins. Lannat wanted to hurt the man in front of him so much it sang in his ears.

A mistake. Wrong.

He shortened the sweep, raking his foot so close it touched the other man's trousers. Continuing the motion, he whirled in a tight circle, ending with a spearing elbow stopping just short of a blinding blow. His opponent was frozen in place, lips drawn back, eyes squinted shut. He opened them when he felt Lannat's grip on his elbow, straightening him. Lannat said, "You're a very dangerous man, my friend. Deceptive. Tough. You had me reaching way down deep in that trick bag you were asking about. I'm looking forward to working with you. What's your name?"

"Retalla. I'll take you next time." The words had a mushy quality, and Retalla spit some blood as if to explain the problem.

Lannat shook his head. "No, you won't. Maybe someday, if you'll learn what I can teach you. But not next time. Not even the time after that. It takes more practice than that." He smiled, stuck out his hand. "It might be a better idea if we took it out on Advisors and kept score."

Retalla considered the gesture. Before he could form a response, the woman named Trey was beside him. Subtly, but unmistakably, she positioned herself with her back to Lannat, between the men. She dabbed at Retalla's split lip with a handkerchief, speaking softly. "Let it go. Learn what he knows. Your turn will come. Now we have to work together."

Only when Trey stopped talking did Retalla reluctantly shift his gaze from Lannat's steady look down to her upturned features. Immediately his long features eased, anger and pain diffused by stronger feelings. Finally he gave his attention to Lannat again. He winced when he shook the extended hand. "You got any stunts will make a black eye go away? You're going to have a beauty." He spat some more blood.

Trey unobtrusively moved to Retalla's side. Lannat almost laughed aloud at the quiet confidence, the way she led her friend away and made it look like his idea.

He wondered if he'd ever really get to know them.

They were returned to the group by then. Lannat noticed frowns but a generally subdued attitude. He said, "Conditioning run commences in thirty minutes. Full equipment. Reassemble here. Dismissed."

With the troops moving off, Jarka said, "You ought to get something on that scrape."

Lannat touched it gingerly. "I'd just sweat it off, running in these hills."

Sul was less concerned for Lannat. "You were pretty rough on Retalla."

"I let him believe what he wanted to believe. To be honest, I didn't think he'd try anything so early on."

Sul managed to combine glare and gape. "You expected that—that exhibition? You set him up!"

Lannat turned on Sul, included Jarka in his cold glare. "He wanted to find out who's in charge. I knew he'd try me as soon as I heard him griping to you. This is no debating team. If I have to break his face to make him understand that, that's his problem. Whatever works, gentlemen. You've stolen my life from me, handed me forty people, and told me I'm responsible for their lives. You think I won't slap the living snot out of any one of you who gives me a reason? Sober up."

They were at the entrance leading to Lannat's underground quarters by then. He lifted a camouflaged horizontal door, complete with bush, and paused before descending the stairs. "I was serious about that background check on all these people,

Sul. Send a messenger to Betak, tell him to initiate the process immediately. And find out if the base is monitored for electromagnetic transmissions."

"We only have three seekums, and they're all in my quarters. The dimenomaps that go with them are there, too. There's no need for the background check, either. These are all good, patriotic Hirans, with relatives in Etasalou's laboratories. They were ready to fight long before they heard your horror stories. Do you know how it hurt them to hear—"

Lannat cut him off. "Tell Betak I want the site monitored for transmissions constantly. Check your people; if they're clean, it does them no harm." He dropped down the stairs, closing the door behind him.

Fuming, Sul glared after him, pounded a fist into his hand. "Jarka, damn it, we've made a terrible mistake. I don't like him. Betak has to know."

Jarka chuckled. "You know what Betak said about our esteemed specialist? 'What an unpleasant man. He's made me think about our revolution in a way I've avoided until now. I'll never forgive him for that.' Then he looked at me, smiled like someone was pulling his fingernails out, and said, 'I never realized how much we need him.' " He winked at Sul as he turned away. "Have to go. I don't want to be late for formation."

CHAPTER 14

Hands spidering softly across the top of the blanket, Lannat felt for the darkglasses hidden at the foot of his bed. Across

from him in the three-man officer's bunkroom, Jarka mumbled
and shifted. Once certain Jarka was again deep in sleep, Lannat
put on the darkglasses and looked about. Sul was no concern,
either, flat on his back, snoring. After dressing quickly, Lannat
slipped out.

The stairs leading outside were made with green lumber. As
it dried, it shrank and warped. Now those minute inconsisten-
cies were a hazard. Each step whispered threat of louder alarm.
No matter how delicately he settled his weight on some, they
squeaked. Not loud. That would be too direct, Lannat thought
as he cursed them. Just like everything in his life now, there
had to be subtlety. And tantalization.

Starlight made the outdoors bright in comparison to the
underground complex. Still, without the darkglasses, Lannat
was practically blind. A flip of the temple switch altered the
mechanism, shifting from thermal imaging to light enhance-
ment. The glasses changed everything to myriad shades of
green. In its color, it was unmistakably forest. In its alienness,
its complete difference from any normal view, it was always a
bit unsettling.

He remembered the thunderous roar of the lyso and admitted that he was perhaps a little more unsettled than usual.

In a few minutes he was at the trailhead leading to Betak's
lodge. He shifted his sword to a back-carry where it was less
likely to snag brush and checked the accessibility of the ceryag
blade under his arm. Next, he removed the bandage on his
damaged cheek. A spray of newskin stopped the bleeding, but
the swelling felt as if he wore a balloon taped to his jaw. The
white cloth was unacceptable, in any case. He scuffed it under
forest litter and struck out.

Approximately two hours later he reached the site he had in
mind. The trail took a steep drop there, a cut through some rotten shale. No one would negotiate that section without making
noise—and being at a defensive disadvantage.

Lannat sat down, back against a tree at the base of the descent, and off to the side. He put his sword on the ground next

to him. Tested the pull of the knife in its scabbard once again. Took a long pull on his canteen, then put it next to his sword.

Then he waited.

Night noise came from all directions. Things moved in the tall trees overhead, hooting softly. Branches thrashed, that rustle mingling with an angry, hissing squabble. Darkglasses revealed moving creatures. Hidden by branches and leaves, they were wraiths that ran their hidden paths with furtive swiftness.

Once something screamed, far away. It was a long, descending cry, as if the screamer felt death's hand tighten. Lannat told himself that was just morbid imagining; it could be a love song, for all he knew.

He exhaled hugely when it stopped.

Minutes stretched into long hours. He wondered at the wisdom of his move and tried not to think about Jarka or Sul waking prematurely to find him gone.

Bits of rock trickled down the treacherous path. Lannat tensed without moving. The disturbance was very slight. Anything could have caused it. An insect. Temperature change. He concentrated on breathing slowly, steadily. Listening. Something came into view, shielded by brush, unidentifiable.

Lyso. The beast's name was an explosion in Lannat's mind. He had never asked how large they were. Or what one even looked like. His imagination flamed.

Stupid. This whole idea was stupid.

The thing continued to advance. A human figure. Wearing darkglasses. Picking a way with great caution, the person still dislodged a cascade of shards. A corner of Lannat's mind noted the sudden silence of the rest of the forest. The figure slid to the bottom of the descent. For several seconds it crouched low to the ground, almost invisible against the scrub background.

Satisfied that all was still well, the person rose and set out down the trail again. Whoever it was carried a sword at the ready. Lannat watched his quarry pass, then moved out onto the trail behind.

His victim either heard the sword descending or suffered a premonition. He dodged, not quite quickly enough. The flat of Lannat's blade cracked down on the skull with a flat, dull report. There was a grunting noise and a soft collapse.

Lannat recognized the man but couldn't remember his name. Working fast, he used the victim's belt and strips of material torn from his trousers to bind him at wrists, elbows, and feet.

Hauling his prisoner up the slippery climb made a tremendous racket. Lannat dismissed it. No one else would be trying to leave the camp now, he was sure. It made no difference if anyone else heard his noise.

Once on the shallower grade above the drop, Lannat lowered the unconscious man to the ground. He grabbed him by the collar at the back of his neck, dragging him behind.

Because he was practicing the blistering lecture he intended for Sul, Lannat almost missed the faint noise off to his right. He stopped instantly. Sword up, he scanned the nearby growth. The sound came again. Something large, approaching slowly. Not uncertainly, though. Whatever it was made steady progress.

Lannat improved his grip on the prisoner's collar. He moved out, interested only in speed. The man he dragged regained consciousness and, groggy, complained querulously. Lannat spared him enough thought to wish he'd gagged him.

The thing was closer. It wheezed when it breathed. Lannat forced a clumsy trot. A thick, heavy smell reached him, cloying Lannat's dry throat, packing his lungs. The smell was sweet, reminiscent of crushed grass. The memory of Jarka saying lysos were herbivores was working across Lannat's mind when the thing behind them roared. The volume was unimaginable. His involuntary shout of surprise was swallowed in the rumble of it. So was the scream of the bound prisoner.

Behind them came a ripping and tearing of brush. The meadowlike smell was constant and stronger. The second roar was closer. Lannat looked over his shoulder. The image in the darkglasses was a nightmare animal, a thing as tall as a man, its rotund body mounted on stubby legs that churned the ground with impossible speed. Horns a yard long speared straight ahead out of a massive head. The mouth was truly terrifying. Saliva in ropes as thick as a man's wrist flailed and splattered from the sides of a huge triangular beak. Flat on the bottom, cruelly hooked on the top, it gaped wide and clashed shut like shears during the animal's closing charge. Lannat flung the prisoner to the side.

Sidestepping, he eluded the horns. The beast skidded to a stop and turned, opening that yawning beak. When it did, the horn slammed into Lannat, flicking him away like lint. The beak snapped shut where Lannat had been. Lannat regained his balance in time to shelter behind a tree. The animal lunged, feinting, trying to flush Lannat from behind his shelter. Roaring constantly, it finally chose a side and bulled ahead. For all its close-coupled appearance, the animal twisted its neck around the tree trunk with startling flexibility. The gnashing beak snapped shut inches from Lannat's shoulder.

The frustrated attack exposed its neck. Lannat stabbed at it, a two-handed thrust that carried the whole weight of his body and every muscle he could bring to bear. He slammed to a stop as if he'd struck a wall. For one sickening moment, he was sure he'd accomplished nothing. A bellowing scream told him otherwise. Nevertheless, the way the sword pulled free confirmed that the beast's hide was tougher than chain mail.

Sprinting, Lannat made for a different tree. A horn grabbed his shirt just above his waist. A twist of the beast's head whisked him off the ground and flung him, spinning. Lannat felt branches break, whip across his face and body. He landed on his back, almost winded. Instinctively he rolled and dug in his toes, not knowing where he was going, but certain that immobility was death. He heard a tearing noise, looked back to see the animal shaking its head, spitting out dirt and litter. Lannat was sure it came from where he had fallen.

The switch on the darkglasses was jarred from light intensification to infrared mode. The new view conjured a glowing monster of the lyso, its exertions creating so much heat the picture wavered. The horns and beak were hardly visible at all, and there was a clear line of demarcation between hotter and colder areas that ran from behind the front leg to the hind leg.

Thinner skin. The difference in temperature could mean only that more heat escaped from the less-armored belly area.

The thing had a weakness—if he could find a way to attack it.

This time when the thing attempted to snake around the tree shielding Lannat, he leaped clear. Crouching, he lunged with the sword, aiming below that telltale line. The impact generated a higher-pitched scream and a crushing blow from a tail that Lannat had ignored to that point. There was no pain. Suddenly, however, he was out of control, caught in the half-world of semiconsciousness. Stumbling sideways, watching the lyso gather its barrel-body for another rush, he felt the sword slip from a grasp that refused to hold. He clutched at branches. Missed. He hit a tree and fell off to the side.

The animal pawed the ground with its ridiculous stump legs and lowered its horns. Thermal imaging transformed it into a wavering unreality. It charged.

Lannat fumbled the ceryag blade free. The knife wobbled from side to side.

The charge veered off, too fast for Lannat's addled senses to comprehend completely what was happening. The beak snapped repeatedly, interrupting high-pitched screaming. Suddenly the animal coughed and made a rough, agonized noise.

Crashing brush marked an inexplicable retreat. Roars and screams dwindled to a hacking rattle. When Lannat heard the crash of something falling he listened eagerly for thrashing and the hard gasps for one more breath. He knew nothing of the animal; he knew well how living creatures die. Nevertheless, he crawled through the brush until he found his sword, and then positioned himself with his back to a tree. He planted the hilt of the weapon against his waist, blade pointed at the weakening upheaval. He concentrated on ignoring pain, exhaustion, fear.

"Val. Val Bordi. Are you all right?" It was Jarka.

Lannat drew a breath to shout, then choked at how much it hurt his chest. "Here. I'm over here. The thing—what happened?"

"It's a lyso. Dead. I can't see you. Are you standing?"

"Getting up." Groaning, Lannat clawed his way upright.

He made it just as Jarka shouted, "I see you. Good man. I thought the thing finished you. What the hell are you doing out here?"

The prisoner. Lannat swore. "I was waiting for someone. Wherever I was when that thing came at me, that's where I left him."

"This way." Jarka hesitated. "Can you walk? You're hanging onto that tree like you need it."

"I'm all right." Lannat pushed away from his support, determined to make the lie work. When he did, Jarka snorted, but he didn't argue. He led off, telling Lannat to stay close.

The prisoner was a few yards away from where Lannat threw him. At first glance, Lannat thought the man was dead, caught in a pitiful attempt to flee while bound. Instead, he was unconscious. Jarka was checking his pulse when Lannat squatted beside him. "Passed out," Jarka said. "Can't blame him. The lyso almost trampled him."

"What happened to it? I was finished when it turned away."

"I killed it." Jarka might have been talking about opening a book. "You have to spear them low, under the armor. Come up, cut into the heart."

"Just like that? That's it? You stuck it with a spear?"

"The heart's huge. All that bulk needs it, you know? Anyhow, it never knew I was there. Its mind was on you."

"It had me. A few more steps, no more La—Val Bordi. You saved my life."

Jarka chuckled softly, slipping an arm under the unconscious figure's shoulders. "You sound like something from a bad holovid."

"Don't be rude. That happens to be my favorite cliché." Lannat took the figure's ankles and helped Jarka lift him. "I'm also glad you decided to follow me. How come you missed me?"

Jarka shifted his grip on the prisoner and started walking back to camp. He spoke hesitantly. "I don't dream much. I had one that woke me tonight. About you. I saw you and knew you were lost. Weird landscape—flat, with knee-high scrub as far as you could see. Funny thing was, you carried a man on your back, but he didn't seem hurt or anything. He was just there, you know? Riding. Then this old woman all dressed in black showed up next to me. She said, 'How helpless he is.' I woke up and you were gone. As soon as I looked outside and you weren't around, I was sure you'd be out here, waiting." He paused, and when he resumed, a touch of his old hostility edged his voice again. "This was another setup, wasn't it? First Retalla, now this poor bastard. You made sure everyone knew you were tightening security. You smoked him out."

"I told two men."

Jarka was quiet for several paces, then said, grudgingly, "That's right. Me and Sul. I didn't say anything to anyone. I suppose that surprises you. You thought we would."

"I depended on it. I was half right. I'm not really happy about it, whether you believe that or not."

Another long silence before Jarka spoke again. "You really think we're fools, don't you?"

"The man who saved my life? No. Nor your friends. If you have a fault, it's subjectivity. Hardly a sin, but a dangerous frame of mind for a clandestine organization. Not everyone who claims to be your friend is telling the truth, Jarka. It's a miserable thing to learn. It's even worse to discover."

Rasping laughter cut at Lannat. At last Jarka said quietly, "I vouched for this man. You think he's a spy. I say he just had enough. He was leaving because you frightened him with all your talk about killing and dying."

"You know better." Lannat recognized the flat dismissal in his own voice as the cruel response of a man grown too wise about other men. He was pleased that Jarka said no more, and more pleased when Jarka stopped to gag the prisoner when he showed signs of waking.

The timing of their return to camp was dramatically perfect. The small unit was milling about in confusion just outside the entrance to the underground complex; the crowd parted for them, as they hauled their bound prisoner down the stairs into the main dining room. The smell of breakfast was an incongruous surround as the two captors put the man on the floor and stepped aside. Sul stood apart from the muttering, anxious group, ashen.

Jarka looked to Lannat. Lannat turned his back on him, limped awkwardly to the tea urn, and poured a cup. Jarka, thrust into the role of spokesman, droned through his tale. When he finished, he looked at Sul. The chunky leader's face was a portrait of stress. There was anger in plenty, and its companion, guilt. No one more visibly expressed the agony of this betrayal. When he spoke, it was defiant. "There's no proof he was running because he's an informer. As soon as it was obvious who was missing, I personally searched his belongings. There's nothing incriminating there."

The prisoner shook his head, making frantic noises through his gag.

One of the women in the group spoke up. "Maybe he just lost his nerve."

"You can bet on that," Lannat said dryly. "Look, you want proof the man's an agent? Find it. Investigate how he came to know about you, who sent him to you. Jarka told me he vouched for the man; that means he tricked Jarka somehow, but someone told him how to do it. Personally, I think the reason you had an Advisor patrol go through this area and not find anything is because they already know exactly where you are.

And this piece of filth is how they know. The Advisors don't want to catch you. Not yet."

The bound man writhed. High screams worked through the gag. It made Lannat think of distant terror.

"If that's true, if they know about this camp, we have to move," Sul said. "Quickly. But what about him?" He used a ludicrously surreptitious nod to indicate the prisoner.

Lannat stepped back. He ached all over, and the cup of tea wanted to come back up. There seemed to be a cold, damp hand pressed between his shoulder blades, and every breath was heavy in his chest. "He has to be interrogated. It's a job for a professional. If this outfit knows one. Your lives, the lives of your families, depend on it."

Thick silence burrowed into each mind in the room and tormented it. Buried fears and doubts suddenly flared, as heat roils up from fanned embers.

Jarka took charge. "We'll take him to Betak. He'll know what to do."

Agreement surged through the assembly. Two men moved quickly to take the prisoner by the arms. One reached to take off the gag; Sul's wordless shout stopped him. Before he could recover, Sul was on him, furiously shoving him aside. "Leave that alone. Whatever he has to say, he can tell Betak. I don't trust myself, or anyone here, to listen to him."

Rigidly erect, Sul glared around at the group as if daring resistance. Finally he looked up at Lannat. "I'm coming with you. This is my command. Any fault is mine."

It was on Lannat's tongue to argue, to remind Sul that the bulk of his command would remain in the camp and that was therefore Sul's proper place as the leader. This was a different Sul, however, a man Lannat had never seen before. There was a hardness in him, the rigid determination one sees in men facing up to the cruelest duty they ever imagined.

Lannat made the trek to the lodge with Sul and Jarka. Fortunately for his bruises and scrapes, they moved with slow caution. There were no hikers to hide from, but they felt compelled to remain under cover in the forest until nightfall before Jarka made his way to the large lodge. He returned soon. "It's clear. Betak's there, but he's got three of his council with him. They're here for a planning session. He wants them to know about this."

Without further comment, the trio manhandled their prisoner into the building.

Betak met them. Lannat was surprised by the man's behavior. Before he had been passionate, fiery. Now he was brightly alert, but no fire burned in him. On the contrary, he was implacable as winter. Three figures in impromptu masks sat with their backs to the far wall of his office. Lannat's companions gaped, making him think of recruits fresh off the elbus.

Again Jarka recounted the night's events. When he finished, Betak looked to Lannat. Lannat muttered agreement.

Betak returned to the prisoner. "You'll stay here. In the basement. I have questions for you. You will answer me. Have no doubts. If you are a spy, you've betrayed your own brothers and sisters. There is no word to describe you. There is but one punishment."

The prisoner moaned. Silent until that moment, his first sound carried the plaint, the plea, of someone so afraid that even hope smells like a trap. He bent at the knees. The sudden shift of weight caught Sul by surprise. The two of them stumbled sideways, slamming into the wall. Face almost touching Sul's, the prisoner made muffled begging noises.

Sul threw him down roughly. His sword was in his hand with almost magical speed. He raised it, bent over the cowering figure. Eerie shrieks, smothered and distorted, boiled through the gag.

Lannat seized the upraised arm. Ignoring that as well as the raised voices of the others in the room, Sul strained to stab the prisoner. Jarka leaped to help Lannat. Between them, they pulled Sul back, held him while he regained control.

With the furor ended, one of the masked men reached up from his seated position to tug at Betak's sleeve. "Do we have to—I mean, you said only one punishment. Isn't that, you know, extreme?"

Lannat made a noise. He pushed past Jarka and the now-limp Sul.

"No one dismissed you," Betak yelled.

Lannat whirled. "Why not? I'm finished. You have your spy. I'm leaving because I'm ashamed to stay. I caught him, and now I have to give him over to people unwilling to accept the responsibility for what they've put in motion, unwilling to do what they know they must do." He took a threatening step toward the masked trio that had them pressing against the backs of their chairs. "You want to lead the glorious struggle? Learn what Jarka and his friends are learning. Any hand that rips power from those holding it is a bloody hand. You think men like us will hand you that power all clean and tidy. Darkness take you."

"We'll do what we must," Betak said. "In the name of our fellow Hirans, in the name of the Seeker who promises us that all who follow in the way shall be all they were ever meant to be. You know nothing of us. We are weapons of our faith. You will see."

Lannat made a noise in his chest and made as if to turn again. Once more Betak stopped him. "As a matter of proper procedure, did anyone search the prisoner?"

Lannat shook his head. "I wasn't thinking. We took his weapons."

Sul spoke up, grating. "I checked his things at camp. It's my responsibility. All of this is." With a glare for the rest of them, he put his sword on a convenient chair and started running his hands over the protesting, squirming prisoner. It took but a moment before he stepped back. His legs were stiff, postlike. Head down, shoulders hunched, he appeared to be protecting something. When he turned, there was a compact rectangle cupped in his hands. He stared as if he held poison.

Betak groaned. "A communicator. An Advisor communicator."

No one had time to stir. Sul threw the communicator from him. Seizing his sword in the same swift motion, he stabbed the prisoner, coming up with the tip of the sword just below the sternum, shoving hard to penetrate the heart.

The prisoner gasped, a sound of great surprise. When Sul heaved the sword clear, the man frowned darkly, an almost comical irritability. Then he looked at Sul, and it was Sul's turn to scream. Dropping the sword, he embraced the man he'd just executed. Crying openly, he lowered him to the floor. On his knees beside his victim, Sul pillowed the dying man's head with one hand. The other covered his own face.

CHAPTER 15

The injury was ugly, terribly dangerous. Nan Bahalt studied the holograph of the patient's fractured skull while slipping her surgical garb out of its clear plastic bag. She continued the examination as she undressed in the privacy of the scrub room, occasionally reaching to adjust a dial and alter the picture's perspective. She absently took a sealed packet from a shelf. The antibacterial-impregnated tunic and matching trousers inside were snug, colored orange and red. All surgeries required senior personnel, which, in turn, demanded Lumin's senior colors. Many objected to the hotter hues, insisting they were exciting rather than calming. Either way, Nan found them insulting. Lumin refused to publicly acknowledge her skills because she was under penance—probably for the rest of her life. Reds, oranges, and yellows in any of their multiple shades were forbidden to her. She wore subordinate blue and green under threat of serious disciplinary action. Still, when medical expertise was required, she was called on to provide it, and that demanded she wear the proper uniform. The hypocrisy bothered her more than the near ostracism and close confinement imposed on her since the debacle on Paro.

Paro. Lannat. They said he escaped from the oneway. Where could he have gone?

Was this her life? Servant to a tyrant, representative of a religion that despised her and left her with faith in nothing?

What if he was dead? What if that were the only escape for either of them?

Nan found herself thinking of Delight, the child who had accompanied the Lumin mission to Paro. A lovely little girl who left bittersweet, haunting memories. Smiling softly to herself, Nan remembered the warm rapport between Lannat and the child.

She took a deep breath, exhaled slowly. Perversely she called to mind a dictate from her nemesis, her uncle: "The surest defeat is surrender." Neither he nor anyone else would live to see that day from Nan Bahalt.

She took her eyes off the holograph long enough to fasten the straps that bound the trousers tight around her ankles, then resumed her study of the injury.

The victim was a young male. A nonk.

In any other culture, a man known to plot against the government would be a rebel. On Hire, the counsellor declared that rebellion was not only impossible, it was inconceivable. The Advisors solved the problem by calling rebels or other disaffected citizens nonconformists. The abbreviation to nonk was inevitable.

Nan despised the term. It had neither dignity nor accuracy. She refused to use it, instead referring to "rebels." The behavior merely convinced her Lumin superiors of her incorrigibility.

She looked at the holograph, and her mind conjured Lannat. The set of the patient's jaw wasn't quite as stubborn. *(Un-*

yielding. Lannat wasn't really stubborn. Too secure in his convictions, maybe, but not what anyone should call stubborn.) The patient's eyes were closer together, too, and Lannat's were a touch larger. Blue. A strange, changing blue, icy and brittle one second, flame-bright and devouring the next. The cheekbones . . .

She shook her head to drive out distractions.

The patient had been injured when arrested. Advisors ran him down from behind. The regulation weapon for urban apprehensions was a plasticoated metal rod two feet long and an inch in diameter. It featured a flexible section between the rigid bar and the hand grip. Timing a blow's impact to combine the full force of muscle and the stored energy of the supple section took practice. The young man was testimony to Advisor diligence.

Entering the operating room, Nan acknowledged the two masked assistants and received nods and mumbles in return. She knew to expect only the most meager interaction with her Lumin contemporaries. She dreaded the day when she came to accept such behavior as normal. As long as it continued to hurt, she was still human.

The patient's skin was barely broken. The injury was a smooth half-round indentation just above the right ear. At its deepest point was a long, blurred scrawl of red, oozing slowly. Nan examined the continuous-image magnetic scan mounted on a wheeled cart beside the patient. While not as all-inclusive as the holo, it more clearly presented the damage to be repaired. Irregular plates of shattered skull, while clearly fractured, were still held in place by tissue, the dura inside the skull and the galea outside. She grimaced, unaware she'd done so; by hammering the skull inward, the blow caused irrevocable injury to superficial brain tissue. Nan manipulated the scan, changing its point of aim. As she did, one of the assistants said, "We checked already, Doctor. The anterior branch of the middle meningeal artery is ruptured."

Nan thanked him. "Most of the damage I see is the temporal

bone, only part of the parietal. Did anyone examine to see if we have ossicle dislocation? Was there any blood in the middle ear?" As she asked, she continued to move the magnetic scan. As the assistants answered, she was already seeing for herself that there was no visible ossicle damage. Almost to herself, she commented, "He's got a long recovery to look forward to, but at least his hearing isn't damaged. And there's no sign of basilar skull fracture." She put on her operating helmet and pulled down the visor. When she bent to her task, a display lighting at the right limit of her peripheral vision gave her a constant readout of patient pulse, breathing rate, heart rate, and blood oxygen. A laser sensor measured the distance to the first solid object under scrutiny and automatically adjusted the lenses to provide the best vision, according to her preentered optometry.

Once started, Nan concentrated utterly. She rarely looked to any of the various screens tracking brain performance. Her assistants were trained to inform her of any unusual activity.

Her primary concerns were to control the arterial bleeding, eliminate the blood and dead brain tissue, and restructure the skull. After cutting the skin to create a flap and gain access, she removed the bone fragments and cut through the dura. With the artery exposed, she clamped it off, then wrapped a fine polymer netting around the damaged area. An assistant sprayed it with protein sealant, then applied a second coat of a protein solution designed to grow new tissue on the structure provided by the netting.

Simultaneously, Nan worked to eliminate the blood and dead brain tissue. She actively disliked the job. The tissue had an unpleasantly mushy quality that made her queasy, and the laser cautery of smaller blood vessels made a stink that never failed to send her stomach into flips. Stopping the bleeding was easy work. Superimposed crosshairs on her magnifying visor pinpointed the target. A minilaser measured the distance; Nan moved the crosshairs to indicate the extent of the target area. The information went directly to the cautery laser. A touch of the control button at her right temple, and a spot of light winked on and off. It made a faint, wet sound. A tiny wisp of steaming smoke wafted upward. Nan was certain every acrid, hot-copper stinking atom of it flew up her nose as if looking for a home. And all the while, the vacuum machine sucking away the dead brain tissue made wet snickering noises. The one bright spot in that part of the operation was that there was less tissue damage than she feared.

Restructuring the skull was practically a relief, after that. The pieces fit together easily. A line of glue along one broken edge and a line of fixative along the other; when they were joined, a two-second hold was all it took to set the glue. The last little piece took a bit of tricky twisting, and then it was done. Nan stepped back, nodding to the assistants to finish up.

Taking off the helmet, she allowed herself a moment to luxuriate in the sheer sense of accomplishment. The young man's color was good, his breathing was normal. He'd need attention to assure there was no undiscovered bleeding, and thus more swelling, but she didn't think there was any chance of that. What little brain tissue he'd lost would never even be noticed. And she'd done it all by hand. No computer-aided cutting, no direct electronic linkage between her helmet and the hospital data bank. The diagnosis and treatment was a product of herself and her team, and them alone.

The rest of the doctors hated her for that. She scorned them as extensions of the machines; servants, not masters.

Before leaving the operating room, Nan made a point of thanking and congratulating those who worked with her. They shook her hand. There was little other response. She knew no other assistants were trusted to diagnose or offer advice to a doctor. Hers would never mention her consideration, much less thank her, even in the privacy of the operating room, but she saw their pride and appreciation.

After showering and changing back into her blue and green robes, she left for Lumin's single women's dormitory alone.

It was a long walk. Court sprawled. A fort in ancient times, its original walls were long ago absorbed into the present warren of offices, bureaus, ministries, and departments. Armed enemies tried for generations to pull down that encircling stone. None ever succeeded. Bureaucracy simply eased alongside the works and, with no furor whatever, gobbled it all up. In the present Court, one needed a map and good vision to discover where the brave old construction once ruled. The new walls—the last of many expansions—were mere affectation.

For Nan, Court had one special place: the Yard. A large area at the southern end of the vaguely rectangular complex, the Yard was a park. Like a polished emerald dropped among coarse stones, its greenery glowed bright relief. Nan was restricted to Court. The Yard was her haven. It offered trees, flowers, a small pond with waterbirds. In short, solace.

From her dormitory window, she looked directly into the branched depths of one massive tree. On her way inside, she stopped to stroke its rough bark, greeting an old friend. That's exactly what they were, she thought—old friends. They'd seen each other through four full seasons.

It shocked her to realize she'd spent less time than that with Lannat. Her face warmed; she had despised him for the first months of that acquaintance, so she could hardly count that time as knowing him. How could she have fallen so completely in love in so little time with a man who? . . .

Once again she forced herself away from those thoughts. She swept into her building and up the stairs to her apartment. Standing in the door, she surveyed her empire. To the right, an entertainment center, the inevitable holovid and, next to it, standard sound reproduction equipment. A doorway leading to the minuscule kitchen. Dining table, two chairs. Picture of Hiran mountains above the table, bookshelves above that. By the window, easy chair, end table, monumentally ugly floor lamp. To the left, sofa and two more matching end tables. Closer to the door, a closet. Next to it, between closet door and sofa end table, the door to the bedroom and its laughably small bathroom. Nice, bright colors throughout; not enough to prevent depression, just barely cheerful enough to make suicide an occasional conjecture rather than a frequent consideration.

Nan went to the kitchen and turned on the radiant under the tea kettle. The original settlers assigned to Hire by the Blood Father had generated a rich lore of herbal plants. Nan silently blessed the intrepid explorers as she sniffed at the ten containers in her cupboard. She chose one she found particularly soothing.

The knock, just as she swallowed her first mouthful, brought a frown. A visitor usually meant bad news. She opened the door. For a moment, surprise blocked speech. She managed, "Doctor Renula. No one told me you wanted to see me."

The woman who brushed past Nan was formidable. One look at her, and any viewer knew that her orange and red robes were warning, like the gaudiness of certain poisonous insects. Marching all the way across the room, she turned, backside almost touching the window. Sunlight through the multiple layers of cloth made her luminous. Nan knew that the doctor's location and the hands-on-hips belligerence were calculated to accentuate her costume and her bulk. The woman easily weighed two hundred pounds, and her movements suggested that little fat was involved. A chin as aggressive as a fist stuck out at Nan, a red shelf between equally red, round cheeks. She plunged a hand inside the robes, where it disappeared between voluminous breasts. When the hand surfaced, it brandished a holodisk. "This just arrived. By starship."

Nan nodded, waiting.

Doctor Renula pressed ahead. "From Sungiver. Herself. Addressed to me but with words for you. I thought it best we listen to it here in your quarters."

Nan was sure she understood the deeper significance of the last remark. Doctor Renula explained anyway. "We've never been able to prove my offices are tricked out with listening devices, but no one doubts it. Sungiver's words to me must be confidential, and we're reasonably certain the rooms of underlings like you are too unimportant to interest them."

Doctor Renula's gift for casual insult was well established. Nan ignored it, reaching for the disk and inserting it into her player. Gesturing at the sofa, she waited until the doctor was seated, then took a place at the opposite end just as the picture came to life.

Sungiver stared at them from inside the holo viewer. "This is a restricted communication. If any unauthorized person dares to view this message, be warned that you interfere with Lumin at its highest office and most holy efforts. Retribution is assured." She paused a few beats. "Greetings, Doctor Renula. I entrusted this to a secure courier. He has given you my instructions: View this with Bahalt, then destroy it. Be sure you obey. I have determined that Commander Etasalou is on Hire. Rumors have placed him throughout the galaxy, but my information is accurate. He is there. Whether this is a collaboration between himself and his niece, I do not know. Despite his claims to hate her and her unscrupulous betrayal of everyone who ever trusted her, including him, my personal conviction is that they will seek reunion and reconciliation. Their primitive determination to place family before any other concern is common knowledge. As a result, Bahalt's atonement must be improved on. She will go nowhere without escort. Her education by Lumin has indebted her to us far beyond her capacity to ever repay. Nevertheless, the debt exists and must be acknowledged. Her skills will be utilized to the fullest. I task you, Doctor Renula, to assure her labors are equal to her obligations and that she is isolated from the apostate Etasalou."

Wild laughter boiled within Nan. Sungiver understood nothing. Forgiveness between herself and Etasalou could never be. Even if she were willing to forgive, he would kill her before the words cleared her mouth. She wasn't sure she wouldn't do the same for him. Until this very moment she had lived on Hire torn by the constant rumors of the fugitive Etasalou's presence. The weight of repetition insisted she believe. Fear made her refuse. Now the danger was confirmed. Sungiver worried she might seek reunion with Etasalou? Reunion with eternal dark.

Sungiver continued. "There is other news from Collegium. In the year since he disappeared, no trace of the traitor Lannat has been found. The Court of Decrees, with the concurrence of Emperor Halib, declared him legally dead. Bahalt, I know your lack of repentance has been founded on your belief that your dashing captain would return to you one day. Perhaps now you can begin your recovery, enter into the true spirit of repentance."

The screen turned black. For a long moment Nan stared at it, caught in the symbolism of funereal nothingness where Sungiver's spite glittered so brightly only moments before.

Lannat. Dead. Pain shot through her chest. *Lannat. Too full of life. He loved her. It couldn't be true.*

Battered emotions twisted everything around her, distorted reality. The click of the holodisk being ejected was transformed to slow, grating thunder. Her heart's beating was a thick rolling sound, a surf of fear. She closed her eyes to thwart tears, forced a deep, reclaiming breath. She would not accept this. She would not fail him. She would be strong and she would wait.

Doctor Renula was not a person to allow silence to go unfilled. "I never approved of you coming here," she told Nan, pulling the holodisk from the player. Her face was redder than ever, lower lip pushed forward in a massive pout. "Now I have to find a way to see you're never left alone. Do you know what a strain that puts on my personnel?"

The self-important pomposity of the woman snapped Nan upright, rigid. Her sorrow stepped aside, making room for icy fury. "Do you know what a strain a complete lack of privacy puts on me?"

Doctor Renula smirked. "Quite a bit, I hope. The difference is, my priestesses didn't create the problem. You did. Whatever happens to you, you earned it. Try to remember that. We always do."

"I'm sure. Petty malice seems to be your strongest quality."

Doctor Renula's mouth worked furiously, but before she

said more, her expression lost some of its heat and turned skeptical, then wary. She huffed loudly, obviously deciding to overlook the last remark, and looked around the room. Her manner was official. "There'll be another priestess sleeping in here from now on. The sofa has to go, and a bed brought in. I'll have to have a watch bill written up, assign people, juggle schedules. How I wish the counsellor had simply exiled you."

"Perhaps he will."

The larger woman turned slowly as the implication sunk in. She squinted, suspicious. "What's that mean? Are you plotting something? I despise that. It's what brought you to disgrace. 'The only truth is Lumin, and Lumin is the only truth.' Even little children are taught that. You never learn."

"None of you want me here in Court. I hate being here. What if the counsellor—who is completely unaware of Sungiver's message—elected to send me away? To Kull, for instance, to minister to the people there. The population always complains that Lumin spends too much effort on Court and sends them too few people. I'd certainly be too far removed from my uncle for any reconciliation."

"Kull. Full of nonks." Doctor Renula sniffed. "Always complaining. You'd fit in with them. Very well, speak to the counsellor, if you choose. Understand, I know nothing of this. It's to be done without my knowledge. Say no more to me, nothing to anyone. I'm powerless to change the counsellor's decisions." She tucked the holodisk back into the seemingly bottomless bosom. Swishing past Nan, she paused, hand on doorknob, suddenly speculative. "You're a strange woman. I suppose liners are as different as they look; I've heard it said. Anyhow, I was watching when you heard that your lover is dead. Impressive control technique. Are all liners like that?"

Clenching her fists until she feared the skin would rip across her knuckles, Nan held her anger long enough to compose an answer that wouldn't get her imprisoned. "We disapprove of the term 'liners,' Doctor. Skin pigment doesn't alter our humanity. We're exactly like anyone else. Capable of the same things. Including violence."

Doctor Renula bounced off the jamb in her rush. She made good her escape on the second try. The door slammed behind her.

Tears poured down Nan's face. She spun away, pounded the wall with her fists. Finally she moved to the sofa and fell on it, surrendering to a year of dread, failing hope, and loneliness. And unacceptable loss.

CHAPTER 16

Counsellor Ullas stalked the Hall of Mediation with stately stride. High above him arched age-darkened timber trusses supporting a roof obscured by distance. Huge chandeliers of polished brass and crystal dangled from the cross beams. Each fixture held a hundred candles as thick as a man's wrist. The suspension chains were iron, with squat, massively thick links.

The central avenue of the hall was twelve feet across. Straight and true, it ranged the full hundred yards of the building. As the candles were unlit, one end was barely visible from the other in the pale light straining through the hall's narrow windows. To add to the light's difficulty in bringing life to the vast expanse, the windows were a full sixty feet away from the center of the main avenue, high in the thick stone walls.

Perpendicular to the outer construction and the central avenue were the Stacks.

Hire revered books. The Hall of Mediation housed the dynasty's accumulated volumes of centuries. Unlike the holdings of Lumin, the hall wasn't sacred ground, nor was it the warm warren of the city's huge public library.

Ullas preferred the hall to any other place. As he walked, he brought hard heels down on the granite floor with exaggerated force, relishing the brittle crack bouncing back from the faraway walls. The next echo was softer, a sound that suggested nostalgia to him. After that, everything came to the ear in a muddle, but briefly, because by then the next heel was pistoning down, and the echo was sharp and hard once more.

Head back, chest out, Ullas paraded in solitary splendor. All around him was the rich, mellow aroma of ancient paper. And leather. The finest leather, treated with rare vegetable oils and refined wax, rubbed to a patina, soft and luxurious as the most pampered, living skin. The leather smell was ever-changing, as some leathers received different treatment from others. Ullas savored them all, his closest approach to indulgence in a narcotic.

He stopped. Profound silence was even more delicious than the echoing steps. In silence, he felt completely confirmed as the ultimate counsellor, the caretaker of knowledge on his planet. *His* planet. Possessing the hall verified his supremacy. Inhaling, he let the power of the books infuse him. Just as his body inhabited the hall, so that which was the hall dwelt in him. They were one.

But his was the greater power. When he walked, when he spoke, even if he merely sighed, the books were penetrated by his sound. There was knowledge in the books; in the counsellor reposed wisdom. In his secret heart, Ullas knew the books were sentient. Ancient as man on this world, they had existed long enough to acquire supernatural characteristics. Because he spent so much time here, alone, Ullas was sure the volumes were cognizant of his strength. No man could know every word of them, and there were times when they oozed sly, mute superiority. Ullas laughed at them, then. Of all the things in the hall, one was animate. The ultimate power was the counsellor's, not theirs. One spark, and the books were nothing.

That was power.

No one before him had used the Hall of Mediation as a formal meeting place. That was because no one understood it as he did. All his life, he had puzzled over that. The dynasty had ruled for generations, and before that, there had been other dynasties, including the one that directed the building of the hall. Yet no one in that long chain of rulers united with the hall. It was unfathomable, since the very name of the building declared it the soul of the culture. Mediation.

Man ruled best when disagreement was mediated out of existence.

Of all Hire's great achievements, it was the commitment to that principle that gave Counsellor Ullas his greatest pride. If there was one constant truth running through all the books of the hall, it was that real civilization was no haphazard jumble of events, but an orchestrated harmony, carefully modulated and supervised by qualified leaders.

Leadership. That was paramount.

History on Hire was rife with instances when decisions created by leaders were resisted by the general population. Sometimes it took the state's most vigorous persuasion to mediate that disagreement. Lamentably, the intensity level of such argument frequently rendered those of negative position organically inoperative. Ullas—like any true social leader—mourned but accepted the heavy burden with the understanding that the cost of progress inevitably weighs heavier on some than others. The bright side of the situation was that, in his reign, everyone agreed that those who refused to submit to fair and considered mediation were noncomformist. There was law to contend with individualistic social recalcitrants, just as Lumin trained doctors to treat physical problems.

The metaphor swept away Ullas's line of thought, concentrated his mind on his reason for being in the hall. Doctors. Doctor Nan Bahalt. He had left orders for her to be admitted as soon as she arrived. The watch in the lapel of his tan-on-taupe striped shirt indicated she was due.

At that precise moment a distant bell rang. He turned, striking a pose, then noted that the lighting at that point was sorely ineffective. He retreated a step and resumed. It was terribly irritating that the best light was between himself and the advancing doctor. It was impossible for him to appear to be moving forward to greet her, of course. He made the best of it, turning one foot outward just a touch, the better to display the exciting contrast between the striped shirt and the pearlescent shine of the beige leather trousers and matching half boots.

As she came closer, her own appearance made him forget to preen. Dressed in flowing, floor-length blues and greens, she drifted rather than walked. Diaphanous material in subtly different shades that overlaid each other shifted and blended, sometimes light, sometimes dense, ever-changing. She wore a pale turquoise material of nubby, rough texture wrapped over her head and tucked under her chin, a stunning frame for dark, syrup-smooth skin. High, curving cheekbones accentuated calm, observant eyes. They, in turn, complemented brows as black and sweetly curved as wings.

Sternly Ullas reminded himself that this was a woman who had betrayed her faith and her family.

She was well schooled. At the proper distance, she stopped, and bowed her head before speaking. "May it please your honor, there is no precedent for this meeting. Permission to approach?"

"You have the requisite qualifications, Doctor Bahalt. Come forward."

Everyone had remarked on her attractiveness; it amused him at the time that everyone unfailingly added some surprised comment about her "unique" beauty. Now, seeing her, he realized what fools they all were. Beauty such as hers demolished comparisons. True, her darkness was unknown among Hire's homogeneous population. Smugly Ullas silently congratulated his wise predecessors. On a planet where mediation solved all problems, government couldn't tolerate such an obvious potential for discord as racial difference. There were no liners on Hire to pursue ethnic identity as a family issue, nor had there been for centuries, when the then-ruling dynasty legislated such breeding patterns out of existence. Ullas smothered a potential frown. By all the light in the universe, her uncle was a perfect argument for eliminating racial disparities; if anything, his skin was a shade lighter than his niece's, but that's where favorable comparison ended. Where she was fine-boned and vibrant, he was scrawny and hyperintense. She extended her hand for him to examine. Again she performed correctly, spreading the fingers exactly right, not as if she were trying to span a plate, the way her uncle did. At his nod, she turned the hand over slowly. As was customary, he reached to stroke it. Normally, the matter of touching was perfunctory. Ullas chose to linger, delighted by the wondrous smoothness of her skin. As fine as any book binding in the hall, he decided, and found himself wondering what other pleasantry she might provide. He said, "We are pleased to make your acquaintance, Doctor. We shall dispense with the more intricate formalities. Consider me your representative."

"As I beg Counsel to consider me a friend of Court."

"Delightful." Ullas favored her with a genuine grin. "I believe we could actually conduct our conversation in the learned mode, if I insisted."

"I couldn't pretend to do that, Counsellor. I am trying to learn, though. If I'm to be a good Lumin doctor, I should understand your culture to the best of my ability."

Ullas wished he could applaud. The woman was as clever as she was beautiful. More than that, what she said had the ring of sincerity. He abandoned his pose, stepped forward to take her arm, and turned her around in order to lead her in the direction of more favorable light. "I should have sent for you much sooner. Hire defers to no planet in respect for Lumin. Religion is constantly on our minds and in our hearts here. We praise the light."

Nan affected a measured nod. "Lumin is honored to be the revealer of light."

"Are your quarters satisfactory in the Lumin dormitory? Do you find working conditions acceptable?"

"My quarters are fine, Counsellor. My needs are few, and my superiors are most generous. Working on Hire is almost too easy. I've never seen patients so grateful for care."

"Probably because Hirans know that health care is a function of government, and government is the result of cooperation. We cannot afford health care for those who willfully obstruct progress."

The faintest line of a frown eroded the smooth surface of Nan's brow. Ullas watched it, fascinated; on everyone else he'd ever seen, a frown was simply a disfiguring wrinkle. On this woman, however, the rich darkness became darker yet, almost black, a powerful warning of inner disturbance. He was pleased to see she was looking away. Preoccupied, he decided, or trying to properly phrase a response. She shattered that comfortable conclusion with her answer. "I have been told that our patients were screened for admission. I cannot approve of medical treatment as a function of social control."

Ullas chose not to be offended. "It isn't your position to approve or disapprove of our customs, Doctor. You seem a person willing to learn, however, so I'll explain. Our culture hinges on the most civilized discourse. I refer, of course, to mediation. Everything—*everything*—must be considered in arbitrating a situation. Those who would disrupt our social fabric must be made to understand how important the services we provide actually are. If we allow anyone to simply take whatever they choose from the rest of us, without contributing so much as conformity, what do we have? Anarchy. Rampant individualism. Your patients aren't denied a thing, Doctor. They are asked to accept the will of the majority as eagerly as they are willing to accept your care and concern. On Hire, we see both as a right. One can reject one's rights, but they must never be taken away arbitrarily."

Blinking, worrying the frown deeper into her forehead, Nan started to speak, abandoned the effort. After a moment she said, "May I speak freely, sir? It concerns my value to Court."

"Of course, Nan. No more pointless formalities, remember? What can I do for you?"

"I wish to be assigned to another medical facility. On Kull, preferably."

Ullas tensed, examined her much more closely. She stood the inspection confidently. He couldn't make up his mind if she was a superb actor or unaware of the implications of her request. If she knew of Etasalou's presence—a secret that seemed to be literally verging on popularity—she was trying to get beyond his reach. If she didn't know her uncle was here, then her isolation within Lumin's community must be truly monstrous to affect her so terribly. Either way, the request reflected a pitiable need to escape her circumstances. He tried making light of it. "Why would you leave us here on Goliphar, absent yourself from our delightful Liskerta?"

"I would be of far greater value to you on Kull. Most of the population is there. There is greater need. And I have seen nothing outside Court."

Pressuring her elbow, Ullas resumed their walk past the towering stacks. He asked her, "Weren't you one of the Exalted's own? On his personal medical staff?"

"Yes."

Beaming, Ullas marveled at the woman: uncomplicated, unassuming. Assigned to the emperor himself, and not a murmur of arrogance or false modesty. Charming. He said, "An amazing honor for one so young. I must ask—please forgive me—was there family influence involved? A crass question, but an obvious one, I think you'll agree."

"As tactfully put as one could ask." She flashed a smile, a dart of perfect white teeth and jewel-bright eyes. Heat steamed through Ullas. He had the mad notion that she felt it, heard it, as clearly as he. But her smile blinked off, and she continued as if it never happened. "You refer to my uncle, the former Commander Etasalou of Lumin's Elemental Guard. He had nothing to do with my career." With that she looked away, but her voice remained as strong as ever. "Except to ruin it and my life. I am disliked by the officials of Lumin, Counsellor. I would apply my skills in some minor facility where I am known only for myself, not for my family history."

They were at the exact midpoint of the central avenue then, the full splendor of the Hall of Mediation in full view whichever direction one turned. Ullas stopped, his tightened grip halting Nan. She turned to face him, looking up with hope.

Drawing himself as tall as possible, Ullas said, "You shall have your transfer. A physician so competent she is chosen to treat the Exalted will not be abused, nor will she be consigned to some rustic clinic, treating farmer's warts and delivering their annual babies. Tomorrow morning come to Chambers. The bailiff will be expecting you."

"I was one of three doctors assigned to the Exalted," Nan said. "A trainee."

A chopping gesture ended her protest. Ullas followed it by waving back the way Nan had come. She retreated a tentative step. He nodded approval, telling her, "As my personal physician, you will have all the staff you deem necessary. All other medical personnel on Hire will answer any request for consultation; it will be their highest priority. Make the arrangements."

"I will do as ordered. Of course. But there are other doctors, more experienced."

Ullas grew stern. He edged backward, half turned. From the corner of his eye, he noted the heightened gleam of the leather trousers. Almost iridescent. An excellent effect. It was a pity she was too distraught to fully appreciate it. "I have known of the treatment you've suffered," he said, and was pleased to see the sympathy was well received. "The enmity of your associates goes far deeper than you imagine."

"I need protection?" Wide eyes swallowed him. A hand

lifted to her cheek, and graceful fingers pressed her flesh. She made his heart pound.

He ached to tell her the truth, to warn her that her uncle lived, here, and wanted her. Instead he said, "You referred to your family history. I can only say that you spoke more accurately than you know. There are forces within Lumin and without that mean you gravest harm. You are under my protection now, free of danger."

Her blue and green robe swirling like pure, flowing water, she hurried toward the distant door. Ullas knew she wouldn't look back; protocol forbade, and she was adept. A small, satisfied smile barely touched his features. She obviously was unaware of Etasalou's presence, despite the unending rumors. Youth and naïveté completely eliminated any chance that she was acting.

It was equally certain that Etasalou meant her harm. Fool—thought he could hide his feelings.

Ullas relaxed his posturing. She was too far away to see him. Once more he resumed his formal progress along the avenue. All was as it should be. He could safely isolate her from Etasalou's anger in Court. Until Counsellor Ullas chose to reveal to each of them how completely he'd manipulated them.

No one—not Emperor Halib himself—could weave a more intricate web.

Emperor.

Etasalou insisted a lightning blow would topple Halib.

Everyone knew there was barely contained revolt on several planets.

Emperor Ullas.

He stopped and put his hands to his temples, wondering how heavy the crown was, how one adjusted it for fit. Even as he squinted about nervously and giggled at his own antics, he considered an ancient motto of his people: Imagination surmounts the impossible.

CHAPTER 17

Nan Bahalt leaned back against the sun-drenched wall of the Hall of Mediation. Recollection cluttered her inner vision with images of Counsellor Ullas contorting himself into attitudes that had to be uncomfortable, but which he clearly thought displayed him at his best. She shivered, despite the heated stone pressed against her back. The man had no "best." Pale to the point of parody, tasteless clothes . . . and the eyes: the manic inquisitiveness of a bird's stare.

She pushed herself away from the wall and set out for the barracks. Once she was moving, especially since she was moving away from Ullas, her spirits lifted. She refused to think about the fact that she'd be dealing with him frequently as his physician. She permitted herself a small smile; it would be a simple matter to refer most of his complaints to specialists. Doctor Renula would be pleased to have sycophants lavishing care on the counsellor.

Relief quickly gave way to more serious considerations.

Why did Ullas persist in the pathetic charade that Etasalou wasn't on the planet? She made a face. How did they expect to keep such a presence a secret? Perhaps the average Hiran didn't know they had the former commander in their midst, but anyone with an ear to gossip at Court certainly suspected. It was always that way; the higher the authority, the more public the private life. And yet those were the people who believed their secrets and crimes could never be discovered. What

Counsellor Ullas and Commander Etasalou were choosing to ignore was that once Emperor Halib tired of this foolishness, he would strike.

But the clash of rulers wasn't her problem. Avoiding Etasalou was. To that end, the morning's visit was a complete success. It was uncomfortable to contemplate being one of Ullas's counters in his game with Etasalou. Still, nothing could be as nerve-wracking as living minute to minute in the Lumin women's dormitory, knowing that somewhere beyond the walls and the inept, not to mention venal, security personnel, *he* waited.

The other thing Ullas's manner told her was that Etasalou knew she was on the planet. Ullas would turn her over without a second thought, but only for a reason. In the meantime, living in the heart of Court offered excellent protection. And there was a tingling gratification in realizing that there would be times when Etasalou was in Court with no idea that his hated niece was practically within reach.

The central core of her plan was far more daring than avoiding capture by her uncle, however. There were times when Nan was afraid to think of her ultimate goal, afraid she might somehow expose her thoughts.

Etasalou's project must be destroyed. Even if the emperor found a way to eliminate Etasalou, someone would resume the work. The idea that the human mind could be mapped, and its ability to create thought measured, analyzed, and then controlled, would tempt the most dedicated scientists. No matter how lofty their goals, such power must inevitably be perverted.

The opportunity afforded was deliciously tempting. Anyone in medicine knew how important the mind was to healing, working miracles no doctor could completely explain. Every student learned that humans used only a small percentage of the physical organ called the brain. For centuries scientists had mapped what it did, but no one had ever penetrated the meaning of consciousness. How could they? There were literally unimaginable numbers of potential synaptic contacts possible.

Etasalou's work had only one goal: to command a sufficient number of those contacts to create a species that behaved according to dictated rules. But what if one completely harnessed the power of those trillions of contacts? What could the mind do if it thoroughly understood itself?

Inexplicably, Nan found herself thinking of Lannat, the child Delight, and the unknown woman the child purported to talk to.

Hairs rose on her forearms and the back of her neck. Her mouth went dry. The need to look over her shoulder was irresistible.

It was broad daylight. She was walking a well-lit, heavily traveled outdoor passageway through the pile called Court. There was no possible danger. Her face warmed with embarrassment.

She determined to think of what she must do. The plan to escape the dormitory had succeeded unexpectedly well. All she had hoped for was to be sent someplace where she could escape Etasalou and make contact with the resistance. Now anything might happen. Including betrayal. She made herself face facts. Betrayal was a given. So long as she served Ullas's purposes in Court, she was reasonably safe there. When she had more value as trade goods, Etasalou would get her.

Unless she destroyed him first.

First the man. Then the work. The project must be ended, its records eliminated. It sickened her to think of so much research wasted. What obligation did a scientist—a doctor—have?

There was no one to help her decide. Just as there was no one to help her do what she must. There were the nonks, of course, but they were a minuscule minority, more concerned with avoiding Advisors than actual resistance.

Once again Nan felt herself grow cold, as if a dead hand squeezed her heart. Humans might be less than perfect, but they deserved to be more than equipment. Unconsciously she looked off in the direction of the mountains that hid her uncle's laboratory. It must be crushed, burned to nothingness, the ashes ground to dust. That was what had happened to the facility on Hector.

Hector. The first experiments.

She wept, huge tears welling from eyes that refused to acknowledge them, continuing to stare into the distance. Once the project was gone, eliminated, then perhaps her own mind would let her remember what had happened to her when she was one of the physicians working for her uncle on Hector. She must find a way. It was her right. Her duty.

Memory refused to grant her access to what had happened during those other years. Still, there was a repeated dream, one she had told no one, not even Lannat. It took her to a laboratory. She felt she belonged there, but it was always strangely unfamiliar. Everyone wore surgical masks and hooded sanitary gear, even the patients. An operation was in progress. She circled the large team surrounding the patient. If she got too close, she was brushed aside effortlessly. No one looked at her or spoke, and when she looked at herself, she wasn't a person but a presence, finer than mist. She always accepted her nonexistence with sad resignation.

She smelled the disinfectant soap, the antibiotic salve, the cooked air, and the burned tissue of laser surgery. The patient was cloaked in a sheet, only the top of his head exposed. The top of his brain, actually; the cranium, removed, rested in the bright clamps of a shining steel apparatus. It made Nan think of a lamp, a pretentious attempt to marry art and utility. Just having such thoughts while a human was being defiled shamed her. In the dream, the unformed, vaporous, thing that was her fled into an adjoining room. What awaited her in that place never changed, either—a woman in a chair, a skein of wires streaming from her skull to a holovid of a brain. The organ itself was a mass of lights the size of dust motes. Pictures flashed on a screen in front of the woman's wide, staring eyes. She wore earphones. At each change of picture, a carnival of different-color lights cascaded across and through and around the electronically displayed brain.

Without looking at the pictures, without hearing what was coming through the earphones, Nan Bahalt watched the careering flood of color-changing lights and read what they said.

She knew that woman's thoughts.

The dream ended when the woman turned her head, agonizingly slow, grimacing terrible pain, and looked toward the door where Doctor Bahalt, in her guise of fog, watched.

Nan Bahalt looked deep into the lost eyes of Nan Bahalt.

Slammed out of her reverie, she staggered awkwardly, arms outflung for balance. A stone wall brought her up short, painfully. Strong hands clutched her shoulders, prevented. Her wits were returning, her eyes regaining focus, when the man holding her said, "Are you all right? I tried to step aside. Are you hurt?"

Flustered, she shook her head, waiting for words to form. "I'm fine. I was daydreaming. Not looking. It's my fault."

Slowly the man's concern melted away, revealing recognition. Fear and anger. "You're the one from Atic, aren't you? The exile." It was accusation.

Nan moved to the side, scraping along the wall. The man pulled his hands back as if she burned. Her harsh "Excuse me" as she twisted past him galvanized him further, and he took a long step backward, almost falling off the curb into the path of a surface speeder. Ignoring the irate honking of the radar-activated warning klaxon, he shouted after Nan. "I only spoke because I didn't know who you are. I did nothing wrong."

Turning, facing him, Nan glared, caught between pity and contempt. Unpriestesslike, she gave in to the latter. She spat on the sidewalk and then continued on toward the dormitory. Dry-eyed. Proudly dry-eyed.

Sunset in the Marnoffar Mountains could be a thing of beauty. The ocean, far to the south, sent moisture boiling upward to form clouds, and the prevailing winds blew them toward land. In soaring thunderheads and sinuous trails, they caught the sun, and their soft whiteness took on warm, promising hues. On a planet that knew only moonless nights, that last view of light was more highly treasured than anywhere else in Lannat's experience.

He hoped his raiding party wasn't distracted by it.

Thirty miles from base camp, deep inside territory far beyond their normal experience, he hoped the team was fixed on its task. People's minds did wander sometimes. To many that was inconceivable, but Lannat had thought it through. He attributed it to stress, an intense, repressed wish to be somewhere else. An unpleasant grin cracked his features. He could write books about the feeling; it was cartwheeling across his mind right now.

Using elbows and toes, scrabbling uphill like a lizard, Lannat reached the hillock's crest and peered down on the quiet highspy base. For the past three days he and the rest of the raid party had used this and other observation posts to plot the small facility's security plan. Actually it was very aggressively maintained. Their problem was complacency. The Advisors methodically checked their sensors, disarmed and rearmed their directional mines, inspected their perimeter wire. They did so without considering that they might be watched while they did it.

Lannat and his raiders were sure they knew the defensive arrangements as well as the enemy. Soon they would test that confidence.

Working his way back off the crest until well clear of the skyline, Lannat then straightened and trotted to the thick brush where the team camped. Most were eating their evening meal, the unappetizing canned protein mixture that sustained them for the entire time they were in the field. Retalla was on watch, and he spotted Lannat far from the site. The lanky Hiran lifted his ration can in wry salute, then continued to spoon away at it until Lannat was close enough to address. He said, "I'm so hungry I'm beginning to look forward to this sludge."

Making a face, Lannat said, "I don't believe I could say that without heaving. We may be able to cook tomorrow night."

"I sure hope so. It's been so long since I swallowed a hot meal my stomach thinks the world's frozen over. You see anything unusual at the highspy base?"

"Not a thing."

Retalla shook his head. "Good lesson there. It's easy to get careless."

"They've had little reason to be alert. That'll change fast. Hire's going to be a different place tomorrow."

"And for the next thousand years. I want my grandchildren's grandchildren to know one of their blood kin was there the day it started. I don't care if the next dynasty is run by a counsellor or a tyrant or a governor, or whatever he calls himself. Just so long as we get freedom."

A chill rippled through Lannat, warning him to retreat. The feeling was so powerful, yet so confusing, it left him with no ready response to Retalla. He pretended to be distracted, buying time to think.

And Astara's voice was in his head.

"Speak to him of ruling himself. Speak to him of communities that are governed by common consent."

He knew better than to give any sign of hearing her. He remained outwardly at ease, but his mind was a volcano. One thing, one thing only, rang clear: Astara spoke of ruling but said nothing of the emperor. It was impossible. Horrifying. He couldn't imagine what she was doing.

Laughter, ancient as mountains, gentle as clouds, interrupted him. Astara's voice said, *"Would I endanger one I love? You know me better, young Lannat. No, I come only to wish you well. And to ask you to put a question for me. Is that so much?"* The soft laughter told him she was gone. He wanted to shout after her, bring her back. There were so many questions. He knew she wouldn't respond, though. She came when she wanted, left the same way. Yet when she was with him, even if only in his mind, he felt comforted. How could that be? She created more questions than she answered. He grimaced, an expression of resignation. And a yearning. It took all his strength to reject both and return to reality. At least she'd explained that her question about government wasn't suggesting treason.

Retalla looked at him, head cocked to the side. "You all right?"

"Just thinking. Wondering if the people here might want to elect a leader, after they get rid of the counsellor." Lannat blurted the distasteful words, getting the incident over with as quickly as possible.

Features utterly still, Retalla stared. There was a weird feeling to the moment. Lannat caught himself thinking of an animal caught in a corner. When the silence broke, however, it came apart on scorn. "Elect? Us? You think we're so foolish we can be led by just any idiot's promises?" Retalla stopped abruptly. He was still vastly amused when he went on. "That'd bring the emperor's Elemental Guard down on us, sure as light. We're a handful of people trying to get rid of the counsellor, and you're asking if we'd do the one thing guaranteed to make us take on the emperor himself. You must think we're pretty good."

Lannat's own laughter marked his relief. He'd done what was asked. "That's the last under light I'd do. As for taking on anyone, good's not our problem. Numbers is what we need."

"That's an interesting answer."

Lannat was on his way past to the main camp. The tone of Retalla's next words stopped him. "I don't think you ever called us 'we' before. Not that way. Not like you're one of us."

Lannat jerked a thumb in the direction of the Advisor highspy facility and told Retalla, "What's coming is the toughest kind of 'we' situation. I'll never be a Hiran. I'm not part of your fight or your culture. I hate being forced into this situation. That hatred doesn't extend to you personally."

"You've worked us like slaves. You worked beside us, though. Maybe we can do something for you, before you leave here."

"I wouldn't be surprised." Lannat sent him a sly wink, then continued on to the camp.

Jarka sat on the ground, the other six members of the team in a semicircle in front of him. Lannat advanced quietly, listening to Jarka finish reviewing the tasks of the two triads. "We—First Triad—are responsible for packing out the highspy control unit. Third, you carry the disassembled highspy. Second Triad, you're at the edge of the defensive perimeter, covering the withdrawal. As soon as First and Third are clear, blow your whistle, then fall back into the forest. Only Second uses a whistle—unless there's an emergency. Any triad that gets into a bad situation, signal with three blasts. If that happens, Second moves forward to reinforce. Remember, Second, when you come out, pick up our cleared-trail markers and reset the Advisor defensive obstacles. Don't forget to rig our own tripwires and spikes at the same time."

Everyone nodded. The hardwood spikes Jarka mentioned were to be set in the forest on the trail, hammered into the ground a few feet beyond tripwires. An Advisor who stumbled over a wire stood a good chance of impaling himself. If he was lucky enough to avoid tripping, he still had to get past the spikes without jabbing one through his foot. The legacy of the Blood Father glorified the use of deception and trickery to foil pursuit; it was a facet of combat Lannat found disturbing. He knew he was naive. He still didn't like mindless objects set to maim and kill.

It startled him to realize he was having trouble distinguishing individual faces. Here, deep in the brush at the bottom of a draw, night fell swiftly.

Jarka turned, rising. "Thought I heard you come up. We're ready, except for painting hands and faces. Outposts come in in about an hour."

"Good. Assemble here when they do."

Lannat walked to his own gear and sat down to check it. The example wasn't lost on his companions. In a few minutes the natural silence of the dark hollow was punctuated by the sound of stone sharpening steel, the metallic clicks and scrapes of equipment being opened and closed. An occasional muffled comment hung heavily in the air, the tension of it far clearer than the words.

When the outposts pulled back, Lannat joined the gathered raiders. The first items inspected were the seekums. Command Communications Modules had been C-COMs in official jargon long before the troopers had christened them seekums. Lannat held his up. "Seekums will not be used for voice communication except in emergency. We'll go over what they do one last time. If you have to send a message, it'll be enciphered and chopped up into electronic segments. The segs are fired out on selected frequencies in random sequence. Every seekum has a receiving module that's keyed to the proper frequencies. Its computer deciphers and recombines the segs. The reason we're maintaining radio silence, unless we absolutely have to break it, is because I don't want any higher headquarters intercepting anything, even gibberish. I want us long gone before the word goes out. It's as much psychological as tactical, so think hard before you transmit. Once radio silence is broken, everyone attaches their seekum to their dimenomap. There'll be lots of talking and we'll need to coordinate."

The hush of the group broke in a nervous flurry of motion. Triad leaders unfolded the new dimenomaps procured by Betak. Lannat hid a smile; they handled the plasticized material as if it were paper. None of them had ever seen one until a few days before this operation. Flat on the ground, the dimenomaps showed the surrounding area in ten-foot contour lines. A small plastic nodule in the lower right corner held the battery that energized the electrosensitive surface. Stylus marks on a triad leader's dimenomap could be transmitted to Lannat; only he could transmit that information to another triad. Another raised surface next to the battery nodule held the optical sensor that read the thumbprint of the approved map owner. If captured, the map couldn't be used by an opponent to pry information from an unwitting link in the chain. Lannat could override that capability, should the designated owner become a casualty and the map remain in friendly hands. Each triad's map presently glowed with the proper blue arrows for friendly route of approach and the red of enemy defenses. Lannat put down his own map. Forefinger like a prophet's wand, he traced the blue line leading to where it pierced the red enclosure. He said, "We've rehearsed this attack a dozen times. We've reviewed our assignments a hundred times. We're going to do it once more. Then it's payday. There'll be no speeches but for this. Take care of yourselves. Take care of each other. Make your companions proud of you."

In a hoarse whisper, Jarka said, "Pray for the Seeker's help."

Lannat responded to the phrase automatically. "May we all come safely to a free truth."

The troops glanced at him curiously, almost suspiciously. He fended off any comments with brusque review questions. In his head, though, he heard a throaty chuckle, and then the voice he so welcomed and so feared. Astara. *"You forgot to mention luck, young Captain Lannat. It's well. They're too frightened to think about anything as capricious as luck. It's not forgotten, however."* The low laughter again, then, comforting: *"Let an old, blind woman pray for you. A greedy woman, who has need of her champion. Let me pray for your luck."*

Lannat said nothing, tried to think of nothing. To acknowledge her now was to admit a need. He couldn't do that.

CHAPTER 18

Lannat inched under the drooping branches of the shrub at the edge of the cleared ground. Directly ahead, the tents of the highspy encampment glowed vividly in the starlit darkness. Despite the amusement-park gaiety of the hemispherical shelters, he fought a stomach that churned mightily. He thought about the untested rebels spread out in the forest behind him and wondered how they were bearing up.

There was no time for that. Not anymore.

Slowly, silently, he moved forward. He flipped the switch on his darkglasses, going to thermal. A sound detector ten feet ahead appeared as a faint smudge. The Advisors had made three mistakes. They placed the detectors in daylight, when they could be watched. They put them where the sun warmed them, making them vulnerable to IR detection in the following darkness. Last, they used the same spot, to the point that trails in the grass indicated where they were. Carefully Lannat disarmed the sonic device simply by cutting its wires. He was practically certain no one manned the sensor control board in the encampment, but there was no sense taking chances.

Rolling slightly, he waved Jarka forward. In the darkglasses, the Hiran materialized like a green wraith. Another gesture sent Jarka forward. The man and woman who made up Jarka's triad crawled past, following their leader. Lannat moved out in their wake after assuring himself the other two triads followed.

Jarka disarmed the next sensor, an illumination device. Lannat turned off the darkglasses while the other man worked. If Jarka made a mistake and the strobe fired, it would fry the fastest lenses made, and those of the Free were far from that. For that matter, the light would permanently blind anyone looking directly at it from this range. Gritting his teeth, Lannat watched Jarka work. Unbolting the plate covering the switch mechanism was damnably tricky.

Lannat kept a hand on Jarka's back; the relaxation of the muscles there told him the job was complete. He signaled the other two people in the team to follow Jarka. Once they were advancing, he waved up the other triads.

The final obstacle was defensive catchwire. The Advisors had laid it out conventionally, two rolls strung parallel to each other on the ground, a third roll piled on top of them. Face down, heart hammering, Lannat twisted to look up at the straplike loops and the pinpoints of light on the barbs.

He feared catchwire more than any sensor, more than the strobes. It would hold a man fast, punishing him mercilessly for any movement. Fight it, and it could kill. Surrender to it, and you were at the mercy of your enemies. Each thin strap—no one knew why the stuff was called wire—had an insulated core, rather like a nerve. A tiny electrical current flowed through that core. If interrupted, it set off alarms. In all likelihood, the catchwire sensory disconnect was connected to all the strobes, as well. Break the wire, and the pitch-black Hiran night would be a blinding explosion of light for anyone outside the perimeter.

There were techniques for ripping wire out or blowing it up, but the Free had neither the machinery nor explosives. Their method was primitive. Triad Three carried rolled-up mats made of woven reeds. Early Hirans had found that particular variety made good floor covering, soft and resilient and tough enough to take years of constant foot traffic. Now such carpeting had pride of place in many luxurious homes.

At Lannat's signal, Triad Three rose, rushed to the wire, and flung their mats across it. Next they threw themselves prostrate on the padding. Their weight collapsed the rolls. Triad One ran across them, storming into the camp.

Stealth was no longer an issue. Lannat wrestled with the idea in his planning. He couldn't be certain the wire wouldn't break under the weight of the breaching technique. Teaching his neophyte raiders to be silent in their attack, only to have it announced by alarms, was almost as dangerous as discovery. In deference to their inexperience—and capitalizing on the similar inexperience of the Advisors in the camp—he opted for violence. If there was to be shock and surprise, he decided, let it fall on the enemy. Furthermore, screaming and yelling was good release for his own people.

War cries tore apart the stillness. The serenity of the Advisor camp turned into a torment of shrieks and yells.

Squashed flat, its clever electrical nerves uncut, the catch-wire failed to set off alarms.

Another Advisor mistake was instantly obvious. The two tents nearest the wire were far too close. One was the communications tent. A single person manned the radio. Triad One swarmed inside. The tent billowed and swayed. Someone screamed agonized despair.

Simultaneous with Triad One's attack, Triad Three bounced off the mats and charged. They caught the personnel erupting from the other close tent. The Advisors ran, but with the confused awkwardness of people who don't really believe what's happening. Jarka, being faster than anyone else, ran to cut down the first two—a man and a woman—just outside the entryway. For a sickening moment, Lannat was sure the other pair of Advisors would get the preoccupied Jarka. He raced to help. Triad Three was there ahead of him, however. They took the Advisors from the side. There was a moment of confused swordplay, some shouting, and then the Free were pounding away for the next tents.

There were a total of twelve Advisors at the highspy site. Charging with the assault, Lannat hoped against hope his raiders would hit the last seven before they got themselves organized. His mind told him they were mere seconds into the operation, but time stretched interminably until they reached the next tents.

The remaining Advisors believed now and understood. Half naked, most of them barefoot, they were outside when the raiders reached them.

The scene was familiar to Lannat. All surprised troops need time to come to terms with their situation. Inexperienced troops, surprised at night, are essentially doomed. There is the occasional born warrior who reacts with natural fury. None of those appeared among the huddled, waiting group of Advisors. Their manner was so forlorn it embarrassed Lannat. His raiders, at least as afraid as the Advisors, had every advantage an attacker could ask for. They had drawn blood. They knew what was happening. They were fighting forces that had oppressed them as long as they could remember.

And the frenzy was in them.

The Advisor who rushed at Lannat from the shadows was the missing primitive. He came silently, determined. Lannat's last-moment shield parry saved his life. Even so, caught off balance, he staggered, flailing to stay upright. His attacker pursued his advantage, hacking away with a two-handed swing that forced Lannat's shield down and kept him too busy defending to counterattack. Still, Lannat was a professional, a man who skirmished with other professionals. His opening came when he ducked under one of the hearty sword swipes. Meeting no resistance whatever, the Advisor was unable to overcome his own momentum; the backhand stroke developed too slowly. Crouched, Lannat caught the Advisor's late returning stroke with his own blade. He drove the edge of his shield into his opponent's crotch. The Advisor grunted, almost collapsed. He took a step backward, obviously fighting through the pain. Lannat lowered his head, leaped up and forward. The crown of his helmet hit the other man's face. Sound and vibration told Lannat of broken teeth and split cartilage. Still, the

Advisor managed another sword stroke at Lannat. It was a much weakened effort. Lannat took it on his blade, letting the other weapon slide along the steel to catch itself in the recurved handguard. Then he sidestepped, twisted his sword. The leverage was irresistible. The Advisor's blade flicked out of his grasp as if greasy. He was still staring after it when Lannat slashed his own weapon back across the man's middle. The Advisor rose on his toes, drawing back from the sight of his guts spilling free. He sagged, sat down hard. He was trying to pick up the ropy mess of his intestines when he fell over on his side, trembling the last bits of his life away.

Lannat turned his back on him, blew his whistle to stop the attack. Somehow the alarm system had been set off, and its blaring horns almost swallowed the shrill pitch of his signal. He tried again. Again.

His people were beyond hearing. He wanted to believe it was the fault of the blaring alarms. It wasn't. He knew what he was seeing.

Close combat wounds more people than the ones who bleed. Perhaps those are the worst injuries of all. Lannat's raiders didn't know that. Yet. And the carnage continued.

Two Advisors saved their lives by falling to the ground. One lay flat, arms crossed over his head, face buried in the dirt. The second curled up in a fetal position, denying everything.

The last Advisor to die was a woman. She raised her hands in surrender. Lannat saw the terror in her rictuslike grimace. The raider rushing at her saw only a raised sword. The raider herself was literally out of her mind with excitement; she had no ability to comprehend that the poor fool Advisor was too frightened to be aware she still held a weapon. It took Lannat a moment to realize the Free woman was Trey. Simultaneously, he understood that what he saw and recognized as the Advisor's fear-distorted features, the aroused Trey saw as a threatening mask, as fierce as her own blood lust. Yelling incoherently, she drove her sword into her victim's center, just below the sternum.

Hard-schooled professionalism stifled Lannat's dismay, and he marked that Trey had struck exactly as taught. She stepped into the thrust, using weight as well as muscle for power. The strike originated in the pivoting shoulders and waist, driving a straight arm. Wrist and elbow locked at impact. Follow-through was flawless, as was the smash to the upper body with the shield that aided blade withdrawal.

The Advisor sprawled backward, her grimace melting, becoming almost a look of disappointment. Her back arched as she strained against a severed artery pumping blood away so fast it was beyond hope. Trey was already past her, looking around, wild-eyed, for more resistance. She never saw the Advisor's heels pounding dents in the ground.

Someone found the control panel, switched off the alarms. In the relative quiet, victims groaned and coughed and wept. In every direction, Lannat heard the panting, heaving sounds of exhaustion. He blew the whistle again. With no one left to fight, his people stood where the sound caught them. Unnaturally glittering eyes blinked rapidly, constantly. Someone spoke. "We did it." Unbelieving. Dumbfounded. Elated. Tension blew away in a roar as everyone cheered. They all looked, counted, then counted again, and discovered that not only were they alive, but so were their friends. Even the three wounded, realizing they weren't seriously hurt, yelled and celebrated.

Lannat went to the two Advisors on the ground. The rolled-up one cried in eerie silence, tears leaking through closed eyelids. The prone figure turned his head just enough to watch Lannat from the corner of a white-rimmed eye. Lannat addressed him while picking up their discarded swords. "You won't be harmed. Tend to your friend. He needs help." He threw the weapons toward the growing salvage pile.

Turning to his raiders, Lannat said, "No more noise. Get what we came for. Triad Two: Get the dead inside tents. Quickly. An elcar may come scouting this place. If they sent out a message . . ." The implications needed no explanations.

Sobered now, trying to hold down voices still too excited to return to normal volume, the raiders moved to assigned tasks.

Highspies came in several varieties. The expeditionary model, used by the personnel in this facility, was an inflatable. Ready to fly, it looked like one of the antique flying machines in the history books, or a child's mechanical bird. The wings didn't flap, but it had the same sleek appearance, with its graceful reach and flared tail. The wings also served as the major power source, with their array of solar cells. Such a highspy could operate indefinitely in clear weather, charging its batteries while the sun was out, then using them to stay aloft during darkness. The large, slow propellor was practically soundless; for maximum stealth the highspy could glide for long periods. Reconnaissance gear consisted of thermal and light amplification video cameras as well as standard video with telescopic range. Field models normally had only limited electromagnetic intercept capability, but Lannat was delighted to discover that this was a newer model, with exactly what the Free needed—both ground and aerial search radar, coupled with radio intercept.

If the Advisors in the camp had used their own equipment to scan the possible avenues of approach to their perimeter, the raid might well have been unmasked and ambushed before it was properly started. Lannat determined to remember the lesson. Highspies were not merely long-range reconnaissance.

The defeated unit fielded two highspies. With all equipment aboard, each vehicle alone weighed a bit more than a hundred pounds. Jarka and Retalla each hoisted one, lashed to backpacks. The control and monitor equipment broke down into lighter loads. With three troopers working at reduced capability due to injury, the team was barely able to pack it all. Lannat drafted the prisoners, giving them loads they could manage with their hands tied in front of them. Last man out, Lannat was picking his way across the mats on the catchwire when everyone heard the unmistakable sound of an elcar approaching.

Lannat reacted instantly, leaping back into the camp.

Grabbing the end of the mats, he threw them outside the wire. The loops sprang back to near-original shape. "Take the mats," he shouted. "Get under cover. I'll handle the elcar if it lands here. Go! Go!"

Jarka moved first. The rest jerked as if waking, then followed at a dead run, loads bobbing ludicrously. Lannat dodged into a tent, mumbling curses as the bodies underfoot rolled and twisted, threatening to trip him up. With the elcar settling onto the tiny landing pad on the opposite side of the perimeter, he cut a slit in the tent material and slipped out, scuttling for darkness like an exposed kreech.

There were two men aboard. They stepped out, swords drawn. One spoke into a handset, his head jerking with the vehemence of his message. The second man shouted names. Whatever response came over the radio, the man with the handset didn't like it. He threw it back into the elcar and took a few angry, tentative steps. He stood there, craning and scanning, while his partner edged toward the nearest tent.

Lannat was elated to see that the handset man wore no dark-glasses—until he remembered the incredible night vision of all Hirans. His heart sank. The dim lights from the tents would be as good as daylight to the pair.

The man advancing on the shelters continued demanding that someone speak up. The shout echoed weakly from the surrounding night, and he immediately turned and ordered his companion to join him. The two of them moved together, tense and alert.

Lannat considered rushing them. Impatience teamed with tension to whisper seductively that, after all, they weren't well trained. Reason triumphed; no matter how poorly schooled, they were two armed men. Instead, Lannat moved on the elcar. There were no communications in the camp, so the vehicle was key. He ran toward it, relying on the bodies in the tent to pre-occupy the Advisors.

One of the men backed out, vomiting. When he turned, he looked straight at the sprinting Lannat. For a startled moment, he simply stared, forgetting his upset stomach. In that time, he realized Lannat's intent. Yelling, he raced to intercept him. The other Advisor was right behind him.

There was no time for Lannat to get into the vehicle. The Advisors slowed their charge when he turned and presented his own weapon. They, too, knew he was trapped against the elcar. Similarly, they recognized that this was no ordinary nonk.

When Lannat feinted, they both leaped back. He tried a bluff. "My friends are on their way back here. Lay down your weapons and you'll be treated as honorable prisoners."

"Like them?" The speaker hitched a shoulder at the tent. His sneer lacked conviction.

"Two Advisors surrendered. They've been taken out of the perimeter. We don't harm prisoners."

The second man lunged, a well-delivered straight thrust. Lannat parried. The other Advisor tried an overhand hack. Lannat rammed his shield into that man's face and continued to drive forward, bowling the man over. Lannat managed to slash at the falling man's knees as he went past him, then immediately spun to confront the original attacker. The man on the ground called to his companion for help.

The uninjured Advisor learned from his companion's misfortune. Instantly very cautious, he concentrated on fending off an advancing Lannat with frantic swordplay. For several long seconds he survived through sheer energy, always an inch, a twitch, from disaster. He made no effort to attack. Eyes intense as glass followed Lannat's blade with terrified resolve.

For Lannat, it was maddening. He felt time slipping away, time he and his raiders needed. The wasted seconds here could mean capture later, assuming the Advisors pursued.

In the end, it was the Advisor's fixed attention on Lannat that undid him.

The first the Advisor knew of Jarka's approach was a sword's point in his back and a voice saying "Drop your weapon."

In the petrified moment of silence that followed, Lannat was eerily certain he knew exactly what the Advisor intended. He tensed, unwilling to shout warning, hoping against hope his intuition was wrong.

Leaping forward, the Advisor tried to get away from Jarka and slash at Lannat in the same move. Blocking the blade with his shield, Lannat simply leaned forward with his own sword. The Advisor essentially impaled himself. His eyes, huge with fright, closed. It was only a blink. Still, when they opened again, fear was gone. He looked deep into Lannat's gaze, almost as if he wanted to share his newfound knowledge. His mouth moved. Before words formed, however, Jarka's thrust from behind drove him ahead again. He fell in silence, taking his discoveries with him.

Yanking his blade free, Jarka stumbled backward and bumped into the other Advisor, who was struggling to rise. On contact, the downed man twisted, looked up at Jarka. Straining to keep his balance, Jarka swayed awkwardly. The Advisor recoiled. He looked up with a haunted, pleading expression that soared to terror when the sword paused at Jarka's farthest reach. Lannat barely had time to yell protest. Jarka grunted. The sword whistled down. It caught the Advisor as he turned away, screaming, and slashed into the back of his neck. The nearly severed head bowed grotesque submission as the man fell off sideways.

The incident took perhaps three seconds.

Lannat turned away from Jarka. He was trembling, too furious to trust his voice. No matter how unnecessary the killing, he was even more ashamed of himself for knowing exactly why Jarka had done it. Explosively released tension. The warrior's perverse fear of not being fierce enough. The expression of other not-to-be-revealed fears. Simple anger. Yet it had been *unnecessary*. Jarka's quick change to iron-hard composure exposed his awareness of the enormity of his mistake. Jerking, stiff-jointed, he cleaned his blade in terrible parody of nonchalance.

Lannat collected his wits. The need to curse Jarka burned in him; he wanted to search out Trey, as well. He imagined himself roaring at them. Amateurs. All nerves and prayers that no one get injured. Until the blood came up.

Lannat swallowed it all and instead told Jarka, "We'll use the elcar. Get one of the wounded to drive. Load as much gear in it as possible. Disable the vehicle's locator device so it can't be tracked. Tell the driver to put it down at the campsite we used before we arrived here at this one. You remember, there's a sandy beach at the bend of the river. It's a good landing place. Plenty of brush close by to hide under until we get there."

Jarka frowned, started to object. Lannat waved it off. "The time and energy we save by hauling the captured stuff in the car will more than make up for what we lose here loading it. Shout our people in; no radios."

Lannat was walking away when Jarka called after him. "What are you going to be doing?"

"Something we didn't have time to do before. There may be papers in the tents that we can use. Information." He faced Jarka again. Jarka clearly disapproved of prowling through the tents holding the dead Advisors. Harshly Lannat added, "I'll be checking the bodies, too. Unless you'd rather take that chore and leave the elcar detail to me. Your pick."

Jarka's shouting echoed back from the nearby forest while Lannat turned to his task.

The overloaded elcar howled aloft. Lannat signaled the column to move out. He took the rear guard himself. They weren't long under way when a figure eased back toward him. At first, he assumed it was someone who'd taken a nick and refused to acknowledge it. The thought infuriated him. The unit couldn't afford someone slowing them down, especially some proud idiot. Appropriate curses lined up in his mind.

Trey's question startled him when she reached him. "Is it all right if we talk and march?"

Lannat considered, then: "Normally, no, and you know it. What's bothering you?"

"You know. You saw. What I did."

"I thought that might be it. Forget it. It's not unique to you, understand?"

"It happened to you? You kill—" Her voice caught. When she spoke again, there was defiance layered over the hurt. "You did something like that?"

"We're not talking about me. I told you to get over it."

"Just like that. Thanks." She lengthened her stride.

Lannat caught her shoulder. She yanked away but slowed. He said, "There's no easy out, Trey. Set your mind to keeping it from happening again."

They walked along in silence for a long time. Trey spoke first. "You've done this stuff before. Everybody knows about the Elemental Guard. I hate them, hate the damned emperor. I started out hating you, too, but you're not like the Guards I saw. We haven't treated you very well, and you've helped us anyhow. But you didn't tell us about going crazy. I thought I'd come out of my first fight excited and proud. Or hurt, or dead. Something. What I am is ashamed. So ashamed."

Lannat didn't respond to that for a while. When he did, he was gentle. "People get worked up. Emotions—instincts—take over. Look, we're doing the right thing. Maybe we're not perfect, but we're right. The Advisors fight for a rotten cause—"

Trey's harsh laughter interrupted. "You think they don't say the same thing about us? What you say is right; I know that. But what happened tonight, back there—what I believe in made me do that. How do I keep loving what I believe in when it turns me into a thing I hate? How do I stay committed and stay sane? When it was all over, when I looked down at that poor woman I felt a piece of my soul tear loose. What about my friends? Is all this worth their lives? Their souls? The Seeker shouldn't let things like what I did happen. Just shouldn't."

Again, silence claimed them. Lannat mulled words, wanting to ease her pain. In the midst of that, a hooting call from some night creature distracted him. With that, the forest seemed to press in on him, pressure him with its secretive, scuffling sounds, its myriad scents.

Suddenly he was smelling Delphi, not Hire. The thick perfume of the temple's flowered grounds filled his senses. He even remembered the name of the small, red ones called dabs, their scent the sweetest of all. Astara spoke to him, and there was a quality in her words he never heard before. *"Her questions are those of a good heart in a world that will not always permit goodness. How many times have you yourself acted, then wondered? Give to her from your strength. Remind her that life is hope, and there is no hope for anything that will not live. She has chosen to be one who pays the price for keeping good alive in the face of evil. It must be done. We know, you and I."*

Lannat stumbled through phrases he hoped were helpful, part of his mind trying to comfort Trey, another part intent on the strange tone of Astara's voice. At the end, he told Trey, "You say you're Seeker cult. Then you know the words: 'Nothing will be asked that cannot be done. No one fails who strives to serve the Seeker, for truth and love are abundant for all. One gives, that all may receive.' "

In the darkness, Trey's upturned face was a dim paleness. Shock edged her words. "That's a quote. From blessing meeting. You're Seeker, one of us."

Lannat bent toward her. "I'm a soldier, loyal to my emperor and his laws. Lumin is the official religion, no matter what you off-world rebels say or do. I teach you to kill and survive. That's all. Now, leave me alone. Face up to your own problems. They're not my responsibility."

Without a word, Trey scurried after the column. Flipping on his darkglasses, Lannat remained in place and watched her, her slight form bent as if breasting a storm.

When he started walking again, he heard something. Thinking it was the cloth scuff of his trouser, he slowed, stopped. The noise continued.

Astara.

No words. A sound, achingly sorrowful. He walked forward again, driving her from his thoughts. Only when she was gone, and the real night noises of the Hiran forest came again, could he admit to himself that he recognized weeping.

CHAPTER 19

First transmissions from Advisor Command refused to believe one of their perimeters had been attacked. Later transmissions insisted that, if an attack had taken place, it had been defeated; the bodies on the scene were nonks, not Advisors. By then the raiders were a full four hours into their withdrawal. The argument continued for another hour before Command finally accepted the facts.

After that, things changed.

Highspies crisscrossed likely escape routes. An Advisor patrol, accompanied by palelen trackers, was assigned to scout the raiders' last campsite and attempt to follow any trail away from the perimeter.

The existence of palelens on Hire was a shock to Lannat. Palelens were native to Syrac, and their presence on Hire was in direct contradiction to the basic law of the empire that no native species from one planet ever be transported to another. The sole exception was for those animals from Home, the rare cattle, dogs, or horses bred and maintained as status symbols among the wealthiest and most influential families of the empire.

Lannat was listening to the captured radio when the leader

of the Advisor patrol reported he was on the trail of the fleeing raiders. He also reported that one of the palelens had slipped its muzzle and savaged his handler before being killed.

Lannat's grim chuckle at the news earned him a questioning look from the woman carrying the radio. He explained, adding "Palelens are excellent tracking animals, but they're a long way from domesticated. You ever see one?"

The woman shook her head, taking her eyes off the trail long enough to look at him.

He went on. "They're big. One twenty to one fifty pounds, every ounce of it carnivorous. If there's nothing else around, or if their territory is invaded, they'll hunt down and eat their own. They tolerate each other only during the annual two-week breeding season, and I'm told that's pretty risky for the smaller ones. Anyhow, they've got four legs, like most animals, but they also have two proto arms growing from the chest area. It means they can run something down, grab it and bite, and never break stride. They don't have to bite very often to do the job; they've got a whole snoutful of long, stabbing teeth. Short, strong claws tear meat off their prey, and they swallow it in lumps you'd think would choke them. Wrapped around all that mean hunger is about three inches of fat, an inch-thick skin, and a pelt of thick, greasy, stinking hair."

The woman gulped audibly. "Those are what's tracking us? You never said anything about them before."

"They shouldn't be here."

Her wordless exclamation was heartfelt agreement. Lannat continued. "Their weakness is they get discouraged. When they realize they're not closing in on us, they'll get distracted and temperamental. Don't worry about them."

The woman's sniff suggested a disinclination to accept the latter guideline.

Lannat considered telling the team that, as long as Advisor Command continued to babble clear transmissions, their security situation was pretty good. He decided not to. So far the raid was a great success. If they could pull this one off, the morale of the entire unit would soar. There was nothing to be gained by telling them that Advisor mistakes contributed greatly to the accomplishment. Confidence was far more important than utter truth.

Lannat wasn't sure that might not be a working rule in most cases.

Advisor radio traffic revealed when the patrol and their palelens stopped for the night. Within a couple of hours after that, the raiders reached the riverbank where their captured elcar waited.

The first order of business was the prisoners. Lannat was determined to release them now. They were already too well acquainted with his personnel and the direction of the base camp. He explained all that to Jarka. "I'm going to give them the elcar. We don't dare use it anymore. As soon as it lifts off the ground, it'll be sensored and everyone on Hire will know right where we are."

Reluctantly Jarka nodded. "I guess you're right."

"We'll turn them loose before dawn. Disable the lights. Rig it for automatic flight; set a course straight back to an automatic landing inside the perimeter. Lock it in and disconnect the manual override. Break all exterior lights so they can't signal."

"Got it." Jarka moved off.

Lannat stopped him with a touch. "Good job tonight. Everyone."

Jarka nodded, smiling faintly, and continued on his way. Lannat wondered if Jarka sensed that his leader was carefully refraining from any mention of the needless killing after the fighting stopped.

Lannat lay on his back, using his shield as a base for his backpack; it made a pillow full of hard lumps. It didn't matter. There were too many things to think through for him to sleep, anyhow.

A hand on his shoulder startled him. He jerked upright. The voice from the darkness-shrouded figure said, "Time to wake up. Jarka's got the prisoners over by the elcar, ready to go."

Groaning, Lannat scrambled to rise. His mind urged performance. His body objected, flopped around like wet straw. The indistinct figure that woke him grabbed Lannat's elbow, and he jerked away irritably, muttering "All right."

The messenger disappeared, leaving Lannat to get to his feet the best he could. Having done so, he staggered through the forest to the river's sandy beach. The prisoners stood beside the vehicle, unbound; one kept his head down. The other peered intently at Lannat. He said, "I don't want to go back."

Not entirely awake, Lannat stared blankly. "Why not?"

It was an appropriate question, but not at all what the prisoner expected. "I-I don't like what I do," he stammered.

"We can't all be happy in our work. What makes you think we'd ever trust you?"

"I thought of that. I'll earn it. I can help you." He glanced meaningfully at the other prisoner.

Lannat turned his attention to that one. "What about you? You want to stay, too?"

"No, sir." A vigorous head shake accompanied the denial. "I've got a wife. Kids."

"Remember that, the next time you're sent out to arrest some poor bastard. He's probably got a family, too. And when you watch your other Advisors pound the light out of him, remember how we treated you. I think you're a decent man. I think you'll find a way to help us, eventually."

The prisoner shifted his weight from foot to foot, saying nothing.

Lannat went on. "I'm letting your partner stay with us. This machine is set on automatic. It'll deliver you to your perimeter. Try to change course before it goes into automatic landing hover, and it'll blow up under you. I don't care what you tell your intelligence people about us, but tell your friends this: We fight for all Hirans, including them. Good-bye. Good luck."

Making no offer to shake hands, Lannat turned away. Movement at the corner of his eye caught his attention, and he looked to see Retalla moving to join him.

"Is it safe to include a prisoner in our group? We're being chased. You sure we can afford a troublemaker?"

"He'll be no trouble. He says he can help us," Lannat replied.

Retalla sneered. "Help us what? Go slow? Get caught?"

"He's got more to fear than we have. What d'you think will happen to him if he's captured? You know his partner's going to inform on him as soon as he's back at the highspy camp." Lannat shook his head. "He's committed. A brave man, I think."

"Well, we'll see," Retalla conceded grudgingly. Then, in the same tone: "I put in some traps last night. You want to see?"

After a long pause, Lannat finally had to answer. "I don't like traps," he said, quickly raising his voice to override Retalla's angry retort. "It may be illogical, but it's how I feel."

Retalla's long face twisted. "Damned right it's illogical. You're supposed to teach us. I was hoping for some advice."

Lannat was torn. If he didn't help, he was not only shirking his job, he was possibly endangering his unit. He shrugged. "Show me."

There was enough light by then to allow swift movement through the forest. Retalla's first trap was only a half mile from camp. Lannat had to congratulate him on his fieldcraft. And his industry. Working alone and apparently most of the night, Retalla had hoisted a rock weighing at least fifty pounds up a tree and wrapped it in a sling. A metlin line, practically invisible, ran from the prop holding the rock in place to an ordinary figure-four trigger and tripwire across the trail.

Retalla said, "I urinated a few yards back. I figure the animals will pull like eltrucks, once they get such a strong scent. The way the rock's set up, it comes swinging up the trail from behind whoever trips the trigger. The arc brings it to within a foot of the ground just a little forward of the tripwire. With luck, we'll take out the animal and the handler, together."

Looking up at the boulder, camouflaged by leafy branches, Lannat shuddered. Retalla had configured his trap well; men on patrol were trained to look behind, but that principle was the first one forgotten. Especially by men in hot pursuit. "You set up more than one of these?"

"Only one like this. The other two are different. One's a hole with a sharp stake in the bottom, the other's a waist-high trip-wire that releases a sapling with a knife attached. I think they'll find that one. I hope so, actually. I don't believe the knife will do much damage, but it'll sure have the point man looking for waist-level wires. This one just above the ground should be a surprise."

"Indeed." Lannat turned to go back to camp, then faced Retalla again. "Did you sleep at all?"

"Not really." To Lannat's amazement, the gawky man sounded embarrassed. When he went on, he mumbled. "I don't need much sleep. I'll catch up on it later. I just figured it'd be a good idea to slow down those people and their animals. It'll make things a bit easier for our people. Won't it?"

"Much easier. You did some fine work. Even if I don't like mantraps."

"I'll take care of it from now on. That way you don't have to get mixed up in it."

Lannat thanked him, smiling to himself. Combat forged that kind of closeness. Especially when one was winning. He wondered what Retalla would be like if the Free lost a few fights.

The entire unit was up, fed, and ready for the trail when Lannat returned. He grabbed some dried fruit and refreshed his canteen while he checked with the triad leaders. They were finishing when the elcar howled to life. The team watched it rise. For a moment it hovered, turning slowly. Lannat looked to the faces of his raiders. To a one, there was longing in the expressions. The prisoner was going home. Somewhere a family would rejoice. The Free had no such option.

Nor did he, Lannat told himself. No family waited for him. The only person who did was as alone as he—in greater danger and helpless against it.

In mental image, she smiled at him. Her manner changed

abruptly. Her gaze left him, focused over his shoulder. She screamed. When he tried to turn, he was locked in place, unable to move so much as a finger. He tried to call to her, ask what frightened her.

Then another voice. *Astara.* He knew it at its first sigh, before there was a word. His mind's eye brought her to him, leaning heavily on her ornate walking stick. The snow-white blindness fastened on him. Waves of sympathy from her rolled over him. And more: pity.

"We are betrayed, my young captain."

In the vision Astara turned her head. Lannat strained to speak and once again could not. His need to understand her cryptic warning was maddening.

"She needs you, Lannat. Her danger overwhelms me. Save her."

"Everyone's ready." Trey's voice broke Lannat's near-trancelike state. She looked up at him. "Don't worry about the elcar. It'll do exactly what you want. I guarantee."

Lannat had the chilling sensation that he was watching himself. He touched Trey's shoulder. "I don't worry about your work. You're a small rock, but a rock, nevertheless. I depend on you." He looked past her and raised his voice so the whole team could hear. "Listen up. We're three days from camp, and every Advisor on Goliphar must be in the Marnoffar Mountains, looking for us. They know we're moving north, so they'll be pinching in with patrols from the east and west to intercept us. We've got trackers behind us, with palelens. There are enough highspies overhead to prevent sunburn down here. We're carrying way more than a normal load. If things get any nastier, I won't believe it. What that tells me is, we've got these Advisor bastards right where we want them. Jarka, your triad's on point. Set a good pace. All hands—at the line. Move out."

There was laughter, and if it carried a tinny edge of nervousness, no one acknowledged it. When someone cheered, it sounded weak, but that was for security's sake—and it was taken up by the whole team. Then they were moving up the trail, marching higher into the mountainous wilderness.

Lannat drove himself, moving up and down the column, exhorting the others, reminding them to take water frequently, to be alert, to keep proper interval. Despite everything he did, however, Astara's three devastating words repeated at his every step: "We are betrayed."

Betrayed? Of course. Which time did she mean?

He longed for his own world. A soldier's life had its own complexities, its tragedy. But it had verities. This world was all cunning and contrivance. Murder passed for glory; evasion supplanted integrity.

A handy sapling offered a handhold up a particularly steep, slippery slope. In a sudden burst of frustration, he squeezed as if to wring sap from the trunk. No more, he told himself. He would do what he promised to do, but he would count his own needs first. If he could expect loyalty from no one, he must be all the more loyal to himself.

The refrain that cadenced his steps was different after that. *Save her.*

CHAPTER 20

Emperor Halib drummed on the massive desk, a disorganized patter without tempo or rhythm. Administrator Ved toyed with the unspeakably rude idea of asking him to stop. The emperor would be enraged. Still, it was hard to imagine him angrier than he was already. And the infernal patter might end.

Saving Ved from himself, Halib raised his hand, using it to pinch pursed lips. The gesture was characteristic. Ved deplored it. It was disfiguring, undignified, and always made him think of a furious vegetable. But it was an improvement over the drumming. Ved offered up a small prayer of thanks. He added a postscript suggesting that some kindness for an old, loyal spy would be welcome.

He was wrestling with contradictions incorporated in the phrase "loyal spy" when Halib broke his silence. "At least you came to me with the news. Most men would have let the matter go, let it disappear."

"Most men are not bred to the emperor's service, Exalted. I'm embarrassed to have failed you, but I am your man. Nothing changes that."

"We're a good team. As were our fathers before us." Halib's features relaxed a little, only to harden again. "What comes after us, Ved? What will be our legacy?"

"We tried our best, Exalted."

For an instant—less than an instant—Halib considered confessing. Of all people, Ved should know his emperor's ultimate plan. Ved would die for him. Would, as quickly, die for the empire. How did you explain to such a man that his every effort was being carefully manipulated to demolish that empire and assure no emperor arose to rebuild it?

Halib concentrated on the matter at hand. "Tell me once more about this man—Mard, you said his name is?—who claims Sungiver intends to eliminate Etasalou."

Ved leaned forward in his chair, relieved to be on familiar ground. "He was one of the men who tried to assassinate Lannat. Finding him was sheer dumb luck. My man who survived the ambush on Lannat's escort team got a glimpse of Mard driving the attacker's elcar; he has a memorable face. Recently the same survivor was conducting a routine Peace/Order camera watch when Mard showed up in the uniform of Sungiver's personal guard. He's a captain now, thank you very much."

"What did your man do next?"

A grin cracked Ved's tough features. "He didn't make a routine report, if that's what you're asking. He's one of mine, Exalted. A member of the Elemental Guard but sworn to my personal secret service. Report channels exist. He used one. Two men besides me know what he saw. I trust those two as myself."

"Someone trusted Mard," Halib murmured softly. "Please tell me how he and his group knew of Lannat's imprisonment and his release."

Ved swallowed hard. Still, he answered without hesitancy or changed manner. "One of my guards at the oneway facility was bribed. An officer of Etasalou's Hector contingent, escaped to Atic, conducted the operation. We captured him attempting transport to Hire. He swears the entire plan was on his initiative. He also says he's had no opportunity to communicate with Etasalou or any of his old comrades since the emperor cleaned out that slime-fest on Hector."

"You believe that? And what of Lannat? This man who was bribed—is he the reason Lannat disappeared on Hire? Where is the traitor now?"

The emperor's near whisper frightened Ved. In his life, he'd never seen Halib so withdrawn, so cold. Through his own fear, Ved worried that Halib's emotions might literally consume him. The empire was too precariously balanced to tolerate a leader not fully in control of himself. Ved was careful to answer with formal constraint. "Since all interplanetary communications pass through the commmbuoys at the passage sites, we intercept everything. What we take in is verified as to content, originator, and recipient. Each message to or from Hire is tested for code and cipher possibilities. I cannot guarantee the absence of couriers, but I am confident there have been none between Etasalou and Hector's fugitives. The man who was bribed is dead. He was—resolutely—interrogated. He was no agent. Just a weak fool. He's been executed."

Silence fogged the room, an air of demolished hopes and broken promises. After a while Halib spoke again, "Why does a betrayed trust so often end in the loss of a good person? What gods can imagine that the execution of a traitor balances off the death of one who is loyal?"

"It's a treacherous business." Ved made a palms-up gesture of surrender, but his sudden grin was malevolent. "Some people never learn to tell friend from foe."

Halib pushed the button that rolled the sumptuous bar out into the room. He opened a chilled wine, selected glasses from a cabinet, and poured for himself and his guest. He raised his crystal goblet, the emeralds studded in the base gleaming fiery green against a liquid that shimmered like gold, and looked into the wine. "I intended to drink some of this later, alone. Instead, we'll use it to salute integrity. And mourn our losses. It's from Syrac, a small vineyard of less than three acres. The vines are from Home, came on the Blood Father's ship. The vintners make the wine for me every year, and I drink it. By myself. This evening wants a friend to share a toast. Two toasts, actually: one now, one later. The first is to you, Ved. May you never trust the wrong man."

Ved drank. His eyelids fluttered, and he sighed. After a pause, he composed himself, launched back to business. "The agent who reported to Sungiver that she saw Etasalou in Counsellor Ullas's Court confirms that Lannat never made contact with the Hiran resistance. The team designated to help him eliminate Etasalou was dissolved and told the mission was cancelled."

"How does she come by so much information? And how do you acquire it from Sungiver's inner workings?"

After swallowing a hefty mouthful of wine, Ved answered. "The woman is an interrogations technician in Court. I would rather not answer the second question, Exalted. There are unpleasant things about the intelligence business I dislike bringing to your attention."

The response was considerate. It was equally warped. Just moments ago they had spoken of a summary execution as if it were on a par with scraping something nasty from a boot. Now

Ved wanted to avoid something he called "unpleasant." Halib wondered what in all light "unpleasant" might be to a professional torturer. He was at once amused and appalled. "Thank you. I understand."

Ved continued. "Which brings us back to Mard. He visits a woman. She's one of Sungiver's agents, but Mard doesn't know that. Nor does the woman know we've penetrated her house."

"One of Sungiver's counterintelligence people? Penetrated? How?"

"Completely, Exalted. Sound and vision. Every room. It's a sieve."

"That's not what I meant, and you know it, Ved. I want to know how you got into the place and did all this without tripping a dozen sensors. Are you employing ghosts now?"

Ved made a face and false-started his explanation twice before putting words together properly. "The woman has a husband. An executive with Transport. Let's just say the woman is very adept at making new friends. When Sungiver wants the woman free to 'entertain' someone, or—as in Mard's case—test someone's security performance, Transport creates a situation that calls the husband away. Recently someone made the husband aware of what his wife was up to while he was out of town. He was very cooperative about wiring his home."

"The husband knows what's going on?"

"He believes the people who tricked out his house are building a case against his wife for Sungiver."

"Enchanting." Halib poured another glass of wine. "What have your technological peepholes exposed?"

"Mard told Sungiver that Lannat escaped the ambush set by Etasalou's renegades. Somehow she's apparently learned that Lannat failed to contact the resistance on Hire. She's very shrewd, Exalted, and her intelligence acquisition is good. I believe she deduced that Lannat was sent to strike at Etasalou. In light of what she assumes was a failed assassination, she intends to eliminate Etasalou herself. Even if she's caught at it, she can expect you to look the other way. She's decided to use Mard for the job. He served on Hector as an undercover operative for Sungiver. He knows Etasalou on sight. The plain fact is, Mard's a kreech, dangerous only when cornered. Sending him is a foolish move, originated in anger, destined to fail even if Mard tries to make it work."

"Sungiver is sending an assassin to kill Etasalou? Why? He wants to bring me down. She helped his last effort."

"And they failed. But she kept her place, and he lost his. He hates Sungiver. She fears him, and wisely so."

"Your plan, then?"

"Apprehend Mard on his way to the woman's place. Turn him, make him work for us."

"What elegant simplicity. What if he refuses?"

"What if he disappears?"

The deadliness of the retort was heightened only by Ved's matter-of-fact sincerity. Halib chuckled. "As ever, right to the heart of the matter. And to the heart of Mard, one might say. Very well; see what you can do." The emperor's amusement slowly faded. Ved waited. When Halib spoke again, his voice was hardly audible. He raised his goblet once more, focusing on it as if the rich aroma of the wine could carry his message to places he could not see. "I believe this is the moment for that second toast. To you, Captain Lannat. Too little known, too soon gone. Forgive us."

Ved's eyebrows jerked up in surprise. The movement was quickly brought under control. Even so, he failed to completely hide his disbelief over the notion of the emperor asking to be forgiven. Ved was his normal self when Halib dismissed him. "Every day we allow Etasalou to live, the greater our danger. Find a way to eliminate him."

Ved put down his goblet, got to his feet. "He's found a perfect hide. Officially, we don't know where he is. Counsellor Ullas gives lip service in support of the empire and sanctuary to our deadliest enemy. You should have enough loyalty within the council of ambassadors to approve a preemptive strike against Hire."

"No chance of that, Ved. The Elemental Guard is committed across the galaxy, what with six planets experiencing unrest. The ambassadors smell blood. They'll wait to see how I come off in this confrontation. I need my Rifles at hand, and I can't depend on reinforcing troop units from any planet."

"You're more than a good emperor, Exalted, if I may voice my feelings. You're the best the empire's ever seen. The things that are happening to your reign are wrong. It shouldn't be like this. There has to be a way to stop Etasalou. We know what he can do. If he's salvaged Hector's capabilities . . ." Ved wouldn't finish the sentence.

Halib nodded abruptly, expressionless. "Of all things I know, Ved, the most certain of them is your loyalty." Suddenly glowering, he gestured sharply. "Now get to work. You sound like some old fool dunking a bedtime cookie in his warm milk. And you make me sound even worse. Go suborn someone. Concoct a scheme. I swear, sometimes I think you're turning into an old woman. Leave me alone."

Ved was relieved to see Halib turn his back, because it allowed him to free the suppressed grin ripping his face apart from the inside. It was reassuring to see the emperor his normal, irascible self. He chuckled all the way to the secret panel and into the passageway behind it.

In contrast to Ved's uplifted spirits, Halib settled into the chair behind his desk with a bleak melancholy weighing his shoulders.

He blamed Astara for much of his trouble. She had convinced his father—How old could the woman be?—and his father had allowed her to preach her vision to his son. Halib reflected that exposing a child to Astara's seductive logic suggested rather predictable results. On the order of guessing what would happen if one pitched an ice sliver into a blast furnace.

Nevertheless, the Seeker's doctrine held many truths.

Self-government, for one.

Halib believed in it. He also believed it must be acquired by people who truly wanted it. The citizens of the empire knew only tyranny. Benevolent at its best, yet inescapably tyrannical. But freedom granted is obliged to wear a mask of thanks. Freedom must be earned. A paternalistic emperor deigning to grant it didn't qualify in Halib's judgment. He had no scientific data to prove that. He believed it in his guts.

Captain Lannat. Halib's thoughts drifted away from Astara and goals, fastened on the young captain. The change darkened his frown. He remembered the broad hint he'd dropped on Ved, practically admitting he saw in Lannat the son he would never have. Lannat, gone well over a year. Swallowed by the intrigues of empire, probably dead in one of Counsellor Ullas's prisons.

In spite of himself, Halib wondered if Lannat was in Etasalou's hands, and he groaned.

"He lives."

Halib yipped, came upright in a rush that tumbled his chair backward. One hand clawed at the holster fastened to the desk's undersurface, appeared with a plasgun. Before it was fully aimed at the intruder, his expression was changing from startled fear to simple disbelief. He choked out a name. "Astara."

Gliding forward through the same door Ved used, the black-robed woman's outline became steadily more distinct, as if born of the darkness behind her. Her serenity mocked Halib's scrabbling efforts to replace the plasgun that she couldn't see. Nevertheless, her words sent chills racing up his spine. "I am not come to strike you down, Exalted. Nor shall any other, if Astara can prevent it."

With words clinging to his dry mouth, Halib managed to say "Reassuring, indeed. You could have called. I would have come to the cavern." The sound of his own voice steadied him. He went on. "What was that you said? Who lives?"

"Captain Lannat. My reluctant champion. Your unwitting friend."

Halib elected to ignore the insult. "The best intelligence-gathering effort in the galaxy declares him dead. You contradict them?"

"I spoke to him."

Gawking open-mouthed, Halib sputtered, then: "He's on—he *was*—on Hire. He died there. Or do you claim to speak to the dead now, along with your other miraculous accomplishments'?"

"Be heedful, Exalted. The Seeker is as a loving parent, and respect is required. Whatever I accomplish is through the mercy and the teaching of the Seeker." She paused, and the elegantly aged features were briefly austere, forbidding. They relented quickly. "I spoke to Lannat, and he heard. Because he will not abandon himself to us, he cannot answer. But I know he hears. As I know he lives."

"On Hire? Imprisoned?"

Astara frowned, faint scrawled lines of concern marring her forehead. The ice-white eyes blinked slowly. "He is a captive, not imprisoned. He—and I—confront a dilemma never experienced by either of us. We are unsure how to contend with our problems. Betak coerces Lannat, forces him to train the resistance movement. Betak doesn't fully understand the obscenity of Etasalou's experiments. He promises Lannat he will be allowed to conduct his mission after the resistance has enough trained personnel and experience."

The shock of hearing his intelligence chief on Hire named as traitor stunned Halib. It didn't occur to him to doubt Astara. After all, he assured himself, Betak was a chronic complainer, constantly pressuring the empire to implement some plan or other against Ullas. And if she knew of Betak's treachery, she knew the truth of Lannat. Even as her knowledge sent fearful chills across his flesh, he believed her. Nevertheless, in accepting, he found himself going quickly from cold to warmth, deep in the pit of his stomach. He lowered himself back into his chair, interlacing his fingers, hands pressed against that growing heat.

Intrigue. Plans within plans, and schemes to twist them all to his ends. That was the highest delight of his life, and Astara was telling him that a unique opportunity was unfolding.

Halib absently told Astara to have a seat. He closed his eyes, considered the players. Lannat and Betak, of course. The woman Lannat wanted—Nan Bahalt. Wanted by Etasalou, as well. Ullas: oppressive, deceitful. And ambitious far beyond his puny skills.

Sungiver. Mard.

What was the word the chemists used? Catalyst. Yes, catalyst. An agency that precipitated a reaction without participating in it. Sungiver and Mard.

The heat within Halib was a fire now, searching, spreading. It sent out long tendrils that touched his heart and made it beat faster, reached into his mind and made him see dozens of interlocking scenarios. For a moment the excitement wavered. Hire was so far away, so much time had passed; people he couldn't begin to name were involved.

Resolve brushed that problem aside. He, Emperor Halib, would put a plan into operation of such finesse that lesser schemers would be sucked into it and play their parts without option—never even suspecting they were manipulated.

"Lannat believes in you, Exalted," Astara said. "He must not be abused. He does not know that Etasalou is aware Nan Bahalt is on Hire."

Halib opened his eyes. He squinted at Astara in her chair, speculating. "What else should you tell me? You calmly reveal that one of my best intelligence chiefs has betrayed me, then natter about a Captain of Rifles and a female doctor as if we were a pair of matchmakers striking a bargain. It's not like you to be subtle. What's on your mind?"

She wasted no time on denial or resentment. "Unless you do something forceful quickly, Hire will be the black hole of empire. More, of humanity." Centering the walking stick in front of her, she clasped it with both hands, leaning toward Halib in her intensity. "Lannat has tried to conduct himself with honor in impossible circumstances. Even I, who love him, cannot expect him to succeed in all he must accomplish. Indeed, I fear the best he can hope for is the vainglorious end all brave fools crave."

Halib lifted an imperious, interrupting hand. Sarcasm glossed his words. "You *saw* his mind? Disregarding the physical impossibility of that entire statement, I detect a suggestion even more extravagant. Your tone, more than your words, has twice implied you were actually on Hire. I accept many things from you, Astara, because I know you to be a woman of enigmatic accomplishments. But would you really have me believe you soar through space at your will?"

"Our archenemy has shown you what can be done *to* the human mind. I would have you learn what can be done *with* it. You cannot imagine my years, Exalted. You cannot imagine my mind. Yet you could have both. Consider: If a handful of metal and plastic can create an image and transmit it throughout the galaxy with a few volts of ordinary electricity, why cannot this incredible engine within each of us do the same? Is it so inconceivable that we might even improve on what the hardware can do?" She raised a wraith-pale hand, touched her head. "In here, in all of us, is a complex that beggars the universe in its scope and mystery. Mankind uses perhaps ten percent of what is there, yet look at our accomplishments. Look what we do by *accident*. We heal ourselves spontaneously. We communicate across impossible spaces, see at impossible distances. What if we learn to employ the mind rather than the brain? That is why Etasalou must be stopped. The treasure, the potential, that is thought makes us unique. It—the mystery that is all of us—must not be prostituted. Must not."

Halib stammered. "I—I sent Lannat. The best man. I'll think of something. You know me. I always do. I—"

"Lannat has been used too often. By me. By you. He must do what is best for him now. Incredibly, he still feels compelled to do your murder."

"There's no need for offensive language."

A resonating bang of the walking stick's end on the floor scorned his protest. "Be honest with yourself, at least. The Seeker will punish us for our present sins, but we can pray our efforts are considered to be for the greater good. If you cannot save Hire and all its people, can't you at least save two young lives?"

There. The challenge defined. A test of massive power tied to the need for most delicate precision. Only Halib could work such magic. A spark of inspiration flickered. He leaned back in his chair. "I'm looking into it." The wonderful fire was in full flame again. He basked, almost too pleased, too thrilled, to catch her next words.

"As usual, the Exalted anticipates us all." She rose, the robes sighing and whispering. Backing into the darkness, she went on talking. Her voice diminished at each step. "All Hiran revolutionaries are presently of the Seeker religion. Across the galaxy, their faith and commitment is a beacon to all other believers. If they fail us, the Seeker is terribly damaged, perhaps permanently crippled. There will certainly be war within the religion. It can only spread to engulf Lumin and the native religions. That is not a fate for our galaxy worthy of your dreams, Exalted. Your goals are finer than that, yet I tell you there is more, much more, beyond even your high vision."

Astara paused. The gloom teased Halib, making him think he saw a flickering smile brighten her face. He leaned forward, squinting. It didn't help. She continued. "We have spoken many times of your goals. To my shame, I cannot remember when we addressed those of the Seeker; undoubtedly, my years betray my memory. However, knowing your heavy burden of concerns, I shouldn't vex you with details at this time. I shall say only this: Imagine your galaxy filled with people whose minds are trained to a level that even a poor example such as I can achieve. That can be the legacy of Emperor Halib. Humankind free to rise to its ordained heights. If Etasalou does not defeat you."

The silent closing of the door left Halib filled with a sensation of falling. For long minutes he was utterly still, thinking, thinking, a white-knuckled grip clutching the arms of his chair.

CHAPTER 21

Captain Mard strutted. Any man who could alter misfortune to position and influence through sheer intelligence earned arrogance. He pictured himself knocking on the door of one of the expensive houses on the pleasant, tree-lined street. The woman would see him coming, of course. The resplendent red uniform and its gold trim couldn't escape notice. He frowned as the image soured. What if she were fearful, pretended not to be home? He knew the type. Frustrated. Burning with envy. Probably watching right now, wishing she had the courage to report an illicit affair.

Mard lifted his chin a notch higher; who cared? If anyone was interested in his relationship with Otala, they'd never dare get involved. Anyway, he was discreet; always walked the last few blocks to the house, always used the side entrance, where he was hidden from view by all but the determinedly curious.

He saw the eltruck parked in front of his accustomed entrance when he turned the last corner, a holovid repair vehicle. He continued on, smiling to himself; Otala wouldn't need holo to entertain her. Not with ever-ready Mard on hand, and her sludge husband gone for a full week.

A repairman in the driver's seat got out as Mard turned to go through the gated entrance. He carried a heavy toolbox. When Mard glanced at him, the repairman waved. Mard ignored him.

Captains in Sungiver's guard had nothing in common with hand workers. He frowned annoyance when the repairman fell in behind him. What if this meant interruption of the afternoon's festivities?

Mard let himself in and was truly angered to hear the repairman follow without so much as a knock on the door. He considered confronting the man but decided against it. It was Otala's house, after all. Better that she handle the matter.

Metal-tapped heels banging on the mosaic floor of the kitchen, Mard stormed into the living room.

Words jammed in his throat. Otala sat at her dining room table. So did her husband. There was a third party, a woman in the same white coveralls as the other repairman. She wore a weird, translucent mask. It made her face indistinct, yet clearly human and feminine. The effect was unnerving.

Mard knew how to handle emergencies. He bolted like a shot. The male repairman was waiting for him. Mard barely had time to register an identical mask on that face before something like a bomb struck him just under the ribs. His breath left in a single gust. Gasping for air, croaking protest, he was quickly lashed to a chair at the table with Otala and her husband.

At a harsh command from the male captor, Otala and her husband rose. Bound hands combined with trembling to make them clumsy. The masked female said, "In the other room, both of you. Don't speak. That's the only warning you'll get. Move."

By then Mard's breathing was almost back to normal. He yanked and strained at his bonds. The trio stopped on their way out of the room as he shouted at the male captor. "What d'you think you're doing? I'm a member of Sun . . ."

The man reached across the table, smacked the heel of a hand between Mard's eyes. His head snapped back. The chair threatened to tip over backward. Mard squawked, struggled to keep his balance.

"Keep your mouth shut, Sergeant," the man said. To his

partner, he went on. "Get those two out of here. They don't need to see this."

Mard found him entirely too cross. He used the correct rank with considerable authority, too. Mard opened his mouth to ask another question— politely—but the man waggled a forefinger at him. The admonishing finger alone Mard might have ignored, but when it curled back to join all its little friends in a truly awesome fist, obedience became his steadfast goal.

Bending to the toolbox, the man rose with something in hand. Mard's heart lurched when he recognized the scanner. From behind, the man grabbed the finger holding Mard's Elemental Guard i-wy. Something stung. Surprised, Mard yelped, tried to pull away. Metlin bonds dug into his flesh. When Mard said, "What are you doing?" a sharp blow on the back of his head reminded him that silence was important.

The repairman moved to the opposite side of the table once again. Still reading the scanner, the man said, "Just so you know who you're dealing with, Sergeant, we're part of Commander Etasalou's hardcore troops. We're stranded here, but we're still faithful, still working to bring back our true leader."

Pausing, he held up another small instrument for Mard to see. He pressed a button on it. A short, stubby needle popped out, back in again. Through the eerie mask, Mard saw a broad smile come and go. The man said, "This thing is just so we know who *we're* dealing with. DNA tester. That was the jab you felt while I was checking your i-wy. Ninety-five-point-one percent accurate, they say."

"That's not fair. What if it's wrong?"

"Hope it says you're Mard. If it doesn't, we have to assume you're a spy, a plant. We can't have that."

The woman returned with Otala in tow. Mard's erstwhile lover looked more nervous than ever. The female captor said, "Otala here tells us you claim to come here from Hector."

Mard nodded, hard. "That's true. You have my i-wy. Sungiver's people checked it, too."

The man sneered. "How do we know it's not doctored?" He

looked to his partner. "We don't need him. Even if he's one of us, he's turned his coat, gone over to Sungiver."

"No one but Guard techs can alter an i-wy. Anyhow, we can use him," the woman said. "Check your DNA; is he real?"

Grudgingly, the man looked at the device. He frowned, and Mard's heart threatened to explode. The man said, "He's who he says. I still say we burn all of them." He spun quickly, bent to put his face into Mard's. "You sold out, didn't you?"

"No!" It was a shout, and the man slapped him to help him keep his voice down. Mard raced on. "Once Elemental, always Elemental. Isn't that right? It was me that was sold out, not the other way round. I was part of the team sent to burn that bastard Lannat. It broke wrong. We fought like devils, I'm telling you—"

Another slap. "Who's 'we'? Name the team."

Mard strained, remembering, adding anecdotal information about every person involved. If he saw the woman aiming her recordat at him, he paid no attention. He finished with "The one in charge, he set up the safe house and all, but he left us. I'm telling you, after I fought so hard, to crawl back there and find no one—"

Another slap. "You lying scum. Back where? You don't even have an address."

Mard obliged. Speech was a bit tricky by then, what with his cheeks swelling from the slaps.

The woman said, "Otala says you're telling Sungiver everything you know about us. She's worked for Sungiver for years. Watching her, seeing who she reeled in, is how we found you. You should've known better, Mard; no one, nothing, gets past Commander Etasalou. We've got so many informants inside Sungiver's outfit they're reporting on each other."

Inspiration seized Mard, flashing a way out of his dilemma. He laughed. It creaked like a rusty hinge, not the strong signal of nonchalance he meant to project. He watched carefully to see how the noise affected his interrogators. The unnerving masks simply stared.

Mard pushed on. "This whore? I knew she was a—a—what you said. You *know*. A plant! Yes, that's it—a plant. I've been using her." He winked broadly.

Otala snarled at him. Mard had no time for concern in that quarter. The interrogators fired questions at him. Every answer triggered another question, each one coming instantly, faster, harsher, unbelieving. Logic told him they ripped at him for minutes. His brain, squeezed for names, dates, places, facts, insisted hours fled past. Sweat dripped from his chin, his nose, turned his proud red uniform into a blotched parody. The stink clogged his nostrils.

He prayed they wouldn't ask about the mission. If they knew he'd agreed to Sungiver's insane plan to assassinate Etasalou—if they even suspected it—they'd burn him in a heartbeat.

Simultaneously, as if their minds were linked, both interrogators straightened and pulled back from the near-contact confrontation with Mard. For a long moment, the only sound in the room was Mard's panting. The woman left, returning with the husband. She shoved him into a chair next to Otala, then positioned herself directly across the table from Mard. Her posture was different now, relaxed, her hand on the back of a chair supporting a body gracefully at ease. When she spoke, her voice was low, kindly. Mard terribly wanted to believe he heard apology in her first words. "We've been very hard on you, Sergeant. I'm sure you understand. The empire needs Commander Etasalou. He is the future. We are the nucleus of his power. Our task is to keep his influence alive."

"Exactly. Exactly. That's what I've been doing. Working for Etasalou's future. Like I said."

Otala made a sound, like a hiss.

From behind the unreadable mask, the male captor's question was as soft as his partner's. His voice was cold. Deadly cold. "If your devotion to our commander is so intense, why, then, did you tell Sungiver you were willing to travel to Hire and murder him?"

Mard jerked in his chair, clamping down his sphincter to halt the burgeoning flow before he disgraced himself. Not absolutely sure if he was successful, he shook his head in violent denial. "It was part of my plan. It just proves how much Sungiver trusts me. Who'd be crazy enough to try to kill Etasalou? Her, that's who. She *told* me, she didn't *ask*. I said I would so I could stay alive." He pushed forward, selling. "Put yourself in my place: Who knows more about Sungiver's plans than I do? I wish you could have heard her. 'Gain his confidence,' she said. 'Make him believe you're on Hire to offer my help.' The old witch thinks the commander will fall for that. I'm not going to Hire to kill him, I'm going there to save him."

The masked female touched her partner's shoulder. They stepped away to exchange whispered conversation. Rumbling anger, the man shook his head in disagreement with the woman's quieter argument.

Mard looked to the bound couple. The husband sat bent over, staring at the floor. Otala was erect, eyes blazing. When she caught Mard's eye, she spat at him. He flinched away, although the froth landed on the table. The interrogators glanced at the disturbance, then resumed their discussion.

Finally they came back. The woman said, "Here's the way it goes. We have people on Hire. You'll be contacted. Until you are, do nothing."

"What if I meet Etasalou? Shouldn't I tell him—"

The man interrupted. "Listen, you dumb son of a bitch—if I had my way, you'd be dead. When he wants something from you, he'll push your button. You do what you're told—exactly what you're told—or we'll cut you in strips. I'm only sorry I won't be on Hire to do it." He half turned, spoke to his partner. "You may be in charge here, but I want this piece of crap watched. I'm sending a message to—"

This time it was the woman overriding the man. Furious, she shouted him down. "Stop. No names. Hold that temper."

The expressionless masks faced each other. When the man at last turned to Mard, the woman gave her attention to the couple. "You were brought in here to watch this so you could see for yourselves how deeply we've penetrated Sungiver's control of Lumin here on Atic. Otala, you'll tell the man you report to that Mard threw you over. He's out of your life now. I don't think it's necessary to describe what'll happen to you if anything about this entire affair ever surfaces. We'll know if it does, just as we know everything else about you. Say nothing, change nothing."

The husband looked up, haggard. "What d'you mean, change nothing? After what you told me about her? After all this?" He indicated Mard with his chin.

The woman was brusque. "Handle it any way you can. But handle it. Let me put it this way: Our plans are much more important than your lives. If you want to get an amicable, uncontested divorce from each other in a year or so, we won't interfere. Make one move that makes us worry about our security—or Commander Etasalou's—and you'll live just long enough to regret it." She paused, giving them all one last view of the dead face of the mask. "We're leaving now. Otala, I think you and I understand each other best, so I'm untying you. Give us an hour, then release these two." She moved to cut Otala's bonds. "Please. Don't make us do something we don't want to do."

Otala's grin was hard, composed. "This isn't over. Another time; we'll see."

The masked woman nodded. Her male companion saluted. They left quickly, calmly.

As soon as the eltruck engine started, Mard struggled against the metlin, but not hard enough to cut himself. He told Otala, "Hurry up and cut me out of this stuff. I have to get out of here."

She came to him, stopped to look down into his face. "They said to give them an hour. You have to learn to listen. Remember this?" She leaned forward, smacked the heel of her hand against his forehead the way the interrogator had. Only harder. Mard yelped once as his chair spilled over backward.

Flat on his back, legs bent to fit the form of the chair, Mard watched her walk away and choked back curses. There was no dignity in yelling at her, he told himself. Better to lie there, cool. Rational. When she came back, he'd glare, give her a look that would make her understand how really cheap she was. He muttered, careful that she didn't hear. "That'll teach you."

Administrator Ved stepped out onto the balcony where the emperor waited. When Halib didn't acknowledge him, Ved announced himself. Halib said, "I'm listening. Where do we stand?"

Ved shifted uncomfortably. "It went as you directed, Exalted. The man Mard will go to Hire expecting to be contacted by one of Etasalou's renegades." He paused, then, as if the words came of themselves: "The man's worse than a cipher, Exalted. He's a scummy coward. He'll cheat anyone, everyone."

Still facing the spectacular view of the city of Collegium and the distant mountains, Halib said, "Send a message to Betak, timed to arrive a few days after Mard arrives on Hire, telling him that Mard is a prospect for recruitment as a spy."

Ved gaped. "Betak? You said you can no longer depend on him."

Halib finally turned. It was painful to watch: the rigid motion of someone weighed down by stress. Ved set himself to show no reaction to anything.

"I can't depend on him to execute my will," Halib said. "I can make use of him, nevertheless. Send the message as directed. Also, Betak is to have no hint that I believe Lannat is alive on Hire."

"But we know nothing of Lannat's situation. He's a loyal, dependable young officer. Betak must be made to understand . . ."

Halib's grim glare stopped Ved. "All must serve the empire, Ved. How they serve, or why, or when—all that is immaterial. They benefit the empire, or they have no value. Lannat was assigned an important mission. He didn't carry it out. Unless he does, he has failed me. I must forget him and search out alternatives."

Ved straightened. "I have always been honest with my emperor. I must be so now. I disagree strongly with this. To send a crawling coward like Mard into a treacherous situation is pathetic. I have heard you speak well of Lannat; I could say you spoke warmly of him. I can't believe he abandoned the mission, Exalted. Something is wrong, I know it is. The only logical conclusion is that Betak has failed Lannat, not that Lannat has failed you."

Halib held Ved's level, worried gaze for several seconds. Breaking that off, he moved to a conchair and settled into it. A weary gesture indicated that Ved should take the one next to him. "I am the empire," Halib said. "My mind decides for every living soul in the galaxy. Even you, as close as you are to me, can never realize the price of that responsibility. Should Lannat not kill Etasalou, his life has no purpose. Oh, there are things that Lannat will accomplish, things he's not even aware of. But elimination of Etasalou is primary. That is how I must measure my responsibility, you see; the empire recognizes no individual."

Unconvinced, Ved refused to quit. "It must recognize character then. There has to be some way for an empire to acknowledge worth."

"That is what I do: recognize character. That is why Mard must go to Hire. Because he is a coward. With luck, Lannat will destroy those who attempt to destroy him. A coward will destroy any who endanger him, and he'll do it without warning. I know Lannat would have carried out his assignment if he could. Mard's self-serving treachery may create the opening Lannat needs. Or, unlikely as it seems, Mard may kill Etasalou. He will, at the very least, bring the pot to the boil."

"Lannat may be among those scalded."

Halib nodded. "And there's the difference. I am the empire. You are not. You care. I must not."

CHAPTER 22

Obscured by the patter of light rain falling on the leathery leaves of hesker scrub, Lannat's crawling progress was part of the Hiran darkness. Retalla was a few yards ahead of him, following in trace of Trey's triad; hers was the lead element of Retalla's squad. One of Trey's people, a man named Keer, took point for the assault team.

The blocky main building of the power station loomed ahead of them, angular against the distant, twinkling lights of Yasil, the continent's second largest city. The muffled rumble of harnessed geothermal energy from the closer building spoke more of force, less of beauty.

Keer signaled for a stop. On the thermal lenses of Lannat's darkglasses, the raised hand was bright against the cold night. Another hand signal indicated activity ahead. According to plan, everyone broke out smoke cloaks.

The captured cloaks were a great asset for a guerrilla organization. The exterior grid pattern of the poncholike device confused the collector plates of all but the most highly refined light-enhancement devices. The cloaks' effectiveness came from construction that featured ultra-thin layers of permeable fabric. They acted as membranes; heat absorbed from the wearer was directed into chemical solutions held between the filmlike materials. The whole generated a coolant dissipation flow. Heat escaped eventually, but at a wavelength that considerably degraded thermal imaging.

The drawback was their cumbersome weight and the masks that allowed only a slit for vision. And the coolant effect failed over time. Nevertheless, a person properly enveloped in a smoke cloak, even when detected, failed to register a clear image on most night-detection devices. In combat, that was treasure.

Lannat thought back over the preceding half year to the highspy raid. The cloaks would have saved lives in that withdrawal. They certainly had on many subsequent raids. Still, the Free had succeeded that first time in spite of the handicaps. Destroyed the pursuit. And the cursed palelens, into the bargain.

Keer signaled to continue the advance.

In Lannat's darkglasses, the two-man Advisor listening post was as gaudy as a circus. A smile pulled at stressed muscles. Despite six months of successful, albeit small and sporadic, raids by the Free, government security remained unconvinced that the major infrastructure was endangered. A perfect example was straight ahead: Although the garrison assigned to the power plant was a full two hundred men, in their imagined invulnerability they took only the most rudimentary precautions. Such as listening post personnel who spent the night chatting.

An indistinct blur to the side of the pair Lannat took to be their smoke cloaks. Two Free recruits would own the cloaks tomorrow. And wear them.

Retalla and Trey inched ahead to join Keer. The other triad member followed. Indistinct, smudged forms in their protective gear, and with the gentle rain to disguise any errant scrape or scuffle, the triad closed to within feet of the listening post.

Following the highspy raid, Lannat had ordered spears be carried by every raid unit. Eight feet long with steel heads like large, grooved daggers, they outreached any sword. Experience also proved that a raging palelen would impale itself on one at every opportunity.

Trey's people lunged in unison.

Lannat was two body lengths away. He heard the dull thud of impact and some muted thrashing.

Retalla squirmed forward, next to Trey.

Lannat wondered how she was handling this action. She'd given no sign of difficulty since the night of the highspy raid. Still and all, Lannat thought, anxieties like that didn't just evaporate.

He rose and twisted to signal the bomb team forward from behind the rocks uphill. Hidden from his view, four more squads were scheduled to move at the same time, creeping downhill to assigned assault lines. Flipping on the dimenomap attached to his seekum, Lannat confirmed their advance.

The bomb team hurried past at a low crouch, taking advantage of the rain's background noise. The hesker plants were excellent concealment. Uniformly four feet high, their bell-shaped forms covered the slope like a collection of umbrellas. Very little other plant life lived among hesker shrubs. Sul had explained to Lannat that the leaves gave off a poison that defoliated most other plants. Strange; the scent of the bruised leaves was very pleasant.

Lannat tried to think about hesker, plant poisons, natural selection—anything.

Twenty minutes. The bomb team had to slip inside the power plant's defenses, plant their explosives, and get back out.

Wait. Avoid useless worry. Check on the position of the assault units. Check again. Once more, just to be certain.

Listen to night noises. Familiar now. The shrieking pack animals hunting downhill, where the trees of the forest started, were called zeebers. Little black things with swirls of white striping. No longer than a man's forearm and no more than four or five pounds apiece, they ran in packs up to twenty strong. Nasty. The man called Val Bordi knew all that. And more. He was practically a Hiran now.

The man who was Lannat, Captain of Rifles, hated Val Bordi. The man called Lannat was real. Val Bordi was a lie, a fraud. But he belonged. He had friends. Lannat was alien here forever. Unknown to anyone. Alone.

Nan.

Lannat checked his map again.

He looked up to find the bomb team retreating through the hesker. They passed swiftly, swishing leaves marking their departure.

A few more minutes.

The explosives in place were Counsellor Ullas's best, stolen from depots and smuggled into the mountains by Free supporters. Tonight Free returned them.

A loud bang was prelude, an opening note. Through the darkglasses, Lannat barely made out the mist of powdered material dispersed by the initial explosion of the Area Blast. ABs weren't the weapon of choice for heavy construction, but the suppliers said the new pyrogen models were a radical improvement over explosive gases.

Lannat quickly turned off the darkglasses and flipped back the hood of his smoke cloak.

Impact was light, sound, and shock wave. What happened next staggered him much more. Lannat understood the principle of the pyrogen effect: The chemical that made up the mist was transformed by the heat of the initial blast into something different, something highly flammable that burned with magmalike heat when the second explosion ignited it. Knowing that basic fact and seeing what it meant in reality were totally different experiences. The powder ignited and fell to earth as superheated, roiling masses of flame. Living fire coated concrete, steel beams, the exposed generators, the pipes and towers. Unbelievably, they burned, melted. Normally flammable materials—wood, paper, insulation—were consumed in explosive billows. In the midst of all that, the freed geothermal steam and water spewed, bellowing, into the turmoil. Air, drawn to the fire's need, created a wind, an evil inhalation that ruffled the already raised hair on the back of Lannat's neck.

Off to the east the light of the fire gilded the two stone

buildings of the Advisor barracks. Men poured out the doors at each end of the nearer one, hands and arms raised to ward off heat. On the side away from the fire, more men leaped from the lower windows.

They raced directly into the oncoming Free squads, down from the high ground and attacking across the space between the buildings.

From his high-ground observation, Lannat had a dreamlike feeling of involvement on one hand and helplessness on the other. It was very unpleasant.

Forty raiders, outnumbered five to one, tore into the growing mob of Advisors with disciplined ferocity. Lannat could only imagine shrilled whistle commands, shouts and screams; thunder from the destroyed power plant drowned out all else. Spears lowered, two squads of shoulder-to-shoulder Free carrying rectangular shields moved with awesome precision. Behind them, peeling off in individual triads, two more squads protected against attack from the rear while dealing with anyone exiting the barracks after the spearmen passed.

Out of sight of the engaged Free, other Advisors organized into counterattack elements.

Lannat raised his seekum and ordered immediate retreat. A moment later the spearmen turned about, raised their weapons, broke into a trot. The flanking triads fell in behind as the ranked spearmen passed, covering the withdrawal as they had covered the advance. Lannat noted Free being carried and cursed softly. Combat required casualties. It was never acceptable.

By the time the Free disappeared into darkness beyond the firelight, the Advisor force was coming under control of its leaders. Quickly, pursuit was under way.

They brought palelens. Lannat counted a dozen of them.

According to plan, the assault unit raced directly uphill, toward Lannat's position. He turned to see the bomb unit carrying out its secondary mission, stringing catchwire through the hesker scrub. It would be practically invisible to the pursuing Advisors.

Lannat rose, retreated. He thought of the other surprises waiting for the Advisors, reflecting on how he'd become a steadfast disciple of boobytraps and ambushes.

With all his troops clear, Lannat signaled the completion of the wire obstacle. The bomb team obeyed, then hurried up into the rocks near the hill's crest. They passed the troops emplacing captured strobe lights and sound generators on the way. Lannat remained with the rearguard element while Jarka led the main body away.

Pained, frustrated yells announced the Advisors' contact with the catchwire. Angry orders rose above the confusion. Palelens roared eagerness. Lannat glanced at the Free crowding down behind the rocks. Fear of the animals was obvious; troopers shifted nervously, peered down the hill.

In minutes the wire was breached. Palelen cries rose to eager baying. Hidden below the domed hesker, only the motion of the disturbed plants betrayed their position. Advisors pounded along behind them.

When the strobes flashed into action, the palelens' nerve-wracking squalls stopped as if cut off. Blinded, those Advisors too close to the obstacles shrieked pain. Others, far enough away to be fairly sure they were merely dazzled, shouted curses. The fear that rang through the cries, the awful fear of permanent blindness, made Lannat's stomach roll dangerously. He was relieved when the sound generators bellowed and smothered that noise.

Sound waves of such intensity dazed humans as effectively as clubs. Even the Free rear guard, protected by distance and hastily inserted earplugs, winced. Palelens were unaffected by the deep booming. To deal with them, the generators had been retrofitted by the Free; after a basso blast, the machines fell silent to human ears. The inaudible high note maddened the palelens. Above the charnel-house screams of the human casualties, the creatures raised an indescribable sound of insane rage. Advisor handlers called for help as their animals went berserk.

"They're finished," Lannat told the rear-guard commander. "Watch for another few minutes, make sure they don't reorganize and come after us. Fall back and catch up at your discretion."

The young man nodded, and Lannat was gone. He reached the prepared ambush position quickly, ordering them to fall in behind him to rejoin the main body. A trooper, a man of long standing in the Free, kept pace with Lannat, saying "It's too bad the sound-and-light show stopped them. If they'd come after us, we'd have rolled them off this ridge like marbles off a knife blade."

Lannat didn't slow, talked out the side of his mouth. "What's your name? Park-something, right?"

"Parkronar. I'm surprised you even hear of me."

"I know of you. You're a good man. Brave. But you're wrong. For us, killing and wounding is the least part of the war. If we let it turn to simple attrition, no matter how hard we fight, we'll lose. The lucky ones will die. The rest will end up in Etasalou's lab. We damage only the people we have to damage. The rest have to come over to our side. We're out to kill Ullas and his government, not his people."

"So what good's it do to blow up a power plant? Ullas'll just rebuild it. And the guys we did kill—their friends'll hate us, won't they?"

"Some will. We're gambling Ullas will make them hate him more than us." Just then they came around a shoulder of the mountain, revealing the huge valley dominated by the city of Yasil. Some lights reappeared now, sporadic pockets of glitter charged by emergency generators. Other lights demanded greater attention, however. Red-orange, flickering like misplaced stars, they spewed smoke that bannered across the silhouetted buildings. Lannat pointed. "Look, fires. Big ones. Our people set them. Those are computer banks burning and the local Advisor barracks. Police stations. Yasil's Peace/Order cameras are being ripped out all over the place. A team of Frees is releasing prisoners from the jail at the edge of town."

Slashing through the smoke and flickering fireglow, emergency and police elcars responded. The latter herded all civilian traffic away from the city, substituting for the destroyed traffic-control center. Firefighting equipment streaked toward the largest blazes.

Impressed, Parkronar said, "Darkness catch us. The counsellor will rip everybody in town."

Lannat chuckled—an unpleasant, grating noise. "And where do you go if Ullas has lost control of your records but continues to torment you? Who'll train you, so you can avenge the loss of family or property?"

"So that's how it works. We bring the counsellor down on them, squeeze them until it's him or us. Doesn't make us sound very good."

Suddenly Lannat remembered talking to Trey in much the same situation, when the heat of battle died out and left a person with a strange, unsettling feeling. Lannat knew it too well: not exactly disappointment, but a deep sense of uncertainty that ate at the soul. He resolved to keep Parkronar talking about generalities. After all, he had been forced into training these people, and psychological counseling wasn't part of the arrangement.

"Point of view." Lannat waved an arm. "Those people out there, they've got perfection now, if it's what they want. No one fails, no one succeeds by too much. Enough competition in the workplace to keep everyone alert without excessive stress. No real poverty, no entrenched upper class to hold people down below a comfort level. Stability. Order. If Etasalou turned their brains into gumballs, most of them wouldn't know the difference. Or care."

For a long while, the two men pressed ahead in silence, glancing over at the distant fires when footing permitted. At last the younger man said, "You hate those people down there in the valley? How come you're up here with us, risking your butt for them?"

Real amusement shone in Lannat's laughter this time,

despite the fact that the conversation showed signs of veering off onto ground he didn't want to cover. "I don't hate them. I think they're fools, but I don't hate them."

"All right, then: Why fight for fools?"

"I don't really know. Maybe I'm a soldier because I'm more like them than I want to admit, satisfied to be wrapped in my own rules and regulations. I hope that's not all of it. I hope I'm fighting because I believe that, if a person's going to be a damned fool, he ought to be allowed to be his own damned fool, and not be required to be someone else's. I happen to believe Emperor Halib's a good ruler, interested in maximum good for the greater number of his subjects."

Again, they walked in silence awhile, and again, it was Parkronar who spoke into it. He was very thoughtful. "It's more than that. You like this stuff. Fighting, and all. I've watched you. I'm here mostly because I didn't like all the rules they've got down there, but it's different here. We've got more rules, and harder ones, than they have, but it doesn't bother me as much. They're for a reason, you know?"

Lannat felt, rather than saw, a quick, intense glance from the younger man before the confiding voice continued. "I think the most reason I'm here is because it's exciting. That's dumb, I know, but it's true. I know I'm on the right side and all that, but I think maybe I was born to soldier." Then, defensively: "I don't think you're so much different."

Coldly, instantly, Lannat told him, "Don't waste your time forming opinions about me. Worry about my opinion of you. Take a message to Jarka: Tell him I said to slow down the column until the rear guard rejoins us. Move out."

Watching the stiff, offended departure, Lannat ached to call the man back. Instead, he muttered to himself, "Sorry. Maybe it's not too late for you to get out of this. Maybe you're not really one of us yet. Get away, if you can, or soon enough you'll learn how badly I lied to you about the people in the valley. The real fools are walking this ridge, and the worst of them are like me."

CHAPTER 23

Several weeks after the raid on the power plant and the city of Yasil, Betak visited the Free stronghold. He reported on increased repressions and explained they were to be expected; the government's data banks were seriously damaged. He hinted at other developments but seemed more distracted than secretive. When the official meeting broke up, he continued to roam about. It was unusual behavior, and it made Lannat nervous.

He mentioned it to those closest to him at the moment, the foursome of Jarka, Retalla, Trey, and Sul. Jarka was sympathetic. "He can be comfortable here. He can trust everyone around him. Anyhow, he's got too many decisions to make."

Surprisingly, Sul scoffed at that. "He's just like the rest of us. We think we make up our own minds, but all we really do is answer up to whoever's over us. People like him and us do what we're told. Or else."

Lannat said nothing. It was too sensitive a subject.

Thoughtfully, Retalla disagreed. "You don't believe that. Losers say stuff like that, and you're not one of them. You're no tool, you're a man. The rest of us are sure of that. I know I'm damned sure about me. I'm worth more than that argument—'All I do is take orders'—and what I believe in is worth more than me. Sure as darkness worth more than some shadowy 'them.' Sure, we follow leaders, but we find a way to dump them when we've had enough. Like the damn counsellor."

Sul stared at the ground, a bit embarrassed. Without looking up at Retalla, he said, "I was just making noise. What you say is right. Sometimes it gets hard to remember, that's all."

The conversation went on, and although Lannat stayed with the group, he heard little more. His thoughts were directed inward. He remembered the contempt and dislike he had felt for these people when he first met them. He still wasn't one of them, not in the way he was a Rifle. No matter what happened, he would always be someone else to them, a man who didn't really exist. But he'd learned to respect and admire them. Yes—to like them.

Betak interrupted his train of thought. "I have to talk to you. Especially you, Bordi." He wasted no time, once he had their attention. "We have a complication. A man named Mard, a captain in Sungiver's personal guard, is on Hire as her personal emissary."

Lannat chose his answering words very carefully. "Before I left Atic, I heard lots of rumors that Sungiver herself was part of the plot to break Paro out of the empire. If there's any truth to that, and I tend to believe it, Sungiver probably sent Mard to advise Doctor Renula. Lumin, under Sungiver, will want to support Ullas, but she can't support Etasalou. One way or another, Mard offers a potential weapon against Etasalou."

Sul was unimpressed. "But a weapon for Ullas, not for us."

Betak intervened again. "Leave those problems to me. I think we can possibly use this Mard. The thing I want you all to remember is that Lumin sent him, and that could happen only if the emperor approved. Something is happening. Mard is more than just another man thrown into the mix. We must work harder, be ready for anything."

Sul's laughter was bitter.

Retalla looked at him from the corner of his eye, grinned wryly. "Maybe you're right, Sul. Maybe all we do is dance to music we can't even hear."

Lannat chuckled with the rest. He wondered if it burned inside them, too.

* * *

Mard sprawled comfortably in a large chair in Doctor Renula's luxurious quarters in Court. Their expressions were a study in contrast. Mard's lean features were relaxed and confident. He maintained a constant faint smile while Renula talked. It altered subtly from time to time. The small changes had the effect of leaves moving in a breeze, frustrating any effort to see exactly what lay behind the constant activity. Renula's brow corrugated in frown, the mouth an unhappy inverted crescent.

Beyond the room, framed in an immense window, was the city of Liskerta. Urban light pollution masked the stars in Hire's moonless sky. Three elcar vortices offered dazzling diversion. Traffic approached the vortex and was given entry permission. Once in a circular flow, drivers received instructions permitting descent, ascent, and departure direction. The patterning allowed elcar access to the city at several points but prohibited random entry. Experience had long ago proven that, even with automatic collision-avoidance radar in place, drivers diving into, or erupting from, city streets without warning generated accidents faster than paramedics could service them.

Neither Mard nor Renula glanced at the spectacle. Renula was saying "Sungiver doesn't understand the situation, the opposition I face. She can't—"

Mard, holding up an interrupting hand, spoke over Renula's protest. "Sungiver is the light of Lumin. We mustn't argue what she can do or can't do. She sent me to express her confidence in you. I told you she considers you responsible for Lumin's continued strength on Hire. Surely that's not a problem? I hear tales of these shirtless Seeker believ___ ___ in the mountains; they can't be important."

"They are important. Dangerous, in ___ ago—just before you got here—they st___ stroyed the regional power plant. In the ___ uncounted population control data. A___ tacked, destroyed. It was terrible." Re___ collapsed in belated realization that M___ a disapproving frown. She struggled to regain lost ground. "We don't underestimate our enemies. If anything, we give them too much credit. Better that than overconfidence, I always say. Counsellor Ullas has redoubled antidissension efforts. Nonks are flowing into Commander Etasalou's laboratories."

Once more Mard gestured her to silence. "Why does Ullas protect Etasalou, the apostate?"

Renula resorted to bluster. "Why hasn't Sungiver done something about Etasalou herself? Don't tell me she didn't know he came here?"

"Sungiver knows everything. Etasalou's presence on Hire is the empire's worst-kept secret." Sudden alarm gripped him at Renula's swift change. Finger to lips, she gestured him to the balcony. Once in the open, she touched a button on the wall; glass doors slid closed behind them.

Renula explained. "The counsellor exercises a healthy curiosity about his subjects' true feelings. I suspect that interest extends to listening devices in my quarters. Those doors are soundproof, and the balcony is inspected frequently. If we're going to discuss controversy, it's safer out here."

Mard's head swiveled industriously. "It's refreshing to know Counsellor Ullas cares so deeply for his subjects. No reason for us to be out here, actually; I certainly wouldn't say anything he shouldn't hear." His voice lowered. "How often do you inspect?"

"Once a week, minimum." Unlike Mard, Renula seemed to take a perverse strength from the situation. She spoke boldly. "You were referring to worst-kept secrets, I believe."

"Yes. Well. A figure of speech, of course." He leaned close, almost whispering. "You're sure we're not overheard? Recorded? Observed in any way?"

Renula shook her head. Mard went on. "Etasalou intends to usurp Lumin, make it his own. Sungiver's adherents will be eliminated." At Renula's shock, Mard nodded sagely. "Most reduced in rank, assigned to menial tasks. Those such as in genuine danger of execution."

Renula recovered quickly. She looked out over the gleaming city. "I should have known that. I've been very stupid. Ullas supplies Etasalou with the very material he needs to overthrow his host." She turned so quickly Mard flinched. "Hire wallows in rumors about Etasalou's laboratory-prison. What do you know about that? Is it true what they say, he does something to those people, changes their brains?"

"The technique was perfected on Hector, but that facility was destroyed by the emperor. No one knows how much of the work Etasalou's been able to duplicate here. Sungiver fears the worst and instructs you to support me in every way as we investigate Etasalou. You will use your covert assets to report. When the time is right, you will assign someone to assassinate him."

Renula stepped back. She examined Mard. Finally, turning away, she paced the balcony's length. Mard strolled to the rail to face the view. Renula joined him. She said, "We provide low-level medical assistance to his facility—additional nurses for the ill or injured, physicians to deal with commonplace complaints his specialists haven't the time to deal with. No one except the counsellor himself has access to Etasalou. You must meet him."

"It's not necessary for me to get close, really. I'm just a messenger, you see? Sungiver wants me to supervise, in a sense, but she trusts you to conduct the actual operation. The honor of the actual blow to save Lumin, as it were. You already know all those people. And the lay of the land, so to speak."

"I see. She told you she wants Etasalou killed? In so many words?"

"I'm afraid so. You can do it. Look at the resources you have to work with."

"None. Lumin has no troops of any kind on Hire. We teach no martial arts or anything remotely like that."

"Sungiver has complete faith in your ingenuity. 'Doctor Renula's faith and determination will carry her through.' That's what she told me."

"Very kind. It was even kinder of her to send an official emissary this far just to tell me these things. One would think a messenger would suffice. But that's what you said you are, isn't it?"

Mard straightened back from the railing. "The phrase was descriptive, not definitive. I am Sungiver's emissary, nothing less."

Coming to full height, as Mard had, Renula looked down at him. Her bulk lacked his grace; it made up for that in suggestion of power. "Absolutely, Captain Mard. Nothing less, and a great deal more."

He reacted to her tone. "What's that mean? You're being very cryptic, Doctor, and if we're to be a successful team, understanding and cooperation are necessities."

"Let me be plain, then. Sungiver didn't send you here to tell me what to do—wonderful person that I am. She sent you to kill Etasalou."

Mard gave a muffled yelp like a frightened dog. He crouched in panicked search for the listening device that would betray him.

Rock solid, Renula continued. "You think I'm a fat fool, assigned to a backwater planet to serve out my years. I'm deeply offended, Captain, and you'll pay for that eventually. For now, we have work to do. You'll receive everything you need to eliminate Sungiver's enemy. You'll complete your mission. I'll see to it."

Mard's sneer lacked conviction. "I told you what Sungiver ordered."

Clapping a hand to her large bosom, Renula said, "So you said. Very clearly. If you'd like, I can send a recording of it to her. Counsellor Ullas can't eavesdrop on us out here. I'm equipped to let Sungiver do so."

"That was cruel. Unfriendly." Mard flung himself onto a chaise. He slammed a fist against a knee. "She had the nerve to tell me she believes some Rifle named Lannat came here to kill him and was killed himself. A fine sendoff. The woman's heartless."

"She is Sungiver."

Awash in self-pity, Mard made weak protest. "Oh, I didn't mean it. Listen, turn that damned thing off, will you? You've already got enough to have me fed to Sungiver's slinkcats five times; what more do you want?"

"Just so we understand each other." Renula turned away demurely, plunging a hand down the front of her robe to inactivate the recorder. Facing Mard again, she said, "Do you have any idea how to do it?"

"You think I sit around thinking about it? I try *not* to think about it. The one thing I can tell you is that we better succeed. And don't think I mean *I* when I say *we*. If we fail, Etasalou and Sungiver will be after both of us."

Renula was genuinely taken aback. "Why me?"

Mard mocked her. " 'Why me?' Because you're here, that's why. Because we both belong to Sungiver. Because if I fail and Etasalou catches me, d'you think for one minute I'm going down alone? So I lied about who's supposed to actually do the thing; you're still my support. Think about it. People like Etasalou and Sungiver use up people like us. The only reason they let us live at all is to do what they want done. I wish I was a sergeant again."

Pacing some more, Renula quickly saw the force of Mard's argument. She decided it was time to initiate self-protection measures. "Not that I feel I'm in any danger from my beloved leader, Sungiver, or anyone else, but because of my undying loyalty to her and to Lumin, I'll cooperate fully."

Mard seemed even more glum. Renula took a different tack. "Did you know Etasalou's niece is on Hire?"

"Everyone knows."

"Etasalou doesn't." Renula allowed herself a moment to relish Mard's astonishment, then went on. "Ullas keeps her hidden from him, right here in Court. The counsellor means to make her one of his concubines, I'm sure, but the resistance has kept his mind on other things."

"We can use that. Good."

"There's more. The emperor's son, the one named Dafanil is here, as well. In secret."

Blinking, Mard blurted questions. "Halib's son? You think we can use him? I mean, he's, you know, the son of the emperor. Wait, though: If we get involved with him, we could, you know, have a problem or something. The emperor. You know?"

"Your eloquence is matched only by your valor, Captain. All I'm saying is, the prince's presence is possibly useful. We'll have to use every advantage to make your mission succeed. Our first requirement is ready access to Etasalou. We'll use Lumin's medical assistance to establish your contact with him."

Reluctantly Mard agreed. "It's a start. I'll turn on the charm. Once he trusts me, we're in the clear."

Not bothering to respond, Renula opened the door, led the way back inside. She continued on, opening the opposite door to the hall. Taking the hint, Mard left without breaking stride. Alone, Renula wondered how the man could be so obtuse about the multitude of previous hints. She muttered to herself, "If I said 'your' mission, 'your' plan once, I said it a hundred times. And the fool keeps answering 'we.' It won't do. Simply won't do."

Luck smiled on Renula. Within days Etasalou requested assistance to deal with a virus outbreak among his technicians. Feigning personal interest, she drew Mard along as part of her supervisory group. When she introduced Mard as a recent arrival from Atic, Etasalou surprised them both with his enthusiastic greeting. He explained, "One grows weary of the same faces, the same sights, the same conversations. I may not be welcome on Atic, but news of Atic is more than welcome here. Captain, would you join me for lunch? Tell me tales of Halib's court, the theater, the museums, personalities—anything."

At first glance, Mard was disappointed by the commander's

lack of height and slight stature. He'd never seen Etasalou in person, and he expected someone large, overwhelming. Nor had he expected anyone so affable. Swaggering, Mard followed Etasalou to a private dining room, where Etasalou ordered a full lunch, assuring his guest that it would take at least that long for a decent amount of news.

Mard strained to hide his elation. If there was one thing he knew, it was gossip. Getting close to Etasalou was practically accomplished.

All through lunch, Mard reveled in his role. Several times, however, he found himself revising a story because of its ethnic orientation. Mard knew no liners. In fact, he'd only met one, a yellow; on that occasion, Mard remembered, it had been impossible to avoid staring at the man's eyes. Sitting across from Etasalou was even worse. No matter where one looked, there was that near-black skin, defying the almost total racial homogeneity of the empire.

They were sipping a superb postdinner native brandy when Mard set his hook. "I have a confession to make, Commander. More than one, to be accurate. I have to tell you I harassed Doctor Renula shamelessly to arrange our introduction." He ostentatiously scanned the room. When he looked back to Etasalou, he took a long, deliberate sip of his brandy before asking "May I assume one can speak freely? One learns quickly that Hire's scarcest commodity is privacy."

Etasalou's gesture was confident. "No one eavesdrops on me, Captain."

"Exactly. Who'd dare? Very well: I have always believed the leader of Lumin should be a man. The Elemental Guard proves my point. The backbone of Lumin, the finest fighting force in the empire. Always commanded by the male leader of the faith. You should have been Lumin."

Smiling gently, but with eyes narrowed, Etasalou said, "I'm not averse to flattery, Captain, but I do expect it to have a point. What's yours? You mentioned confessions."

"Your niece, Nan Bahalt, is on Hire."

Sudden brightness in Etasalou's gaze lasered across the table at Mard, reached into his brain. Utterly immobile, silent, Etasalou stared.

Mard thought of steel. He wondered how he had ever thought of this bolt of black lightning as amiable. Listening to his guts shift in agitation, it suddenly occurred to him that the hundreds of pictures he'd studied had failed to hint at the magnetic force within the lean, compact figure. Worse, he smelled evil. He tasted it, a foulness coating his tongue, clotting on the roof of his mouth. He cursed himself for being afraid of Sungiver before knowing Etasalou. This was fright of another magnitude. This was being consumed.

Etasalou finally spoke, threat heavy in the slight voice. "I know Doctor Bahalt is here, so it's a pity: You've exposed yourself as an untrustworthy person, and to no purpose. Your effectiveness is ended before it began. Sungiver will be quite disappointed. You'll have to leave Hire."

"I can't go back there. I mean, not for quite a while. She wants . . . That is, Sungiver ordered me, said keep an eye on the niece. Doesn't, you know, trust her. That is, Sungiver didn't know about you when she sent Bahalt here . . . Doctor Bahalt; excuse me . . . and she—Sungiver, that is—she's afraid you two will get back together and the niece will be your agent. Help you, I mean. You know."

"Counsellor Ullas is quite wisely waiting for me to prove my loyalty to him. Meanwhile, he keeps Nan Bahalt's location a secret from me. It grieves me, but I can't blame him. Good security. As you would say: You know." Etasalou's smile turned almost sad.

"I know where she is. I can get a message to her. Arrange a meeting. Maybe. I think I can do that. I know I can speak to her. Take a message. You—" Mard had the presence of mind to bite down on the babble. He finished lamely. "I don't care about Ullas. I want to prove I'm loyal to you."

Etasalou was thoughtful. "Perhaps I misjudged you. I was shocked by your abandonment of Sungiver, but I rather displayed a similar flaw, didn't I? We have something in common. You know? But of course you do. And you know where my niece is hidden. Let's not have any messages to her just yet. In fact, don't let her know you've spoken to me. We'll surprise her later."

"I have other news."

"More? What a box of surprises you are, Captain."

"The man who opposed you on Paro—the Rifles captain named Lannat. He escaped an ambush on Atic. Some of us, loyal to you to the death, made the attempt. I alone survived, knocked unconscious." Mard watched carefully.

Etasalou leaned back a bit, cocked his head to the side. "Unconscious. Frightening. How did you escape capture?"

"Uh. Oh, they captured me. It was Sungiver's people who ruined our ambush, see?" Mard warmed to the story; Etasalou was paying close attention. "We had an elcar. The man driving panicked, left us. Sungiver's best interrogated me. Weeks. I don't have to tell you . . . I don't want to brag, but I fooled them all. I played along. You have lots of loyal supporters on Atic. I gave Sungiver names." Mard tried to wink. It turned into a nervous tic. "Dead people. I threw in some troops I knew made the escape to Hire. But no one she could get her hands on. She thinks I'm her man now. And she believes Lannat's dead. I don't."

Leaning forward, Etasalou closed on Mard, enjoying the way the other man paled. Smoothly, as if it were his sole purpose, Etasalou picked up the brandy flagon and served both glasses. He smothered laughter at Mard's sickly grin and trembling thanks. Etasalou said, "My congratulations, Captain. Very impressive. You'll forgive me for being so security conscious, but before you leave your i-wy will be inspected."

Shaking visibly, Mard nevertheless hoisted his glass with bravado. "Served on Hector, sir. One of the last off that rock. That is, to leave the post."

"Sungiver knew that, too, did she? You must have tricked her completely. I'll wager your real mission from her is to penetrate my laboratory, get details on what we're doing here. Am I right? Did I guess it?"

"More than that, Commander. Much more. That's the other confession I mentioned. She sent me here to kill you."

Backed hard against his chair, Etasalou widened his eyes in exaggerated disbelief. "She didn't. She wouldn't."

"I'm afraid it's true, sir. 'For the good of Lumin and the empire,' she said. Women. They don't understand anything."

"I'm afraid you're wrong about that. They're very dependable, once they know what's expected. Exactly like men. But I must excuse myself for a moment, Captain. Enjoy your brandy. We'll talk more when I return."

Mard's instincts fired off alarm signals like an electrical overload. It was difficult mustering enough strength in his knees to rise out of his chair. Etasalou waited patiently. Mard caught himself remembering the caged slinkcats inside Sungiver's compound. He heard himself blithering again. "I'm late getting back to Renula. Doctor Renula, I mean. You know—she brought me here? Lunch, we said. It was wonderful. Thank you. Look how the time's gone. Who'd believe it? I don't believe it. She expects me. We, you know, have to get back to Court."

"Wait. I insist." The whip-crack of Etasalou's words dropped Mard back into his chair like spilled grain. His forgotten brandy snifter tilted, dribbled aromatically on his bright scarlet jacket. Not even the closing *click* of the door latch stirred him.

CHAPTER 24

Laughing merrily, Doctor Renula entered the room on Commander Etasalou's arm. She immediately caught Mard's expression. Simpering amusement wobbled through several stages of degeneration, coming to rest, dull as a lead coin, in a worried frown. Etasalou disengaged her arm and eased her into the chair directly across from the captain and his stained jacket.

Mard offered no greeting.

Etasalou took position at the head of the table. "You have no idea how pleased I am to discover I have two such good friends at Court. Now, how can we be of service to each other?"

Renula glared at Mard, created an ingratiating flutter for Etasalou. "I'm not sure what you mean, Commander."

"You're too modest, Doctor; it's obvious you arranged for Captain Mard to meet me because you two have something in mind. I have the captain's word he was sent here as Lumin emissary specifically to murder me. You, as senior Lumin official on Hire, brought him here. If your goal is, indeed, my death, then strike. I'm here, unarmed. Or is it poison? Not that, surely; you wouldn't desecrate this fine brandy?" He refilled his glass, then Mard's, and got one from the bar for Renula. Pouring hers, he said, "I'll drink first." His look was enough to bring the other glasses high. Mard downed his in a gulp. After seeing that, Renula sipped hers.

Etasalou said, "I want my niece. That is a manner of family

229

honor and must be attended to. Remember that at all times. It exceeds all your inconsequential goals."

Mard answered enthusiastically, "That is our plan. And more."

Interrupting with a gesture, Etasalou rolled his eyes at Renula. "Such an incredible fellow. Always 'more.' An unending fountain. What else could there be?"

Renula seized the opportunity. "I must speak. If Mard hadn't confessed his assassination assignment, I would have informed you. I am a physician and a faithful servant of Lumin. I could never raise my hand against one of our leaders. Nor see one killed."

"But I am apostate, Doctor. Anathema. How can you not raise your hand?"

"Sungiver jeopardized my very existence by ordering your death. If I aided Mard in such a plot, Counsellor Ullas would have me executed. She knows that. Nevertheless, Ullas's days are numbered."

Etasalou's feigned unconcern evaporated. "And mine?"

Twin red spots lit up Renula's cheeks. Her hands twitched. "Ullas: I'm talking about Ullas. The people lose faith in him. The Seeker cultists who rebel against him grow strong, may well overthrow him. He will take Lumin down with him. I must prevent that, at any cost. The only person on Hire strong enough to crush the pagan rebels is yourself. I'm placing myself at your service. So is Captain Mard." She sent Mard a venomous glance. It went unnoticed because Mard was so fixated on Etasalou that his mouth hung open.

Etasalou told Renula, "Practical. I like that. What do you expect of me, after I overthrow Ullas?" He returned to Mard. "Don't look so shocked, Captain—or whatever you are. The time for shock is past. You're up to your gaudy epaulets in high treason now, and you'll perform or die."

Mard wanted only to please. "Captain now, sir. Sergeant on Hector."

Etasalou was already back to Renula. "I've told you I will have my niece, Nan Bahalt. Knowing that, what's your plan?"

"You said you knew Nan Bahalt was on Hire. I must assume you know Prince Dafanil is here, as well. I can drug him, make him appear ill. Ullas can't afford to have the emperor's son die while on Hire. The counsellor has high regard for Bahalt. He'll listen to me when I tell him I need her to minister to the prince. When we have the pair properly situated, your men can kidnap both. The counsellor will blame the resistance. And the Seeker cult. There will be vengeance."

Indeed there will, Etasalou thought. More like massacres, with attendant unrest. He dismissed that concern; the sabotaged data banks were being repaired quickly; information was available from many subsidiary sources. It was only a matter of time before even greater control of the population was possible. He returned to the matter at hand: Renula's plan was workable. He made a mental note to infiltrate an informant into her personal circle.

Letting his guests stew in silence, Etasalou considered the probable effect of kidnapping Prince Dafanil. Basically, it defanged Ullas, even if he correctly identified the kidnappers. The mere possibility of Dafanil's death would force Ullas's cooperation. If Ullas chose not to cooperate, it would inconveniently accelerate the date of his murder, but it could be accommodated. It would also cut the time available to properly restructure Dafanil.

The very notion was thrilling. Dafanil as surrogate emperor. What man ever had an emperor as servant?

From the sublime to the tawdry; Etasalou next considered Mard and Renula. They seemed malleable enough, albeit inept, although Renula showed raw cunning in her concept of a dual kidnapping. Mard was another matter. Shrewd, like most cowards, and absolutely amoral. Etasalou almost snickered, seized by an image of Mard transformed into a fearless fanatic. It was quite rich, really.

Surprisingly, it was Mard who broke the silence among the

trio. "People are saying your troops will be going into the field to destroy the Seeker rebels. Will you have enough personnel to stage the raid called for in Renula's plan? Is there time to train such a unit?"

"A good question, Captain. I see you were wasted as a sergeant. To answer both questions—yes." Etasalou wished he could tell them how easy it would be to dedicate a team to the plan. Sometimes the knowledge that, of all men, only he controlled the mind-altering facility was overwhelming. Not this day, however; not now. Today was dedicated to the delightful certainty that empire was within his grasp.

He scolded himself. First things first. One brought down an emperor patiently.

One also allowed time to savor the smaller victories as they were won.

Nan Bahalt. Traitor to family and cause, caught at last.

Lannat. Alive. On Hire.

Sungiver. She was probably right about Lannat. And if he lived on Hire, that explained a great deal about the effectiveness of the Free.

Yes. Nan Bahalt would provide more than revenge. She would bait Lannat.

What a joy. To see them transformed into willing slaves.

A surge of determination jerked Etasalou upright in his chair. "You are committed to me now. You, Doctor—you think you can dabble in this pool, then stand clear while Sungiver and I settle our differences. You, Captain—I have known many like you. Ambitious men, greedy to improve their lot. Those who remain true to my cause have suffered, but Etasalou shall lift them to triumph. Those who thought their ambitions more important than mine are dead. Or envy the dead. Remember that, and obey. What has passed between us here is forever secret. Absolutely. Neither my loyalists nor Lumin will ever know. Whatever plans either of you had to use this situation to your advantage, forget. We shall work well together. But you shall serve me."

White-faced, Mard and Renula swore loyalty in a spluttering explosion. They glanced at each other, seeking confirmation, reinforcement. In the expression of the other, however, each realized the full measure of their mutual helplessness. Stunned by how terribly their vision of this meeting was changed, they listened to Etasalou tell them they must contact him only through an intermediary. "The eltruck drivers who bring supplies to the laboratory are my men. Any of them will pass on a request for my attention. My medical personnel will deliver any instructions I have for you. Mard: You say my loyalists on Atic said some of their comrades escaped to Hire. If they contact you, have nothing to do with them. They can only disrupt my plans at this time."

Half the trip back to Court in Renula's elcar passed in aching silence. As the suburban houses grew closer together, Mard found his voice. "You should have waited until we knew him better before telling him we could deliver Bahalt and Dafanil. I could have talked him into concessions."

"Oh, sure." Renula leaned forward to close the window between themselves and driver. To further assure privacy, she turned on a music channel, loud. Leaning toward Mard, her continuing sarcasm was blistering. "Had him eating out of your hand. Moron. You actually told him you were sent here to kill him? Talk about rushing things. It's a good thing I had my plan. One more word from you and we'd never have left that place. You, an assassin. You're so stupid you can't kill time."

"Who're you calling stupid? If you hadn't butted in, I'd have talked him into doing the whole job for us. Now we have to drug an emperor's son, arrange for Etasalou's own niece to nurse him, and then kidnap them. Thank you very much, Doctor Volunteer."

"At least I had a plan. All you could do was snivel."

Mard snorted, turned to look down on the city rushing past underneath them. "Every suicide has a plan. Well, I'm not dying for yours. Or his. I've survived by turning other people's ambitions to my own advantage, and I'll do it again here. From now on, Captain Mard will know who's doing what and how. Etasalou may get to be emperor or he may not, but I'm going to live, no matter."

To her own surprise, Renula found herself agreeing with Mard. His survival was proof of considerable underhanded skill. She jutted her jaw, balled her fists. If Captain Mard thought he was the only one determined to survive and benefit from all this, he was in for a very rough ride.

Counsellor Ullas looked down at Prince Dafanil, so still on his hospital bed, and moaned softly. For a moment, Ullas looked worse than the patient. Without changing position, he spoke to Doctor Renula, who stood opposite him. "What is it? How soon will he be well?"

"An unknown virus. We're working to identify it. We're treating the symptoms: low-grade fever, recurrent nausea, dizziness, general weakness. These things tend to run their course in a few days. He should be fine in a week, two at most, with proper care."

Ullas huffed indignantly. "You'll see he gets proper care. Anything. This is the emperor's son, you understand? The emperor doesn't even know the boy's here. If I have to inform him that his son is ill, has been on my planet for months, unreported—" He broke off. "Light, look at him. Two days ago he was sturdy as an eltruck. How lifeless his hair is. Blond people always look sicker, don't they? Their hair goes lank. Unattractive. You're sure he'll be all right?"

"Quite sure." Renula frowned. "My only concern is a secondary infection. This is a hospital. There are other people, other diseases about."

"Move him then. What's wrong with you? Get him out of here." Ullas gestured. "Doesn't all this equipment do anything? Disinfect the place. Sterilize the air. You staff people: Get out. You, close that door behind you." He glared at scurrying backs.

Renula remained commandingly calm. "I anticipated your

concern, Counsellor. Rooms are prepared in the old Imperial Quarter built for the prince's great-grandfather's visit. The southwest corner of Court gets full sun, and six floors up, there's always fresh air, which reduces troublesome secondary infection problems. It even has its own dispensary. Antiquated, but it's being equipped for our needs. I do have one unfilled need, however."

"Name it."

"Full-time care. Although I dislike the woman personally, we have a superior caregiver on hand in Doctor Bahalt. She was on Emperor Halib's personal staff, you know. I'm sure the prince is in no danger, but should something unexpected occur, it would be well if we could assure the emperor that someone he trusted was in attendance."

"Trust? He exiled her."

"Not the emperor, Counsellor; Sungiver. Purely as an example. Anyhow, I'll be supervising constantly."

Reluctantly Ullas conceded. "Use her as you see fit." He waved at the staff gathered in the hall. "Get the prince moved. I have things to attend to."

By sunset Renula and Ullas were together again, standing at a window in a luxurious suite. Silhouetted in the far southwest, the uppermost peaks of the Marnoffar Mountains scarred the horizon. Renula wondered if someone of the Free stood on one of those peaks, looking back.

Ullas intruded on her thoughts. "The first floor is cleared of all occupants, as are the two floors beneath this one. Advisors are billeted on all three vacated floors. All stairs and elevators are sealed off. So are all first-floor windows and the rear door. Above us, on the roof, is a railgun with radar and IR aiming controls. You and your caregivers will come and go by elcar, just like the upper-story Advisors."

Renula felt sick. She tried not to think of Etasalou's reaction to such tight security. Still, he would demand an answer; it would be better if she could quote Ullas, put the blame on him. "Are my personnel in danger?"

Chewing at his lower lip, Ullas hesitated. "It has nothing to do with Prince Dafanil. It's her." He jerked his head to indicate Nan, busy with her patient in the adjoining bedroom. Ullas pulled Renula closer. "Commander Etasalou hates her." Renula pretended disbelief. Ullas went on urgently. "She broke away from family; he can never forgive that. So long as I hold her, she remains a valuable bargaining chip. I put nothing past him. Protect her. And yourself, of course."

The last was such a belated afterthought it infuriated Renula. The desire to repay this last insult, as well as decades of slights and other insults, overcame good sense. "Trust our zeal, Counsellor. May I say, I admire your personal courage." That got his attention. She pressed ahead. "If anything happens to Doctor Bahalt, Sungiver herself will be personally involved. Remember, she sent Bahalt to your planet to pursue her atonement. We of Lumin know and love Doctor Bahalt because she resisted the apostate Etasalou. You've protected her out of pure altruism, not even troubling Sungiver with confidential notice that Etasalou shelters with you. That takes great character, especially since we all know how unreasonable Sungiver can be. Some have said vindictive; I feel that's far too harsh. Don't you?"

Ullas looked to the ceiling as if wondering if the railgun there was sufficient protection. He told Renula, "Prepare to leave here. I want her and the prince on Kull."

Renula cursed herself. Transferring Bahalt to Kull would make the situation tenfold worse. She reached out a pleading hand, almost touched Ullas. "So far away? Could you be comfortable, knowing two people as important as the prince and Doctor Bahalt were out of your sight? Beyond your immediate control?"

She saw his eyelids flicker and forced herself to shut up. The argument is made, she told herself, repeating it, over and over.

Ullas turned, took two steps toward the door. Facing her again, he scanned the room to be certain no one was within earshot. He bent forward to speak, snarling long face projected on the end of the long neck. "I have always been a faithful Lumin adherent. I will not lose what I have worked for over a disgraced doctor. You are Lumin. You will protect me by protecting what is mine. Heal the prince. Safeguard Bahalt. Fail me in any particular and you fail Lumin. Only I shall live to make your excuses to Sungiver."

CHAPTER 25

Her robe a swirl of Lumin's senior reds and yellows, Nan swept into the room. The young man lying on the bed glowered. Before she could speak, he said, "I slept well. I kept down my dinner. Breakfast was awful, except for the fruit, which was merely unripe. It seems to be staying down; however, I took my medicine. Is that it? Did I get the morning catechism correct? Everything in order?"

Keeping the smile in place, Nan continued on to the bank of monitors ranged on the bedroom's former bookshelves. "Perfectly, Highness. Lowered temperature—still above normal, though. Good blood pressure, respiration." She turned to face him. Blond hair framed a pale face. His eyes, a neutral blue-gray, peered at her from under a pronounced brow and slim, carefully contoured eyebrows. A small, bud-shaped mouth held a surly pout. The latter, and the arrogant assurance of the calculating eyes, irritated Nan more than the complaining voice. She frowned, pointing at a black box. It displayed small numbers in purple lights. "Muscle tone. As soon as you're on your feet, I want you getting more exercise. A young man like you, with those readings—shame on you."

Anger flashed across his face. "Prince Dafanil. How dare you address me without name or title? Where is your training? No one scolds me."

Concentrating on the monitors, Nan answered, "I apologize for informality, Prince. As for scolding you, it is my duty in Lumin to make well the sick, heal the injured. I'll scold you and your father, as well, to perform that duty. You'll scold me quick enough if I don't hold up my end of the bargain." She faced him then, defiant.

Prince Dafanil colored. The reaction only lasted a moment, and then the reddened features sagged. To her great surprise, he mustered a wan smile. "I'm sicker than I thought. It's terrible to be so weak that even anger weakens one. Still, it was not any wisdom in your words that disarmed me, Doctor. It was the image you created in my mind. I'd give anything to see someone stand up to my father."

The sudden bitterness, as much as the weary surrender, brought Nan to his side. Solicitous, she touched the c-button attached to the head of the bed. The red transmitter light blinked on. Nan ordered a stimulant bath, then told Dafanil, "Mentioning your father was the greater error, Prince. I broke our agreement."

"About not mentioning him?" Dafanil found another smile. "It's impossible for me to have a conversation without him becoming part of it. You're not the only one sensitive to his rather pervasive presence. Or eager to bask in it."

Because she was so conditioned to expect insult, Nan took instant offense. "I was honored to be on your father's medical staff. He's a gentleman."

Now Dafanil's ego was threatened. Renewed irritation put acid in his tone. "Are Lumin's hot colors so important? Are you afraid you'll be taken off my case and reverted back to junior blue and green?"

Rigid, hands bunched in fists at her sides, Nan glared. "That's a lie."

Rolling his head to the side, facing the wall opposite Nan, Dafanil suddenly seemed very vulnerable. "I know about family difficulties, Prince Dafanil. I understand your pain."

Dafanil's voice was hollow. "Doctor Renula made it perfectly clear that your permission to wear the senior colors is a function of your assignment to my case. Think about that, Doctor Bahalt. Everyone touched by my life measures success or failure by that contact. Yet the source of that godlike influence over human lives isn't within me. My father is the power, and he despises me."

Nan marched around the bed, stood arms akimbo, looking down at her patient. Then, as if coming to a decision, she sat heavily on the windowsill. "All right," she said, "spit it out. I'm tired of slipping and sliding around the issue. You've been in this room over a week, and at least once a day, I get the long sighs and the 'poor-me' drill. Talk to me. What's the problem between you and your father?"

Shock twitched back and forth across Dafanil's face. It was a wildly comic expression of surprise, and Nan had trouble keeping a straight face. Dafanil spluttered. "The imperial family doesn't air its concerns. Certainly not with Etasalou's disgraced niece."

Fear sharpened Nan's thinking. She forced calmness. "Exactly what do you know about me? My situation?"

"Prettily phrased: 'situation.' You people are all alike. You grow so used to having things your way you can't believe it's possible that everything isn't as you wish. Half the people in Court know all about you. Everyone knows Etasalou's running some secret laboratory out in the Fols Hills. What very few people know is that Etasalou knows you're here. He just doesn't know exactly where. I believe that's all that's keeping you alive."

Dafanil's sly threat was comically insignificant. What could he know of the true horror of Etasalou? Laughter touched the back of Nan's throat. It burned, the touch of hysteria. Scenes that refused to come in focus swirled past her inner vision: patients, strapped to skeletal beds of gleaming metal and crisp streets, shaved heads studded with cranial probes. Wires, like obscene puppetry strings, trailing away to looming machines. Dials, luminous displays, the electronic noises of monitors. And screams. Every vision, every muddled memory, punctuated by agony and misery, screams that cried unspeakable abuse.

In the midst of that, she heard her uncle's voice, cutting, wounding: "This is science, Doctor. We create for Lumin. For our family's glory. It is why you were born."

How many times had those terrible, suggestive wraiths drifted across her memory, just beyond her grasp?

Never before in those rememberings—*never*—had she heard her uncle.

"Answer me. Are you all right?" Dafanil was up on an elbow, pale with exertion. Concern twisted his features.

The demand jerked Nan back to the present. With Etasalou's words ringing in her ears, she mumbled assurance. She said the first thing that came into her mind. "How did you find out about me?"

"Once again, your assumed superiority fails you." Dafanil sprawled back on his bed. Slowly recovering her own composure, Nan noted he seemed a bit more alert. Evidently, conflict brightened his outlook. Particularly when he controlled the game. He continued. "Do you know my reputation?"

Irritated now, Nan answered with asperity. "Prince Dafanil is reputed to be a playboy."

He winked at her. "Accurate, as far as it goes. I prefer authority. I'm an authority on all human appetites. My life work is to discover what people like. Especially what *I* like."

"I see no connection between what you like and how you ever learned anything about me."

Holding up a chiding finger, Dafanil said, "The finest thing in the world—from my perspective as the world's greatest authority on my likes—is a woman. *Women*, actually. The prettier the better, of course, but one learns not to penalize one's self; appearances do deceive. Surprise abounds."

"Charming."

"If one would learn, one must study. Counsellor Ullas has servants. He has no idea what they hear, much less what they talk about."

"You seduced one of his female servants?"

"You have a genuine talent for crudity hidden under all that primly medical blather. I did not question. I listened. And certainly not just any servant. Light above, what do you take me for? A person with experience in these matters seeks someone with access. His private secretary's maid is quite attractive."

Nan stood up, arms crossed over her chest. "You're a spy."

A quick flash in Dafanil's eyes warned Nan she'd struck a nerve. Nevertheless, he answered easily. "Everyone is. It's a particular necessity for me, as the most important homeless man in the empire. Anyhow, the woman tells me things Counsellor Ullas says in private."

Nan nodded. "I only met your father once. Still, I think he'd be very disappointed."

Dafanil laughed so hard it set off a coughing fit that doubled him over. Nan offered a glass of water. He swallowed some, got his breath back. "My father despises all three of us. None of us ever had a chance to prove we're capable."

"Your mother—pardon me; mothers—have so little influence?"

"Less than none." Dafanil's sudden willingness to speak of his family surprised Nan. "Three brothers, three mothers; if anyone ever doubts that power corrupts, they need look no further than the three wives of Emperor Halib." He paused, sent her a sharp look. Then he turned spiteful. "You asked why I'm here on Hire. The clearest lesson I learned from my parents is that I'm not wanted. My father says I'm not fit to take his place. My mother says I failed her because I won't be emperor. She blames me for her loss of favor. What that tells me is that I must find favor elsewhere. Everywhere. She taught me to enjoy myself, Doctor. The counsellor offers me great entertainment. It costs him very little, in the grand scheme of things, and if I do somehow gain the throne, he thinks I'll remember and be kind. The ruler of every planet in the galaxy hosts me and my brothers on those terms. Except Syrac. I won't go there."

After a long pause Nan said, "You've been convincing Counsellor Ullas that you need support. For when your father dies."

Dafanil fixed her with a gaze that was doubly frightening for its completely unexpected coldness. "That would be called treason. A person could find theirself beheaded."

Nan swallowed past a suddenly tight throat. She determined to hide her growing concern. Archly she said, "Which does Prince Dafanil intend as the greater threat, beheading or a continuing onslaught of atrocious grammar?"

The persistent peeps and tweets of the monitors chipped at Nan's nerves as Dafanil's gaze continued probing at her. She fought growing concern by analyzing him. He had no power, yet all feared him because of what he might become. Unwanted, distrusted, seen by all as something to be controlled. Nan found herself pitying him. Even so, she knew she would never turn her back on him. When he spoke, there was amusement in his manner, but he looked very weary again. He said, "Sometimes—very infrequently—I meet someone who makes me wish I could be an ordinary person. Normally I hurt them immediately. It's a kindness. It forces them to get as far from me as possible. This time has to be different. We are both prisoners here. This miserable sickness confines me. Your uncle's hatred throws you in here with me. That, and your skills. Whatever else comes of our incarceration, nothing must come of our association. We will not 'get better acquainted.' " He inhaled sharply as he finished, launched another fierce coughing spell. Once more Nan quelled it, got him to sip some water. When he finished, his breath rasped and sweat beaded his forehead.

Nan ordered humidifier therapy for the cough to be followed

by a medicated bath. He thanked her with a slight nod, and she put on a smile she knew must be as false as paint. She said, "We'll get some soothing material down into your throat and lungs. The bath will be mildly stimulating. I'll be back to check on you right after."

Dafanil shook his head. "I've been sick before. Never like this. You don't know what's got its hooks in me. It's not like Renula to entrust my care to a subordinate, no matter how well qualified you are. We both know that. So tell me: Has she been openly speculating on the chances of my death?"

"Don't be melodramatic. You're sick, but there's nothing whatever to suggest you won't be better soon. No, we don't know the cause. We're treating symptoms. But you're nowhere near death, and you won't be. You're my patient, and the word doesn't distinguish between nobility and poverty. You'll be cured because I damned well say so."

Dafanil's lips twitched in what might have been a smile. "Leave one absolute ruler and walk right into the clutches of a tyrant."

The arrival of two nurses stopped Nan's retort. Both nurses were burly males. Lumin trained a select group to act as security personnel as well as qualified caregivers. They were quite handy sometimes, Nan mused, as they swung into action. One fitted a transparent mask over Dafanil's nose and mouth. A hose led from the device to a small machine that looked like a food blender. After a quick consultation with Nan, the nurse used a pipette to pour minute measures of three liquids into the blender. A few drops of water completed that job. At the flick of a switch, a high, barely audible whine filled the room. The liquid in the glass container trembled for a moment and was transformed into an opaque mist. It migrated up the tube, became part of Dafanil's breathing. At first contact, he frowned slightly, then relaxed.

The second nurse finished inspecting the monitors and making notes. He, too, spoke to Nan. "The inhalant will stabilize and correct the respiration anomalies. My interpretation of blood chemistry, pressure, respiration rate, and EEG records makes me think he's suffering stress and short periods of depression." He held up a band of paper, covered with multicolored squiggled lines. "Look at these brainwave patterns; see if you agree with me."

Nan's throat worked convulsively. The EEG charts, so suddenly thrust in her face, triggered a repeat of the terrifying memories at the depths of her mind. She looked away from the chart, fought them back. "I see. You're right."

The nurse shrugged. "Only natural, under the circumstances. I'd suggest we try a brighter, livelier light color in here. I'll requisition psychocolor bulbs for the light fixtures and rig a connection to the EEG. When signs of depression show up, it'll adjust the illumination for hue and intensity. I can do the same thing with a warm-fuzzy lighting for stress indication, if you'd like."

"His stress levels are well within acceptable norms. Let him work that out himself. You have something in mind for bathing?"

"A sponge bath, as soon as the inhalant's finished." He grinned. "Not much point in aromatherapy if his nose is stuffed full of that other junk. His chart indicates a rising depression level the past few minutes. Whatever you two were talking about bothered him. More than he showed, I suspect."

Nan made a face. "These machines know too much. A bunch of tattletales."

Tactfully, the nurse merely continued. "I think a mild skin stimulant bath—in keeping with the improved breathing, you know? A mild scent, nostalgic. Meadows, forests—something outdoors, natural?"

"Not for this man. Make it very light, but he'll be most at home with rich foods, fine wine. A hint of one of the milder narcotics."

The nurse's eyebrows rose. "You want an inhalant narcotic in the bath medium?"

"Absolutely not. Just a reminiscent scent. Do you have something in your medkit?"

"Sure. Any preference?"

"Your choice. I doubt if you can find one he won't know."

They exchanged knowing looks, and Nan made her good-byes to Dafanil.

It was late evening when Nan returned to make her final call of the day on him. He looked up from his book, put it aside. She felt his eyes on her as she checked the various monitors. When she turned, he gestured at the chair beside his bed. "I have to talk to you. I wasn't entirely honest with you earlier today. I neglected to tell you something I think you should know."

"I suspect there's a lot of that in your life," Nan said dryly.

"Quick mouth. Outruns good judgment. Perhaps I'll just keep my thoughts to myself."

The voice and manner were light enough, but something about the set of Dafanil's jaw warned Nan that there was genuine cruelty buried in his words. She made amends. "Idle conversation, Prince. From what you told me—"

He interrupted. "What I told you assumed you wouldn't throw my confidences in my face. Don't do it again. Now I want to talk to you about your friend Lannat."

Taken completely by surprise, Nan stepped back, fist to her mouth, stifling an exclamation. The reaction pleased Dafanil. He beamed. "More friend than most, I see. I thought so. You were told he escaped on Atic? No one's ever been identified as one of his accomplices. Nor has he ever been seen again. I assume you've been told he died."

Nan shrank under the rapid-fire telling of Lannat's tale. Her voice cracked. "He's alive. I won't believe he's not."

"Good for you. You should believe. I believe."

She was beside him in an instant, hands fluttering, only discipline preventing her grabbing him. "You've heard something? Seen him?"

"Nothing so concrete, I'm afraid. But I know my father. He

admires your Captain Lannat very much. If my father lost a favorite ring, he'd turn Atic backward on its axis until he found
it. Yet Captain Lannat goes missing and, after a decent interval,
is pronounced dead. Oh, there was an investigation. Going
through the motions. I believe he lives. I believe my father had
further use of him." He stopped and looked out the window,
signifying the conversation was ended.

Nan was having none of it. "There's more. I know there is.
You didn't open this subject just to tell me to have faith. I want
the rest."

He turned back to face her very slowly. "I'm trying very
hard to be pleasant with you. I'm the emperor's outcast son but
his son nevertheless. You do not make demands of me."

"You're talking about someone I love, someone who may
have been taken from me. What do you expect? I *care*."

Dafanil nodded. Very softly he said, "Oh, I understand that.
I think I hate you for it. But I'll be patient. This time. Very well,
then; here's a question for you. If you were emperor, and your
deadliest enemy had just escaped your clutches, taking with
him scientific secrets that could destroy your empire, wouldn't
you want to get rid of that enemy?"

Nan nodded, uncomfortable with the changed drift of the
conversation.

Dafanil went on. "Your captain was instrumental in Commander Etasalou's downfall; the empire sings his praises for
that, despite his subsequent disgrace. Why, of all twelve planets, would the emperor approve this one for your penance?
Could he have known Etasalou was here? And, knowing that,
would the emperor dispatch someone to terminate the commander? Someone who knew how desperately the commander
hates the niece who abandoned her family, her liner tradition,
to fall in love with a nonliner enemy of her uncle? Try to imagine it, Doctor, envision the tiny pawns, spread out on the board,
all racing about, convinced they're doing the right thing. No,
no, dear Doctor, take my word for it; your Captain Lannat is
here on Hire, waiting for his opportunity to kill the wicked

ogre—that's your uncle—and save the damsel in distress—
that's you. I wonder if you'll both live happily ever after."

Stammering, too frightened to remember Dafanil's warning
about manners, Nan said, "Y-you're making this up. Imagining. That's . . . that's diabolical. That's inhuman."

Dafanil beamed. "That's my dad."

CHAPTER 26

While appearing to stroll casually along the street separating
the area called Old Town and Court's outer wall, Mard studied
the wing housing Nan Bahalt and the emperor's son. Helter-
skelter Old Town, with its unique winding streets and odd
buildings, was a popular shopping destination and tourist at-
traction. Mard's concentration was reserved for Court, and his
quarry. He was ill-prepared for the approach of a man who was
clearly trying to appear casual—and failing badly.

The man said, "Friends sent me to contact you. Act as if you
know me. We're being watched by the Peace/Order camera on
the roof behind me. *Don't look at it.*"

It took all of Mard's will to keep his gaze fixed on the nervous face in front of him. The possibilities of the situation
showered down on him. Burning memories of Sungiver's deceit insisted this man was sent by someone—Renula?—to pro-
voke him into some sort of admission. Could this be something
staged by the emperor's Advisors? Etasalou had warned that
only he could initiate contact; could this be it? More likely the

idiot hardcore loyalists, the ones Etasalou insisted must be avoided.

Indecision coiled in Mard's guts like a snake.

Before the man could say any more, Mard indicated they should walk, making a jerking movement with his head, rolling his eyes. He stepped off. The man fell in beside him. When he tried to speak, Mard cut him off abruptly. "Whatever you want to discuss will have to wait. I don't talk out here in the streets." He cut a warning glance at the reptile-eye of a Peace/Order camera swiveling atop a light standard. His new companion nodded.

At each step, Mard found his quandary worsening. If he asked the man who sent him, and it was Etasalou, the commander would flay him for asking a question that might expose his liaison man. If he didn't ask, he couldn't be sure what to say or how to say it.

Mard looked at the man, trying to glean some clue. Instead of that, he suddenly realized the man was studying him. Although nervous himself, the man managed a slight smile. He sounded reassuring. "We think you can help us. Any man who was on Hector is important. I was sent to tell you we could use your help."

Mard gnawed the inside of his lip. Of course. The contact picked the meeting place. That had to mean it was under surveillance by any number of associates. It didn't make any difference if they were Sungiver's people, or the emperor's or Ullas's, or . . .

Pain ripped across Mard's stomach. What if the man was a rebel? The Peace/Order cameras had them on film.

Trap. *Trap.*

Mard searched wildly, determined to find the surveillance team. Whining, hissing, an elbus came to a stop in front of him. Seizing the moment, Mard grabbed the man responsible for his trouble and practically threw him aboard just as it started to leave. He followed so closely the pressure of his body almost tumbled them both into the driver's lap. Mard was too busy assuring himself no one followed to notice. Even as they extricated themselves from a tangle with the fare box, Mard was inserting his buy card. By the time the contact regained his balance and swung about angrily, Mard was pointing at a seat. For several blocks they rode that way, touching each other and worlds apart, silent.

But Mard's mind enjoyed no respite. He thought of how many times he'd been betrayed, how his every effort to serve the powerful resulted in treachery. Was it Sergeant Mard who botched the attempt to kill Lannat? Absolutely not. It was only his own finely tuned skills that allowed him to escape. And then what? No one to turn to, nowhere to hide. Who could blame a man for seeking refuge? So what if it was within the enemy camp? What could Etasalou expect from a man abandoned? After all, it was Sungiver who had recruited him to spy on Etasalou in the first place. But did Sungiver treat him right? That was a laugh.

Now this. Did this man represent opportunity? Or was he just another agent of betrayal?

They were clear of Old Town by then, well into Liskerta.

A huge building loomed ahead. The library. Like Court itself, the accumulated construction of generations. Mard had seen the inside once, during one of Renula's familiarization tours. Despite crushing boredom at the time, one image remained clear in his mind. Seemingly unending aisles, intersecting, crisscrossing, dimly lit, stretching for light-only-knew how many miles.

The perfect place for an unobserved conversation.

Mard rose and stepped to the exit. When the other man followed, Mard's confidence soared; he was now in charge. He even smiled, although careful to keep it hidden. For all their dishonesty and bullying, none of those powerful adversaries had really bested Sergeant Mard. He frowned, corrected himself: Captain Mard.

This problem would be handled, too.

Someone was in for a hard lesson.

The contact man wasn't a complete fool. He moved away as soon as they stepped down from the elbus, making his way to a nearby shop. Pretending to examine the merchandise, he watched Mard cross the street and climb up the steps into the building.

From inside the library, Mard watched him come. No one followed or appeared interested. Mard prided himself on being just that extra little bit careful. It marked the true survivor in the world of intrigue, he told himself, as he led the way into the maze of aisles. Slowly, giving the other man a chance to follow, he hiked deeper and deeper into the building's heart.

Mard stopped at a peculiar little cul-de-sac, an almost hidden research room with a small reading desk. It had a chair attached. A ridiculously dim reading light gleamed from a wall fixture.

Only someone walking the short aisle perpendicular to the entrance could possibly see in.

Positioning the man behind the desk, Mard said, "All right, let's get to the heart of this. Who sent you to me?"

Swallowing, the man said, "I'm here to speak to you as a member of the rebellion."

Drawing himself erect, Mard glared. "I should call for Advisors right now. Why would I have anything to do with you rabble? I'm loyal to Lumin. You people are all Seeker cult."

Bending past Mard, the man peered up and down the aisle, assuring no one was close by. When he straightened, rehearsed speech poured out of him. "Our information tells us you were Elemental Guard, even serving on Hector, but you come to Hire as emissary for Sungiver. You've had audience with Counsellor Ullas and Commander Etasalou. You must have discovered by this time that neither Ullas nor Etasalou trusts you. The surveillance on you is occasional so far, but be assured that, as you grow more important to them, the 'security' around you will become ever tighter. More than that, you know, as we know, that Ullas's reign on Hire is collapsing. You must also have heard, as we have, that Commander Etasalou's project is consummate evil." The rote presentation broke off. In its place came an equally stilted closure. "We of the underground favor the Seeker, but we have no quarrel with Lumin. There is room in the light for all. The Free suggest that you consider joining us."

The utter stupidity stunned Mard. He had no idea how long he simply stared, catching himself only when the expression in front of him turned from nervously determined to quizzical. Mard acted a cool cynicism he didn't feel. "You expect me to believe you're one of the hill-fighters I hear about? You're no warrior."

Discipline broke under insult. "Not everyone carries a sword, Captain. Without information, any organization is blind. An infiltrator can do more harm than a hundred armed men. I'm sure they taught you that."

Mard felt hot, as if he stood in front of a device sending rays into his body, setting his blood afire.

"I'm sure they taught you that."

Spoken in anger. Inadvertent. How could the underground have learned of his connection with the Guard? Certainly they couldn't know of Hector! The meeting with Ullas was common knowledge, and anyone could have heard he went to Etasalou's facility with Renula.

In a flash of comprehension, Mard understood that, no matter what he said or did, even if he called for Advisors to arrest the man, his freedom was gone. From this moment forward, someone would own him. He would be a prisoner, held to one truth, with nowhere to run when that truth became untenable.

There was a way out.

There was no surveillance on the contact. No one followed them to the library, or inside. If the Peace/Order cameras caught anything, it was inconsequential. Simple denial of any actual meeting would stonewall further investigation. "This foolishness is over," he said. "In fact, it never happened."

As the contact had done earlier, Mard leaned out of the

cubby, looked down the aisle. He popped back inside, eyes wide. "There's someone coming. Is he one of yours?"

Pushing past the desk, coming abreast of Mard, the man peeked around the corner. He said, "There's no—" and stopped on a weird, high-pitched grunt.

Quickly Mard grabbed the man's collar at the back of his neck and yanked him upright. At the same time, he pulled back on the handle of the dagger jutting from the man's abdomen. When the weapon came free, Mard slammed it back into the unresisting figure, an up-angled blow just below the sternum. The aim was perfect, the slim, sharp blade penetrating all the way through the beating heart with little more effort than slicing a roast. The victim gasped, rose on tiptoe. Mard stepped back, withdrew the blade, prepared to strike again.

The man sagged. His eyes rolled up until nothing but white showed. Mard let go of his collar. The man was dead when he hit the floor.

With a jittering speed and thoroughness that surprised himself, Mard tidied up the scene. There was practically no blood on his victim and the slightest smear on the polished blade. Mard wiped the stained weapon clean on the corpse's trousers. He inspected it carefully before replacing it. Next he lifted the body onto the chair and laid it out in a natural sleeping position. With his handkerchief, he wiped down everything he might possibly have touched, including the outside edge of the wall where he pretended to look for the false intruder. Forcing a deep breath, he stepped back, surveyed his handiwork.

Something was wrong. He twitched impatience, darting looks along the aisle, trying to think what didn't look right.

A book. A man sleeping at a reading desk should have been reading. Mard yanked one from a shelf, meticulously wiped it off with the handkerchief, and placed it, open and facedown, by the body's right hand.

Then he fled.

CHAPTER 27

Counsellor Ullas frowned at the knock at the door of the Hall of Mediation. With a heavy sigh, he touched the c-button at his lapel. "Speak."

"A message, sir. From Sheriff Plon. He humbly requests a meeting in chambers."

"Why?"

"A security matter, sir. Very important, he said."

Ullas curled a lip. Sheriff Plon's definition of importance lacked balance. Still, the man was thorough and dedicated. It wouldn't do to disregard him. "I'll be there in a while. Get out."

When he ambled into the official chambers, three people waited, Sheriff Plon and two Advisors. Plon was almost a caricature contrast to his master. Where Ullas was tall, spare, and pale, his chief security officer was short, broad, and florid. The younger men were unremarkable, save for natural nervousness. Plon's barely contained excitement surprised Ullas. Normally the man was as stolid as bricks.

"Well, Sheriff," Ullas said, "what news is so heavy it takes three of you to deliver it?"

Positively swollen with importance, Plon blustered. "I'd rather show you, Counsellor. We've set up a screen and a holovid." He pointed to Ullas's right. Ullas didn't like surprises, and he despised people who arranged them. Anticipating the lecture to follow this impertinence, he sat down without another word.

In seconds, the Advisors had the room darkened, the projector running.

Captured in living color, Captain Mard strutted down the street, taking in the sights. Ullas was forming the words to question this waste of time when the sheriff said, "Watch the man in the green jacket, Counsellor. Coming toward Captain Mard. See how his attention is on Mard, how he ignores everything else?"

Unimpressed, Ullas held impatience in check. Suddenly his eyes narrowed, watching Mard initiate the scramble to board the bus. As the pair acted their way into the library, he muttered under his breath. The screen went black.

Ullas rose, spun, and snarled at Plon. "Where are the pictures from inside?"

"On another disk, Counsellor. It'll only take a minute."

"Minute be damned. I want to know what they did, what they said. Move."

Voice quivering, the sheriff said, "We have footage of them wandering about. They show nothing that seems important. Then we have this." The screen leaped to life. Ullas settled back into his chair mechanically, completely immersed in the scene unfolding in the tiny reading alcove. The voices of the agent and Mard echoed through the vast space of Chambers, adding an eerie, cinematic aura to the already horrific action. Only when Mard disappeared, backing out of camera range, did Ullas speak. "My city library. Right there, among books. The filth committed murder in a library. Desecration. What kind of beast is he? Get him. *Get him!*" After the shout, Ullas shivered, gripped the edge of the table. Voice fallen to a near whisper, gaze still fixed on the empty screen, he said, "Have these two Advisors bring him to me. They will tell him nothing. Get him."

Several minutes later, seated again, but still looking only at the screen, Ullas asked, "Who is the dead man?" He had to turn from the screen to get a response.

Stammering so badly he sounded as suffering hiccups, Plon said, "H-his identification p-papers are f-false, sir. We-we're investigating. F-fingerprints, retina scan, and D-DNA are all c-correct, according to the l-lifeline on the b-body, but it's not really h-him. The name on his d-documents is really that of a c-child killed in an accident over t-twenty years ago."

"This isn't possible. How could he have papers? Fingerprints, retina scans, and DNA samples are taken at birth, entered in the computers. Everything required in a lifeline is linked to that information. You tell me we have a man with a false lifeline, a man not in our computers? Have you lost your mind?"

"No, sir. Please, Counsellor, understand; we just found the body a few hours ago. The Peace/Order diskers were able to produce the recorded data from the library alcove within minutes, naturally. It took a great deal longer to backtrack through all the other library cameras to discover when both men entered the building. Then we had to examine hours of disktime to catch them getting off the bus. Then—"

"A matter of minutes. All you had to do was feed either man's image into a disk reader. The computer can pick a suspect off a Peace/Order camera disk in seconds. Everyone knows that. What's wrong with you?"

"Nothing, sir. I mean, my diskers have no readers in that district. We asked for them in our last budget request, and—"

"No excuses, Plon. Results. I will have results."

Plon forged on. "Sir, we located their original meeting, before the bus. My sincere apologies for the time it took. Nevertheless, sir, we used that unfortunate delay to check personnel files on the central computer to establish the dead man's identification. That's when we discovered it."

"It? Discovered it? What?" Ullas gripped the table.

Gulping, Plon said, "The central data banks. Penetrated. The backup system, too. Records altered. Known deceased purporting to be living people. Living people recorded as dead. We're investigating."

"You mean Yasil—the attack." Ullas made a threat of the statement.

"No, sir. Central. Here. Liskerta."

Dangerously calm, Ullas asked, "You're examining all signs of access to the computers?"

By now Plon was bathed in sweat. He mopped at it as he responded. "When the Free attacked the computer facilities in Yasil, someone knew how to link with Central. They also knew how to make the computer erase any indication of trespass, as well as any records altered. We only realized what was happening when today's cross-check of names brought up the dead boy. The man killed by Captain Mard made the mistake of claiming the same hometown as the boy whose name he took. As soon as we discovered the fraud, we investigated further. It turns out that no one knew the murder victim longer than three years. Beyond that, nothing. All other personal history in the data bank was a complete fabrication. It's as if he were born full grown, three years ago."

"This is a pivotal moment, Sheriff. We are confronting a crime that cannot be mediated. The security of our culture is at risk. You are in charge of the mission to save it. All computer data files will be verified. Everyone on the planet must be cross-checked. I want technicians in here before the hour is out. I want a terminal here for my personal access to central data. While you arrange that, bring me a printout of the murdered agent's lifeline."

With the alacrity of a man scenting possible redemption, or at least escape, Plon burrowed into a pocket, produced a neatly folded sheaf of paper. He extended it to Ullas with the expression of a scolded spaniel. "I thought you might want to see it, Counsellor. I brought it with me."

Ullas took it with a short nod. The sheriff beamed. Then he trotted off on his errands, heavy footsteps thudding into the distance.

It took no more than an hour to hastily rig the computer access Ullas demanded. In that time, and to the consternation of the assembled technicians, the security personnel, and the counsellor himself, all record of the dead man was gone from the data banks. It was as if he never existed.

Counsellor Ullas bellowed threats at the just-returned Sheriff Plon. He cursed everyone in sight and many not present. It did no good. The crowning blow was the search, purely unauthorized and improperly initiated, for Sheriff Plon's own data. The young technician responsible looked up from his screen, shouting. "Sir. Sheriff, sir. You're gone. In the computer, I mean. It says you were never here."

Quicker than Plon, Ullas was beside the man in two strides. The sheriff hustled to a place at the technician's other shoulder. Hoarsely he told the technician, "Run the request again."

Voice trembling, the technician gave the machine instructions. Twice it flashed messages admonishing the young man to enunciate clearly. Satisfied, it hummed busily. The screen flickered. Then the message: PERSON THAT NAME NOT ENTERED. CENTRAL FILES DENIES EXISTENCE.

Plon's cry of disbelief echoed through the room. He bent toward Counsellor Ullas, making no pretense of protocol. "It's not true. The system's been abused. I'm here."

Ullas recoiled, looked at him coldly. "There can be no doubt of your presence, Sheriff. Control yourself. You know I hate displays of emotion."

Plon managed some dignity. "I'm a loyal subject, Counsellor. I officially protest my erasure."

Small red smudges tinted Ullas's cheekbones. He closed his eyes, composed himself. His color returned to its normal pallor. "And a worthy protest it is. Now, listen carefully." He paused, sweeping everyone in the room with a penetrating gaze. "Listen, all of you. The resistance has infiltrated our computer system. The compromise of Hire's information system is akin to destroying our society's brain. Effective immediately, security of all government files and the buildings that house them is to be increased. Every living person on the planet is to be checked against our existing records. Anyone— man, woman, or child—found with a false lifeline will be summarily executed. Sheriff, see to it."

Plon executed an about-face. While he gathered the crowd around to issue specific instructions, Ullas typed name after name into the now-vacated terminal in front of him. Many of his senior officials had been given the same treatment afforded the sheriff; as far as the computer was concerned, they were never born. On a hunch, Ullas went back to a name that had checked out correct when he first sat down. In that short time, the woman was no longer in the system. Ullas swore under his breath. The erasure program was working while he watched, silently prying loose his grip on his subjects, freeing them from the instant identification that was the keystone of his control. Looking over his shoulder, he found Sheriff Plon waiting.

The sheriff said, "I have a question, sir."

"What is it? You have your mission."

Plon glanced around, assuring himself no one had slipped up on them while he waited. Confidentially he asked, "You said to verify everyone for the computers, sir. You didn't really mean everyone, did you, sir?"

Swearing, Ullas reached up, grabbed Plon by the throat. "You brain-dead stump. If I didn't want—" He checked himself. Awareness touched his expression. He clamped down on the sheriff's throat all the harder, ignoring the darkening cyanosis of air-starved lips. Glaring into bulging, watering eyes, he said, "You know full well there are exceptions. Would you destroy? . . ." Then, realizing he was saying too much, Ullas pitched the sheriff away like a rag.

Plon left at a wavering gallop, massaging his throat, croaking at the few personnel left to leave ahead of him. The door's slam cut off more roaring curses from Ullas.

Almost immediately, the sheriff was back, calling through the door for permission to enter Chambers. Ullas shouted at him to come ahead. Hurrying to where Ullas sat at his computer console, Plon saluted. He rasped, "Captain Mard is here, sir. The two men you sent brought him."

"His escort will bring him to the door, then direct him inside. You and I will greet him as if nothing is wrong. The men will wait outside, in case of trouble."

Respectful, formal, Mard was at ease. He strode past Sheriff Plon to where Ullas waited at the head of the long table. Mard either didn't see or chose to ignore the holovid screen mounted at the far end. When he reached Counsellor Ullas, Mard executed a bow replete with the latest style in hand flourishes. When he straightened, Ullas smiled, gestured him to a seat. "I hope I didn't send for you at an inconvenient time, Captain."

Mard reassured him. "I am here to do Sungiver's work, Counsellor. I am at your disposal."

"Ah, yes; Sungiver's work. Lumin assigns many unusual duties to true believers. I find even I'm surprised by some of them. Have you had any unusual duties to perform recently, Captain?"

Laughing lightly, Mard made a face. "Everything about this assignment is unusual to a man like me, Counsellor. I'm just an ordinary soldier, not the sort for diplomatic fanciness. I don't mean that as critical, sir. It's just that I'm a direct sort of person."

"Just as I expected. Plain-spoken. I was telling Sheriff Plon, just before you arrived, that I was sure you'd have direct answers to the questions I have of you."

"Anything at all, sir. How can I be of service?"

"Watch a disk with me, Captain. I'd very much like your opinion of it." Ullas snapped his fingers. The projector splashed light on the screen. The scene on the street was suddenly alive at the end of the table. Even in the dimly lit Chambers room, Mard's sickly loss of color was apparent. His mouth fell open. He coughed, half rose. "That man," he said, and the next word was a loud obscenity that rang with surprise and pain. Ullas had a fold of Mard's upper arm flesh between thumb and forefinger knuckle, pinching hard.

Speaking with conversational ease, Ullas told him, "Please don't interrupt, Captain. Let's see this out and then discuss the totality of it, shall we?"

"I'll be glad to."

Counsellor Ullas released him.

When it was over, Plon brightened the lights. Mard had the look of a man who was sorry to see his darkness taken away. Still, he found bravado. "I acted without full appreciation of your population control measures, Counsellor; I never suspected cameras in the library. My compliments, sir. As for killing the false recruiting agent, I have no remorse. You heard what he said about my service on Hector? I told you I was there." He raised his left hand dramatically. "Surgically implanted in the bone of my ring finger is a thing called an i-wy. That's short for identification wire. Only the Elemental Guard has the technique to imprint information on an i-wy; only the Guard can read it. Removing the wire permanently damages the finger. 'Once Guard, forever Guard.' The dead man was no rebel. He was from Etasalou. No one else could know of my service on Hector."

Ullas pounded irrhythmic fingers on the tabletop. Finally he said, "These are perilous times, Captain. Truth is more important than ever." Then, with unexpected quickness, he was on his feet, headed for the door. "Come with me," he said. "You, too, Plon. Bring the two Advisors who brought the captain here."

Mard knew he was a prisoner, with Sheriff Plon carefully positioned to forestall any quick reach for a sword. More to the point, the two silent Advisors fell in behind. Still, the counsellor had listened to the story without comment. That was a good sign. The longer they meandered through passageways and halls, the more Mard was convinced that his spur-of-the-moment excuse for killing the man in the library was essentially true.

The door where Ullas stopped was a satin-finished gleaming steel panel. It hung on thick hinges of the same material. Ullas nodded at Sheriff Plon, who advanced, raised a shining brass knocker, banged it once. The door swung open. As it did, its thickness was apparent. Smiling over his shoulder at Mard, Counsellor Ullas waved at him to enter first.

A man in tight shirt and trousers of dark rust appeared in the gap created by the partially open door. Mard thought the costume particularly ugly, its color reminiscent of dried blood. Inside by then, Mard turned his attention to the large room. Windowless, it shimmered with light from room-long illumination tubes overhead. Their glare reflected from tile. Floor, walls, ceiling—all was white as salt. More than that, the only furniture in the room seemed to come directly from a hospital, scintillating curves and angles of chrome and steel.

Mard's stomach collapsed in on itself. He realized that the shining instruments weren't medical equipment. Not in the conventional sense. He turned to Ullas, fighting rising bile.

Gesturing broadly, Ullas lectured. "This is our Chamber of Facts, Captain, and its perfect cleanliness symbolizes my love of truth. Humankind's most important concept, yet the most abused of all, wouldn't you say? Here is where we bring those who withhold truth—or give us reason to believe they are doing so."

Over Ullas's shoulder, Mard watched the door swing shut. It moved with awesome slowness.

Ullas continued, unaffected. "All law seeks truth. Lies are the weapon of those who would destroy the calm and rational governance of Hire."

The tenor of the conversation in these surroundings frightened Mard. His voice pitched upward. "I have the feeling your remarks have a deeper meaning, Counsellor. I hope not. As Sungiver's personal emissary, my personal integrity is assured. Perhaps I should have reported today's unfortunate incident, but my solution was a plain soldier's response to a dishonorable proposal. I erred. I concede it. Still, the reason for not reporting the incident is equally plain and straightforward. As your friend, and as Sungiver's agent, it was my plan to wait, to say nothing, and to lure Etasalou into a larger, more easily proven treachery."

"Oh, yes; you erred. We can agree on that. We're here to find out in what way. How often. In whose name." Ullas's gaze shifted from Mard to someone beyond him.

Mard turned. Ranged beside Sheriff Plon were eight men in the costume of the man who opened the door. They advanced. Mard raised his hands, backed away. The two Advisors caught his arms from behind. The eight rushed forward. The sheer speed and irresistibility of the action stunned Mard. Resistance was no more than mumbled disbelief, weak warding motions. In seconds he was stripped naked. When his captors tried to move him farther into the room, however, panic demanded he act, protest.

Struggle was as fruitless as declaiming innocence. With an ease that spoke of long practice, the men grabbed arms, legs, head. Rocking and swaying easily while controlling his thrashing, they shuffled past gleaming tools. Mard tried not to see them. He failed. Their bright malice spurred him to start yelling his innocence again.

A coarse cloth stuffed in his mouth ended that.

Mard saw the steel table and knew that was where he was going. He redoubled his efforts to break free. His carriers didn't even slow. Smoothly they swung him up, dropped him flat on his back on the frigid plastic surface. While muffled cries begged Ullas to believe him, the team strapped him down. When they finished, Mard could tense his muscles and wiggle his fingers and toes. He could breathe, blink, twist his head a few degrees left or right. That was all. Then his gag was yanked free.

Pain in one finger drew Mard's attention, clipped off his renewed shouting. Rolling his eyes, he saw a metal clip biting into his flesh. Wires from the clip led somewhere, out of his vision. There was more pain. The other hand. Just as it occurred to him that no one had spoken since Ullas signaled for all this to happen, the first electric charge slammed him. Muscle and tendon turned to stone, then convulsed. He screamed, felt his head and heels uncontrollably banging the hard plastic table surface. The metal beneath the insulating plastic boomed like a gong.

Then it stopped. The clips were removed. Attached again. Lower lip. An ear. The current came again. For one shattering instant, Mard thought his eyeballs were ruptured.

The current ended. Blood splattered when he tried to plead with them. It took a full two seconds for him to connect the blood with the pain of a bitten lower lip.

When he felt the electrode clipped onto his genitals he literally lost all control. A sewage stink rose around him, quickly hosed away by an expectant attendant dispersing icy water. Aching, overstressed muscles instantly cramped at the shattering chill. The shock of the current combined with that agony to shut down his autonomic nervous system. When the charge stopped, his heart was fluttering wildly. His lungs refused to work properly, pulled in tiny puffs with weak panting gasps. Gore and saliva clogged his throat. He choked, gagged, so used up he lacked even air to clear the passage.

His own fluids were suffocating him.

Death would end the torment. He wept as blackness swaddled him, sweetly delivered him from pain.

CHAPTER 28

Mard's mind struggled to grasp the significance of the sound. It was important. He was certain of that. It had something to do with the pain.

Steel on steel. A door. Opening. Closing.

Silent men, dead faces. Electrodes, pinching. Then . . .

He screamed, coming fully conscious in one wrenching instant, calling for help, begging to be freed. He couldn't stop.

Once more his mouth was stuffed with cloth.

Counsellor Ullas appeared at his shoulder. Pale, intense eyes peered deeply into Mard's, whose own gaze washed away under a flood of self-pitying tears. Ullas asked him, "Would you care to speak to me, Captain?" and Mard grunted desperately into the muffling gag.

Glinting metal tongs flashed across Mard's blurred vision, plucked the cloth free. "They never asked me anything. I'll tell. Anything you want to know. They never asked. Just ask me a question. I'll answer. The truth. I swear it. Anything. Don't let them hurt me anymore."

At the last, Ullas leaned a bit closer. He was stern. "I am not here to discuss your pain, Captain. Perhaps you haven't learned as much as I hoped." He shifted his gaze and, from the corner of his eye, Mard saw one of the rust-red uniformed men moving forward with the electrode clamps dangling from his hand.

"I learned. I understand. I won't mention the pain again. All

I want is to tell you what you want to know. Ask me. Please. For the sake of the light that saves us, just ask me."

Ullas smiled, straightened. "Much better, Captain. You're learning mediation's subtle practices. One endeavors to think of ways to accommodate those with whom one is in disagreement. Or where suspicion exists. So let us be honest with each other. Let us mediate our misunderstanding. My goal, as counsellor, is a smoothly run state. Your goal as Captain Mard and emissary of Sungiver—forgive me for speaking bluntly—is to survive this discussion without permanent physical damage while improving your status in imperial society. I can guarantee both of your goals, but only if you work with me. You must help me by telling all you know about any situation that might interfere with my goal. You see how easily we can mediate the situation so we both win? Isn't that better than a silly legal confrontation? Not to mention brute force."

Mard told himself it was all Etasalou's fault. If he'd never sent the false recruiting agent, none of this would have happened. With that thought foremost in his mind, Mard told Ullas his history, from his enlistment in the Elemental Guard, his agreement to spy for Sungiver, the real reason for his mission to Hire. "There's another thing. I had to tell Etasalou about his niece. I think he already knew she was here, but he made me tell him. I didn't tell him where she's assigned or anything like that. Just that she's here. No more. I swear it."

One secret remained locked in Mard's head. He held back the details of his alliance with Renula and their agreement with Etasalou. A lifetime of betrayal and self-interest conditioned him to hide something.

Sweating, panting as if finishing a race, Mard reached the end of his tale. Ullas shook his head, whether in disbelief or disapproval, Mard had no idea. He was sure only that Ullas told the waiting figures in rust red, "Release him. Let him bathe and dress." To Mard he said, "You'll be my guest here tonight. I think it best you remain here until late tomorrow afternoon, so we both have time to think through our new relationship. Now that we've learned we can resolve our differences so satisfactorily, I see an interesting future for us to share. I suggest you invent some cover story for your absence. That should pose no problem for a man of your competence. We wouldn't want our conversation to be known to anyone, would we?"

"No, sir. Our secret, sir." The words were a hymn of gratitude.

Ullas used the long walk back to his quarters to compose himself. Once he was at his desk, he scribbled careful notes. He decided Mard was right; the recruitment came from Etasalou. The telling fact was the knowledge of Hector. Ullas stroked his chin. It was like Etasalou to weave such a complicated plot. If Mard accepted, he was trapped by his own duplicity, and Etasalou held him to account forever after. If he refused, Etasalou merely proved to himself the loyalty of an underling.

How best to confound a mind so devious?

A smile as thin and forbidding as rime ice worked its way across Ullas's face. Mard supplied the answer: ". . . a simple soldier's straightforward response . . ."

Simplicity. Kill Etasalou.

Without Etasalou, the technicians at his facility would have nowhere to turn. Except Lumin, and that meant the redoubtable Doctor Renula. Ullas shrugged. An accident could be arranged for her.

Suddenly the smile was gone. Ullas remembered Etasalou's troops. What if Etasalou were taken from them? What instructions were planted in those altered minds?

Greed crept into Ullas's evaluations. He wanted control of those people. He wanted the secrets of creating them. Etasalou was a mere man. The techniques he was perfecting were the key to divinity.

Let Etasalou live, then. Control him and control his secrets of the human mind. Control that, and control humankind.

Three days later a supply elcar driver was ushered into Commander Etasalou's office. Standing at rigid attention, gaze fixed on the wall above the seated Etasalou's head, the man reported. Etasalou nodded. "What information do you have?"

"My Advisor contact is unavailable, Commander. We were directed to report any change in agent activity."

"So?"

"My contact works in personnel security, sir. I suspect a problem."

That coincided with other reports of intensified activity at all levels of population control computers. Etasalou determined to pursue it. Accordingly, he dismissed his trooper and arranged an elcar for Court. Ullas greeted him warmly, but Etasalou detected a false cordiality in the counsellor's gaze, in the way he failed to preen and posture.

Nevertheless, Ullas seemed frank enough in admitting some errors in the computer system. His show of temper was disarmingly real. Etasalou waded through some inconsequential chitchat, then made his way back to his laboratories.

He immediately alerted his men to seek out Mard and direct him to report to the revamped factory.

When no one could locate Mard, Etasalou worried. He sent word to Court, and specifically to Doctor Renula, that he was ill.

Renula reported to Counsellor Ullas. She bowed low, head averted. "Commander Etasalou requests medical assistance, Counsellor. Permission to visit him?"

Ullas wanted to exult in his foresightedness. Etasalou and Renula might pretend to be in conflict, but they were both Lumin. Etasalou would play on that. With Mard confined to his quarters, allowed no visitors, Etasalou must seek his information elsewhere. Who but Doctor Renula might know Nan Bahalt's location?

He told Renula, "You will attend Commander Etasalou personally. You will record every word. Send for Sheriff Plon; his technicians will equip you. Come directly to me when you finish with him."

Renula paled, then turned red. "Counsellor, you intrude

on Lumin's most sacred rights. The relationship between leader in the faith and believer, the sanctity of doctor-patient relationship—you ask me to breach them? I cannot."

"No one has supported Lumin more faithfully than I, Doctor. Lumin is indebted to me, and I will have that debt paid. Choose, Doctor; do you serve Etasalou or me? Sungiver's Lumin, or the disgrace that is Etasalou? He is an enemy I tolerate because I have use for him. I will tolerate no others."

Renula spluttered. "I didn't know, Counsellor. I mean, I didn't think . . . You're right, of course. I see my responsibility clearly now. Thank you, sir. May I withdraw?"

Ullas leaned forward, sent her a thin smile. "You may leave my presence. You will never withdraw from my service. Our pact transcends all others, except your oath to Lumin. Although we both agree they're the same thing now, aren't they?"

Too confused to disagree, Renula conceded, feeling the last vestige of her power slip away with the words. Once out of Ullas's sight, she gave way to the storm raging inside her. Rumbling down the halls, she brushed people aside. If Bahalt had stayed on Atic, none of this would have happened. Not all of it, anyhow. What wasn't Bahalt's fault was certainly Mard's. Liars and cheats, both of them. No morals, no ethics. Conspirators.

She ground her teeth, completely unaware that several people heard the noise and turned to stare at her heavy-striding passage.

As bidden, she called Sheriff Plon. The indignity of standing in her undergarments while three disgustingly impertinent female Advisors equipped her with microphones and a covert camera nearly undid her. She trembled with fury, a condition only worsened when one of the technicians said, "There's no need to be nervous, Doctor. This is a routine procedure. You'd be surprised where we've put these mikes sometimes."

Another of the Advisors hooted, adding "And you'd die watching some of our holovids. Make you duck, they will."

When it was over, Renula's jaws ached. That pain, and even the shame of being handled so rudely, was quickly forgotten when she stepped out of the elcar at the entrance to Etasalou's compound. On entering his office, however, Renula was so nervous she barely got through the exchange of greetings.

Etasalou stepped to the side, regarded her with pitying scorn. When Renula moved to open her medkit, he took her by the arm and practically threw her out the door. Stumbling down the hall, she heard him say "We're going to the laboratory, Doctor. It may be the source of my problem. An allergy, perhaps."

Walking there was torture for Renula. She'd treated some of the people who lived there, before and after they were handed over to Etasalou. Although they seemed perfectly normal, there was no question they were *changed*, and it frightened her to know they were changed but not know *how* they were changed.

She kept telling herself Etasalou wouldn't dare harm Lumin's senior representative.

In the lab, Etasalou stepped away for a moment, returning with a white lab robe. It covered her from neck to ankles, and Etasalou himself zipped it together in front for its entire length. With that he said, "Now we can talk."

Too frightened to speak, Renula managed to fake a quizzical look she hoped made her seem innocent.

Etasalou waved lazily. "The detectors in my office counted both your microphones and the clumsy attempt to disguise the camera peeking out of your Lumin medallion. Sewn into the lab coat lapels you're wearing now are batteries, a receiver, and a transmitter, all controlled by a computer chip. The receiver measures the frequency of intercepted sound waves. The computer directs the transmitter to pump a matching signal through the sound-transmitting fibers woven into the coat's material. If you listen very carefully when I speak, you may hear a pleasant little hum. It's quite harmless. Which is more than I can say about your motives, Doctor."

Hands flapping dismay, Renula protested. "Not my motives, Commander. We're working together. I wanted to warn you. How could I?"

"A simple handwritten note suggests itself." Etasalou smiled. Renula wished he hadn't. He went on. "From now on, we'll assume you're an unwilling accomplice rather than an ally."

"I can't openly resist Counsellor Ullas. But it's you I want to help. Really."

"Wonderful. Tell me about Dafanil."

Renula caught her breath. "He's where we said he'd be, in the Imperial Wing. He's closely guarded." Exposing the prince crystallized her deceit within her. What had been nothing more than a vindictive, anger-fueled scheme suddenly had dreadful weight and substance. The wires, the camera—those were indignities, but she felt them to be symbolic bonds between her and the most powerful figure on Hire. All that was gone. Reality was in place now.

"My niece is with him?" Etasalou asked. "At all times?"

"She sleeps in the adjacent rooms. I don't think any attempt to kidnap her could succeed. The security . . ."

"I will succeed. With the help of yourself and the inestimable Captain Mard." He moved to Renula's side, linked her arm over his. "I will need to know everything about the guard. How many are there? How many are on duty, and at what times? Where are they stationed? Tell Mard to learn how I can disable the city's radar traffic controls. How can I cut off power to the apartment building? Are there auxiliary generators? What communications does the guard have? How can I jam them? Don't try to memorize it all, Doctor. I'll give you a list. And I'll know if my questions reach other ears; some of my troops have families in Liskerta, and they're very eager to help their sons and daughters by spying for me."

Grasping at that straw, Renula said, "It makes no difference what you know. Counsellor Ullas isn't protecting an intended concubine, he's protecting the emperor's son. The boy may be useless to his father, but any attempt on him is an insult the emperor cannot forgive. Is any advantage worth that risk?"

Once more Etasalou forced Renula to look away from a malevolent smile. "You can never know all I want or don't want. No one can. No one living." Then, with a bright cheerfulness so inappropriate it bordered on madness, he went on. "Now then, let's go to my office. You seem a bit weary."

An hour later, with Etasalou's requirements written on a tiny sheet of waterproof paper tucked between her cheek and gum, Renula left. Etasalou chuckled to himself at the way the heavy, sturdy woman moved. There was a ponderous sway to her that spoke of crumbled morale. It occurred to him that control of another's mind wasn't always a matter of neurons and synapses.

With that, he was reminded of Dafanil.

It was odd, Etasalou mused, how a figure standing in the wings could suddenly become instrumental in a drama.

Capturing Nan Bahalt to make an example of her to the rest of the extended family was a matter of honor. Etasalou was honest with himself; it was also a matter of simple revenge. He must be on guard, not let that interfere with the ultimate goal. Nevertheless, the empire must know that their new emperor was not to be offended. Not even by blood kin.

Capture Nan Bahalt. And Dafanil.

Force Lannat and the ragged Free into the open. Again, a thrill raced up his spine at the prospect of vengeance. He shrugged free of it. Vengeance would come, surely. It must wait its turn.

That evening Etasalou relaxed in one of Ullas's comfortable office chairs, enjoying his host's obvious tension. He was careful to hide that enjoyment. The net grew smaller every day; it was vital that the prey not be alerted.

Ullas was saying "I've assured that Dafanil receives the best treatment possible. Personal physician in attendance . . ."

"Personal physician?" Etasalou interrupted to show great

approval. "A very wise move, Counsellor, if I may say so. Someone highly regarded, I'm sure."

The wince barely touched Ullas's features. It was enough for Etasalou; his smile oozed good fellowship.

Ullas continued. "If the fool dies, everything is ruined. I'm arranging transport to Atic. Let him die on his father's hands, not mine."

Leaning forward, lowering his voice, Etasalou said, "I don't think we need concern ourselves any longer with the prince, dead or alive."

Speechless, Ullas waited. Etasalou obliged. "Just about now, the starship returning your son and his third of the Hiran Cultural Sibling Group is leaving Atic. Think of that, Counsellor; it means more than getting your son out of Halib's hands. By relinquishing a hostage without so much as a warning about harboring me, Halib admits he's too weak even to protest our activities. Now's the time to strike. You want Geren and Pylos. Take them."

Sarcasm laced Ullas's red-faced retort. "You expect me to flap my mighty wings and fly there? We have no—" Comprehension stopped him in midsyllable, left his mouth in a startled round. He recovered quickly. "The starship? You mean to actually attempt to capture it?"

"We shall. And its cargo. A full third of each Cultural Sibling Group from Geron and Pylos will be aboard her. Don't you think that will make the rulers of those planets more receptive to your terms?"

"A good point. Very good. Still and all, Halib will come. He'll sacrifice those poor, innocent lives without a second thought."

"Let him. We'll be ready."

Ullas's scorn was gone. He remained skeptical, however. Etasalou explained. "On the day the CSG starship arrives, Starship *Achilles* makes a routine cargo stop here. The next day Starship *Socrates* hits orbit. Three starships in two days; that may not happen again in ten years."

"All three? Capture all three?" Ullas barely trusted his voice.

"All three. We claim the rebels have damaged the spaceport power supply and control equipment. That holds the CSG ship and *Achilles* in orbit while *Socrates* arrives. Then we send up the lighters, filled with your best Advisors. In a few minutes you and Emperor Halib will be the only men in the empire to command interstellar flight. In a few weeks you'll be the only other emperor in the galaxy. After that—who knows?"

Ullas was calmer by then. "It might work, Commander. You've given it considerable thought. Tell me, though; while my Advisors are capturing the starships for my empire, where are all the fine, restructured troops you've created?"

"Destroying the Free. Forgive some unpleasant truths, Counsellor, but my units are the only ones fit for the job. Your Advisors are noticeably unwilling to engage the Free. They get mauled in ambushes when they attack or pursue, they get surprised when they assume the defense. Population control measures are weakened by attacks on the data centers; even when those control measures are most vigorously applied, they drive the survivors into the Marnoffar Mountains or into the underground resistance. My troops are without concern for anything but your triumph. They will kill without pity. Take your starships, Counsellor. When they land, it will be on a planet with no living dissidents."

Rising, Ullas paced. Head bowed, hands behind him, long legs whisking him back and forth, he considered. Etasalou waited, practically lounging. Finally Ullas said, "It takes five months for the starship to travel from Atic to here. That's how long you have, Commander. If the resistance isn't destroyed when the CSG returns, I shall satisfy myself with control of Hire. There will be no attack on any starship, no conquest of other planets. I have ambitions, but I do not have insane ambitions."

Etasalou stood. "It shall come to pass, Counsellor." He saluted, executed a stiff about-face, marched out. Once he was outside and in the elcar headed home, he permitted himself a small smile of satisfaction. He knew better than to appear too satisfied; all the elcars were equipped with hidden transmitters and cameras. It was better to know they were there and behave accordingly than to defeat them and incur ever greater ingenuity in their placement. So Etasalou smiled to himself, expressing himself only in his thoughts: " 'It shall come to pass.' True, true. But you shall have passed first, Counsellor. And isn't that a dirty shame?"

CHAPTER 29

Lannat darkglassed the open ground between the lodge and the forest one last time before sprinting from cover. Bent to a near crouch, he strained to hear past his own footsteps and the whispering rush of high grass against his legs. Far off, an animal moaned. Insects called smallsaws buzzed in the treetops. All of it grated on unaccountably raw nerves. He knew men who simply ran down. It was a disturbing memory.

Pressed against the wall of the lodge, he signaled in the others. Jarka and Sul dashed toward him. They entered together. Lannat kept his hand on his sword hilt until they were in Betak's small office. There he sat with his back to the wall, watching Betak at his desk, the door, and the sole window.

As soon as the trio was seated, Betak spoke into an intercom. "They're here. We're ready."

Draped in black robes, head obscured by a hood, a figure slipped into the room. Cloth whispered as if sharing secrets.

The newcomer settled on the remaining chair. Lannat was sure it was a woman. His mind filled with memories of Astara. This woman's movements were supple, her voice young. And blunt. "I asked to meet with you three men. You must make a decision. I want to hear it for myself."

Sul told Betak, "This woman must be one of your informants. This is a terrible break in security."

The woman answered. "You'll never know who I am, and I only know you by reputation. I've earned the right to hear your answers."

Betak agreed. "None of you is as brave as this woman. She confronts danger at every heartbeat, watching, listening, asking. Hear her out."

Unruffled, the woman continued. "Prince Dafanil is ill. He's been moved to Court's Imperial Wing. Doctor Nan Bahalt is assigned as his personal physician." Lannat was certain the eyes hidden within that shrouding hood were aimed at him. He clenched his jaws. She went on, unemotionally detailing Dafanil's unexpected illness and his hurried, security-ridden transfer.

Already tense when she finished those revelations, Lannat listened to the woman report that Doctor Renula was behaving strangely, and exploded. "Doctor Bahalt is at greater risk than ever. How can Ullas think to keep this from Etasalou? If we know of it, he knows of it." He whirled away, disgusted. Then, facing Betak, he forced calmer words. "Once Etasalou has his hands on Bahalt and Dafanil, Ullas is finished."

"Etasalou doesn't know," the woman said. "The precautions for the prince's safety are impenetrable. There are at least a hundred Advisors, with a railgun on the roof."

"Etasalou knows, I promise you," Lannat said. "And any static defense is vulnerable to determined attack. Ullas has constructed his own gallows."

The woman shook her head, but Betak cut her off. "What Etasalou knows about Prince Dafanil's health and security isn't as important as what I've learned."

Cutting a glance at Jarka and Sul, Lannat saw that his companions were more curious than alarmed. His own sense of apprehension refused to quiet, however. Once again, without even looking at the young woman in black, Lannat found himself thinking of Astara. Sounds, indistinct suggestions of her voice, came to him. He remembered how she spoke once of a soldier's luck and the thought that some men seemed to live under an almost mystical protection.

All soldiers who lived long enough wondered about that. Those who survived enough close calls rarely spoke of it. They dared not risk damaging the luck. Hair on the back of Lannat's neck tingled. He sensed that whatever Betak had learned would endanger the man named Val Bordi.

A sinister question picked at Lannat's mind: Would Lannat's luck extend to Val Bordi?

"Free supporters in Liskerta took two of Etasalou's eltruck drivers captive," Betak said. "The woman died as soon as she was bound. The man was unconscious, and when our people saw the way the woman died, they immediately drugged the man. I had him brought here."

Sul pointed at the hooded woman. "First her, and now a prisoner? Why don't you just get Etasalou on the comfone?"

Betak ignored the question, spoke to Lannat. "I never really believed what you said about Etasalou and what he does to people. I didn't want to. What our Free supporters said about the woman seems to confirm your tale. That's why the prisoner is here." He pushed a button on his intercom.

Three men carried in a long, roughly cylindrical object. When they lowered it, it proved to be a man wrapped in blankets. Exposed, he wore one of the new black uniforms. Betak said, "He's got enough sedative in him to kill a normal man. It makes him sleep. Even now he lashes out from time to time, which explains the wrapping." He nodded at the three who brought him, and two stepped back. The third prepared an injector.

"That's a stimulant, specific to the sedative. We can—" Betak hesitated. Once more he directed that odd look at Lannat, and once more Lannat felt danger weigh heavily in Betak's words when they continued. "—we can interrogate him."

At that, Lannat understood. Betak had been told how the prisoner's female partner had died. Lannat's palms were suddenly damp.

The man giving the injection rose, exchanged glances with his two companions. One said, "We'll be outside. In front of the building. Call when it's over."

Slowly, comprehension livened the prisoner's features. He struggled to sit up, hampered by the fibermet binding his wrists to his waist. Ankles were also secured. He focused on Lannat, speaking very clearly. "Am I a prisoner?"

Ice closed Lannat's throat. He pointed at Betak. "Talk to him, trooper; he's in charge."

Betak reasoned gently, "You're one of us. All we want is information about Etasalou, the foreigner. He's your enemy, too. We want a free Hire, a place—"

"I can't tell you anything." The man was equally reasonable. Still, there was a monotone, removed quality to his voice.

"You'll be saving lives, man. Your own kin, your friends."

The man squirmed a bit. "I can't tell you anything. I fight for Commander Etasalou."

"That's what your partner said—the woman. She died."

"Everyone dies. The fortunate die with cause and glory."

"Your cause is wrong. Etasalou is wrong."

Suddenly transformed, the man raged, actually forced himself upright. He roared. "I live and die for the commander. Win or die."

Lannat walked to the door. "I won't watch anymore. He'll do it if you keep this up—he'll turn himself off like a lamp. He's dead already." He addressed the prisoner. "Tell them, for the love of light. Tell them."

The prisoner wilted. The rage was gone as quickly as it came. He looked from Lannat to the others. "I'm a prisoner? Alone?"

Death sounded in the words.

Betak reacted badly. Clearly frightened, he blustered. "That's right. Your service to Etasalou is over. You might as well answer our questions."

Jarka reached out, caught Lannat's arm. "You know about this. Don't let him die."

"I can't stop him. It's in his mind. He can't stop himself."

Sul cried. As if unaware of his own tears, he looked at the prisoner and wept. The woman ran past all of them, gagging. It was her escape that seemed to break the prisoner completely. His voice strained. "We are a whole, and the loss of one is as nothing. Our only crime is to fail the commander and remain alive."

Lannat pulled at Jarka's grip. Jarka hung on. The prisoner's agonized scream stopped their burgeoning struggle. They stopped, transfixed.

Betak shouted. "Don't! Stop that. No more questions. I swear."

Searching the face of each man with an expression of infinite loss and despair, the prisoner buckled. Bound hands, tied to his waist, strained to reach the lowered head. Long, trailing screams hammered at the walls, driving back those watching him.

The shrieks stopped. The man coughed. Blood gushed from his nose and his wide, silenced mouth. Convulsing, he fell to the floor.

Sul moved quickest. Sword flashing, he cut the man's bonds and rolled him onto his back. But even as he turned the man's head to the side to prevent him choking on his own blood, it was obvious there was no need. Glassy eyes stared from a contorted, blue-gray face.

Lannat was still in the doorway. He broke the silence. "There you see it, Betak. Death on demand. If you'd helped me when I first arrived . . ."

"Enough!" Sul's sword angled upward as he whirled. Lannat backed away. Sul's wide features were almost as twisted as the dead man's. Even in his present emotional state, however, he couldn't maintain fury. The threatening weapon lowered. His expression softened. "We didn't know. We didn't want to believe."

It was on Lannat's tongue to ask Sul how many lives that denial had cost. Instead, he addressed Betak. "Etasalou's too strong for direct attack now. We can make him come to us, though."

"Just what we need," Jarka said. "Bring him down on us. With a couple of regiments of those." He jerked a thumb at the corpse.

Sul turned to Jarka, angered all over again. "Don't say that. He was a man. Probably a good man. He deserved respect. And pity."

Betak's quiet authority quickly calmed things. He picked his way past the dead man, left the office. A few moments later he was back with the prisoner escorts. Wordlessly they bent to carry the body away. In the deep silence after their departure, Betak addressed Lannat. "You want to make Etasalou attack us? That makes no sense."

"He's going to attack. We have to dictate the conditions of the battle. It's our only chance. We start by disrupting his plans. We capture his niece and the prince."

Jarka made a harsh noise. "There's a tactical asset—a female doctor and a puke prince."

Jarka couldn't know how close he was to dying, couldn't imagine that the man he called Val Bordi loved Nan Bahalt. Lannat contained his fury only by repeating to himself that his love for Nan belonged to a different world. It took a moment, but he answered patiently. "Doctor Bahalt represents a personal affront that Etasalou cannot tolerate. He hasn't moved against her yet simply because he needs Ullas. Capturing Prince Dafanil offers us two possibilities. Etasalou will be cautious about endangering a prince of the blood. A second alternative is more likely. Once the emperor knows his son is captured by rebels, he has to try to get him back. He can't be seen as so weak he'll do nothing to rescue his own child. He'll dispatch Rifles and Elemental Guard units immediately."

"This gets better and better," Jarka scoffed. "The emperor sends troops after us? How's that help?"

"When Etasalou hears an imperial task force is headed for Hire, he's got to try to eliminate us and make Dafanil his own bargaining token. The emperor fears Etasalou far more than us. Once Halib has Dafanil in hand, he'll destroy Etasalou. There's another thing to consider: You just saw an example of what Etasalou is. Can you still believe he means to remain Ullas's faithful servant? If we have Dafanil, we can bargain with Emperor Halib. If Etasalou has the prince, he holds every card in the deck. Our only hope is to force Etasalou into a hurried campaign, so we can destroy him."

Surprisingly, Sul was first to object. "You're guessing. You don't know any of that. You talk like you know everything they're thinking." He gulped, looking down at the bloodstained floor. Pale, staggering, he bumbled past Lannat, retching.

Betak listened to the noise recede in the distance, then: "It makes sense. As much as anything." He slumped in his chair.

"If we can get the doctor and the prince out of there, maybe Etasalou and Ullas will hurt each other," Jarka suggested. "That certainly helps us. And having hostages can't put us in worse shape than we're in now." He, too, looked down at the fouled floor. Unlike Sul, Jarka showed a mix of fear and loathing.

Betak caught it. "How different are we, Jarka—the dead prisoner and us? Aren't you willing to die for what you believe?"

Jarka refused to answer.

Lannat tried. "You choose to risk your lives for a cause. As sure as light, there's a difference. Don't forget it."

"The Bahalt woman is Lumin," Betak said. "I want no conflict with them. I say we bring back the prince and leave her. If Etasalou harms her, he distances himself even farther from Sungiver and the rest of the religion. That could be to our advantage."

Lannat forced calm logic. "The prince will be Etasalou's prime political objective, but if we're going to really rattle him, we have to be able to taunt him with his niece. She's the whip to flog him, make him careless."

Listening to himself, he thought of poor Sul and the woman spy, overcome by the horror of watching a man willing himself dead. What would they think of Captain Lannat, a man so submerged in guile that he made a lure of the woman he loved?

What would Nan think?

Jarka agreed. "I'll go along. If we take one, we take both. Let Etasalou see what it's like to know someone important to him is at risk."

Fortunately, Jarka and Betak were looking at each other and failed to see the impact of Jarka's analysis on Lannat. There was surprise in the moment, as well; Lannat realized that he cared what Jarka thought of him. And what Sul thought. Trey and Retalla. Someday—if they lived—he'd have to know. Could they call Lannat friend? Or would they mourn the loss of Val Bordi?

It was unfair. Lannat looked at Betak. A thief. Like Halib, like the unnamed spymasters on Atic. They had done this to him. They had stolen his life, his *self*.

Movement jarred him out of his thoughts. The hooded woman entered the room. Chin up, studiously avoiding seeing the floor, she said, "You called, Betak? I can't stay in here . . ."

"We're going to take Doctor Bahalt and Prince Dafanil," Betak told her. "Val Bordi will tell you what he needs to know."

CHAPTER 30

On the trek back to the Free's mountain hide, Lannat took the last position in line since he was so much more dependent on darkglasses. As last man, he had only to keep Sul's broad back in focus. The group was on the narrow trail for a couple of hours when Lannat noted Sul drifting back to take position beside him.

Lannat almost laughed out loud. He wanted to ask Sul if Hirans had some strange compulsion to save confidential conversations for dark walks on wilderness trails. It occurred to him it was really a function of privacy. A unit in the field enjoys little of that, and the Free lived in the field. Still, it was funny. First there was Trey, then the youngster, after the raid that took out Yasil's power plant. Lannat tried to remember the trooper's name. He couldn't. When he had been with Rifles he had known every soul in his command.

He had no time to dwell on that unpleasant truth. Sul said, "What you said about that dead man back there—about causes, and all. That was good."

Unsure where the conversation was aimed, Lannat merely made a noise in his chest. Then, as afterthought: "Is it safe to talk? I've seen enough Hiran wildlife."

Sul chuckled. "We're less likely to be attacked if we don't surprise anything." He sobered. "The raid will surprise Ullas. He'll order reprisals."

"It can't be helped."

"Oh, I know. It makes us more like that prisoner, though, don't you think? I mean, he had no choice. Not after Etasalou."

The bitterness in his own voice surprised Lannat when he answered. "We all make bad choices. The dead guy's choices were made for him. Maybe he was better off."

"Did you ever ask yourself how many choices we actually do make? They all grow out of someone else's decision."

"Some truth in that. If we surrender the power to say yes or no, we lose . . ." He stopped. The word "ourselves" died in his throat.

Sul fell silent. The conversation ended.

Back in the underground camp, sleep refused to come to Lannat. Unrelated thoughts spun across his consciousness. No single idea remained still long enough for him to concentrate on it. Until he envisioned Astara.

His eyes flew open. There was only darkness, and the sound of someone snoring softly. He closed his eyes again. Slowly, like fog coalescing into solid, she returned. She spoke. "Please, young warrior, let me stay. Don't send me away."

Lannat thought, and heard his own voice in his mind. "You tried to claim me before. I am farther from you than ever. Leave me to myself."

"Can you not understand that distance from me is distance from everything you love? Where is the confidence, the self-determination I admired? You are a different man, changing more and more. Ask yourself: If you are lost to me, then by whom are you found?"

"I'm still true to my feelings. I was never yours. Or Lumin's. Or anyone's."

"What of Emperor Halib?"

"This *is* me. My oath. I have not abandoned it. As you threaten to abandon me."

The old woman's voice took on a steely sharpness. "Make up your mind. You reject me, then accuse me of desertion? What liar's tongue fills your mouth now, Captain?"

Embarrassment spawned words Lannat regretted even as

they tumbled out. "I told no lie. This is our same old argument. I will not belong to your Seeker. I was friend to your cult out of honor and responsibility. You wanted to see more, so you did. Now you see yourself losing a recruit, so you weep over me and threaten at the same time."

Astara's chin rose. Her free hand, the one not holding her tall walking stick, moved fitfully. Lannat had the disturbing sensation that he was watching physical indications of boiling anger. Fear touched him, the prickle of things beyond his comprehension. Yet Astara was calm-spoken. "You observe your oath too well. You become what you are not. The soldier gives way to the schemer." She paused, sighed before continuing. "Love makes me no less prisoner than you. I cannot cease caring. Wherever the man Val Bordi takes my friend Lannat, I must follow."

"If you will." Now hurt added to Lannat's shame. He retreated farther into himself. The image of the old woman lost precision. He hurried on, giving pain as he felt it. "I will be whoever, whatever is necessary. Nan Bahalt was sent here. I was sent here. The evil I was ordered to destroy is allowed to flourish. You and those like you—you with power—have no right to complain about how I do what you want done, nor any say in how the act benefits me. Or Nan. I'll save her. I'll kill Etasalou. And you'll be unsatisfied. You always want more of us."

"So." Astara's image shimmered, a thing caught in heat waves. Impulsively Lannat reached, wanting to tell her he wasn't changed, that he was still her friend, too. He ached to reassure her that his words were simpleminded resentment, that he was still the man she called her young warrior. While he struggled, mute, she continued. "I must leave you. I give you my blessing. We shall see what comes of it—and many things. Later we shall judge our choices."

Lannat felt her departure was retreat. Loss descended on him, pressing consciousness from his mind. He slept. The next morning was torment until an excited call from Sul forced him to confront the world outside himself. "It's from Betak. He's sending information on the Imperial Wing. He has an architect's holomodel. Security data should be available in a few days. He must have every Free agent and nonk in Liskerta working for him."

"That many more mouths to spread the word," Lannat muttered sourly. His next remark was clearer. "I want to see this place for myself. Words and pictures won't cut it."

Sul blanched. "You mean go there? Court?"

"I have to look at approaches, escape routes. I won't stage a raid without knowing details."

Sul's excitement gathered others. Trey was among them. She said, "You shouldn't be going at all. You're too valuable."

Lannat nodded. "I'm valuable because I know how to do the job. After this one, others can lead."

Jarka stepped out of the group. "I'm in." Tone and manner dared Lannat to deny him. Similarly, Retalla ambled over to join them. The lanky man slouched alongside the bristling Jarka, his half smile and attitude barely short of insolent. He said nothing but winked at Lannat. In his way, Retalla was as determined as Jarka.

They brightened Lannat's mood. "The three of us, then. A reconnaissance. Get that right. No excitement."

"I'm coming along," Trey said.

Darkening, Lannat disagreed. "Not this time. If it comes to escape, we may have to fight."

"What happened to 'no excitement'? What makes you think the three of you, stumbling around like drunken lysos, are going to blend in better than Retalla and me, a couple shopping and taking in the sights?"

A glance at Jarka and Retalla told Lannat they were enjoying his discomfort. He faced Trey again. "It's a bad idea."

Instead of temper, she gave him reason. "I'm nonthreatening. I can ask questions where you'd scare people off, go places you're not even allowed."

Before Lannat could argue further, Retalla said, "She's right

about that." In response to Lannat's swift glare, Retalla raised
a hand. "I'm not saying you should take her. It's your mission,
your decision. But what she's saying's right. You know it is."

Trey tried again. "When you first came here, you used me to
make a point about everyone carrying his or her own weight.
Or were you just talking?"

Lannat tried to restrain a wince, but the faces of his companions told him he was too slow. "All right," he said, and
shook his head. "But it's against my better judgment."

When Lannat walked away, Retalla followed. When they
were alone, he said, "I know how it grated on you to back
down just now. You did the right thing."

"You think so?" There was more than disagreement in Lannat's manner. There was challenge, as well.

Retalla was immediately defensive. "She's as tough as any
man. I know about her talk with you, how she worries about
not measuring up. We all feel that way sometimes. But she's
one of us; she has a right to be treated like anyone else."

"Very pretty. Her rights." Lannat looked away, shook his
head. "I may have to send her into something I know she's not
coming out of. I'll do that, Retalla, and not because it's my
right but because it's my duty. When that happens, I won't be
thinking about her rights. I'll be thinking about how many
people may pay for them if she fails. You said you want me to
treat her like anyone else; you remember that when the pressure's on. I didn't exclude her because she's female. I did it because I'm not certain about her attitude. Now she's in. We'll
see what happens."

In his customary, and very misleading, slouch, Retalla said,
"You said I wouldn't be able to take you on my second try. I
may have to chance that, you unpleasant bastard. Don't you
have any feelings at all?"

Lannat looked over to where Trey was in animated conversation with Jarka and Sul. It wasn't all that long ago he'd worried what Sul, Retalla—all of them—thought of him. Now that
was pointless. "You people brought me here to use. Like a

weapon. I'll listen to your foolishness and I'll answer you like you had good sense. But don't you ever talk to me about how I feel. Never. Is that clear?" He whirled, leaned toward Retalla.

To his credit, Retalla maintained his same posture, continued to meet Lannat's hard glare. Nevertheless, a subtle change, an undefinable shift from aggressive to wary, altered the lanky man's manner.

Lannat's hand dropped to his sword hilt. "I asked you a question. Answer me."

Retalla's sneer wavered. "It's clear enough."

The words weren't what Lannat wanted, and the tone had a face-saving defiance that grated. Nevertheless, he walked away.

He was shaking. For a few heartbeats, he had considered killing Retalla. A man he wanted to consider a friend. Now this.

What had he become?

Renula watched Mard pace the examination room. He stopped abruptly, scanning the walls. Renula sighed and answered his question before he could voice it. "No, there are no listening devices in here. I've told you a hundred times. My people inspect it constantly."

Mard made a face. "Ullas doesn't believe your drivel about that lab coat muffling your chat with Etasalou, you know. Neither do I. You're not fooling anyone."

Protest turned Renula wide-eyed and innocent. "It's the truth. You should try telling the truth some time. Remember, it was your lies that got you channeled."

Opening his shirt, Mard glared at the taut strap encircling his chest. "This is degrading. It's worse than being in prison. All my bodily functions, constantly recorded on a damned monitor."

"It must be just awful." Renula oozed mock sympathy. "It could be worse. What if it channeled everything you say as well as everything you do? Have you tried exerting yourself? They say it's awful the way it draws tighter, squeezes your lungs so you can't breathe. Imagine, gasping, pleading for a breath, and—"

"Just shut up. It's bad enough, without your yammer. Are you sure it's explosive? Has anyone ever tested one?"

"Many people. I heard some lived. Test it yourself. Just walk outside the Imperial Wing. Or should I say, spread out outside?" She laughed cheerily.

Mard ground his teeth. "I could tell Ullas about our conversation with Etasalou. Then he'd know you're lying about that damned lab coat. He'd put *you* on his electric gurney for a while, like he did me. How'd you like that, Doctor?"

"You'll tell no one anything. I know you. Etasalou's your only hope of survival on this planet, and I'm your only access to Etasalou. Counsellor Ullas says you're to stay here where you're well guarded, along with our other celebrity guests."

"Don't forget who sent me. You're required to help me."

"I am sworn to Lumin. There is no other loyalty. Not even to myself. I was tempted, but I have repented. The danger to Lumin is from all sides. I will protect the faith against all. That includes you. Counsellor Ullas thinks he's drained your poison. I think not. I shall watch you. And them." She gestured. Mard knew she referred to Bahalt and Prince Dafanil.

"Oh, there's a dangerous pair. Hold the empire in their hands, they do." Sneering, Mard buttoned up his shirt. "They're as helpless as me. Or you."

Renula walked to the door, posed there. "You're wrong about everything. The counsellor complimented me for maintaining my composure when Commander Etasalou made me wear that coat. I gave the counsellor a full report of everything that was said. He does trust me. And he knows you for a liar. As for Dafanil and Bahalt, they're counters in a game I don't pretend to understand. Nor do I care. My sole task in these times is to protect Lumin."

She swept out.

Mard stormed about the examining room. Yanking open the shirt again, he plucked at the channeling strap binding his chest. He was careful not to pull too hard. The man who had put it there warned that it could be set off by excessive tampering. In his fury and frustration, he whined in a high, nasal tone that stopped only when he began to curse.

For her part, Renula strode the hall in great good humor. Perhaps Counsellor Ullas hadn't exactly complimented her performance at Etasalou's labs, but he'd understood there was nothing she could do. She thought back: At first his calmness in the face of such disappointment had been unnerving. Still, he'd been very polite. Almost pleasant.

Everything was going well. Calling Bahalt and Dafanil counters was a neat turn of phrase, she told herself, because that's what they really were. So was Mard. None of them was quite as smart as they wanted to believe. If they were, then how had Doctor Renula ended up holding the three counters that the two supposedly big players both wanted so much? And why didn't the two supposedly big players even suspect that Doctor Renula was just as big as they were?

It proved the power of Lumin.

Now that she saw the error of her ways, it was so obvious that only Lumin could deliver her to her proper place. Her superior intelligence and pure-hearted dedication meant nothing if Lumin wasn't paramount in her every thought. Protect Lumin. That was what she had to do.

And Lumin would protect her.

That faith took a terrible blow when she entered her office and found Commander Etasalou waiting for her.

Tight smile underlining eyes that burned with intensity, he waited while she struggled to regain her composure. "There's no one else here, Doctor," he said. "I sent them away. I told them I am unwell and must see you alone."

"Why?"

Dark features taut, Etasalou told her, "Counsellor Ullas has isolated Prince Dafanil, my niece, and that lying double agent, Mard. There will be an attempt to take my niece and the prince from here. It must not succeed."

"What . . . what are you going to do?"

Etasalou relaxed. The crimped lines at the corners of his eyes disappeared. "Many things, dear Doctor. Many you do not wish to know about. Just as you wish you didn't know Mard's true mission on Hire."

Renula steadied herself. "He is Sungiver's emissary. Nevertheless, I would never have let him do it."

"Yes, you would. You are loyal to Sungiver, but you don't know her true nature."

"I will not hear blasphemy nor sedition. I—"

"Talk without listening." Etasalou interrupted, continuing "I would offer the faith of my restructured personnel to Lumin. Not to Sungiver. She plotted to see me ruined. Now, by planning my murder, she disgraces her title, reveals herself as nothing but a common courtier. I would give my services to a worthy leader."

Renula felt sweat accumulating at the small of her back. "These are very dangerous words, Commander."

He was quietly triumphant. "You see? Your intuition is so strong it tells you my thoughts. Help me, and Lumin will be the only religion on Hire. You will be her leader. You, Renula. Alone and supreme."

"Sungiver?" Renula couldn't bring herself to ask a full question. She whispered the name, trailing it across the conversation like a lure, hoping Etasalou would tell her what she needed to hear, say the things she dared not think.

His answer tore the breath from her body. "It is our holy obligation to keep Lumin pure and honorable. I must have Dafanil, I must have Hire. When I have them, the empire rests in my palm. My empire will have no place for the one who now calls herself Sungiver. That role would be for one I trust. A partner." He rose, came to her, took her hand between his. "Help me."

CHAPTER 31

Lannat and Jarka stepped from the elbus without a glance for each other. Jarka went briskly to the right. Lannat strolled, window-shopping. From the corner of his eye, he watched the elbus stop at the next corner. Retalla and Trey got off, turned right, and proceeded toward Lannat. He, in turn, moved off in Jarka's wake, a half block away already.

Peace/Order cameras swiveled and scanned all activity from high above the quartet. Mounted on rooftops, streetlight stanchions, and windowsills, the unblinking, unforgetting lenses recorded everything. Advisors, working in pairs and wearing the gold-on-black costume of Identity Police, randomly stopped passersby to demand lifelines. Lannat passed three such teams. Each time his nerves jangled.

Reflections in windows provided more shocks; Val Bordi looked back. Since his arrival on Hire, Lannat had never once seen a mirror larger than the hand-size metal one he used for shaving. It showed his face in small squares, like parts of a puzzle. Now he saw himself in total. His focus darted back and forth between the place of the absent scriptlike scar and the strange new one. Peculiarly, the latter made him feel disfigured. Lannat had the sensation of looking at someone he'd met briefly long ago. Someone he didn't care to remember.

The rest of his appearance was ordinary enough. The clothes fit well; shirt of rough material under a lightweight leather jacket. The jacket worn loose enough to hide the ceryag knife and scabbard strapped under his left arm. Trousers, boots, and wide-brimmed hat. The hat was an afterthought. Retalla had pointed out how weathered they all were and suggested they conduct their reconnaissance disguised as farmers. Sul had agreed, adding "The Peace/Order cameras and the Identity Police are concerned with urban people, not rural types. They won't give you a second look."

So far, Lannat mused, Sul was right. Occasionally a small child, surprised to see someone wearing a hat, stared curiously. To everyone else they were bumpkins, come to gawk.

Half right. Lannat smiled to himself. The foursome were most certainly gawkers. He crossed the street to spread out the group a little more.

The town that had grown up around the walls of Court had moved with every expansion of the old facility. Ironically, the carefully measured and executed construction of Court's additions never extended to reconstruction of Old Town. It simply grew back, adjusting to the new dimensions of Court, like scrubbrush next to a garden. Streets were a jumble of narrow ways and alleys. They wandered past buildings built to whim, rather than code. Far beyond that haphazard mess, separated from it by encircling parkland, was the proper city grid and its surround of planned suburbs. Everyone considered Old Town quaint.

Except a raiding party that had to contemplate negotiating it in the dark while escaping pursuit and carrying captives.

That thought was rankling Lannat's mind when the two Identity Policemen appeared in front of him. One of them, surgically neat, extended a hand inside a wide-gauntleted glove. "Lifeline." Boredom made the demand an insult.

Lannat extended his papers. The IP took off the gloves, thumbed through the pages, ran the cover's magnetic strip through a handheld reader. Lannat couldn't see the screen. When the IP frowned and tensed, Lannat braced himself. The IP looked up to study Lannat's features. His partner, alerted by the irregularity, stopped watching the crowd and concentrated on Lannat. The first IP said, "What's the name of your central data bank?"

Shrugging, Lannat looked confused. "I don't know. The data-takers come, ask questions. I don't know what they do with the answers."

The second IP pressed forward. "What d'you think they do with it, Dirt?"

"Put it in a computer." Lannat acted properly offended.

"Where? That's what we asked you; where's your central?"

"No one ever told me. In the city, I guess. I don't ask questions about the government."

The second IP turned to his partner. "Dirt's not as dumb as he looks." Looking back to Lannat, the amusement disappeared. "What're you doing in this neighborhood? Why aren't you in the computer?"

Lannat scratched his chin. The move put his hand inches from the hidden weapon. "Everybody knows there's been computer troubles. I'm just walking around, looking. Nobody told us this is a restricted area or anything." He gestured with his left hand, hoping to distract possible attention away from the right; it ached to grab the knife, put an end to this suspense.

The first IP pointed at a storefront down the block. "There's a new lifeline checkpoint in that building. I want a better read-out on you. Come along."

"What's wrong, cousin?"

Trey's voice, bright and cheerful, hit Lannat like thunder. A small shoulder bumped him off balance. His reach for the knife was aborted.

Trey said, "Officers, we've only got a couple hours before our elbus. I know your duty's important, but there's so much to see, and we don't get to town but maybe twice a year."

"You with him?" the second IP asked. "Where were you before?"

"Just there." Trey half turned, presenting an excellent figure to advantage.

The IP lost a great deal of hostility. "You called Dirt here 'cousin'?"

"Val Bordi. We grew up together. He brought me to town, special."

The IPs exchanged glances. First IP said, "I'll bet he did," and stuck out his hand. "Lifeline." Lannat noted how his fingers slowly trailed across Trey's hand as he took the offered papers. Lannat nervously sought out Retalla. The rangy figure was up the street, behind the IPs. The byplay between Trey and the IP was hidden from his view.

Handing back the papers, First IP said, "You check out. We still have to verify cousin Dirt. You want to come along?"

Lannat spoke before Trey had a chance to answer. "No sense in both of us losing our sightseeing. You go along. I'll catch you at the elbus stop."

"Please." Trey moved closer to First IP. She also pressed against Lannat's right side, effectively blocking any attempt at the knife. "Val's nobody, done nothing. Why does he have to go with you?"

Second IP smiled. "He didn't answer a question correctly."

Trey put a hand on Lannat's arm. "Well, what did you expect? You saw his readout. It says about the accident, it gives you his rating."

After another exchange of glances, First IP told Lannat, "Not a word out of you, Dirt. Not a sound." Lannat realized immediately he was to say nothing to Trey about the missing computer information. The IPs knew how to bait a trap. Second IP drew his weapon, the flexible bar capable of so much bludgeoning damage. He stared coldly at Lannat. First IP stepped closer to Trey. Hiding the truth—that he had learned nothing about the man called Val Bordi from his computer trace—he ran his bluff on her. "You mean his service draft rating. I didn't notice that."

"Well, it explains everything. On the farm? The harvester hit his head? He's draft exempt. He forgets things all the time." She turned sad blue eyes up at Lannat. "Isn't that right?"

Truly fuddled by the changed course of events, Lannat goggled at her. "What?"

First IP swore, spoke to his partner. "Light. A dummy. Wouldn't that lard-butt sergeant like to see me drag in a mental case for background check? He'd fry me." Facing Trey again he said, "You saved us some trouble. I'd like to buy you a drink, get better acquainted. There's a place one street over where they know me."

Trey was shy. "It's nice of you to offer, but I've never seen Court; the walls and Old Town and all? Could I find your place by myself, after?"

Smirking, First IP told his partner, "I'm going off duty for a few minutes to show a helpful subject some consideration." He offered an arm to Trey, turning his back on both Second IP and Lannat, who followed them to the tavern. "We can't stay in one place long," he told her. "We've got plainclothes people around, watching. They tightened security around here. We don't let anybody without special passes on these streets after dark."

Impressed, Trey moved closer. "Really? They're watching us? Why?"

The IP bent toward her, brushed her hair with his lips, whispering. Lannat pretended disinterest. He hoped Retalla was able to do the same. "Something about a nobleman. They even moved a railgun onto the roof. I heard there's another one hidden inside."

Little by little, Trey picked bits of information from him. Advisor forces in the city were strained to their manpower limits by the requirement to fill whole floors of the Imperial Wing with security guards. "Orders direct from Court's Sheriff," First IP confided. Trey gave a tiny squeal of conspiratorial delight, begging to learn more. Listening to her, Lannat formed an image of a seedling, imperceptibly expanding, one cell at a time, until it cracked solid rock. By the time they arrived at the bar, Lannat was sure that everything the IP knew about Court's security system had been transferred to Trey.

Once inside, with beer flowing freely, the IPs combined to convince Trey she should choose one of them to go home with. Lannat, consigned to the bar, listened to their crude suggestiveness and ground his teeth in silence. When one of the IPs rose and walked toward the back of the small establishment, Lannat assumed he was going to the restroom. Instead, the man worked his way under the Peace/Order camera and reached up to hang his cap over the watchful lens.

Customers, not especially numerous in the first place, thinned out considerably before the IP even made it back to his seat. Those who remained behaved as if the trio at the table didn't exist; no one so much as glanced in that direction.

Trey's laughter tightened as the jokes grew coarser. She rarely lifted her glass from the table, taking only tiny sips. It was well she kept her hands free; she needed them to fend off groping that was rapidly becoming brute force. The anger boiling in Lannat grew stronger every second. Still, Trey gave no sign of asking for assistance. Forcing himself to stop watching in the bar mirror, Lannat stared at the scarred, stained wood, the bubbles in his glass—anything.

He couldn't hold the attitude. He raised his gaze to the mirror again and straightened with surprise. Aside from himself and the trio at the table, the room was as empty as a drum. The bartender obviously had some sort of bolt hole, and the customers, true Hirans, knew exactly when and how to disappear.

Retalla walked in. Before his second step hit the floor, he was a vision of destruction. His chin drew down. His torso bent forward. Fortunately, Jarka was right behind him. Coolly he yanked his friend sideways, slammed him into a seat.

For a few minutes, that situation held.

It ended when each of the IPs grabbed one of Trey's shoulders, and First IP half rose from his chair to hold her head steady to kiss her.

Later Trey would steadfastly maintain she was at all times in perfect control of the situation.

At the moment, it seemed otherwise to her companions. Retalla covered the distance between himself and the struggle in three long strides that suggested avalanche. From behind, he fetched First IP a kick between the legs that lifted that gentleman bodily, almost assuredly providing an effect very unlike any kissing experience in his past. Lannat, too, was moving by that time. As he closed on his own target, he noted the noise coming from the collapsing First IP. It sounded rather like underwater yodeling.

Jarka and Lannat arrived at Second IP from different directions at almost exactly the same time. Second IP was still entranced by the sights and sounds of his partner. Worse, the avenging demon responsible for First IP's sorry state clearly had further mayhem on his agenda. Second IP, burdened by those considerations, was grossly unready when Jarka's fist slammed into his head from the right side. That impact rendered him all the more unprepared for Lannat's contribution from the left. Imperfect timing caused the head to snap first one way, then the other. Unlike First IP, who continued to coddle his crotch with both hands and hoot strangely while scooting in a tight circle on his side, Second IP said a weary, questioning "Mommy?" and dropped facedown in spilled beer.

Trey leaped back from the table, knocking over her chair. Brushing at herself, she said, "Look what you've done. I just washed these trousers and you knocked my beer over. It spilled all over me." Rubbing at the stain, she continued to complain, pointing at First IP. "Somebody put a sock in that one, please? He's enough to wake the dead."

"And if we don't get out of here, we'll be among that number," Jarka said. "Come on."

Retalla stood firm, glaring at Trey. "That's the thanks I get?"

Trey's mouth flew open. Her eyes flashed. Still, she paused, reconsidered her answer. Surprisingly softly, she said, "Of course not. I do appreciate it. I couldn't have done it without knowing you were there."

Lannat thought Retalla might explode with pride. He shoved

the man toward the door. "Take Trey out first. Jarka and I follow." To Jarka, he said, "We have to tie up these two so they can't call for help or come after us."

As from a distance, a voice said, "Get going. We'll take care of them." The bartender rose from behind his bar, apparently surfacing from his hide. He went on. "They won't be doing anyone any more harm." He tilted his head at the Peace/Order camera and its blinded eye. "When their partners come looking for them, we'll tell them they did that so they could duck out the back way. Deserted. Threatened to kill us if we told."

"Who's 'we'?" Jarka asked.

The bartender stared back, as if the words had never been uttered.

"Let's go," Lannat said. "We're finished here." On his way out, he said, "Thanks." The bartender remained as stony as ever.

The walk to the elbus was an eternity. The ride to the outlying town where their elcar waited was even longer. Once they felt clear and able to talk, the debate started. Lannat listened, more than participating. He already knew how the operation must be mounted. There was little time to acquire equipment, train, rehearse. He listened to the ideas of the others, including, discarding. Pieces fell into place.

After a good night's sleep in camp, the trio that accompanied Lannat seemed more enthusiastic than ever about the mission. They joined Lannat in the small underground room that acted as command post for the captured highspies.

The controller was named Multran, the same man who'd defected to the Free on the raid that had captured the equipment. He greeted the trio warmly. Sul was already there. Lannat, sipping from a postbreakfast cup of coffee, asked Multran, "What d'you have for us this morning?"

Multran moved to give the others a better view of the monitor. "We got a report of unusual activity in the military camps near Etasalou's lab—down in the Fols Hills. The highspy's on the—Whoa!" In response to a sudden bleat from his console, he leaped forward and jerked on the control stick. The image on the screen went wild, suggested a rising earth rather than a machine's dive. At the last instant the flight leveled off. There was a blur of trees whizzing past, startlingly close. Nose practically touching the screen, Multran maneuvered his machine expertly. Retalla turned away, eyes rolling, mouth slack. He mumbled about fresh air and rushed outside.

The galling noise from the console stopped. Multran fiddled with his controls and leaned back in his chair. He heaved a monstrous sigh. "Ta-dah! Cheated death again."

Sul glowered. "What was that all about?"

"A tail chase. The rear-seeking detectors picked up something closing on us. I didn't think it'd pursue. No matter; we lost it. Probably hit a tree." Pride bloomed in the last.

"We've been lucky to keep that thing flying this long. You're good," Lannat told him.

Multran's grin broadened. "I'm pretty careful. I stay inside radar shadows most of the time. When I come out, like just now, I try to parasite on an Advisor highspy. Most radar ops can't separate one target from two, if you keep close enough."

"How do you see anything worthwhile, if you're cruising along with one of their machines?" Jarka asked.

"A lot of their missions are flown to check up on their own activities. Second, I can aim my cameras and detectors any direction I choose. He looks for things that interest him, I look for things that interest us. Simple."

"Sure, simple. If you know what to look for and you're skilled enough to fly that thing up a lyso's beak and back out again," Lannat said. "Now, what's this about unusual activity?"

"Let's see where we are." Brow furrowed, Multran punched at his keyboard. Numbers superimposed on the monitor. He tapped more keys. A map appeared on the screen, with a flashing dot at its center. "Good," he said. "I can move south a bit and show you this." The map disappeared, and a sideways pan came on, revealing strings of eltrucks departing a huge campsite. Multran narrated. "You've seen Etasalou's base camp any number of times. We've caught them going out for training before. This is different. More trucks. Gone a long time before they come back."

"Where are they going?" Sul asked. "Can you follow them?"

"Too dangerous." Multran was talking to himself, his companions forgotten. "They're not going to worry about being intercepted or attacked. They'll go right to their destination." Decisively he tapped on the keyboard again. He whistled softly, then looked up at Sul. "I just put in course and estimated speed, and asked the computer to work out coordinates. I don't think we're going to like what comes up. There." He pointed at more superimposed numbers, then bent to his controls. "Be just a minute," he said.

His estimate was overly optimistic. For a good five minutes, the small group was treated to a travelogue. When they recognized their own Marnoffar Mountains on the horizon, closing, the silence grew tense. Lannat was first to see the actual target site. He pointed. "Look. Eltrucks, rising." Mere dots, it took a moment for the others to spot them. Multran selected an observation point amid some trees. Tilting the highspy, powering up the engine, he managed a fairly steady hover. Compensators on the detection systems damped out any erratic motion.

As one, the group voiced concern. Retalla walked back in as Trey was saying "That's a permanent camp they're building. That peak's no more than thirty miles from here. Look at all the digging, the construction. You could put fifty people in a place that size."

Lannat said, "We saw enough eltrucks to carry more than that work crew and their equipment. Look around for another site, Multran."

Within a few minutes Multran jabbed a finger at the screen. "Just like the other one. A mountain peak. Construction. Farther along, too."

"It's started," Lannat said. "Etasalou's finally got enough people restructured to start a ring of bases around us. Our raid on Court just moved up." Still staring at the screen, he put a hand on Multran's shoulder. "You did well. We'll have lots more work for you from here on."

Multran thanked him. Retalla asked Sul something. Conversation filled the small, dark room. Lannat heard none of it. All he could think of was Nan and the raid. Was equipment even available? A training site? Time?

The thought that Etasalou might seize Nan first was a knife in Lannat's guts.

A dark-blue flag snapped in the breeze over the dark-green cloth tent. Orange letters spelled out LEGION in large, exotic script. Under the word was a smaller numeral one.

Inside the tent, Etasalou slouched in a large chair. There was a desk in front of him. Strewn papers gave it a busy look, and a computer terminal on a swivel looked down at the commander as if studying him. In front of the desk stood a small woman in camouflage uniform. She held to rigid attention. Similarly dressed men and women moved around behind her. Etasalou asked her, "You lost the enemy highspy? It eluded you?"

"Yes, sir." The petite features were composed. Still, there was a sense of something wrong about the woman. A look into her eyes made one think of inexpressible sadness, while the precise, proper words carried a suggestion of emptiness.

Etasalou went on. "What happened?"

"I chased it. I crashed."

Pointing at a man in the background, Etasalou snapped his fingers, gestured. The man, also in camouflage uniform, hurried to her side, snapped to attention. Etasalou asked him, "Your highspy camera kept contact with the enemy highspy?"

"Yes, sir."

"You saw where it went? Was it in position to observe our construction?"

"Yes, sir."

"That's all. Dismissed." Etasalou nodded at the two young Legionnaires' salute, watched them about-face and march off. He spun his chair around to face the wall. A thin smile split his features. He tented his fingers in front of him. "I know you're out there with your damned Free, Captain Lannat. I know you saw us. You know the true hostilities are about to begin. If you're to rescue the fair maiden, your time grows short. Come for her, Lannat. I wait."

CHAPTER 32

Betak paced his office, head down, hands jammed in trousers pockets. Lannat simply sat in a corner. Only storm-dark features suggested his own high emotion. Betak finally said, "It's too early."

Whatever else he intended to add was lost in the crash of heavy boots hitting the floor and a chair skittering backward. Lannat was on his feet, leaning across the desk. "Now. No more delays. Since I arrived, I told you she was the key to influencing Etasalou."

Something unpleasant, an oily change of expression that came and went too swiftly to identify, slipped across Betak's features. Too bland, he said, "That's true. But I'm not as sure about that as you."

Lannat retreated more from the urge to strike than any sense of defeat. He pretended he didn't see Betak's hand creep down to rest on the pommel of his sword. He said, "I'll tell you this: You're looking at a mutiny. The Free trust me. Don't force me to play on that trust, Betak. I'm trying to help you. Get in my way and I'll help myself." A sound like laughter rumbled deep in his chest. "We're wrapped up together as tightly as that poor bastard who came here trussed up in blankets."

Betak shot a glance at the floor in front of his desk, winced, then looked to Lannat. He sagged. "I don't see why this move of Etasalou's—after all, it's only two small base camps—means we have to rush into something as dangerous as this raid."

"I've explained already. Those sites look down on our major supply routes, just when our needs are increasing. They'll build more sites. Etasalou will have constant patrols out looking for us. Not Advisors, no one we can intimidate. We're going to be dealing with utterly fanatic troops who fight to the death."

"You make it sound hopeless."

"The camps are isolated. We can hit one and be gone before the other can move to provide support. By the time reserves come from the base camp, way over in the Fols Hills, we'll be halfway home. Aggression, Betak. We're the little guy; we need speed, unpredictability, and constant aggression to keep Etasalou off balance."

"We don't need the Bahalt woman for that."

"We need her to keep reminding him we have her. It'll drive him crazy."

"Why? Why do you keep insisting on that? No man is that family conscious."

"He is. And don't forget the value of Prince Dafanil. The prince puts Etasalou in a circular quandary. He'll want to hit us as hard as possible in order to get his hands on Bahalt, but he has to worry about harming the emperor's son."

The suspicion was back in Betak's eyes. "And if *we* harm the prince?"

"History is written by the winners. If something unfortunate happens to Prince Dafanil, dead men won't contradict the stories of the living."

Leaning back in his chair, Betak's upper body drifted outside the glow of the desk lamp. His face was a pale blur. Lannat wondered if he purposely hid his expression.

Silence clouded the room, drew the walls, the ceiling close. Lannat caught himself taking in air in heavy gusts, like a man surfacing in cold water. When Betak spoke, he was thoughtful. "You would never have said a thing like that when you first came here. Have you considered the innocent who'll suffer for your desire to capture this woman? Let's stop pretending. She's more to you than you admit."

It was a confrontation Lannat long awaited. Now that it was here, he felt cleansed. His answer was ready. "When Etasalou learns who holds his niece, he'll erupt. I'll say no more."

"I wish you'd said something earlier. Does anyone else know of this? Anyone here?"

"Only you. Keep it that way."

Betak frowned, but he nodded. "Are you all in agreement on your readiness?"

"Total. Even Sul. He was the last to come around. When he did, it was with enthusiasm."

"Sul enthusiastic?" Betak chuckled, sat up, bringing himself back into the pool of light. "I'm impressed. He's my cautious one." Then, suddenly pensive, he let his gaze wander. He went on. "They say one must strike decisively or not at all. Let's hope what we're doing is bold enough to clear the way for a rational progress. We must reduce the suffering of the people. May we bring light and peace from darkness and bloodshed. Execute your plan."

Once outside, Lannat paused. He couldn't resist peering into Betak's window. Betak was still at his desk, leaning forward. An elbow on the desk provided bracing for his chin-in-hand pose. His enigmatic smile was a slight curve of the lips. Faint as it was, the expression ran ice-fingers across Lannat's neck. Sinking to a crouch, he darted off into the night and a future that suddenly seemed far less dangerous than the small room he left behind.

* * *

Four elcars spiraled down to blend into the suburban surface traffic pattern. Each waited patiently for an approved radar-controlled insertion into the stream of vehicles bound for the shopping center. The vehicles had no discernible involvement with each other. The sole similarity was their passage load. Driver and passenger sat up front. Three people sat in the backseat. When the elcars parked, drivers sauntered off, leaving their four companions to make their way to elbus stops. Oddly, having just arrived at the mall, the passengers already carried loaded shopping bags.

The shopping center, being quite large, was served by several elbus lines. Sixteen Free fighters with their disguised swords and packages of explosives boarded elbuses at three different locations. Some changing of routes would be necessary. All would arrive, on foot, at the designated assembly point. Each Free wore tight black clothes under normal civilian dress, and each carried a hidden black hood and black gloves.

Almost an hour after the elcars offloaded their passengers, a fifth elcar lifted off north of the city. The small landing port served a well-to-do neighborhood. There was nothing remarkable in the driver's request for a high-altitude course and speed clearance for distant Kull. When queried by Traffic Control, the driver responded with proper credentials and a legitimate business contact. The elcar loitered, hovering, while Traffic Control placed the obligatory call to the stated destination to verify that the person requesting such clearance was expected at the other end. This last step was a precaution initiated by Counsellor Ullas. It assured that any flight cleared to pass over Court had a legitimate reason for doing so.

Neither Counsellor Ullas nor Traffic Control could know that the comfone call to Kull was intercepted and answered by Betak's intelligence network. Nor could Ullas or his Advisors know that the businessman supposedly making the trip to Kull was presently seated on his sofa with his wife and two children, engaged in strained small talk with two very large men holding very large knives and a young woman doing her best to lend an air of civility to the event.

In the businessman's elcar, Sul received clearance. He turned to Retalla and Trey, in the backseat. He ignored Lannat, next to him. "That's it, Retalla. This is your last chance to talk Trey out of this. It's just too dangerous."

Trey answered. "It gets old, Sul. I appreciate what you're saying. I really do. Just quit saying it, please. Get going, or Traffic Control's going to get suspicious. They're all getting paranoid."

Beside her, Retalla laughed. "They've got good reason."

Lannat spoke up. "Just get us on site, Sul. Argue with her when this is over."

Sul gunned the engine. The elcar surged forward.

"Mind your speed," Lannat chided softly. He busied himself checking the buckles and straps of a harness across his chest.

Sul slowed to his prescribed velocity. It seemed no time before he said, "Here we go." Rising sharply, stalling, the elcar whined distress. The rush of air outside stopped with ominous abruptness. The silence inside the vehicle seemed to weigh it down, send it sliding off to the right. Sharp and loud, Sul called to Traffic Control. "Trouble, Traffic. Have to land. Emergency one-eighty to home. Now."

Falling, the elcar picked up speed. Despite safety harnesses, the trio of passengers grabbed overhead handles to maintain themselves. Sul yanked the control yoke, stomped on pedals. Screaming complaint, the car caught itself. Barely making headway, it was at a near hover when he yelled "Time! *Go!*"

Doors flew open. Lannat launched himself. Below, like malevolent stars, city lights waited for his hurtling body. He gulped air when the chute rustled open. The harness tugged solidly. Slipping the darkglasses over his eyes, he quickly picked out his companions, closing on him.

That done, he searched for his target, shifting to thermal. The dazzle of city lights kept him twisting and turning for a clear view. He spotted the roof, confirmed it by the heat rising from the railgun's active fuel cells. The crew's tent showed up, as well. The lone watch stood under the gun's muzzle at the waist-high roof wall.

Lannat tugged on his lines, correcting his course. Trey and Retalla followed. The chutes and the coveralls they wore were undetectable to ordinary traffic radar. If they bunched up, search radar would signal an anomaly.

The larger fear was chute proficiency. His companions' only practice consisted of static leaps from a cliff.

Lannat worked his chute hard, angling to land flat and fast. The perimeter wall rushed at him. It was too close, too high. He pulled his knees up to his chest. His boots scraped the wall, pitching him forward. Straining, he straightened, let go the lines, windmilled his arms to keep his balance. He ran, awkward, out of control. Now the railgun loomed in front of him. He threw up his arms to cushion the impact.

The lone watch, alerted by Lannat's clumsy landing, hurried to investigate. Bowling ahead, almost out of control with forearms raised against the prospect of slamming into the railgun, Lannat plowed into the Advisor, who flew backward at the collision. His head hit the base of the weapon. It made a solid, cracking noise. There was no other sound as he slumped to the ground.

Lannat's headlong stumble stopped instantly. He was disengaging his chute when Trey and Retalla charged past him, attacked the three men just coming out of the tent. Trey clubbed the lead man to the ground as he attempted to draw his sword. Retalla crouched in front of the other two, sword pointed at them. "Don't move. Make any noise and we'll kill you. Get on the ground, facedown. *Now!*"

Swiftly Trey circled behind them, pushed them to obey. They dropped. Lannat hurried up, stripping off his pack. He took a coil of metlin out, and in seconds the prisoners were all bound, gagged, and stacked against the wall.

Lannat ran to the opposite wall, carrying the pack. Cautiously he peered over the edge, surveyed the street below.

Gesturing Retalla and Trey to him, he pointed out the Advisor watch standing outside the IP post almost directly below. Then he indicated two roving two-man patrols. While they watched, another appeared at a distant corner. Whispering, Trey said, "You'd think they'd be smart enough to turn off the street-lights, wouldn't you?"

"Defense-minded," Lannat said. "They believe the light's their friend." He reached into the pack as he spoke and hauled out two pieces of wood and a metal tube. When he fitted the wood into the tube and stretched cord across the arced ends, he was holding an ugly, handmade bow. That was followed by an equally unimpressive trio of arrows. He attached the thin metlin line to the end of the arrow, back by the feathers. Retalla had the coil in hand, reeling it off to spread it on the ground in large, loose loops.

Fitting the arrow to the bowstring, Lannat drew the missile to the head, aimed it in the general direction of the Marnoffar Mountains. Slowly he let the weapon go slack. Putting his back to the wall, sitting down, he scuffled in the pack for his seekum and dimenomap. The only light on it showed his own position. That was disappointing. It meant Jarka and his teams were delayed.

Or something.

Lannat took a deep breath, steadied himself in order to project calm confidence. He hoped Retalla and Trey believed it was real. He told them, "Well, that's it. Now we sit and wait for Jarka and the rest to come to our party."

CHAPTER 33

Moving with shadowy swiftness, the black-clad Free scaled the Peace/Order camera tower at the edge of the park. For him, the steel trusses and slats were like stairs. He was at the top in seconds.

His fifteen companions hid in bushes. When the man atop the tower dropped a roll of electrical cable, one of the Free darted out, grabbed it, and quickly attached it to a small machine. Jarka loomed beside him. He whispered to the technician, "Is it working? Is it all right?"

The technician said, "I think so." He jerked a thumb upward at the other man. "If he taps in without setting off any alarms, we'll be fine. The Advisor monitors will be watching our canned holofilms of the park instead of real time."

Jarka looked past the technician and the camera pylon; the irregular roofs of Old Town blurred against the looming black of Court's high wall. He could barely make out the angle where Lannat hid with Retalla and Trey. Breaking out his dimenomap, Jarka turned it on. Next to the raised surface that indicated the battery location, tiny digital numbers ticked away. Jarka read them and winced. The operation was off schedule by a full ten minutes.

Above, the man working on the camera moved with infinite caution. Peace/Order cameras were designed to detect tampering. According to the side plate, this was an old model, with no contact or movement detector installed. That left only the armored cable. The man cut into it gingerly. There was a small green light on the frame of the hacksaw. He concentrated on that, pulling and pushing the blade with slow, easy strokes. The light flashed red. Instantly the man yanked the saw away, wiped sweat from his brow. Buried under the armored outer cable, something carried a tiny electrical charge. The saw was designed to detect that; thus the red light.

Delicately he cut some more, stripped away armor and insulation to expose the encased wires. From his kit, he brought out a small, rectangular box. He placed that beside the exposed wires; it read current flow through induction. Protection policy for Peace/Order cameras included a randomly timed query through the power line. A chip within the camera responded. If a query failed to get through, Advisors were dispatched immediately. The man on the tower couldn't prevent such a signal. He would know only that he was discovered. That was something, at least. It should earn them enough time to escape.

He dried his hands on his tight coveralls and went back to work.

Working on the breached cable, he quickly found the line carrying imagery back to the Peace/Order monitors. It took seconds for him to tap into them. A soft whistle from below told him the connection was working. Then, just as the man reached for his current reader, the needle leaped violently: a query signal.

There was no response from the camera. Frantic, the technician ran fingers across connections, tried to think where he'd gone wrong. He bent over to shout to his companions.

From the corner of his eye, he saw movement. The needle. It twitched. Then again. He sagged, limp with relief. The thing was an old model, practically antique. The chip within had to read the signal, then trigger an answer. A matter of two seconds, perhaps three.

Noting his pounding heart, the technician took consolation in knowing that, back in Advisor HQ, some diligent monitor was watching images he thought were the real world. On his way down, the man reflected that it would all be very funny if it weren't so damned frightening.

Jarka hurried everyone across the park, keeping well within the cone of vision of the disabled camera. They exited at an alley leading into the darkened Old Town. Jarka assigned his two best swordsmen to point duty. Silently, dodging from shadow to shadow, they preceded the main body. Jarka let four more Free go ahead of him. He longed to be one of those on point, able to see everything first himself. Leadership demanded he be in position to control the larger number of his unit. He cursed his responsibilities.

Well within Old Town, they disappeared through a doorway. In the gloom of a storage room, the raiders quickly uncovered a cache of slim poles. One raider voiced the surprise and dismay of all. "This is it? The ladders?"

Jarka was harsh. "Don't worry about the dark-blasted ladder. Just do your job."

The man subsided. The doubt remained. Redoubled fear thickened the room's close air. Jarka knew the slender shafts were the finest carbon fiber. Far stronger than steel. Betak and Sul personally assured him that, at the lengths involved, the ladders would support at least three people, four in an emergency.

Jarka hefted one. It was *very* slim. Very light.

He snapped at his team, "We're late. Let's go." Jarka led the way. In the utter darkness of the building's interior, even the Hirans were forced to use chemoluminescent wands. They filed upstairs and doused the wands, exiting onto one of Old Town's few flat roofs. Back outdoors, they saw well. Too well. Three rows of buildings stood between them and Court.

"Assemble the ladders," Jarka ordered. It was at least sixty feet to the cement street. He tried to think about anything but those poles.

Men appeared with the assembled ladder. The crossbars between the main shafts were six feet apart. The twin columns stretched vertically into the darkness, disappeared. Jarka inspected the grapples at the base. He wished he was more certain they'd hold.

He turned on his dimenomap. The streets and buildings between himself and Court leaped to life in schematic outline. Small points on the map glowed red. He pointed at the closest. "There, just across the street: Betak said the underground would rig lines for us to hook. Lower the thing."

For all its lightness, the length of the ladder—now technically a bridge—made it awkward. As if threading a needle several feet away, the men handling the ungainly frame guided it into place. Their initial failure to hook up with the grapples did nothing to reduce tension. When they finally secured contact, the sight of the ladder, sagging, swaying, trembling, was even worse.

Without a word, Jarka slung his sword onto his backpack and moved onto the shafts. Prone, the twin poles provided support to his upper body, while his feet, positioned outside their span, gave a bit of added security. Hand over hand, he pulled himself forward.

The technique was familiar. They'd rehearsed many times, in camp. Not with the carbon fiber poles. There they used heavy saplings; they bent, of course. So did the poles. Incredibly. Alarmingly.

When the rhythm of his advance triggered a sickening belly-up/belly-down movement, Jarka clutched the poles to him, not with precisely balanced pressure. That induced a sideways sway in complement to the continuing vertical bounce. Jarka forgot all about the requirement to never look down. When he did, his stomach did all it could to ram dinner back up his throat. He worked just as hard to prevent it.

He won. Barely. Now he used the bounce to advantage, scooting forward busily while the flexible support flung him upward, holding fast when he dropped—however fearfully—toward the forbidding cement. Scrambling onto the blessed firmness of the target roof, he almost whooped relief. Until he remembered there were fifteen people behind him and two more crossings to make. Using the seekum, he reported his experience to the remainder of the team, adding "Forget what they said about three people on this damned thing. Even it if would hold us, we'd probably shake each other off like ripe fruit. Send the next person. I'll tell you when to start the next, and so on. Reply."

The seekum said, "Understood. Ending."

On the roof of Court, the trio of Lannat, Retalla, and Trey peered over the edge. Lannat examined his dimenomap. He looked grim. "They're late and falling behind. If this keeps up, we could still be here at daybreak."

Trey dropped back behind the wall, looked to Lannat. "We can't possibly get out then. You said it yourself—surprise, speed, and darkness; we have to have all three."

Lannat tried to smile. "Two out of three's not bad. We'll be all right."

Retalla took her hand. "Jarka knows what he has to do. Anyhow, both of you are forgetting the diversionary attack. That'll draw off most of the city's Advisor force. While they're fighting fires in the north, we'll be getting away to the south."

Everyone nodded agreement. No one commented.

For Jarka, the second crossing was a vast improvement over the first. The third went so smoothly the entire team buzzed with self-assurance while they disassembled the ladders. They made their way across roof crests until Jarka signaled a halt. Looking at the height of Court's wall and the wide street intervening, he said, "This is it." He spoke as if to himself, a mix of awe and determination. Around him, the Free were silent in their own thoughts.

Jarka attached his dimenomap to his seekum, marked his location.

In seconds, Lannat's blunt arrow thudded onto the far end of the room. While team members drew coils of heavier line from their packs to be pulled back across the street, another arrow carrying thin line dropped on the opposite end of the roof. Soon after the third arrow landed. Three heavy cords were secured rapidly. The rise from Jarka's position to the top of Court's wall precluded hand-over-hand crossing. From Court's side, looped straps slid down to Jarka's people. Metlin lines led from the loops back to Court.

Behind the wall, Retalla and Trey were just completing construction of a small machine. While Trey fished the last parts out of her backpack, Retalla hurriedly fed the end of one metlin line into the multiple pulleys inside the machine's frame. Leaving the parts, Trey moved to connect the device to the fuel cells of the railgun. Retalla turned from his work, nodded at Trey, pushed a button. The electric motor growled. Pulleys spun, pulling on the metlin. Retalla faced Lannat. "It's ready."

"Right." Lannat spoke to the seekum. The crossing cable next to him suddenly flexed. It whispered stress where it rubbed the stone wall. The smaller metlin line hissed agreement. Across the street, hanging onto the strap, Jarka dangled in midair. The electric motor hummed industriously, dragging him up and across.

Eager hands lifted Jarka over the wall. He dumped his pack and secured his sword to its belt. The strap was released, to be retrieved by the raiders waiting across the street. The second metlin line was fed into the small machine's pulleys. A second raider stepped out into space.

Everything went fine for the first three crossings. Then the fire alarms went off in the distance.

The street below erupted with Advisors. Disorganized, they whirled like windblown leaves. Bared swords glinted in the glow of streetlights. Shouts echoed between Old Town's buildings and Court's walls. Above the confusion, pale and wide-eyed, a Free raider hung onto her strap loop, halfway along the cable. Trey extended wishful hands, yards short of any assistance.

Lannat grabbed the raiders already across. "Guard the roof entrance. Let no Advisor up here."

North, a red glow scarred the darkness. The diversionary attack was right on time. Lannat wished the same were true of his own effort. The suspended Free raider came over the side of the roof, gasping. Lannat practically tore her out of Trey's supporting grasp. "Get over there with the others." He wasted no time on sympathy or congratulations. Those things would come in abundance later. For the survivors. As the woman ran off, he turned on Retalla. "Can't you make that thing go faster? Twelve more people means two hundred and forty seconds before we're all here. We may not have four minutes."

Retalla didn't look up from where he was feeding the next line into the pulleys. "We may have enough time. We don't have any more power." The quiet whine of the little motor doing its job underscored his finality.

Lannat watched his frightened comrades sway and twist across the gap. He watched the scurrying Advisors, so unaware of what was taking place over them. He supervised the last-second preparations of the team. It was all unreal, a dreamscape. His thoughts were for Nan Bahalt. A few yards away, nearer than she'd been in over a year, since the few minutes they had spent together in the accursed oneway.

Now the doubts swarmed, foul and disgusting. Was this all really to protect her? Or to satisfy his own needs? Was Betak right to doubt him? Did a thinking man so gravely risk the life of the woman he loved? Could he offer her better protection in the fastnesses of the Manoffar Mountains than she enjoyed here?

What if the raid failed?

A touch on his arm startled him so badly that he grabbed his sword. Trey said, "The last one's coming over the wall." She pointed at the increased glow to the north. "That has to be the data bank, because power to the city's not affected yet. We're going in anyhow."

Lannat led the way down to the next floor. There was a guard post at the bottom. When the door to the stairs opened, he barely had time to lift his head from his book before Lannat cut him down. The only sound was the muffled thud of the body.

A shock team of four raced past Lannat, bound for the rooms designated sleeping barracks. Their task was primary; they must capture the Advisor communications equipment intact. The raiders could allow no calls for help yet must be able to turn aside questions. Jarka followed the first four. Running after him, Lannat checked over his shoulder to see the rest of the team, with Retalla and Trey in the rear.

Lannat rounded a corner into a hall just in time to see the guard post overwhelmed. A comfone flew through the air, smashed against a wall. Jarka salvaged the dying guard's seekum, clapped on the headset. When Lannat arrived beside him, Jarka gave a wolfish smile and a thumb's up.

The sounds of pitched combat already escalated from within the sleeping quarters. Lannat turned to the doorway, where Retalla and Trey were hurtling into the room. With Jarka and his men hard behind, Lannat joined them.

Advisors, waking to the shouts and screams of their companions, offered little resistance to the swift, deadly efficiency of the black-clad intruders. Those who did went down quickly, demoralizing the rest. Again, the grinding, repetitive rehearsals in the Marnoffar hideouts proved their worth. Before the stunned guard force was aware how greatly they outnumbered the attackers, survivors were on the floor, facedown. Designated raiders bound the captives, gagging them with strips torn from the handy bedding.

Leaving two men to guard the prisoners, the rest of the team sprinted for the stairs leading down to the rooms housing Nan and Prince Dafanil.

The back of Lannat's neck tingled. He was irresistibly drawn to look back up the echoing stairwell. They had to go down three floors. Every intelligence report insisted the building was absolutely vacant, save for the top floor and the two lowest, set aside for the Advisor guards, with the captives on the fourth from the top. Nevertheless, he threw open the door at each landing and checked the long, dimly lit hallways. He saw nothing but still carried with him a nightmare feeling that something lurked there.

The team reached the target floor as the lights flickered once, twice, and went out. It proved the diversion was working. Another power plant down, more computers and data eliminated.

They were in the main hall that served the rooms used by Nan and the prince when the lights came on again. Jarka signaled a halt, spring-wire tense. After peering about for no more than two or three seconds, he resumed the advance.

Lannat moved with the rest. The prickling at the back of his neck was suddenly worse. More, the memory of those long, deserted halls was so strong it crowded out even the urgency of the moment.

Lannat told himself there was no reason for concern. If the Advisors had moved in an auxiliary generator, it was a normal precaution, nothing more.

Jarka reached the door leading to the medical facility, threw it open. The duty nurse screamed, falling backward over her chair in retreat. Lannat noted how her stark white face gleamed terror against the bright blue and green robe.

Lannat held Jarka in place, addressed the nurse. "Where are the guards? The security?"

Drawn tight against the wall, hiding behind a shoulder, she shook her head, made no sound.

Foreboding redoubled, Lannat told Jarka, "Pull half of our people. Have them wait in here until we send for them. The rest come with us. Check every room. Something's wrong."

Confusion twisted Jarka's expression, but he made no protest. Even as he turned to issue the orders, Lannat was on his way, trotting, overtaking the lead element. He forced his way to the front. The door at the end of the hall was the one, the entry to Nan and the prince.

His joy would not be restrained. He was here. They would get away, be together again. He burst through the door so quickly the latch ripped clear of its niche with a shrill, grating sound. He stepped in and froze.

Across the room, a naked sword against her throat, Nan stared back at him. Next to her was Prince Dafanil. Behind Nan, a sharp-featured man in the red and yellow of Lumin peered out. Dimly Lannat noted an Advisor lieutenant holding Prince Dafanil in the same manner. The two captors smiled confidently.

CHAPTER 34

Confused yelling and the unmistakable clash of sword against sword erupted behind Lannat. He took a step toward Nan. Mard made a warning grunt, moved his weapon. Nan jerked, winced. The hard blade-gleam contrasted brutally with the soft darkness of her skin.

For Lannat, time seized. His head roared like distant, echoing thunder. There was nothing in the universe but Nan. Anyone could see her obvious fear and confusion. Lannat felt he was observing her at microspeed, seeing details of facial expression no ordinary person could comprehend. Part of his mind scoffed at such conceit, but he wanted to believe. He told himself he saw a question in her eyes, then uncertain recognition. Another change followed, swift as light. Withdrawal. Dismissal.

"It's over, rebel," Prince Dafanil said. "You're captured. There are thirty more Advisors behind you." He gestured loosely at Mard. "I suggest you surrender to Captain Mard here. He's quite willing to butcher all of you, Commander

Etasalou's niece included. Her death will publicly be blamed on you, of course. It's quite hopeless, you see?"

Dafanil's voice barely carried over the distant noise of combat. Lannat said, "Are you Prince Dafanil?" He watched Nan, praying for recognition of his voice. He saw no reaction.

Before the prince could do more than nod, the sharp-faced man said, "He's not in charge of this situation. I am. Drop your weapon."

Lannat raised it instead. "It's not that easy, Captain."

"Of course it is." Mard gloated. "That racket you hear is the lieutenant's guard force attacking your raiders from the rear. I thought you might try some derring-do. Everyone else said you'd come through the ground floor. I convinced the lieutenant we should prepare our own defense plan. I never thought you'd use the roof, but I fully expected you to enter above the second floor. The point is, you've been outgeneraled at every turn. The Advisors have you and—" He gave Nan a shove. "—I have these."

The fight behind Lannat was a good bit quieter by then. Mard heard the change, as well, and his smile gained confidence. Lannat kept his own expression flat. If no one from the raider force called for his help, then the diminished racket could only mean the Advisor force was losing. No matter their numbers, only four could fight abreast in the hallway. Lannat was confident his better-trained personnel could cut up the limited front of Mard's ambush. Especially if the eight men took Mard's people from behind, in their turn.

As if to stretch Lannat's tension to the breaking point, the noise of the fighting in the hall suddenly increased. There were shouts, cries of pain, of effort and triumph.

Then the scream. Even as he watched Mard flinch, Lannat knew it was no Advisor. He knew exactly who it was: Trey.

Her subsequent cries drowned in a sound that lifted the hair on Lannat's neck. It was a chorus, like beasts after prey. It lasted but seconds. As quickly as the intensity had risen before, now it slacked. Within moments of that frenzied roar, the hall-way was almost silent.

Then Trey's voice rose again, anguished. As before, Lannat knew: Trey wasn't injured. Retalla was. Remaining at the ready, he kept his gaze fixed on a now-uncertain Mard.

Trey approached from the rear. "No! No. Help us. Some-body, help us." There were shouts, confusion. From the corner of his eye, Lannat saw her stumble into the room, Retalla's gangling frame draped over her. The hand not wrapped around her shoulder was clamped over a bloody wound in his side. Stopping just ahead of Lannat, Trey lowered Retalla. He collapsed facedown. Sobbing, Trey bent to touch his cheek, raised her eyes to Mard. "He needs help. A doctor. He'll die."

Lannat said, "Trey. Stop it. They want us to surrender. What happened in the hall?"

Jarka forged into the room, stopped beside Lannat. Flushed, chest heaving from exertion, he said, "They quit. You were right. We boxed them. Only a few really wanted to fight at all. It's over."

Trey refused to acknowledge them, continued begging. "I don't care what the Free says, what Val says. It's not worth it. Help him, please." She dropped her sword and unbuckled her sword belt. Arms fully extended to her sides, she went on. "Look, I'm deserting. Me and my friend are deserters. We sur-render. Please. I'll tell you everything, I swear it. Just don't let him die."

"Shut your mouth," Lannat snarled at her, reached out.

Nan's gasp stopped him, held him fast. Blood welled where the blade bit into her flesh. Watching Lannat, Mard spoke to Trey. "We can help each other here. Help me talk some sense into your leader. If you don't surrender, I'll kill these prisoners. You'll be blamed. You'll all go directly to Etasalou's labs. I think you know what that means. Surrender to me, and I'll pro-tect you. There's a dispensary right here. A nurse. Doctor Bahalt can save your friend."

"You're a liar," Lannat told Mard. "You'd never kill the emperor's son, Etasalou's niece. If they die, so do you. Here."

Lannat saw Nan strain, try to lessen the pressure of the edge at her throat. He couldn't bear to meet her eyes. His bluff could never stand up to that. He could only hope the man called Mard couldn't guess how empty the threat was.

Mard went on. "You have no choice. Surrender honorably, and I promise none of you will go to the labs. You'll have to be jailed, but in our cells, not his. Decide quickly. The rest of the guard force will be here soon. Then it'll be too late."

Trey half turned, looking to Lannat and Jarka. "You heard. He'll help us. Help Retalla. We have to do as he says."

Calmly, reasonably, Lannat said, "We can talk about it. Just step back, Trey. You're making him nervous. See, he's cut the doctor." He was sure he appeared calm. He willed it, ached with the need to make the charade work. Inwardly he coiled tightly, waiting for the instant when Mard would be watching Trey's move.

Looking directly into Lannat's eyes, Trey seemed to read his mind. She skipped away, toward Mard. "This is all your fault. If Retalla dies, I'll curse you beyond death."

Groaning, Retalla reached for her ankle. He was barely audible. "Don't. They lie. Don't."

Coaxing, Mard said, "They don't understand. I meant what I said. As soon as it's safe, Doctor Bahalt will tend to your friend. We'll do everything for your other injured, as well."

"Thank you, thank you." Trey rushed to him. "Hurry, please. He's bleeding. Hurry." Without pausing or without any changed inflection in her voice, she jammed her fingers in Mard's eyes. At the same time, she reached up with the other hand and heaved back on his wrist, immobilizing the sword. The latter move was unnecessary. Blinded, Mard screamed and fell back.

Retalla, reacting as quickly, scooped up Trey's dropped sword and lunged past Prince Dafanil. The Advisor recovered too soon for him. Deflecting Retalla's weak blow with his own weapon, he smashed a fist to Retalla's forehead. Retalla dropped in a heap. Prince Dafanil was moving by then. Whirling, he flicked out a hand in what seemed to be no more than a warding gesture. Nevertheless, the lieutenant staggered away. Both hands went to his throat, his forgotten sword clattering to the floor. When Trey picked up his weapon and turned to engage him, Dafanil grabbed her shoulder and stopped her. "That's unnecessary," he said. "He's dying."

That said, Dafanil walked to where Lannat had an arm around Nan's shoulder, supporting her, dabbing at the small cut on her neck. The Advisor lieutenant fell, choking and kicking. Dafanil ignored him. To Lannat, he said, "Congratulations. You were right, you know: That insect wouldn't dare harm me. But now I think you'd best think about leaving here. I assume you cut off communications with the force waiting downstairs; they'd be here otherwise. As Mard said, though, it won't take them long to discover something's happened up here. Before you rush off, however, I've a favor to ask."

Ingratiating as fine weather, Dafanil completely overwhelmed Lannat's need to tell him he was still a captive. Lannat heard himself answer, thought he sounded like a flustered child. "I'd be honored, Highness. Anything I can do."

"Stop being so ridiculously heroic and kiss this poor woman. She's talked about nothing but her precious Captain Lannat since I met her." He paused, flashing the smiling charm that dazzled the courts of the empire. "You really are her captain, aren't you?"

Etasalou threw aside his blanket and turned on the comfone irritably. "What is it?" He showed no interlude between sleep and full awareness, aside from a squint brought on when his voice triggered the automatic lighting.

The slight woman on the screen answered apologetically. "Sheriff Plon's office reports a Free riot, Commander. It appears to be very large, but spontaneous. There are fires. No armed Free units are involved."

"Very well." The incidents were becoming epidemic. Every move by the Free underground destroyed more records, injured more Advisors. Worse, it increased desertions by the spineless idiots. A moment's curiosity moved Etasalou to ask "Where is it this time?"

"Northeast sector, sir. It must be their turn; they've had no trouble until now."

Etasalou bent forward, glared into the screen. "How long has this been going on? When did it start? Is it continuing? Never mind; get me Plon's office. Immediately."

"Yes, sir." The woman obeyed so swiftly she cut off the end of the last word. Etasalou didn't notice. He was reaching for his clothes, calling for brighter light. When the comfone chimed, he was pulling on his boots. The face on the screen identified himself as Captain Larem, Duty Officer.

"What's the situation at Court?" Etasalou asked.

"Nothing unusual, Commander."

"What's being done about the northeast sector riots? How long has the condition existed?"

"Trouble started almost two hours ago. The rioters are being very stubborn, sir. Aggressive. We break them up, they run, then regroup and start more trouble. Sheriff Plon sent reinforcements to the Advisor Post. We'll have everything under control soon."

"When's the last time you checked the guard on Prince Dafanil and my—and Doctor Bahalt?"

The duty officer visibly relaxed. "The duty officer's not responsible for that anymore, Commander. The Imperial Wing detail was reinforced two nights ago. They have their own officers on duty round the clock. They report directly to Sheriff Plon."

Etasalou grabbed the screen with both hands, as if trying to strangle the man on the other end. "Two nights ago? Why?"

"Sheriff Plon's orders, sir." The duty officer leaned away from his comfone.

"There's been nothing unusual happen there tonight?"

"No, sir. Not a thing since last phone check, sir."

"How long ago was that?"

"They call in every time the watch changes, sir. That was 2000 hours."

"What? Almost four? . . . *Idiots!* I'm giving you a direct order. Get to the Imperial Wing immediately. Tell that lieutenant to report to me, tell him to expect a roof landing by Legionnaires within minutes. Do it now, you imbecile. *Move!*"

Etasalou ran from his bedroom.

Lannat fixed his gaze on Prince Dafanil, unwilling to look into any of the questioning eyes around him. "I've heard his name, Highness. A Rifles officer. Court-martialed. I'm Elemental Guard myself."

"Of course." Dafanil waved a languid hand. His tone might have been sarcastic. Or bored. Any number of things. He turned to Nan. "This is where we part company then, Doctor."

Coughing softly, Lannat corrected him. "With all respect, Highness, I'm afraid that's not true. You have to come with us."

Dafanil turned quickly. His weakness betrayed him, and he swayed, fighting furiously for control. "I am a prince of the blood."

"I don't have time for argument, Highness." Lannat pointed at two raiders. "You and you; help the prince." When Dafanil resisted, pushing at them, Lannat bent close to him. "I won't have anyone killed for your pride, Highness. Cooperate, or you'll be carried like a sack of grain. Can you run, with help?"

"Damn you. I'll see you flayed. Yes, I can run."

Dubious, Lannat told his men, "If he slows you down, pack him out. Keep up." Then, to another raider, a bulky man, he said, "That one, who calls himself Mard. Bring him. Maybe he's just a souvenir, but I want him." He grabbed Nan's arm, pulled her out of the room, past the raiders in the hall. A clump of seated Advisors formed an island of uncertainty between the raiders. A few were bandaged, as were some Free. Lannat told the prisoners, "Eltrucks are coming to lift us out. We welcome anyone who'll fight with us. Think about it." Over his shoulder, he said, "Jarka, take rear guard. See everyone keeps up."

Looking back at the crowd mounting the stairs, he saw Retalla, making hard work of each step, but managing. Lannat was more startled to see some of his men helping wounded Advisors keep the pace. Similarly, two of his own personnel, too badly injured to walk, were each carried by a team of one Advisor and one raider. Once on the roof, however, the Advisors were herded together, guarded by raiders.

Nan came to him. She had trouble looking at him. "There are badly wounded people here. They shouldn't be forced to travel."

"It's that or get turned over to Etasalou. Give them a choice. Most will take their chances with us. Wouldn't you?"

She winced as if struck. Without answering, she fled to the wounded. Cursing himself, Lannat called to Jarka and led him to the railgun. After turning on the firing switch, Lannat pushed the button operating the loading mechanism. "Watch," he told Jarka, grabbing one of the ceramet slugs from an ammunition box. "This is all you do to load. Drop the round in that receptacle. Now, come." He leaped into the gunner's seat. "See this crosshair ring? Put the cross on your target. This is the firing button. When the light is green, the way it is now, all you do is hold the sight on the target and push the button. These slugs take off making over fifteen thousand feet per second, so anything you can see is just about point and shoot. You got that?"

Jarka was thunderstruck. His question was a croak that matched his expression. "Missile weapon?"

Lannat blushed. He was glad it was dark. "The emperor says it's all right to use them in defense of the empire. I figure we fit the definition. Do you remember what I told you?"

Jarka nodded. Lannat went on. "Good. You're the loader. I'm the gunner."

"Loader?" Jarka couldn't find anything in this scenario that was believable.

An Advisor, followed by a raider carrying a ready sword,

came to Lannat. He said, "There's another of these things. Down on the next floor."

Lannat sent Trey and a work party to bring it to the roof. They were just reappearing when another raider pointed north. "Look. Over at the Fols Hills. Vehicles lifting."

Lannat nodded. "Etasalou. Smart bastard. I was afraid you'd figure it out." He turned to Trey's work party, snapped orders. "Set it down there. Jarka, show them what I showed you. Hurry. We've got two minutes, maybe less. Trey, get over here."

Trey put a tentative hand on the insectile-looking railgun. "You're actually going to use this?"

"Absolutely." He looked past her. "Where the hell are our eltrucks?"

"Did you know that these people knew we were coming?" she asked him.

"You're sure?" Lannat asked.

She nodded. "The Advisor prisoners all say so. They weren't sure when or how. They moved in an emergency generator two days ago. Increased the guard."

He leaned against the railgun controls. "Now we really have to wonder about our eltrucks. First things first, Trey. We bust these incoming vehicles."

Her apprehension slipped away, surrendering to the grim smile of someone stepping off the edge of reality and into the maelstrom of combat. Quickly he showed her and another trooper how to load and fire. Returning to the gunner's seat of the first railgun, he watched the elcars streaking toward them.

His seekum beeped. The mechanical voice was terse: "Eltrucks. Headed in."

There was time for one last look at Nan. Mere yards away, she knelt beside a coughing trooper, comforting him. Turning back, Lannat ran a finger across the firing button. He inhaled, savored electrified air, the unique scent of fuel cells and oiled metal. Under his breath he said, "I beat your creatures once, Etasalou. I'll do it again. You'll never get her. Not while I live."

CHAPTER 35

The five elcars spread out in a diamond. The lead vehicle accelerated. Lannat said to Jarka, "They're sending in a scout. How far away is our extraction team?"

The answer came slowly. "They've dropped out of sight."

Lannat put a good face on it. "That's smart. They spotted the elcars."

Jarka made a noise. Lannat said, "Stand by with a second round. It takes a few seconds for the fuel cells to build to full charge. Trey, when I fire, you take out the last vehicle in the formation. The senior man will probably be in that one."

The scout vehicle slowed. Lannat shouted, "Everyone who can stand, do it. On your feet. Hide the wounded."

"What difference if we knock out the senior man?" Trey asked. "They don't think, you said."

"They think as well as they ever did. They have a mission. They'll execute."

"What if I miss?" The question was jagged, high-pitched. "I've never even seen a railgun."

"Neither has the guy in the elcar. Do your job."

After that, there was silence. Soldiers who had tried to kill each other a few short minutes before now stood together in shared uncertainty and anticipation.

Silhouetted against the distant glow of fires, the scout drew closer. As soon as Lannat heard the antigrav power up for landing, he fired. The blue-red course of the ceramet slug blasted an unerring line. So quickly the mind barely comprehended, the elcar exploded. Everything at the point of impact was transformed into incandescent mist. The glowing mass expanded, then fell, its beautiful horror fading into the blackness of the night.

Trey's shot followed an instant later. It struck the target vehicle at the forward edge of its wedge shape. The vehicle cartwheeled backward, spraying liquefied metal. Then it, too, exploded.

The three remaining vehicles cranked into violent turns. Lannat centered on one, watched anxiously for the ready light. He fired. The vehicle exploded. Trey got off her second round. The fourth elcar became a plunging fireball.

A man shouted from the gathering on the roof. "Our eltrucks!"

Lannat concentrated on the last elcar. Lights out, it dipped swiftly behind buildings. "Jarka. Supervise loading. Bring the other railgun. I'll keep the other elcar off."

The extraction eltrucks swept in, nearly running over people with their landing. As soon as they settled, four Advisors broke free, rushed at one. The driver alertly lifted. The foursome turned and faced the others on the roof, already in pursuit. One of the four yelled, "Our families will end up with Etasalou's labs. We have to stay here."

Another Advisor shouted back, "They'll get our families anyway. We can at least fight for them."

Lannat was relieved to see one of his troopers quietly positioning able-bodied Free behind the arguing Advisors.

Jarka stepped between the two forces. "All Advisors who want to stay, move out now. Get downstairs." He pointed his sword at the four. "You. Lead the way." He took a threatening step forward. The men ran, and as they passed the others, several more joined them.

The hovering eltruck landed before the last departing Advisor was out of sight. Feverishly troops wrestled the railgun aboard. Prodding, cursing, Jarka forced people into eltrucks, had them stacked on top of each other. Even as he scanned desperately for the hiding elcar, Lannat wondered how the prince was taking to being squashed among the masses.

He tried not to wonder about Nan.

Someone called his name. Lannat recognized the trooper from the Yasil raid, Parkronar. The man said, "Jarka says come now."

With perfect, malevolent timing, the elcar rose into view, then immediately dropped back under cover. Lannat cursed it, told Parkronar, "Tell Jarka to lift. When he sees me nail the elcar, come back."

"He won't leave."

"It's an order, damn it. Tell him." Lannat looked toward the Fols Hills. More elcars rose, with larger eltrucks in trail. When he checked, Parkronar was leaping into the last remaining vehicle. It lifted off.

As Lannat expected, the hidden elcar pursued. It would easily overhaul the burdened eltrucks. With a close pass overhead, engine downblast would tumble the target machine. The effects of the antigrav on human physiology would assure no effective reaction from those aboard.

Once more the incandescent streak speared out from Lannat's railgun. The stink of ozone, of fried air, washed over him. The elcar turned into a multicolored ball of flame, plummeted.

An eltruck slogged back toward Lannat. In the seconds before it arrived, he dropped to the roof and grabbed his pack. There was pliable explosive in there. He yanked the service plate off one of the boost stations that propelled the weapon's slug along the rail. The sheet metal was searing hot. Lannat dropped it, gritting his teeth against the pain. Burned hands fumbled for a blasting cap. He held his breath, sweating heavily. Clumsy, hurting fingers bobbled the sensitive cap, finally plugged it in the soft explosive.

Jarka grabbed his shoulder. "They're coming fast."

Lannat slammed the service plate in place, then grabbed his

pack. The two men flung themselves into the back of the already moving eltruck.

A Legionnaire elcar made for the abandoned roof at full speed. The laboring vehicles of the Free ran. Personnel in Lannat's eltruck screamed for the driver to dive for cover. Up front in the cab, unable to hear them, unaware of the danger, he continued on. Lannat and Jarka tried to calm the others, explain that the railgun was sabotaged. Panic had its teeth in them. In a culture that considered a thrown rock a dishonorable act, the prospect of dying by missile was a terrible thing. Lannat could only wonder about the scene in the other vehicles.

Two eltrucks lowered toward Court's roof. The railgun erupted in a dazzling blue-green orb below and between them. The explosion swelled outward. The eltrucks flared bright red and yellow, crashing to the roof. A closing elcar, hammered by the shock wave, slewed sideways, crashed out of sight behind Court.

Lannat forced his way past cheering troopers to the front of the cargo space. He banged on the window. The driver half turned, rolled down the window, and shouted, "Quit yelling back there. I'm going as fast as this lump will move."

Lannat shoved his dimenomap forward for the driver to see. "Tell the other drivers we're going past the original drop site. You lead. We're going here." He pointed.

"Are you crazy? Who are you?"

"I'm in charge."

Blinking, the driver said, "We'll never make it." He jerked a thumb to the rear. "They're gaining."

"Get lower. Lose them."

Grudgingly the driver touched his c-button and spoke to the other drivers while sending the truck into a howling dive. Leveling off, he checked his rear-vision radar. From the side of his mouth, he said, "You a gambling man?"

"Depends on the odds."

"You try to land and unload, those people behind us will be on you before half of you touch ground. There's a hill up ahead. It's between the place you showed me and the original drop site. I can hold a lead until we get there. We can swing around behind the hill and hit the ground. That bunch should burn right past us, on up the valley into the Marnoffars. By the time they miss us, you'll be under cover and we'll be far away from these eltrucks and headed home."

"Do it." Lannat spoke to the seekum. "Debark on my command. Changing drop site."

Trey responded immediately. "Received."

Lannat grinned. Tough lady; no questions.

The driver finished instructing the other vehicles to close on him, then spoke to Lannat. "Original drop site coming up." He hit a switch. The forward-looking array on the control panel lost color, went to green and black. Neatly arrayed forms lined three sides of the small clearing. The driver swore. "You knew it, didn't you? Waiting for you." Before Lannat could answer, the machine dropped even lower, skimming treetops. Hanging on, Lannat barely had presence of mind to note the similar action of the other eltrucks.

Behind him, Jarka yelled outrage. "What the hell's going on? We've got wounded."

The driver said, "Whoever was waiting for you down there won't be right for a good ten minutes. Antigrav downblast scrambles brains like eggs. I wish we could've got lower."

The vehicle twisted into a hard right turn. While still sliding sideways, the driver nosed up, powering into hover mode, and dropped. Lannat's order to offload was more stutter than anything. The troops needed no urging. They erupted onto solid ground. The wounded were handed out. Trey's voice was the only one raised, yelling unloading instructions for the railgun. The eltruck drivers left on foot.

Lannat's personnel streamed into the nearby forest. Once there, he called a halt, gathered everyone. Trey and her gun carriers arrived last. She asked, "Did you see the people chasing us go by?"

Lannat shook his head. "I don't know how I missed it."

Other voices rose. No one saw or heard anything of their pursuit, wondered at their disappearance. Lannat said, "Whatever happened, it's good news." He raised his voice to address the entire group. "Jarka, you and three Free take the point. Trey, you and three more—rear guard. The rest with me in the main element with our guests." He pulled six former Advisors clear of the rest. "You'll shoulder the railgun for the first hour. All the rest of you just joining us, I want your swords on the railgun carriage. Once we reach camp—or if anyone tries to intercept us—you'll get them back."

From the darkness, a voice rose in accusation. "We risked our lives, our families, to join you. You don't trust us."

"Damned well told. A little while ago, you were trying to kill us. Nearly did, some of us. You'll get plenty of chance to prove your loyalty. For now, do what you're told and keep your mouths shut."

Murmurs trailed through the group, tentacles of resentment and uncertainty. Lannat shouted over them, "Jarka, move out. Parkronar: Supervise disarming the newcomers. You six: Lift that thing. Ten-minute break in an hour."

Lannat turned. Nan stood a yard away with Prince Dafanil, lending him a shoulder in support. Thermal imagery made them glow in shadings of green against black. Even in that extreme, her expression of distaste was clear.

Etasalou's elcar settled onto the roof of the Imperial Wing. The declining whine of the antigrav was mood music for his appearance. The slight, electric form leaped out. He inspected the scene, seeing everything, revealing nothing. Legionnaires stood in orderly ranks by the wreckage of the railgun. Wounded lay in rows near the wall. Advisors gathered away from them, close to the stairs leading below. When Etasalou at last acknowledged Counsellor Ullas, he said, "Your actions cost me almost a hundred Legionnaires."

Sheriff Plon exclaimed at the unimaginable rudeness.

Ullas was rigid. "There are no Legionnaires. The people I

have allowed you to mold to my goals are Hirans. You have no authority to name them or employ them. You abuse the sanctuary I provide you. You will direct your personnel to take orders only from my appointed Advisor leaders."

Etasalou trembled. He paused, seeming to digest Ullas's ultimatum. "If that is your desire, sir, I can say no more. I must point out, however, that it was your personal order that directed me to land my Leg—the pursuit force at the supposed Free drop site. Your Advisors attacked us."

"And your robots murdered seventeen good Advisors. Such a thing will never happen again."

Arms spread wide, Etasalou bowed his head. He flashed a crooked, deprecating smile when he straightened. "I am ashamed. I mean only greater glory for Hire. The gathering of the starships grows imminent. Eagerness causes me to overstep my authority. I humbly apologize. You have my word; my goal is to raise you to the highest possible state."

Skepticism pinched Ullas's face tighter than usual. He squinted at Etasalou, probing for insincerity. Seeing none, he relaxed a bit. "I shall hold you to your word. We have much to repair."

"They escaped with a railgun, I understand. As well as Prince Dafanil and Doctor Bahalt. Do we know how the Free managed entry?"

"Over here." Ullas indicated the wall facing the street. "Sheriff Plon's investigators found parachutes. Whoever landed managed to get lines across the street and the rest joined them."

"How many?"

The answer was a touch too forceful. "At least fifty. They overwhelmed the security."

"Yes. Security. Please, Counsellor; may I ask how you knew where the Free drop site was?"

"You may not."

"Perfectly understandable. But my instructions to send

my—the pursuit there came directly from you. Surely you don't control every aspect of your intelligence net personally?"

"It's none of your concern." Ullas's smile was all teeth. The rest of his face was scorn. "Your only concern is my ascendancy."

"And it shall be." Once more Etasalou bowed, this time with flourishes much like Captain Mard's. Moving forward, the bow suddenly a crouch, Etasalou clamped his arms around Ullas's lower thighs. Lifting, the smaller man hoisted the taller with surprising ease and swiftness. A half step, and they were at the waist-high wall. Ullas's buttocks barely cleared the top; it was enough that they did. Unbalanced, the long torso bent backward, over the street. In one smooth motion, Etasalou pulled his hands from under Ullas's legs, thrust them against the chest.

Ullas screamed.

Flailing, clawing empty air, he tipped over. He shrieked terror until the sidewalk cut off the noise with shocking abruptness.

Etasalou had his sword to Sheriff Plon's stomach by then. Crackling with intensity, he said, "I have raised Counsellor Ullas to a higher plane, exactly as I said I would. My dynasty begins here. I'll have your loyalty or your bowels, Plon. Now."

Without waiting for Plon to collect enough composure to speak, Etasalou shouted at the unmoving Legionnaires. "Any of those Advisors who offer objection to my rule, kill them." Drawing a seekum from a jacket pocket, he flicked it on, ordered, "Execute dynasty."

The seekum's mechanical voice said, "Received, Commander."

Etasalou turned off the instrument. The tip of his sword still rested on Plon's belt. "Do you serve me willingly, Sheriff? Or shall I arrange perfect loyalty?"

"No!" Plon shook his head so hard his whole body vibrated. "I acknowledge you. Sir. Commander."

Etasalou sheathed the sword. Turning away from Plon with

a casual air that said more than any language, he addressed the Legionnaires' leader. "Detail teams of four Legionnaires to personally contact all senior Lumin and Advisor personnel in Court and Liskerta. Sheriff Plon and his men know where to find them. All dignitaries report to Court tomorrow morning at eight. Failure will result in imprisonment and confiscation of all personal property. Punishment for any resistance to my rule is execution."

Returning his attention to Plon, he said, "Send a message to all Advisor forces: Ninety percent of all Advisors on the continents of Kull and Sardeg are transferred to Liskerta, to arrive no later than twenty-four hours after receipt of my order. You will see to the logistics of the matter, Plon. Be efficient. We have a tight schedule. In ten days, the Free must be a memory. I must have Prince Dafanil. Alive, if possible. Dead, if need be. Ten days. You hear me?"

Plon saluted. He was breathing too hard to answer.

CHAPTER 36

For two days the raider column made its way back to the base camp. The march was slowed by Lannat's insistence on full security measures. Scouts preceded them. Flankers protected. The rear guard hung back, protecting against possible pursuit, keeping alert for signs of infiltrators who might fall in behind the main body. The march avoided Betak's lodge/headquarters and labored along obscure trails onto the higher ground.

Through it all, Lannat rested very little. When he did, Nan avoided him. At first he attributed it to lack of opportunity. Then he made it a point to speak to her. Politely she made it clear his presence was unwanted.

He was too bruised to press her. He told himself this wasn't the time or place. In the dark reaches of the night, however, listening to the murmurings and cries of the forest, he admitted the truth: With all her earlier references removed, Nan Bahalt found nothing in him to attract her.

They arrived in camp under cover of darkness to the sobering news of Ullas's death and replacement. Sul reported constant overflights of highspies. Worse, reports from the coast indicated heavy concentrations of Advisors; supply levels indicated they were in position to conduct long operations.

It was a clear picture. The Marnoffar Mountains occupied a large peninsula. It afforded plenty of cover and space for maneuver, but it was a finite area. With Advisors blocking the peninsula's shoulders and patrolling the coast, escape by sea was greatly restricted, if not completely prevented. The Free safe zone was appearing more and more like a trap.

Exhaustion failed to bring Lannat sleep their first night back. Slipping out of the room he shared with Sul and Jarka, he stepped into the richness of a clear-skied mountain night. Even now, however, feeling as secure as he had since leaving this same place, he was careful to keep canopy cover between himself and open sky. He settled himself against a broad, rough trunk to watch the stars.

Within five minutes, Sul called softly. Lannat responded, and the shorter man joined him, saying "I'd think you'd be too tired to breathe."

"Still unwinding. Lot of things to go over in my mind."

Sul was almost apologetic. "What you said about an informer; the increased guard and the drop-site ambush? I've been thinking about that."

Lannat's sharp bark of laughter stopped Sul momentarily. "You think I haven't?"

Sul chose to not answer. There was indignation in his tone when he continued. "You know we've been careful. I think it was all coincidence."

"The auxiliary generator and the increased guard—maybe. The ambush? Not possible. They knew."

"Then why didn't they know exactly what night you were coming to Court? Why didn't they intercept your extraction eltrucks before they left the ground? You see? Ask yourself who could possibly have informed, in the first place. Then ask yourself why Counsellor Ullas would defend against the raid the way he did. There's no sense to what happened. Remember, you went over that drop site at a pretty fast clip; you may just think you saw an ambush in place."

"I saw what was there. And the only reason the raid didn't get burned is because we surprised them. Even so, until Trey messed up that guy Mard, we were looking at a hard fall."

"All right, let's say you're right. So, who informed?"

"We may never know. Let's hope whoever it is can't tell Etasalou about our movements. We're in for a bad ride, just the way it is."

"You think we can beat him?"

"Head to head? No. We stick, run, and hide, Sul. We don't plan to win. We plan to endure."

Sul sighed. "Well, you can give up sleeping if you want. I've got to turn in. I'm glad you made it back, you and the others."

Lannat thanked him, settling down, his back against the tree. He tried to think of the best way to use his captives, his newly acquired bargaining power, to deal with Etasalou. The need to concentrate guttered, burned out. His thoughts came from his heart, not his mind.

Nan was gone. The man she loved no longer existed, and she had no interest in the one who'd taken his place.

He fell asleep there, slumping to the side, knees drawn up. His dreams were bleak and empty. He woke at first light knowing he dreamed, but with no real memory of the dreams.

Later that morning he was watching the highspy monitor

with Multran when a trooper came in saying Prince Dafanil requested his presence. Lannat smiled at the language, but he went. Dafanil waited aboveground. Nan was with him. Lannat forced himself to concentrate on the prince. Surprisingly, the younger man seemed better for his long hike. His color was up, his manner more solid. He greeted Lannat quite warmly, then got right to business. "I've been asking about you. Since you're not Captain Lannat, I decided I needed information. Elemental Guard, they say. Not at all like my impression of the rest of them. I'm also told there's some mystery concerning exactly why you're here. That strongly suggests my father's delicate hand, but we won't go into that. The point is, you're obviously in charge of operations. You kidnapped me, Doctor Bahalt, and that fly speck, Mard. You mean to use us in negotiations with Etasalou: Is that correct?"

"As far as it goes, yes, but—"

Dafanil cut him off. "You've wasted your time."

"Why, Highness? Do you think Etasalou won't bargain?"

"Of course he will. You won't."

Lannat looked mildly quizzical. "Again, Highness—why?"

"I don't know." Dafanil cocked his head to the side, and for a moment, Lannat felt as if he were looking at a holo of the emperor as a youth. Bright, probing eyes held Lannat's, but when Dafanil spoke, there was an arch tone that Emperor Halib would never affect. "You had nothing to gain and everything to lose by arguing with Mard when he outguessed you on your raid. A true rebel would have cut him down. Doctor Bahalt and I would've been just another pair of casualties. You seem to exercise some conscience; I don't believe you'll give us to Etasalou. And if you try, we've promised each other we'll commit suicide. Doctor Bahalt has seen what happens to people restructured by her uncle." He stopped, seemed to wrestle with his next phrase. After a sidelong glance at Nan, he went on. "Whatever you've heard of me, I will not be used against my father. My so-called father."

Lannat's smile broadened. "I think I smell a suggestion coming."

"Very clever, I'm sure. A few days ago you could have used me as trade bait, played off Ullas against Etasalou; neither could afford to let the other control me. That's over. You'll get nothing for me from Etasalou but promises, and you'll end up dead. If you're lucky. Let us help. I know something of fighting. Doctor Bahalt will be invaluable, caring for your injured."

"With all due respect, Highness, I'm not aware of your combat record."

"I'm not a soldier. I'm a prince. Very good with a sword. Test me yourself."

Remembering the Advisor lieutenant who had died of a blow that seemed no deadlier than a slap, Lannat believed Dafanil. He said as much, then: "I won't put you at risk, Highness. Not until I'm satisfied there's no other choice. You're probably right about Etasalou, but I have to wait and see. You didn't mention what your father would do to me if you were injured fighting beside us."

Prince Dafanil tried to smile. It was painful to watch. "Injured? He would say nothing if I were injured. Should I die in your battle, however, and you should live, he would make you one of the grandest heroes in the history of the empire." Slowly, subtly, the expression transformed itself, turned cruel and taunting. "You showed me you have a keen nose for scenting out suggestion. How are you on opportunity?" Laughing aloud, he turned his back on Lannat and walked away.

Still watching the arrogant departure, Lannat almost missed Nan's words. She was saying ". . . keep your medical supplies? I should know what's available."

"This way." He took her arm. The contact triggered an avalanche of memory. After so many months, so much darkness, she was here. He touched her. The woman he loved. He could hold to his lies no longer. He said, "It's me. It really is. They operated, changed my face, my fingerprints."

Revolted, Nan pulled away. "You don't even know him.

He doesn't bargain with people's lives. Or souls. Don't ever touch me."

"I had to tell them I needed you to bargain with. How else could I get them to help me free you? Ever since I got here, that's been the only thing on my mind. All the rest is what I had to do."

"The emperor sent you to train rebels so they could overthrow a ruler so oppressive his people couldn't dream of fighting the empire? You insult my dreams, you insult my intelligence. You're as foul as you are stupid."

"I wasn't sent here to train anybody. These people were supposed to help me in my mission. They said if I didn't train their fighters, they'd give me to Etasalou. I decided my only chance of rescuing you was to train them, then use them. It worked. You're free."

"You just admitted I'm nothing but property. We're all probably going to die. I understood what was said last night about my uncle's plans for attack. Just have someone show me the medical supplies. Stay away. Your lies sicken me."

"Nan, please." He smothered the urge to reach out to her. "Remember the oneway. We talked about children, about our own home. We joked about both of us knowing the emperor, how it might help us get stationed there on Atic, and we'd have our honeymoon in the mountains, then have all of Collegium to explore. How would I know that if I'm not Lannat?"

Pale, shaken, she refused to believe. "Anything that's said in a oneway is overheard. That's how you know." She turned away, fist to her mouth as if fearing she'd be ill.

Lannat surrendered. He waited for her to get herself together, then told her, "This way," and moved out toward the stores. At the entrance, he pointed and left her.

The campaign started that same afternoon. The highspy detected numbers of elcars appearing at the Advisor camps on the coast. As the machine sent pictures back to camp, the vehicles rose lazily, spreading out to patrol the beaches and all access to the sea. Simultaneously, a Free patrol sent a priority seekum message about a large column of Legionnaires heading directly for the Free base camp from one of the Legion advance bases.

Lannat left first with a small team to select an ambush site. The Free patrol kept him informed of the column's progress. When Lannat first spotted the Legionnaires in the distance, they were dispersed on the banks of a small stream, enjoying their noon break. They were relaxed, bathing their feet in the cold water, eating, lounging. Outposts were well positioned and alert, however.

Lannat and his team ate while they waited. When the column formed up and moved out, he noted the posting of flankers, the maintenance of proper interval between individuals, the constant supervision by noncommissioned officers. Sourly he conceded this unit was well trained. Any of Etasalou's units would be well disciplined. These people had polish. The more he watched the distant figures trudge up the valley, however, the more they puzzled him. For all their technique, there was a peculiar eagerness about them. They were way too far off for him to distinguish facial expression, but there was something manic about them.

Lannat spoke to his seekum, waited for response from the ambush group. He told them, "I'll meet you at the place we picked on the map." On acknowledgment, he signaled his team. Low to the ground, keeping to concealment, they withdrew.

The ground chosen for the ambush was on a downhill slope. The valley approach used by the Legion ended in a narrow pass some three hundred yards above. At the selected site, the path offered good cover on its eastern side; the assault would be able to close swiftly. On the western side, the ground rose gently at first, then the grade increased. So did cover, provided by large boulders and thick scrub. If all went well, the Legion would take the first blow and retreat to the west to regroup.

That was when the second element would strike downhill from their covered positions.

If all went well.

The column descended from the pass with commendable caution. Still, Lannat couldn't shake the notion that the Legionnaires were daring anyone to interfere. When the point walked past the ambush trigger without seeing anything, and when the ambush itself escaped observation by the flankers, Lannat knew the operation was a tactical success. The strange sensation hung on, regardless.

When the first troops of the main body reached the ambush trigger group, the hidden Free rose, screaming, charging. So did the long arm of the ambush, parallel to the path. Spears lowered, they came like some many-fanged animal, raging.

The Legionnaires carried no spears. They had shields, however, and good sword defense skills. The momentum of the charging Free forced them back but failed to scatter them. Shouting their own commands and war cries, they fell off, straining to maintain a cohesive front.

None broke and ran. Chills rattled up and down Lannat's spine. No unit took the shock of an ambush without *someone* coming apart. These people didn't. They dropped of horrible wounds, screaming in pain—and slashing at the legs of their attackers with the last morsel of their strength. Lannat saw one man, impaled, roaring curses, flailing his sword at the unbelieving Free on the other end of the spear.

The second element leaped from cover and bowled into the rear of the struggling column. With complete surprise in their favor, they wreaked terrible havoc. Legionnaires fell like windstruck straw.

But the fight continued. Desperately. Until there were no Legionnaires. What should have been victory was more. And worse. It was massacre.

It was a disaster. For the Free.

Panting, soaked with sweat, Lannat looked at the heaped, sprawled bodies. He saw streams of blood mingle, flow, disappear into trampled plant growth like obscene rain rivulets. He counted five dead Legion for every dead Free.

He saw the future of his troops, and tears scalded his eyes. That was the swagger of the Legion column. They knew. They took the field to kill as many of their enemy as possible before dying. They fought with the fear of death, in order to fight effectively, but they had no intention of leaving the battle while one Free remained alive and they had the power to kill.

The campaign was started. The first attack had no purpose but to illustrate the objective: extermination. It was to be a campaign the Free could not win, would not endure.

CHAPTER 37

The Free refused to understand.

In the forest's dusk, with victorious warriors standing to the side, what Lannat said was unacceptable. Yes, there were casualties, but they were being tended. They were tired, but rest would bring them back. Of course there was sadness for the dead, but their triumph was complete, flawless. A good cause had glory to blunt its losses.

Yet Lannat said, "Etasalou means to run us down, grind us up. Elcars and eltrucks will hunt us from the air. Patrols will comb these mountains. Those who made the attack today can tell you: The Legion comes only to kill, and doesn't care if they live. Anyone who has a chance—or thinks there is a chance—to escape must take it. For the rest of us, we fight. The Legion wants no choice. We have none."

It was a death sentence.

Debate burned through the evening and into darkness.

Groups, pairs, even individuals wrestled with uncertainty. In the morning, when that night's two-party listening posts checked in, eight of the twelve teams reported the sound of people leaving. Roll call revealed thirteen troopers missing. The number itself generated as much nervous commentary as the departures.

Lannat went to the underground hospital. Nan was there, at a small table having tea. The Lumin robes were gone, replaced by drab blouse and trousers, high boots. Her hair was drawn back. She watched him come, reserved.

Her beauty consumed him.

He sat down across from her. "I spoke to Sul earlier. He has family on Kull. It's one of Hire's three continents. Primarily rural. He thinks he can smuggle you there. We're putting together a group. Educated people, capable of contributing to an underground. I want you to go. I think the prince should, too. Can you talk him into it?"

Sipping the tea, she studied him over the cup rim. "You really think my uncle won't track us down?"

"He'll never stop trying, granted. Stay here, and he won't have to look any further."

"After all the trouble I've caused him, it's only right I make things easy for him this once. Don't you think?"

Lannat looked away from the grimace she meant to be a mischievous smile. She read his reaction perfectly and responded with anger. "You claim to know something of me; if you did, you'd know why I can't survive on a planet he controls."

"Sul's people will hide you. You'll have a different identity."

"This entire planet will be one mind, one consciousness, within a decade. There'll be no hiding." She shifted uncomfortably. "Anyhow, I don't trust Sul."

"What?" Shocked, Lannat was loud. "Have you even met him?"

"Obviously. He came to me as soon as you finished talking to him."

"Why didn't you tell me? Why let me hope?"

The latter question stung her. She blanched. "I meant to tell you, but I wanted you to hear my reasons." Then, defiant: "I still don't trust him."

Lannat thought back to Sul's crazed rage at discovering the traitor among them. He shook his head. "You're wrong. I understand why, though. It's for the same reason you're wrong about me. I'm not the same person I was. I know that. They've used me. I don't know what's left. But you're different, too. When I knew you, you wanted to believe in people, in things. You were more afraid of hurting someone than being hurt. That's not so anymore. I guess I don't blame you. I loved you, Nan. You loved me. The way I feel, the worst that could happen to me already has. Stay if you like. I'll promise you one thing. Etasalou will never capture you, so long as I live to prevent it."

He expected her to say nothing when he left, and she didn't. It was well. He couldn't think of turning, that she might see his face. His throat made speaking impossible.

He found Prince Dafanil on the surface, supervising sword drill. Stripped to the waist, sweating, he was a whirlwind. Calling troopers forward, he demonstrated on one, then another, carrying on a running commentary. "Footwork," he said, dancing from under an overhand slash. "Feet are as important as hands." To prove his point, he parried the next looping blow with his blade. Pivoting, he kicked. His foot stopped an inch short of the knee bearing the trooper's weight. Dafanil lowered it, stepped back. Chagrined, the trooper sent the prince a queasy smile.

Dafanil clapped a hand on his shoulder. "Don't look so down. I'm one of the very best. Now you know one of my tricks." He was grinning when he caught sight of Lannat. Turning the practice over to another man, he joined him. Lannat told him of Sul's offer.

Dafanil was noncommittal. "No mention of Doctor Bahalt?"

Lannat hesitated. Prince Dafanil hadn't impressed him as particularly concerned for others. As quickly as Lannat said, "She refuses to leave," Dafanil snapped a retort. "It surprises you that I ask about her? Wouldn't you?"

Tone implied much more than actual words. Lannat clenched his teeth. Dafanil watched, waited. At last, Lannat shrugged. "I've told her. I might as well tell you. I'm Captain Lannat."

"Didn't I say so? My father *did* send you, didn't he? Why?"

"To kill her uncle." Self-consciously, Lannat reached to touch the false scar, describing his physical alterations. That done, he explained his mission in briefest terms.

"Good plan." Dafanil nodded judiciously. "Not like my father to be tripped up by someone like this Betak. Any chance Betak gave away your raid?"

Lannat rejected that, then reconsidered. "He wasn't very enthusiastic. And he knew all the details. I don't see what he could hope to gain, though."

"Consider your own situation, Captain. Two years ago, would you have imagined yourself doing the things you've done in the past year? Are your goals the same? Are they known to anyone else?"

Heat boiled around Lannat's collar. "Even an emperor's child is expected to exercise some manners, Prince."

"Another false assumption." Dafanil waved airily. "And don't waste your temper. There's nothing you can do or say to concern me, unless I so choose. Our stations forbid it."

"Insufferable—" Lannat bit back the rest.

Dafanil agreed. "My prerogative. I enjoy it quite a bit. Are you going to tell your Free friends who you are?"

"No."

"Very well. Our secret, then. Yours, mine, Doctor Bahalt's—who doesn't believe it—and the filthy Mard."

"Who?"

"Aha. Surprised again. Too easy, really. But I concede I'm guessing. He's said nothing to me."

"He's hardly spoken since we brought him here. Whines about the food and his cell. What makes you think he knows?"

"When he held us, he was more attentive to the doctor than to me. He suggested Commander Etasalou—evil little insect—was more interested in her than me. And, of course, Doctor Bahalt dithered endlessly about the wonderful Captain Lannat. As long as I'd listen. Other people's romance is so trite, I find. What little I know of your background, and my intimate knowledge of my father's machinations, strongly suggested the mysterious Free fighter from Atic might well be yourself. And who else would attach more significance to a common doctor than me?"

"I could start at any point in the galaxy and work in either direction, naming names," Lannat said. "All the way around, Highness."

"Temper again. No one mentioned you're a slow learner. What d'you intend to do about Mard?"

"Talk to him. Try to learn more about Etasalou."

"Kill him. If there's a way to foment trouble, he'll do it. Get rid of him. And there's nothing to learn about Etasalou. You said it yourself: We're to be exterminated."

"You take it well."

Once again Lannat had a glimpse through a crack in Dafanil's facade. "Some of us have more curiosity than fear about death. Like your temper, your opinion of me isn't an issue."

Lannat's own bitterness strained to break through. He kept it to himself. "You looked to be at ease with those troopers. We fight in teams of three, called triads. Three triads and a leader make a squad. Three squads, with a supply NCO and a platoon sergeant make a platoon. That's our primary tactical unit. If you're staying with us to fight, would you want to lead one?"

"I would, yes. Close combat would be my most effective contribution." He darted a grin at Lannat. "What a sly bastard you are. I, who should be emperor one day, find myself thanking you for allowing me to die at the head of one of your little platoons. It's no wonder my father thinks highly of you."

Lannat saluted. "We bastards have to stick together."

Dafanil was chuckling as Lannat left.

From Dafanil, Lannat went to have Mard brought up from his underground cell. Squinting against the brightness of daylight, Mard bowed, nodded, reached tentatively as if to take Lannat's hand. Lannat thought of abused pets.

"I'm no good to you here," Mard said. "Let me go. I'll tell Etasalou you're too strong for him. He'll want to negotiate." He bobbed his head. "I can be very convincing. He'll think there are thousands of you. I can tell him—"

"Be serious, man. You'll go directly into his laboratory. He knows you're responsible for his niece and the prince being captured."

Mard groaned. "Doctor Renula, then. She's Lumin. Sungiver sent me here. Doctor Renula will protect me. Let me go. I'll get to her."

"Why did Sungiver send you?"

Mard thought it over, gestured helplessly. "She wanted me to assassinate Etasalou. She's crazy. I never had a chance."

Lannat smiled. The expression offended Mard, and he blurted his feelings. "You think I'm a coward because I want to live. All of you—strutting, so brave and cocky. Inside you're as scared as I am. I'm honest about it, that's all. Let me out of here. Let me go back to Lumin."

"You said you'd cut Nan Bahalt's throat. I want you where I can see you." With his sword at Mard's back, he prodded the man across camp to the railgun. Calling for metlin binding, Lannat ordered Mard's right wrist lashed to the front of the carriage. He said, "You're part of the weapon now. When it moves, you help move it."

Mard wailed and yanked at the metlin. It bit deep into his wrist. He stopped pulling, continued to demand his release. A short, wiry Free walked over to him. He said, "If our lieutenant hadn't listened to you at Court, some of my friends would still be alive. If you get loose, a lot of us'll be waiting for you." The man looked up at Lannat and grinned. "To see he doesn't escape, right?"

"Exactly that," Lannat said. "We save this one for a proper trial."

The short man's grin disappeared. He looked Lannat straight in the eye. "Justice for all, right?"

"Right." Lannat met the bold challenge. The man almost smiled, went back to his unit.

The first elcar swept overhead not long afterward. Trey leaped into the railgunner's seat. Forcing himself along behind her, Retalla took over the loader's job. Lannat yelled at her to stay under cover and hold her fire. Joining her, he explained, "We save our shots for eltrucks. An elcar may carry six people; a truck may carry five times that number. There are three more railguns on Hire. Etasalou will have them by now, if the underground didn't wreck them. You're our strength, Trey. Protect the gun. Above everything."

The next morning, the lone Free highspy caught the first offensive move by Etasalou's Legion.

Foot columns moved out from the advance bases, with elcars scouting ahead and to the flanks. Far to the rear, eltrucks rumbled along in trail of the columns. Lannat assumed they carried supplies and reserve troops. His suspicions were confirmed when the columns stopped for the day. The eltrucks descended into the perimeter, discharged rested personnel and construction material, and lifted back to base with the men who'd marched since morning. By nightfall, the Legion camp was ditched, surrounded by a shoulder-high stockade.

The Free, moving all night, closed on the western base before dawn. They struck thirty minutes prior to daybreak.

Lannat was well aware that the Legionnaires were immune to the normal concerns of humanity. He also knew that, without a basic urge to survive, they would be mere suicides, and useless as fighters. He saw the troops of the ambushed column handle surprise with few problems but believed specific conditioning predetermined such response. He wondered how these troops would react.

Explosives breached the base's palisade wall in a stunning blast. Free troops charged the smoking gap.

For the first few minutes, Etasalou's reconstruction techniques warred with that instinct to survive. Free troops watched in horror as some Legionnaires stumbled from their tents and fell to the ground in shrieking heaps, their tampered brains unable to respond to the conflicting needs of an unanticipated concept. What might have been panic in similar circumstances became mental overload, and the minds simply shattered.

Most, however, recovered well. The Free cut their way through disorganized resistance into the center of the camp, tossing hand bombs into elcar and eltruck parks, fuel supplies, and buildings. With the base ablaze from end to end, they retreated at full run, carrying their wounded and dead. Within minutes, they were deep under Hire's double canopy, moving at a steady jog, ignoring the angry howl of elcars and the tinny whine of highspies. Teams fell out to set traps, then ran to catch up.

Some time later eltrucks appeared. Lannat assumed they were from the other advance camp. The rumbling vehicles hovered over peaks. Legionnaires rappelled to the ground. Minutes later massive blasts toppled huge trees, creating landing sites. The eltrucks returned, landed. Troops poured out to search for the raiders.

The Free buried their dead, then pressed on.

That pattern of the Marnoffar campaign was set. From that moment on, the action was unending.

Three days after the first Free raid on the Legion advance base, two Legion columns bulled through Free resistance to close on the underground camp. Forced to retreat, the Free were pushed too far from Etasalou's fortified positions to strike at them. Undaunted, they harried the columns. Hitting, running, placing traps on every possible route of advance, the Free slaughtered Legionnaires. They lost one for five, for seven, sometimes one for twenty.

The Legion replaced its losses.

Firing the railgun required a bitter decision. Trey never missed. Every round, however, brought violent retaliation; the entire area was rapidly saturated with Legionnaires. Also, Etasalou had a railgun. During any search for the Free's weapon, it fired at anything remotely suspicious. So far, their nearest miss was, conservatively, a mile off target. Many Free were caught in the infantry sweeps, however. The railgun carried a high price.

A few more days into the campaign, Free troopers reported something shattering, unbelievable. They identified dead Legionnaires with wounds so severe they looked like deformities. Yet they were recently healed. When some Advisor recruits recognized people from their own previous units, a wild desperation settled on the Free. In those casualties the Free saw that the future of their people was to become units. Even if broken, they would be repaired, used up, disposed of. After that, battles were unspeakably brutal.

Many times Lannat asked himself if Etasalou hadn't already transformed them.

Inexorably, the Free were driven down the peninsula.

One dawn, following a twelve-hour march to escape a Legion encircling movement, Lannat woke on a south-facing slope and saw no more mountains between himself and the waiting sea. He rose swiftly. Despite clear skies and bright sun, he felt a brooding quality in the day. Normal routine offered escape. He took a small basin from his pack and washed up as best he could on the limited water ration. The ceryag knife worked to hack off whiskers, trim the hair dangling over his ears.

He was on his way to breakfast when he noticed Jarka being tended by Nan. The Hiran was on a stool outside the tattered hospital tent. He changed course, walked over to them.

Nan rained indignation on him on sight. "This fool waited all night to get this treated."

Lannat peered at the cut. "Looks clean. Nice patch, I'd say."

Nan fumed. "That's not the point. It could be infected. He should have come to me immediately."

Long-suffering, Jarka told Lannat, "I told her: We were rear guard." He turned to Nan. "I was busy."

Then, with hardly any pause whatever, he was speaking to Lannat again. He didn't look at him, however. It was more as if he looked through him. His voice had a distant, musing quality. "You don't know what day it is, do you?"

The change in the man was so swift, so radical, Lannat wasn't sure how to respond. "Day?"

Jarka appeared not to hear. "Did you know I have a girl cousin in the Hiran Cultural Sibling Group?"

"I didn't know that. Is it her birthday?" Lannat pulled a face at Nan. She nodded, uneasy.

Jarka went on. He shifted, stared out to sea. "Prettiest girl you ever saw. Sweet, too. We hated to see her go—three years, that's a long time. We were sort of proud, too, though. She's turned out to be brilliant musician." His sudden turn toward Lannat startled him so much he stepped back. Jarka didn't notice. His eyes were full of tears. More ran down his cheeks. "Her part of the CSG came home yesterday. She's in hell with the rest of us."

Lannat and Nan exchanged glances. Lannat said, "Maybe the emperor held them on Atic. He knew there was trouble here."

Jarka dredged up a smile. "I wish I could hope for that." He added a jarring false laugh to the smile as he stood to leave. "Well, might as well eat while it's quiet."

After a moment, Lannat said, "I guess we're all pretty much like that, aren't we?"

Nan busied herself cleaning up. Tossing her head to indicate the sea behind her, she said, "Not much farther to run." She straightened, faced him, not even an arm's length away. Once again Lannat saw something—that same frightened, questioning expression—touch the rich brown eyes, the full lips, her sweeping brows. As before, his heart told him he saw it. His mind said it was all daydreams, a physical tremor he wanted to believe was a statement. He barely heard what she was saying. "You're a good leader. Whatever happens, all of us are proud of you."

He started to thank her, changed his mind. Words boiled out of him. "I want you to know I'm sorry about what's happening here—what's coming. I'm not sorry about us, though. I mean not sorry we had time together. Good time. I know we're here because I'm who and what I am. That hurts. All the rest, though—being with you, sharing, trusting—that was the best thing in my life. I wanted to tell you."

She rose, brushing at her trousers. The look she gave him was as vacant as the sky above. Lannat didn't try to contend with it. With a schoolboy wave, he turned, set about his duties.

Twenty-four hours passed without enemy contact. It seemed the Legion needed rest as badly as the Free. Lannat woke several times that night, as was his custom, and sensed the darkness, sniffing, darkglassing, listening. Nothing disturbed the quiet. The sense of foreboding, however, was ever stronger. More than that, each time he woke he found himself thinking of two things. One was Jarka's cousin, the CSG. Thinking of the girl made him wonder if Etasalou was celebrating the arrival of new material for his technicians. The second, and more powerful, thought was of Nan and her total disinterest in his early-morning declaration. When he remembered the emptiness of her eyes, he found himself wondering why he ever cared what the next day might bring.

CHAPTER 38

Following the day and night of rest, the Legion moved into attack positions with almost leisurely deliberation. From their high-ground advantage, the Free watched with stoic resignation.

Their flat-topped mountain afforded plenty of stone and timber, which they put to use. A small fort with log walls ten feet high rose behind a four-foot-deep ditch at the center of the crown. Sharp wooden spikes studded the ditch bottom. Small ports at knee and chest level allowed spear thrusts from inside the walls. A battlewalk circled the interior. It was crude. It was ready.

That morning the highspy reported Advisor troops shifting inland from their blocking positions. Many moved down the peninsula to act as reserve; others actually lifted north in eltrucks.

Sul reacted badly. "They're going home. They think we're finished. They mean to end it today." He slumped. "There was never real hope. I've been a fool."

Prince Dafanil put a hand on his shoulder. "It's the fools who don't have hope. Today may be Etasalou's. There will always be tomorrows for those who *will* hope, in spite of everything."

The words appeared to strengthen Sul, though he made no response. When Dafanil left Sul's side, Lannat spoke to him.

"You should be careful, Highness. You're wrecking your rotten image."

Dafanil sniffed. "In a better world, I'd love to see you flogged. Shall we continue to watch our doom take shape?" He nodded at a different observation point.

They set out. Lannat said, "You're a riddle, Highness. I always knew there was a chance I'd die in combat, but part of me never believed it. Now that the magic moment's here, I'm having a little trouble accepting it, I don't mind telling you. But you don't seem to give a solitary damn. In fact—"

Dafanil talked over him. "Captain, can you never learn? You must not presume your betters care what you think of them. I, on the other hand, am obliged to point out your simple errors. Your problem is denial."

"Denying what?"

"You've denied your mortality all this time. At least now you've adjusted. Unlike Doctor Bahalt."

Lannat stopped, then hurried to catch up. "What's that mean, exactly? No more jokes."

"I never joke; occasionally I speak in obscure parables. Never mind. Doctor Bahalt still loves you."

Lannat was too startled to take offense. "How can you say that?"

"Because I'm intelligent."

They were at the overlook then. Distant elcars droned faintly, a muted hymn of power. Below them, black helmets and spearpoints glittering, twin infantry columns snaked across a meadow toward parked eltrucks. Perhaps in response to the scene, Dafanil's pause preceded a softened manner. "She's very frightened, Lannat. We all are, but hers is far deeper. You think she's rejected you because you're different. That has nothing to do with it. She's doing it because she knows you're Lannat. She can't allow herself to find you again, only to lose you for all time. She can accept Val Bordi's death, not yours."

"I told her the truth. She won't believe me."

Dafanil's stare was direct challenge. "Who cares for your

truth now? Are you so eager to make her certain of the end of this day's work?" He pointed at the Legion. "We all know what that means."

Lannat nodded. He didn't dare speak further of Nan, had to think of other things. He told himself he was being selfish, that he had responsibilities to others. He changed the subject. "I keep thinking I should say something to our people. Leaders are supposed to say important things before fights like this."

Dafanil eagerly reverted to his public character. "It is so depressing to face eternity in the presence of an ignorant ruffian. Walk with me; we'll gird ourselves to meet the foe. Meanwhile, try to understand: A leader makes a speech. He does not 'say important things.' We are not about to 'have a fight,' we are engaging in battle. Never mind; don't damage yourself attempting to think about it. Writers come up with the really good speeches anyhow, years after the event."

Lannat laughed. "You feel as bad about me as you want, Highness. I'm glad you're with us." He checked, waved both hands. "That didn't come out exactly right. I'm just saying you're the kind of man I'm glad to have on my flank."

Dafanil nodded, surprisingly sober. "Thank you. That's high praise from a man like you. I'll remember it as long as I . . ." They looked at each other and howled laughter. Troopers watched them walk into the fort. There were many bemused expressions. Even some worried ones.

Not long after that the eltrucks lifted.

Lannat's defensive plan hinged on maximum benefit from the railgun. Three raised mounds inside the fort provided firing positions. With its scissors-legs folded, it squatted below the wall. To fire, it rose, retracted. To avoid counterfire, it was to be hauled immediately to ground level and readied for action. Trey's primary target must be Etasalou's railgun.

Obstacles outside the fort channeled advancing troops into areas where the Free planted explosives. Other charges were secreted in likely preassault assembly sites, armed with the last of the Free's radio-controlled detonation devices. The bulk of the explosive material was saved to break up the inevitable mass attacks on the walls. Some considered hand bombs missiles. Still, the Rifles issued them for combat in built-up areas. He decided the Blood Father could argue it out with Emperor Halib.

Lannat watched the eltrucks gain altitude and looked over his shoulder for Nan. Her raggedy hospital tent fluttered in the breeze beside her. She waved to him, white smile sun-bright. Lannat waved back, marveling at her courage and mourning her presence.

The eltrucks came at speed, rumbling like surf. They used cover well. Trey burned only one. The troops debarked, mustered behind a rock outcrop.

Retalla's explosives placements featured a bag holding tightly packed rocks around the explosive itself. He had one by the outcrop. The detonation was followed by screams. A hidden eltruck exploded. Carrying ladders, the surviving Legionnaires, some visibly wounded, made for the wall.

More eltrucks landed troops on all four sides of the fort. Trey blasted them and shouted at the crew to move her. Lannat noted Mard, his utter terror apparent even at a distance. Retalla worked right behind him, helping carry the weapon and assuring Mard's dedication to his task.

The first wave of Legionnaires reached the wall under Lannat. Crouched on the battlewalk, he darted to where the first ladder shafts appeared. A red, straining face under a black helmet appeared. Lannat drove his sword through the exposed neck. Almost as soon as that man was gone, another face appeared—a woman. She died the same way.

Something clutched at Lannat's chest, slamming him backward against the wall. He looked down. The prongs of a grappling hook gouged at his chest, ripped into his flesh. Yelling, he slashed over his head, chopping at the line. Weight pulled the prongs deeper. He continued to yell, slashed harder. Mercifully, the line parted. He jerked the thing free and threw it to the ground inside.

Legionnaires were at each wall. Some already fought on the battlewalk.

Jarka's reserve force dealt with that. Determining that the wall opposite Lannat was most threatened, Jarka led his troopers up the steps and onto the walk in a bellowing rush. Spears swept the attackers off.

Explosives boomed outside the walls. Lannat peered over the top. Sickeningly, smashed victims of the charges clawed themselves toward the fort. Some carried their swords. One, obviously blind, scrabbled on all fours in the wrong direction. Two more were empty-handed; still, the compulsion to continue attacking drove them.

The wall seemed to leap backward. A sound like a giant slap disoriented Lannat momentarily. He made no sense of the sudden appearance of smoke and flame, the tortured wail of high-speed fragments. Nor could he imagine why troops of the reserve force were screaming. Trey's shouting cleared his head. She stood in her gunner's seat to see over the wall. "By those trees. Railgun. Turn me, give me an angle."

Below her, Free scrambled to help those wounded by splinters from the shattered logs. An elcar screamed in, following the contour of the ground, almost scraping the wall. Free close to that path dropped. Another railgun slug crashed into the fort, this one narrowly missing Trey's weapon. She squinted through the hole.

More ladders thudded against Lannat's wall. Below him and to his left, Legionnaires hacked at the broken, burning logs, enlarging the gap. Jarka's spearmen counterattacked. A few thrusts, and five Legionnaires were thrashing in the dirt. Jarka and his people were barely clear when a third slug smashed into the logs.

Lannat engaged a Legionnaire charging at him on the battlewalk. Ducking a blow, Lannat was struck from behind. It hit his helmet. He leaped forward, tried to spin with the first Legionnaire. The man held to him, screaming for his companion to cut Lannat. Parkronar appeared, carrying a spear. Features contorted, he leaped high, thrust down past Lannat and his foe. Someone shrieked. Lannat heaved, pitched his enemy backward off the wall. Parkronar's grab kept Lannat from going over as well.

As Lannat straightened, Trey's railgun fired. He turned away. Down the hill, the blue-green flames of a vaporized railgun testified to her skills.

There were more eltrucks, more Legionnaires. The battle became brute labor. Obscene work, where admitting exhaustion meant being killed, where the product was agony and stench. There were no particular sounds, but a world of endless, senseless roar. Men and women hacked at each other, lost the power of speech and growled like animals, bit, scratched, gouged. Wounded and dying cried for water. For an end to pain. Many received the latter from a bloody-eyed deliverer with a sharp weapon.

It ended as if the thing itself were dying, a falling off, a diminishing energy. Propped against the wall, soaked in blood and sweat, Lannat listened to voices croaking orders to withdraw. Head hanging like a stunned beast, he stared stupidly at retreating backs. It took both hands to steady him so he could look behind. The hospital tent was flat, a smoking log from the fort wall thrown across it. A small, pitiful hand stuck out from under the smoldering cloth. It was very dark.

Stumbling, shouting incoherently, he moved to her. At the bottom of the steps he recognized Parkronar. The broken blade of a Legion sword jutted from his back. He still held his spear, its point buried in the stomach of an enemy. Another downed Legionnaire, coughing past a ripped throat, cut at Lannat as he passed. Not even slowing, pure reflex guided Lannat's parry and killing counter.

A Free woman pushed ineffectually at the log as Lannat approached. He heard himself scream loss and fear. He bent, tossed the timber aside in one convulsive heave. The woman immediately uncovered the figure. Eyes closed as if sleeping, Nan lay still, exposed. Lannat dropped to his knees beside her.

The woman said, "I'm a nurse. Give me room." She fumbled in Nan's medical sack, found a diagnometer. Skeptical, the woman tried to turn it on. She muttered when it worked, immediately scanned Nan's body. Looking up to Lannat, she said, "Her internal injuries are serious. I can set the broken bones, give her painkillers."

Lannat felt himself come apart. "She's dying?"

The woman turned her head, jerking her chin in angry gesture. "I can't help. We have nothing. Look at us."

Jarka called his name. "It's a white flag! Etasalou wants a truce."

A hand gripped Lannat's shoulder. Dafanil said, "You have to see what it's about, Captain. Your duty."

"Damn duty. Nan's hurt. She could be dying."

Gently Dafanil pulled on him. "Get up."

Listless, Lannat obeyed. He scanned the interior of the fort, the scattered bodies. Smashed walls gaped, as if joining the moaning of the wounded. Able Free tended to their injured, cautiously skirting living Legionnaires, who snarled and lashed out at anyone who came near. Bitter experience had long since drained the Free of any mercy for them.

The grounded elcar was almost five hundred yards down the slope, at the end of a long, roughly rectangular open burn scar on the mountain. By the time Lannat neared it, he was changed. Shoulders back, head up, he marched. Beside him, Dafanil kept in step. They were unlikely ambassadors, foul with blood and dirt, hollow-eyed with fatigue. It was obvious that pride alone held them erect. They unbuckled their sword belts, let the weapons fall.

Etasalou himself waited, a guard of four immaculate Legionnaires ranked behind him. "I have an offer for Prince Dafanil and the woman Bahalt. I recognize you, Highness. Are you the one called Val Bordi?"

"I am. Your offer?"

A quick shake of the head dismissed Lannat. "You are not involved. My congratulations, Highness; a worthy defense.

I'm glad you survived, because your spirit has moved me to offer you your life. As we speak, my Advisors are boarding three starships. A small but auspicious start toward my own corner of the empire. Your father is certain to resent my ambitions. I propose to let you return to him. No negotiations, no conditions. I wish peace and coexistence. Compassion on my part is a necessary proof of intent."

Alone with the railgun on its firing mound, Mard strained to reach the dead crewman's sword. It tantalized him. He whined, pulled hard enough to dig the metlin binding deep into his flesh. He pinched the tip of the handle, drew the blade to him. Sawing at his bonds, he watched everyone else, concentrating on the meeting downhill. The cord fell away.

Lannat tried to get the image of Jarka's young CSG cousin out of his mind. He said, "We need medical assistance. Water."

It was as if he didn't exist. Etasalou spoke to Dafanil. "Bahalt comes with you. She cannot leave Hire."

"She needs medical treatment," Dafanil replied. "I must see her receive it."

Lannat said, "You're listening to him? We can't trust him."

Etasalou flinched but remained fixed on Dafanil. "I came prepared to prove my sincerity." He snapped his fingers. The elcar driver ran forward with a camera. Etasalou had it handed to Dafanil. "A transvid. Assure yourself it's in working order. We take pictures of you agreeing to my proposition. The information is instantly sent to a commmbuoy, relayed to Atic. Incontrovertible evidence of our agreement and your condition. If anything should happen to you, I would be known to be at fault."

"And if I don't accept?"

"The offer is a courtesy. You have some value."

Lannat interrupted again. "I need some indication of good faith. We need—"

"Stop." Wide-eyed, nostrils flaring, Etasalou raged, transformed. "You are dead, whoever you are. Lannat, Bordi—it doesn't matter. When I finish speaking to Prince Dafanil, you will all be cut down. Do you understand? *Killed.*"

"I'm going," Dafanil told Lannat. "I'm taking Nan. It's her only chance."

Lannat shook his head. "No. He lies. He'll make you the same as these things he's restructured. Light knows what he'll do to Nan."

Arguing gently, Dafanil said, "Even if you're right, I have to do this. I was born to rule the lives of a galaxy. That won't happen. So who am I? Just another man, my friend. A good one, I hope. This is a chance I take for me, as much as for Nan. You see?"

Lannat looked away. "I told you once, us bastards have to stick together."

Etasalou frowned uncertainly when they smiled.

Mard wiped sweat from his eyes. Slowly, inch by inch, he traversed the barrel of the railgun, raising it simultaneously, twitching uncontrollably at the least change of sound in the gears. The hand not on the controls played delicately across the firing button.

He almost laughed aloud. Whatever made Etasalou think he needed to negotiate with the remnants of this band of fools? He, Mard, would solve the problem. One shot, and the arrogant Val Bordi would be gone. A quick dash out of the fort while those idiots on the battlewalk were trying to guess what happened, and life would be good once more. They would learn that Captain Mard—Who knew what promotions lay ahead for the man who killed the rebel war chief?—was no pack animal. Indeed, they'd learn who was.

Centering the crosshairs on Lannat's back, Mard unconsciously hummed. The point of aim was directly over the heads of some of the Free spectators. With luck, concussion would kill some.

* * *

Lannat shook Dafanil's hand. "I'll have stretcher bearers bring Nan. Be sure he takes those pictures. Now."

Dafanil nodded. Then, taking Lannat completely off guard, he snapped to attention, saluted. "It's been a pleasure serving with you, sir. Until next time."

Lannat felt awkward returning it. He hurried away. When he reached his sword belt, he glanced back. Etasalou was posing against the elcar, with Dafanil a few feet to his left. A man aimed the camera at them. Lannat bent down for his gear.

He felt the railgun slug burn past him before he heard it. There was a resounding blast from the fort and another, closer, behind him. He whirled around, drawing his sword. The elcar was a flaming mass. Etasalou was nowhere to be seen, but bits of disgusting material like torn meat lay everywhere. The guards were sprawled on the ground. Dafanil struggled to rise. Lannat ran to him, had him on his feet when they heard the shouting. Mard pelted toward them, calling Etasalou's name at the top of his lungs. His legs continued to churn for several steps after he realized the two men watching him were Lannat and Dafanil. His expression when he skidded to a halt was pathetic. He screamed, falling to his knees. Behind him, enraged Free ran down the slope.

Lannat ran to him, got between the weeping, cringing figure and the Free. They weren't too hard to calm down. Mard had frightened them witless but harmed only his supposed benefactor. They were willing to let him live.

Brushing at himself, Dafanil joined them. The discussion was over by then, and in the relative quiet, he cocked his head, listening. "Is it my ears, or is something making a noise?"

The group listened. The pause gave Lannat time to reflect on how few there were. Trey and Retalla had survived. For a moment he couldn't locate either Jarka or Sul, but then there they were, so weary that they were leaning on each other. The nurse was missing, busy with her charges. "It's probably more eltrucks," Lannat said. "We better get back to the fort." He passed Mard off to two troopers.

Reluctantly everyone turned, started up the hill. The sound was louder then, and it tugged at Lannat's memory. He looked back anxiously to check on the Legion. They seemed lethargic, unwilling to move. The noise interrupted his speculations about that. And then he shouted, "Landing sleds! Sleds! That's sleds! Where? Everybody look. Where are they?"

Dafanil stared at him, tense. Lannat laughed aloud, threw his sword in the air. "Landing sleds, damn it. Rifles' landing sleds, for putting troops ashore. Listen!"

There was no longer need for listening. Dull green, slab-sided, wedge-shaped machines flew up the valley in tight formation, most dropping on the lower slope of the mountain. Three roared to a stop within fifty yards of the Free fort. Rifles poured out and ran to surround the group. Whatever they had expected, they received welcome. In the midst of near-hysterical celebration, a stocky, broad-shouldered older man approached Lannat and Dafanil. He saluted the prince, saying "It looks like we didn't get here soon enough, Highness. I'm Colonel Vonta, Imperial Rifles. Commander Etasalou's Advisors told us where you were."

"When? How?"

"Emperor Halib sent us instead of the Cultural Sibling Group. There are more of us off the other cargo starships. Some are in reserve, the others are headed for the other two continents. I wish we'd arrived sooner." His gaze slid off to the fort.

Lannat grabbed his arm. "We need doctors, Colonel. We've got wounded. Inside the fort."

Vonta barked orders into a seekum. From the back of the formation, people ran for the fort. Lannat took off after them.

He was at Nan's side with a young, coolly efficient doctor who had just finished his examination when Dafanil and the colonel arrived. The doctor readied an injector. "I think she'll be all right. Can I use a sled for casualties, Colonel?"

Again Vonta gave orders. When he finished, there was an incoming message on his seekum. He listened, then said, "Repeat that," and turned up the volume. He held out the device. A metallic voice said, "We've had a couple of these Legionnaire people just fall down and die. Others talk to themselves. Most act like they were clubbed. Tell them what to do, and they just do it. Don't say nothing. It's spooky, sir. What'll we do with them?"

"Disarm them, centralize them," Vonta said. "I'll arrange transport." Dafanil was talking to the doctor when Vonta finished, so he addressed Lannat. "I have instructions to find a Val Bordi. Is he among you?"

"I'm called that, but—"

A returned Dafanil interrupted, arm draped across Lannat's shoulders. "This is the man, Colonel."

Sticking out a hand, Vonta interrupted Lannat in midsalute. "I have some questions I'd like to ask you. Could we step over to my command sled? Some of it's confidential."

Lannat exclaimed aloud, jumped, and slapped at his shoulder. Embarrassed, he said, "Something just stung me. I don't . . ."

The colonel's features sagged, ran like batter. Lannat's knees buckled. He grabbed Dafanil for support, looking up to search his face for explanation. He managed, "What? . . ." and Dafanil was disengaging his grip, lowering him onto his back. There was an injector gleaming in Dafanil's other hand. Lannat didn't care. He never felt so warm and protected, one with the universe. From a vast, wonderful distance, he heard several Dafanils harmonizing. They sang, ". . . sent here on a mission by my father. He failed miserably. More, I believe him to be a traitor. He's my personal prisoner now, and I want three Rifles guards on him, full time. There's your real hero, sitting over there. Poor devil's fought himself to mental and physical exhaustion. That's the man who killed Commander Etasalou."

A tiny voice told Lannat that this was all terribly wrong. A grand, soft blanket of serenity drifted down across the nasty nagging, however, to muffle it and all the world completely away.

EPILOGUE

Emperor Halib leaned back in his library chair, chuckling. "He injected him, did he? Lannat's mind must have gone nova. And the touch with Mard; a beautiful stroke. The boy's changed beyond belief."

Administrator Ved shared the emperor's good mood. Still, he disagreed. "Do you really think it's wise to make such a hero of Mard? He's completely amoral, Exalted. There's no character there at all."

"The whole point. He saw the tapes of the interrogation at that woman's house? The murder on Hire, and Ullas's interrogations?"

"As you ordered, sir."

Halib spread his hands. "Then he understands. If Sungiver ever sees any of that material, he'll be dead meat by lunchtime. In fact, he'll be lunch. She can't be identified with assassination or assassins. Never mind that the empire thinks Mard killed Etasalou in a moral act. We know both issues are lies. And he knows someone else knows. It's a perfect knife at his throat."

"I just don't like it," Ved said sourly. "To you, using Mard is just setting out manure to draw dungbugs. I'm the one who has to dabble his fingers in it."

"I've always said, Ved, you've the soul of a poet. You're wasted as a spymaster. Speaking of which, has Dafanil discovered the informer in the old Free organization?"

"No, sir." Ved frowned. "I'm troubled about that. Once the boy claimed Ullas's throne for himself and used your Rifles to establish order, he sought out your old intelligence chief, that Betak person. They work together. Frankly, Exalted, Dafanil makes too many broad statements about his 'independence' and people participating in their own government to suit me. There's a tinge of radical in him, if I may say so, sir. I suspect Betak's a bad influence."

Trying to appear judicial, Halib agreed. "Have to watch them. Good for you, Ved. See to it." He rubbed his hands together. "The lovely Doctor Bahalt is tending to her patient?"

After a glance at his watch, Ved said, "The bandages come off today. I'm told her psychological problem practically cured itself, once she was back here on Atic with him. A touch of hypnotherapy, some mild treatment. I didn't realize how dangerous her physical damage was until recently. Almost didn't make it. Recovered rapidly, though. Rugged stock—as we know all too well. Anyhow, they've been practically inseparable since their return. You're turning into a matchmaker in your old age."

"Whose old age?" Halib bristled, then laughed. "It's more fun than juggling idiots and self-serving thieves, I'll tell you." He stood up and walked out onto the balcony and into Collegium's bright sun. Ved padded along after. Halib stood at the railing, soaking up the view of the gleaming city against the softer purple-green of the distant mountains. He said, "I never suspected Dafanil would have the presence of mind to get Lannat back to me with his cover intact. Not after all that happened. Convincing the doctors to keep him semiconscious until you could get your hands on him was intuitive genius." He turned, faced Ved. "Have I made many mistakes, Ved? Be honest."

"I would say yes, Exalted. Being honest. Speaking as a prudent man who has attended beheadings, I would have to say no."

"Droll. We'll give young Dafanil his head. He's certainly

calmed Hire." The lines fanning out from Halib's eyes deepened. His lips thinned. "I am emperor. There will be no challenges. From anyone. How many Rifles has he again?"

"One company, sir."

"That's enough. You've got a plan to get Lannat back into proper status as Rifle? You're claiming a health problem, if I remember correctly? He'll be indistinguishable from before?"

"Yes, sir."

Halib paced, hands behind his back. "I don't like the Bahalt woman knowing about the Val Bordi thing. That's a loose end."

"I should have five people in my control who are as trustworthy as Nan Bahalt."

Stopping, Halib looked at Ved as if examining him. "I have one trustworthy person; it's all I need."

"It's my life. I'm proud to serve."

"We did good work, Ved." Halib returned to the wall. An expansive gesture, like a dancer's arm movement, encompassed Atic and all the sky above. Halib went on, arms raised. "We have to deal with ourselves honestly. To fail to appreciate what we've accomplished, we demean ourselves. I've raised a son brighter than I dared suspect. We thwarted a particularly vicious rebellion, destroyed secrets that posed an unimaginable threat to mankind. We must admit it; we are brilliant." He lowered his arms. His head dropped, as if he prayed.

Ved bowed low, notwithstanding that Halib faced the other way. Holding the position, he said, "The pity is that we must hide our cleverness as industriously as we exercise our modesty."

Halib continued to gaze out over the city. He said, "It's a good thing I was born without a conscience. What man could live with two? You may withdraw, Administrator Ved."

Still bent over, Ved shuffled backward, off the balcony, into the library, all the way to the secret panel. He shook and snuffled suspiciously the entire way.

* * *

In another, distant part of Collegium, Lannat felt the last of his bandages fall away. Nan Bahalt said, "You can open your eyes now. It's over."

Lannat hesitated. "It's all right? Am I? . . ."

Nan laughed softly, happily. "Are you what? Captain Lannat again, handsome as ever? Of course. I made them promise."

He smiled and opened his eyes, wincing immediately. His hand went to the old, familiar scar that ran across his brow from over his left eye to drop across the right. Carefully a fingertip traced its course over his cheekbone, down to where it disappeared on his jaw. "That's tender," he said. The smile was tentative this time, a bit lopsided. "Make up your mind. Either I'm Lannat, or I'm handsome. You can't have it both ways."

She kissed him, quickly, lightly. Then, faces almost touching, she said, "I can. I do."

"Give me a mirror."

She turned to the small chest of drawers. Aside from the bed and a chair, it was the only furniture in the room. A translucent skylight and overhead light tubes exposed everything as dull and functional. It took her only a moment to pick up the small, square mirror and head back with it; that was plenty of time for Lannat to survey his surroundings. Not that he hadn't done so a thousand times during his stay in the hospital. Everything was exactly as it was on his first examination. The place was so featureless it was obviously designed for that purpose.

The thought of release was a complex of concerns. It would be wonderful to get away from a building that was no better than a prison. Still, going back to the Rifles meant lying to everyone he knew or would ever meet, men and women who valued his honesty as highly as he did. But what choice had he?

He wished he understood all the machinations involved.

On second thought, he told himself, don't even think about it.

Nan held up the mirror, wrong side to him. "Are you sure you want to look? You're still a bit swollen and discolored from the operations. You look exactly as you did before they changed you, but you also look like you lost a nasty fight."

"Then how do you know I'll look the same when the swelling goes down and the bruises go away?"

"Trust me. I'm a doctor."

He grabbed at the mirror. "That does it. Give me that."

Enjoying herself hugely, she let it go. He peered into the glass, then relaxed. "That's me."

The last should have been just another ordinary remark, but Nan heard the hidden strain, the horror, buried in it. She pushed the mirror aside and kissed him again, hard this time, with a passion that drew his arms around her. When they parted, she gave him no chance to speak. She said, "The past is over. All of it, finished. We're free and clear now, the two of us. We're ourselves."

In that instant, the words barely uttered, they both stiffened as if seized by electricity. Lannat sat bolt upright and took Nan in his arms, face twisted in a snarl. She stared at him, her own features a mix of fear, curiosity. She whispered hoarsely, "Music. Women, singing. There aren't any women in this place. What's happening?"

"Seeker." The word sounded as if torn free. "You shouldn't be exposed," Lannat said then. "She shouldn't do this, not to you."

"She? Who is she?" Nan looked away from Lannat. Fear was clearly gaining the upper hand in her voice, her manner. "The singing; someone, something's in my head. My mind."

Lannat held her tighter, closer yet. "Don't be afraid," he said. His voice betrayed him.

"Hear him," a soft soothing voice said. "I am his friend. I would be yours. I pray you each will be mine."

Choking, Nan pulled against Lannat's strength. He held her as if desperate.

"It's Astara, a woman of the Seeker cult," he told her. "She can speak to your mind. She won't harm you." As he spoke, he felt Nan's tension ebb. Her near-frantic struggles slowed, stopped. Her face suffused with wonder. Like her, ⎿ relaxed.

Astara was almost cheerful. "There. That's better. Doctor Bahalt, I apologize for intruding on you so rudely. If you would be more comfortable with me, please close your eyes. Imagine an old woman in black, with long, silver hair, carrying a long walking stick. You shall see me. You, too, friend Lannat; I would have you with me while we talk."

Lannat was abrupt. "You frightened Nan. I have nothing to say to you. I never did." Nevertheless, he watched Nan as he spoke, and when she closed her eyes, so did he.

A mind-image of the broken temple on Delphi shimmered before him. Beside him, Nan gasped. "The flowers, Lan; so red, so beautiful. A carpet. And this temple; it's beautiful. Is it real? Where? . . ."

She was turning to him when a bright light flared between them and the tumbled stone of the shrine. Astara stepped out of it, and it faded away. Chin lifted slightly, she faced the couple, blind eyes aimed straight at them. She said, "We must know each other, Nan Bahalt, because we love the same man. For you he is a mate, to share your life. To me he is many other things, all needed in the service of the Seeker. He resists me, but we must have him."

"And I will never give him up." Nan took a step forward, out of Lannat's grasp. "I know some little of you, Astara. I've seen him troubled and worried by something he wouldn't explain. It was you. You torment him."

"I do." It was a wry confession. "Neither more nor less than he torments me. But I cannot stop. My cause is the good of all people, and we need hearts like his. That is why we must know each other. It gives me joy to see him find the woman with whom he would travel this life, and I wish you every happiness. Nevertheless, you have chosen a man marked by fate. All of us serve history. Most of us learn too late we have done so in ways we never dreamed possible. Lannat, for reasons none of us will ever know, is an unwitting catalyst, an agent of change. Like it or not, he is become a central figure in an epochal struggle between good and evil. I am come to you, Nan Bahalt, with a plea, with a vision, with a warning. Love your brave Lannat. Love him the rest of your life with all your heart. But understand that you must share him. The Seeker needs."

Lannat stepped up beside Nan. Together, they faced the beauty and threat of the hazy, wavering figure before them. "I am of no cult," Lannat said. "I am not what you say. I'm a man, an ordinary soldier."

Nodding slowly, Astara said, "The Seeker understands that. Perhaps better than you, my friend."

Nan interrupted. "Listen to me; I will never share him gladly, you understand? Try to change him, or take him from me, or play tricks with his mind—or mine—and I will fight you. I don't understand what or who you are. You frighten me. Still and all, I will beat you. I will. But you call him friend. Tell me, then; do you protect him? Will you always?"

Lannat pulled away from her side, the better to stare, jaw hanging slack.

Nan made a gesture of impatience. "Don't try to understand. This is women's business." Then, coloring, a bit flustered, she faced Astara again. She set her jaw. Lannat noted her hands were balled in fists. "Well?"

Astara chuckled. "I loved him first, child. Yes, I do and shall protect him. As best I can. You already know I have limits. Not where my need of him is concerned, however. I will not lie to you about his importance. Or my determination."

For a long time, the three of them were still. The delicate red flowers, oblivious to the boiling turmoil of the humans, reached for the gentle breeze to create a scented, carefree dance. Suddenly, jarringly, Nan was moving, advancing through them to Astara. Stopping within arm's reach, Nan raised her hands. Astara, in response, leaned her walking stick against her body, extended her own hands. Eerily the older woman unerringly linked her fingers with Nan. She smiled. Nan said, "Perhaps

we can never be friends. We must never be enemies. Cou.
be sisters, do you think?"

Astara laughed, the sound musical against the sigh of the
breeze. "A perceptive suggestion. I believe we already are."

Offended, confused, Lannat objected. "There's more here
than two women coming to terms. Those terms concern me—
my honor. Don't forget that. And you both know my only am-
bition is to serve my emperor."

Changing her grip, Astara took Nan's hands in one of hers.
Leaning heavily on the walking stick, she advanced through
the bobbing flowers and gave Nan's hands into Lannat's. Only
then did she speak to them, as a couple. "I leave you now. A
meeting such as this—it tires me too quickly. And you must return to your secret hospital and your interrupted lives. Carry
one thought from here, however: We three—with our treasured, so-important goals—may someday realize we were
never so far apart from each other as we thought."

Lannat and Nan were still sitting beside each other, un-
speaking, strangely distant, when the masked figure who daily
coached them on their cover story entered the room. He found
his audience curiously preoccupied during the session.

✎ FREE DRINKS ✎

Take the Del Rey® survey and get a free newsletter! Answer the questions below and we will send you complimentary copies of the DRINK (Del Rey® Ink) newsletter free for one year. Here's where you will find out all about upcoming books, read articles by top authors, artists, and editors, and get the inside scoop on your favorite books.

Age _____ Sex ❑ M ❑ F

Highest education level: ❑ high school ❑ college ❑ graduate degree

Annual income: ❑ $0-30,000 ❑ $30,001-60,000 ❑ over $60,000

Number of books you read per month: ❑ 0-2 ❑ 3-5 ❑ 6 or more

Preference: ❑ fantasy ❑ science fiction ❑ horror ❑ other fiction ❑ nonfiction

I buy books in hardcover: ❑ frequently ❑ sometimes ❑ rarely

I buy books at: ❑ superstores ❑ mall bookstores ❑ independent bookstores
   ❑ mail order

I read books by new authors: ❑ frequently ❑ sometimes ❑ rarely

I read comic books: ❑ frequently ❑ sometimes ❑ rarely

I watch the Sci-Fi cable TV channel: ❑ frequently ❑ sometimes ❑ rarely

I am interested in collector editions (signed by the author or illustrated):
   ❑ yes ❑ no ❑ maybe

I read Star Wars novels: ❑ frequently ❑ sometimes ❑ rarely

I read Star Trek novels: ❑ frequently ❑ sometimes ❑ rarely

I read the following newspapers and magazines:
❑ *Analog*   ❑ *Locus*   ❑ *Popular Science*
❑ *Asimov*   ❑ *Wired*   ❑ *USA Today*
❑ *SF Universe*   ❑ *Realms of Fantasy* ❑ *The New York Times*

Check the box if you do not want your name and address shared with qualified vendors ❑

Name _____

Address _____

City/State/Zip _____

E-mail _____

prisoner within

PLEASE SEND TO: DEL REY⁽ᴿ⁾/The DRINK
201 EAST 50TH STREET NEW YORK NY 10022

Don't miss this exciting new series by Brian

SMOKE ON THE WATER
GammaLAW Book 1

Though they contemplated a final suicide mission of blood, guts, and glory, the Exts knew their warrior superskills were no match for the LAW—Legal Annexation of Worlds—who were sent into space by the mighty Periapt potentates to colonize new populations against the evil, alien Roke.

Among the Ext draftees bound for Periapt were Allgrave Burning, his technowizard cousin Lod, and beautiful, death-scarred Ghost, all sworn to a greater purpose, destined to fight in a star-torn war like none other. For a mysterious, danger-shrouded planet beckoned them—along with a disgraced starship captain and a powerful high priestess—for the greatest battle of their lives . . .

Published by Del Rey® Books.
Available in bookstores everywhere.

STARFIST
Book I
FIRST TO FIGHT

by David Sherman and Dan Cragg

Stranded in a hellish alien desert, stripped of their strategic systems, quick reaction force, and supporting arms and carrying only a day's water ration, Marine Staff Sergeant Charlie Bass and his seven-man team faced a grim future seventy-five light-years from home. The only thing between his Marines and safety were eighty-five miles of uncharted, waterless terrain and two thousand bloodthirsty savages with state-of-the-art weapons in their hands and murder on their minds.

But the enemy didn't reckon on the warrior cunning of Marine's Marine Charlie Bass and the courage of the few good men who would follow him anywhere—even to death . . .